ALL FOR ONE CHILD

THE BENEDICTION OF PAUL
BOOK THREE

PATRICIA MCCLURE

WAYZGOOSE PRESS

Paperback ISBN: 978-1-961953-17-8

V021025

Cover design by GetCovers.com

Family comes first.
To my family, who support me in the process of writing, and even read when it isn't their genre.

CONTENTS

CHAPTER I
ABBOT ELECT

The monks of St. Alberic's were choosing a new abbot. Paul sat in his room listening to them on the baby monitor he had snuck into the chapter room. They still treated him like he was four instead of fourteen.

They seemed to forget that. Sometimes they would remind him, saying, "You're not vowed. You don't wear black. You are just living here." Like he needed reminding.

"You are one of us." Those were Brother Mellitus's words. Paul remembered the envelope Brother Mellitus had handed him before he died. Our last crusade together, he called it. Paul had raced into the chapter room, handing the note to Abbot David. This abbot, appointed to witness the election, lived in some abbey back east.

Now, Paul paced in front of that closed door in the dimly lit hallway.

Visions of the old, white-haired monk that Paul had loved filled his mind. Brother Mellitus, but Paul had named him Merlin, had three years together before the monk died, and Paul still missed him.

Two novices struggled with boxes as they entered the monastery. That meant someone was leaving, arriving, or had died.

Paul followed the men to the elevator and held the door open. There were only six boxes. He wondered who was moving. A dead monk would have more containers.

"Whose boxes?" Paul listening for the squeak of the chapter room door.

The novices set the boxes down. Novice Alcuin peered over his glasses, scolding him for speaking in the hallway. They were in an elevator; Alcuin was so irritatingly pious.

"So, you're leaving?" Paul asked, as he blocked the door from closing. He flipped open a box and noted the sparse contents of books and papers. This didn't belong to Alcuin.

"God no," Alcuin blurted out, standing straighter and pulling on his scapular, a long cloth that covered the front of his habit, which moments ago was wadded in a ball on a box.

Novice Reginald chuckled.

"The boxes belong to Father Jacob," Reginald said. "His cell is on the third floor, right?"

Paul considered sending them to wonder about the monastery, since the doors lacked labels.

"At least he won't be staying long," Paul said, having listened to the rumors that his return was only temporary. Even though Abbot Gordon had helped to wash away the anger, the pain, the sting of Jacob's two-year absence still hurt. Things were fine when Jacob was nearby. Pius could not harm him.

When Jacob ran off, leaving him vulnerable to Father Pius, nobody explained what was going on. The abandonment simmered and turned to hostility. Now, Jacob was back. Or was he?

"Unless they elect him abbot. He is the superior choice," Alcuin said with an air of seniority.

Paul fought the urge to punch the young man. He wondered why all novices were so naïve.

The elevator dinged softly, signaling its impatience.

"Novice, you are breaking the rule of silence. Do not make me report you to the Novice Master," Paul said as he pushed the button to all the floors before exiting.

"What the hell?" Alcuin said as the doors closed.

The halls were empty. Paul ran to his cell, kicking the doorstop aside and letting the door slam shut behind him. The KISS poster on the wall flapped in the breeze. The baby monitor crackled.

"We have a new abbot. Congratulations Father Jacob Mackenzie-Knows the Song."

"What?" Paul grabbed the monitor, pressing it to his ear.

"Ah, no, are you sure? You must have miscounted," Jacob said. "Oh, this is hilarious, guys. It's a joke, right? Are you teasing me? No, you're scaring me."

"I say recount," Paul said, sure he had heard wrong.

"Father, I assure you, this is no joke. You are the Abbot Elect. May the peace of God strengthen you." The community answered amen, with such conviction that Paul felt his knees weaken.

"I, oh my God. What do I do now?" Jacob's voice said.

"Say no," Paul said. They had to be kidding. Maybe, he thought, they found the monitor he had hidden in the flowerpot. "Merlin, is this your doing? Did your note tell them to play a joke on me? Jacob would never stutter like that."

"Well, Father, most accept the office," Abbot David said.

"I have a choice?" Jacob said.

"You have a choice."

"Someone has to lead us and save Paul's soul," Father Pius said as chuckles filled the room

"You're an idiot," Paul said, dropping the monitor into the trashcan. "You just wanted to be abbot."

Paul forged his way through the clothing on the floor and yanked on his door, nearly dislodging his shoulder. He had forgotten that he had set it to the lock when it closed.

"Damn you, Pius, you're the reason for this lock." Pius was the monk who had bruised and terrorized him for years. His anger rose to full boil as he realized the community almost elected Pius as abbot.

"May I pray about it?" Jacob's voice quivered.

"Please do, Father," Abbot David said.

Paul groaned, unlocking the door. He shuddered in disbelief, wondering if the sudden death of Abbot Gordon had messed with their brains. He ran out of his cell into the hall, crowded with monks, who were all chattering like chickens.

"He had a wife and children. Can we have sex now?" Brother Flavian asked, holding onto Brother Ambrose's arm.

"Well, you're not my type, Brother, but thanks for the offer," Brother Ambrose said to the ancient monk.

Paul rolled his eyes. Flavian was always so confused. Jacob had been married with children. Everyone was aware of that and his tragic loss, five deaths in three days. Jacob claimed that was how he entered the monastery, by default. Those events were before Paul lived at the monastery.

"You're a monk, Brother Flavian. You can't do that. Not now, not ever," Paul said. His tolerance for the naïve young monks and the old faltering ones was running thin.

Ambrose harrumphed and shook a thick finger at Paul. "Be nice, the judgments you hand out could be your own someday."

"That's not the child, is it?" Brother Flavian asked.

"No, that's just a visitor from Mars," Ambrose said.

"What's going on?" Paul asked, ignoring the massive man's scolding.

"Like you don't know," Ambrose said, his eyes narrowing under his dark brows. "We elected an abbot, Father Jacob. I guess Mellitus had the last word."

What had Mellitus done? What had he done? Father Joannicus's warnings from his childhood rang in his mind. Learn to say no to Mellitus.

Paul stuck his head in the chapter room, which carried the heavy odor of men, cologne, and coffee. The chairs were being stacked, and the box with the votes sat next to Abbot David. Paul fought the urge to take the box and run. The whiteboard displayed the tally, Jacob had won, but where was he?

Paul exited the door leading outside, scanning the area for some sign of Jacob. Paul ran to the parking lot between the weave shop and the brewery. Jacob's motorcycle was still there.

Where was the newly elected abbot? Paul stood poised to run, but in which direction? Thoughts of conversations of conversion, a vow that monks took, came back to him. He knew conversion wasn't magic, but it was magical.

Paul hoped the words of the election hadn't yet made their way to Jacob's soul. For he knew that could happen. A young man visited the monastery and changed. Paul wasn't sure how it happened, but it happened. By the time they entered the novitiate, their brains had stopped working, and they got starry-eyed and idealistic. He had watched the young ones move from novices to juniors. They stumbled over their virtues and ideals, most of the time, making fools of themselves. On the day of their profession, they transformed. He had witnessed it. That memory sent a chill down Paul's spine.

Paul raced to the guesthouse and flung open the door. The smell of fresh bread filled his nose as he listened for voices. The doors labeled with names of saints stood open. Novices were cleaning the room.

His mind raced to the last profession he saw.

A grown man lying prostrate on the floor of the church in front of family and friends, offering himself, his body, mind, and soul to an abbot, the community, and God. When he stood, a transformation from the inside out had occurred.

Paul ran across the courtyard, back to the monastery and up to the third floor and held his breath, listening outside of Jacob's door. If he couldn't sweat, where would he go? To the white man's house of prayer, the church, so Paul raced down the stairs, slowing as he entered the hallway leading to the atrium. The incense for Mass lingered. Inside the atrium, he skidded to a stop, his chest heaving. A sigh echoed in the church.

Father Jacob sat with his head in his hands, his long hair unbraided, forming a black veil, concealing his face from the world. As he looked up, Paul stepped back. Those blue eyes were always penetrating, startling. An Indian with blue eyes. That was not normal. He was Apsáalooke and Catholic. Was that even possible?

"Not now, Paul," Jacob said.

"I'm not here to congratulate you," Paul said, sitting in the chair in front of Jacob and glancing at the Abbot's empty seat. A great sadness filled Paul as he stared at the space. He missed Gordon.

"You're not accepting, are you? This isn't God's doing. You should say no thanks."

Squeaky sandals and heavy breathing announced Brother Ambrose's entry into the atrium of the church.

"Come now. There is time for another vote. Nobody has left yet," Paul said.

Ambrose chuckled as he came into the church. "Little One, I know Father Joannicus has explained how this works. Ten percent man, ninety-nine percent God. It is over and done with."

"That doesn't add up to one hundred," Paul said. Stomach acid hit the back of his throat. "He can't be abbot. He doesn't want the job. Pick someone else."

Brother Ambrose stood with his hands looped in his habit belt, causing his habit to show a hairy leg. "You don't refuse God's request, Little One. Besides, if we had that attitude, you would be in an orphanage."

"That's not true. Abbot Gordon said it was bigger than him and all of you. We should wait, vote later when things have settled," Paul said, wondering if this was what Brother Mellitus expected. They had voted to care for him, but this was different.

"Fine, God played a part, but can't God make mistakes?"

"We need an abbot," Ambrose said, raising an eyebrow.

"We've been okay without one," Paul said. "You should have elected Father Joannicus."

"We couldn't. Father Joannicus took his name out of the running," Ambrose said.

A frightening thought gripped Paul as his stomach clenched. Why would Joannicus withdraw his name? Was it more than a summer cold?

Jacob tapped his foot. "Paul, I need time to think, without unnecessary influence, and that means your opinion."

The images of Abbot Gordon sitting in his chair during Vespers on June 26th danced around the room. Gordon had looked like he was asleep, but he was, in fact, dead.

The words of Psalm 17:5 echoed in his heart. "The waves of death rose about me, the torrents of destruction assailed me, the snares of the grave entangled me, and the traps of death confronted me."

Paul had lost them all, his mother, Brother Mellitus, and Abbot Gordon. Fury rose inside as he ran his hand over the back of the chair.

"You left me. That was wrong. You weren't on sabbatical. I know the truth," Paul said. "This isn't your kind of job. Go be a chief to your tribe. You can't knock off the Abbot and then take his place."

The entrance door banged open, and voices floated in from the atrium.

"Excuse me?" Jacob said.

"Paul, that was out of line," Ambrose said, shaking his large, bearded face like a buffalo.

"It's true when you left Abbot Gordon was upset. You never said you were sorry. You avoided him. That hurt him. I told you Father Pius would ruin everything. Abbot Gordon tried to fix things, but you were too stubborn," Paul said, not sure he was making any sense.

"It's time to return to your cage," Ambrose said as Father Jacob stood. Brother Ambrose put a hand on Paul's shoulder.

Hurried footsteps echoed as the voices evaporated. Whoever had entered was making a hasty retreat. He had to hold his ground and speak the truth.

Paul shrugged the heavy hand off and stood. Jacob was a tall man, and Paul stepped back, feeling a chill run through him.

"Please go to your cell," Jacob said calmly.

He wasn't four, they couldn't send him to his room. He would leave, run away. That would show them. There were four exits in this octagonal church. A clear path to each of them. He was faster than them, he would make it out before they knew he was gone.

"I don't have to listen to you."

"Oh, yes you do," Jacob said. "Do not challenge me."

As Paul's anger drained, spite filled his heart. "You're being a jerk. Maybe I'll leave this time and go live with my grandfather, Terence. At least I know he loves me."

Paul's sharp words seared through Jacob with incredible speed, and as if punched, Jacob sat. Triumph filled Paul. Jacob's stepfather, Terence Mackenzie, always evoked a reaction.

"Enough," Ambrose growled, clamping a meaty hand on Paul's upper arm. "I think you're right. Let's elect someone else. I vote for Father Pius."

Jacob slumped back into the chair. Paul's anger returned. Although the community forgave Pius his offense, and the physical abuse ended, Pius was still with them. That was wrong, too.

"See, he doesn't want the job. So let me go." Paul shook off Ambrose's hand.

"Why are you siding with him? If Pius is abbot, I will leave."

"Jacob the abbot. There's only his side," Ambrose said, crossing his arms and exposing a rip at his shoulder, telling all he was wearing polka dotted long johns.

"That is right. I am the abbot," Jacob said, raising his head and pushing his hair back. The warrior gazed out at Paul. The argument was over.

"Paul, go to your cell and remain there," Jacob said, his voice taking on a tone of authority.

Silence. Paul half expected them to count, as they had when he was four.

Paul waved his arms and stomped out of the church. "I'm calling my grandfather. I get one phone call."

"Do you want me to stop him?" Ambrose asked.

"I am sure Father Vincent has already spoken to Terence."

Damn, thought Paul as he paused in the atrium. He had forgotten that Vincent was zealous with news of the monastery. Also, Vincent was Jacob's half brother, so calling about a family member seemed normal. Paul took a step closer to the church proper.

"Don't mind the boy. He speaks out of grief and hormones," Ambrose said.

"Do not make excuses for him, Rose. He must face the consequences of his words."

Had he heard right? Did Jacob say his words were powerful? Perhaps he had won, and Father Jacob would not be an abbot.

Abbot Jacob's voice resounded in the empty church. "Sometimes pain is necessary to learn."

Ambrose harrumphed.

"It is time for a change, Rose. Take some boxes to his cell and have Paul pack up his stuff."

Boxes? He can't kick me out, can he? He was the abbot, and it sounded like he wanted to be the abbot. Paul ran to his cell, his life twisting like a sheet in a tornado.

CHAPTER 2
FATHER JOANNICUS

Psalm 89:12
Make us know the shortness of our life
that we may gain wisdom of heart.

Abbot Elect Jacob Mackenzie-Knows the Song wandered the church after prayers, thinking about what Paul had expressed. The boy is right.

This is not man's doing, it is God's.

Then you had better step up. His wife, Faith, would say that. *If you join the God parade, you better march.*

Jacob's stomach clenched. Ten years ago, that small, orphaned boy, Paul, full of hope and expectations, looked to him for answers. Those eyes, so innocent, had reminded him of his children, his significant losses. Fear had overwhelmed him.

Not again. Don't trick me into loving again.

That had been foolish. He knew it then, and he realized it now. He had fallen in love with Paul, and he would lead this community. The only real problem was how. Already, he could sense that his days would be full of appointments and those seeking his approval or blessing.

A shift in power positions. How many more wrinkles needed ironing out?

Jacob walked down the hall to the abbot's office, his office. He opened the door. Someone had placed Indian artifacts in the showcase. A pipe, a colorful beaded vest, nestled in with the traditional Catholic and history items of St. Alberic's humble beginnings. A stack of notes lay on the shiny desktop. A handsome obsidian holder displayed a miniature of the Apsáalooke Nation flag, with a sleek pen for signing those important documents abbots sign. That was a gift from the tribe.

A knock on the door drew him from his thoughts. Abbot David's smiling face appeared.

"Checking it all out?"

"This does not seem real," Jacob said, sitting in the black leather chair behind the desk.

Abbot David approached. "It will soon enough. Don't let it get mundane. So, have you selected your Senior Council?"

"Yes, I have chosen Father Joannicus and Brother Ambrose, and we need a young one for balance. The community is choosing Father Pius and Brother Barnabas. Our prior will still be Father Hilary and sub-prior Brother George."

"Excellent. I have something to discuss with you."

Abbot David pulled an envelope out from under his scapular. "This is a request to release you from your vows as a Benedictine, dated before Abbot Gordon passed away. I'm assuming that I should disregard this?"

"Sure," Jacob said, biting his lower lip. "There might be a

bigger problem than my request to be released from the priesthood."

Abbot David grinned. "I don't think so. God and his minions took care of that for you."

"What?" Did the envelope get returned for lack of postage? He had a second thought. Ambrose snatched it before the mail left the monastery. Or maybe Joannicus.

"I'm going to enjoy watching you as abbot. St. Alberic's appears to delight in the unusual," Abbot David said as he walked out of the office.

Jacob pulled open drawers on the enormous desk, familiarizing himself with the contents. The drawer on the bottom right didn't open. Locked. He ran his fingers under the rim of the desk. No taped key. A knock on the door and Father Joannicus entered.

"Hey, I was just thinking about you," Abbot Jacob said.

Father Joannicus fingered the large manila envelope before placing it on Jacob's desk.

"Hopefully only good thoughts," Joannicus said, pulling his black sweater tighter around himself. "I heard Paul is giving you grief, and that you banished him to his cell until he is thirty-five."

Jacob rose and walked to the cart that held a thermos of hot water.

"If Paul thinks that's best, who am I to argue with the teen wisdom? I must get my house in order, so to speak. A lot of Paul's suffering is his own fault. Is it time for a lock on the outside of his door?"

"Seriously, you were the locksmith? Paul never told me who did that."

"Guilty as charged. It was just to give him security. I had spare keys hidden everywhere," Jacob explained, thinking the precaution didn't work, for Pius still got to Paul.

"You're forgiven."

"Now that I am abbot, I get to ask about your health." Jacob poured hot water into two mugs as the tea bags floated to the top.

Joannicus tapped the envelope before setting it on the desk.

"Okay, official shit. Just tell me." Jacob didn't want to read that. If he had believed what doctors said, he should have died as an infant. A person's heart and mind produced more miracles than any medical treatment.

Father Joannicus accepted the mug and took a deep breath. "Cancer. Testicular to be exact and, from what I've been told, treatable. I've got a good chance to beat this."

Jacob tried not to wince. "What are they planning on doing?"

"Seriously, it will mean surgery. They are taking only one unless the other is cancerous. More times than not, it's only one. Don't look so pained. It's not as if I'll miss the sperm."

Jacob wanted to laugh, but the seriousness of the word "cancer" chilled his humor. "You will have one left."

"It will be useless after the chemo and radiation. I'll be sterile. Treatment in Bozeman begins after you've been invested."

"That is far away," Jacob mused, as he noticed the art in the office. Gone were the icons with funny eyes. Replaced with a blue-and-white painting of Calf Woman and White Buffalo. On the wall over the philodendron was an artistic interpretation of Jesus and the twelve with native faces and shoulders draped in colorful blankets. Jacob stood and walked over to the painting and looked closer at the faces. It was icon art, and he realized his sister Rebecca had purchased the piece. He shook his head. She, like Paul, had a knack for discovering monastic news before it became public.

"Seriously, Bozeman is closer than Missoula, and what isn't far in Montana? I have enlisted a junior to be my treatment partner. There might be prolonged stays. Will you come and visit? I'm aware you don't care for hospitals but see it as a house of healing."

Jacob shivered at the shadow of fear, a wolf hidden in the corner of his soul, hospitals. "I do not want to watch you die."

"Father Abbot, we all die. I've readied myself for that."

Joe's calm face told Jacob the man was ready. Joe might be ready, but Jacob wasn't.

He set his tea down and moved to sit in a chair opposite his friend. The deaths of his wife, Faith, and his four children had caused him to avoid hospitals and cemented in him that time with loved ones was always too short.

"I know," Joannicus said, his voice gentle as he leaned over and touched Jacob's arm. "Seriously, I'm not dying in a hospital. If I die, it'll be here at home."

"So, you have spoken with God, and he has assured you of this?"

Joannicus shook his head. "No assurances. It's not my time. I fear that being away from the community will, well seriously, I'm afraid that it might test my faith, so get over your dislike of hospitals and visit me."

"I will be there," Jacob said, hoping that his words would strengthen his conviction to face the formidable bricks of a hospital. He could almost smell the antiseptic.

Father Joannicus shifted in his seat. Jacob wondered what Joe's pain level was.

"I have a favor to ask," Joannicus said.

Jacob leaned forward. "Anything."

"Don't tell Paul."

Jacob leaned back, crossed, and uncrossed his long legs. Keeping secrets from Paul was dangerous on so many levels.

"Are you sure about this?"

"Yes," Joannicus said. "Paul has dealt with too many losses. His mother died of cancer. When he hears that word, he'll become unreasonable. Don't you remember when he was little how every illness was cancer?"

"More so than he already is?" Jacob asked. "I believe he can manage your illness. You said it was curable. His mother had a brain tumor. It is similar, but different."

"I know how they found Paul before they brought him here. Barb told me. He spent the holiday with her unconscious body. He thought his mother was asleep. By the time the caregivers returned, he was dehydrated, scared, and hungry."

Jacob inhaled deeply. The vision of a small boy curled up next to a corpse disturbed him. He stood and walked to the window.

"I remember when Brother Mellitus died. Paul cried for days. If it gets to the point of goodbye, we can revisit this decision. Paul's still dealing with Abbot Gordon's passing. It may look like he's managing the loss, but sometimes his face holds such suffering. In case you weren't aware when you left, Paul was miserable, and you weren't even dead. I wish to spare him any more pain."

The guilt card, not fair. Paul has never been alone.

"All excuses," the warrior in his mind chided. Jacob smoothed the material of his habit.

"Fine, we can take it week by week. If you die and I am left telling him, I will be furious with you, bring you back from the dead."

Joannicus laughed. "Okay, I can deal with that."

The clouds parted, and the dimness of the room vanished. Joannicus looked pale and worn in the bright light. This is a horrible idea.

Jacob reached over for his mug, sat down, and took a sip of the warm liquid.

"What are we going to tell Paul?"

"Tell him I'm on sabbatical. He won't be thrilled, but he'll understand that."

Jacob leaned back in his chair. "How about I send him to visit monasteries, a new one every week?"

"Are you trying to ruin his affection for the monastic life? That is crazy."

"Yeah, that's what the others said," Jacob said, still thinking it could work.

"I can tell that you have done extraordinarily little traveling in your monastic career. As abbot, you discover that visiting is exhausting. Gordon hated it."

But he wouldn't have to deal with a surly teen.

"I'll talk to the community. They'll keep their thoughts to themselves and voices away from Paul," Joannicus said.

He'll run away to be with you every chance he gets.

Jacob worried he would spend his time chasing after a willful teen. Paul had to go on sabbatical, too.

Jacob crossed his arms. "Why am I abbot if you have the power to quiet gossiping? We elected the wrong man."

"We didn't choose the wrong man. You've more influence than you know. Trust me on that one. Besides, it was pre-ordained. Even Mellitus knew."

Jacob sighed.

You are a Warrior Chief of the Benedictine tribe, crowed the Elder in his mind.

"I want something, too. Once you are well, I will resign and then we can pick you."

Joannicus laughed, and his laugh turned into a cough. Jacob waited, saying a prayer that begged God not to cut short this man's life.

Father Jacob retired to his cell early, yet sleep took on the qualities of a wrestling match with the sheets, so Jacob rose, and in the pre-dawn light made his way to the barn. The scent of hay and manure greeted him as Brother Ambrose looked up from his task.

"Father Abbot, are you lost?"

Jacob shook his head. "No, I need to do something physical. I am searching for answers."

"Gertie is a good listener," Brother Ambrose said, cocking his head toward the Australian Shepherd as she nursed her brood of puppies.

Jacob cut the wire on a bale of hay. Ambrose took a sickle from the wall of museum-like tools and sat at the foot-powered grinding stone.

"Worried about Paul? Well, don't be. Aliens have abducted him. They will return him shortly. I was going to check for crop circles later this morning."

"He is unhappy and appears to be taking Abbot Gordon's death harder than most," Jacob said as he stuffed a trough with hay. The cow mooed, and Jacob caressed her boney head. The light aroma of disinfectant wafted around her as her tail swished.

"Never mind. Paul is fourteen going on four. He needs to be bricked in until he turns seventeen. I'm sorry he takes it out on you."

"Nothing different there. Do you remember how he used to push the limits when I was here?"

"Yeah, guess he knows you can take it, and in the end still love him."

Jacob ran his hand over his braid. "It is okay that he vents to me, but he will have to do it behind closed doors. I do not think others understand Paul is not acting disobediently."

"He's obedient now, hasn't left his room since you banished him," Ambrose said with a wink as he tossed Jacob a broom.

"That is not obedience, it is stubborn defiance. He hopes he can outlast me."

"True, but he'll become defiant at some point. They all do. Maturing has something to do with hormones and mating, over-throwing the alpha male. I tried to explain that to Abbot Gordon, but he said Paul wasn't an animal. Gordon trusted in benevolence, and frankly, I see nothing positive coming from that. Self-absorption just makes everything soggy."

Abbot Jacob chuckled, watching the stone sharpen the blade. Sparks flared like an electric rooster's tail. Ambrose shook his wooly head.

"What the boy needs is stability, God, and community. That's what we all need. How's Joannicus? Should I pray harder?" Ambrose asked.

Abbot Jacob leaned on the broom.

"Rose?" Jacob said, using the familiar form of the man's name.

"I'm not saying but," Ambrose scanned the space as if the sheep were taking notes. "Joe is ill, hence his absences. It doesn't take a Ph.D. to figure that out."

"Who knows?"

Brother Ambrose mopped his forehead. "You, me, the sheep, and everyone."

"He does not want Paul to know."

A living wish, which was better than a dying wish. Protect Paul. The irony didn't escape Jacob. He had once held that thorny gauntlet.

Ambrose touched the blade, then counted his fingers.

"Everyone knows Joannicus isn't well. There are rumors. Out of respect for Joe, nobody asked. Not even Paul. This secret keeping will be tricky."

Jacob pushed loose strands of hay around the floor.

"Yes, monastery magic to work. Speaking of which, what happened to my Rome papers?"

"Rome." Ambrose ran a calloused hand over the crown of his head. "Moses needed help, so I took care of it. I guess I just forgot. Good thing too, seeing that we elected you."

Jacob closed his eyes and shook his head. He hadn't forgotten. "Ninety-nine percent man and ten percent God?"

Ambrose laughed. "Yeah, something like that."

Ambrose stood and scooped a lost puppy who wiggled away from the warmth of the pack. The runt of the litter, Jacob realized, judging from the size of the siblings.

"Paul might be oblivious, but he's going to it figure out."

"We will have to keep him occupied," Jacob said, wondering if they had a daycare camp for teens.

"Nobody can be kept that busy," Ambrose said, placing his hands on his hips.

Jacob swept the stray hay to the side, contemplating Joe's plan. As well-meaning as it was, Jacob knew it would hurt Paul.

"I have an idea." Jacob lifted the broom to knock a spider's web from a corner stall.

Ambrose sliced twine into even lengths.

"An idea. I have heard of this idea of sending Paul away. It'll not make your job easier. He can't see every single monastery. Even if he did fifty-two, one every week, he'd develop cloister phobia. The idea is absurd."

So much for gossiping and secrets.

"You are being a jerk. I never considered fifty-two monasteries. That was a joke," Jacob said, banging the broom on the hard floor.

"Joke or not, what female community would take a teenage boy? That's even crazier than us raising him." Ambrose turned and snatched the broom.

Jacob felt oddly disabled, stripped of a task. "I have four who are willing. So there."

"What did you do, bribe them?"

How did he know?

"Okay, I'm listening." Ambrose hung up the broom and blade.

"I am considering sending Paul away for a year and giving Joannicus a chance to heal. But nobody believes in this promising idea. I am sending him to trusted communities, and where we know the members. He will not be alone. Do you expect the lawyers to go for it?"

"Reasoning with lawyers, funny one." Ambrose walked to the stall, letting the cow out.

"I plan on using the argument that Paul needs experience in the greater world, the world he will someday live in. They can't deny that."

Ambrose's eyes narrowed. "I don't want him to go."

"Rose, be reasonable. Help me pick the communities. One year is not that long. It will be good for him."

"Won't be good for me," the man growled as he picked up a bucket and dipped it into the feed bin.

"You can call him every week," Jacob added. Worries of what could go wrong loomed, and he pushed them away.

"I guess if you can submit to being abbot. Warrior Chief."

"I am not a Chief."

"Wrong. You have fulfilled all the requirements. After disarming Judith, you left her alive. You touched the enemy. You rallied us into a war party so many times."

"I have not stolen a horse." Jacob paused as he remembered the blue mustang he had taken in a fit of anger toward Pius.

"You're the one. You took Pius's pony."

Jacob hung his head. Confession time had finally come, and he was abbot. A chill trembled his body at the thought.

21

"I should probably give it back."

"You still have it? Just place it in the parking lot. We can call it the miracle of the pony."

Jacob nodded, wondering what condition it was in after years of nonuse.

Ambrose grinned.

"This is the will of God. Father Abbot, you need to work on surrendering to God what is God's. Try a little humility and trust. Don't mess with things that aren't broken."

The title scraped on his ears as he watched the giant man walk away toward the pasture, his rubber boots squeaking with each step.

"This is not God's will."

"You don't know that." The large man laughed and lumbered to the barnyard.

CHAPTER 3
EXCOMMUNICATION

Psalm 80: 12-13
But my people did not heed my voice.
And Israel would not obey,
so, I left them in their stubbornness of heart.

"Go to your cell." Those were Abbot Jacob's words, and Paul kicked himself for obeying, for not arguing more.

"I'll leave when I'm ready. I can spend a week alone," Paul said to the closed door as he spent the day isolated.

Twice there had been a knock on his door and both times there stood Novice Alcuin with his superior glare, handing him a tray of food. Paul couldn't bring himself to say "thank you" because of the sneer on Alcuin's face.

Paul turned to the wall that held a black-and-white portrait of Trent Reznor, the founder of Nine Inch Nails. Trent peered out from drapes of hair, casting an evil spell on those who entered. Wooden angel's wings flanked Trent, making him appear to have sprung from goodness. Hadn't Alcuin seen Father Joe's cell, which was knee deep in stacks of papers and books? Brother Ambrose had seedlings growing in his space. Paul pictured Alcuin's room, empty with a mattress on the floor, wondering if he can sneak into his cell and turn his crucifix upside down. Knowing that would freak the novice out.

But Alcuin was a judgmental cretin.

Paul expected boxes to arrive with an order to pack up and leave.

"You're being paranoid," Paul said, looking at his reflection in the darkening windows. Jacob couldn't send him away.

A knock came on his door. Paul checked the time. Too early for a meal. The door pushed open. Paul held his breath, expecting Father Joannicus, but Novice Reginald entered carrying boxes.

"What the heck?"

"I was told to bring you these," Novice Reginald said, glancing around the room. Paul suspected he was trying to verify Alcuin's claims. "Paul has so many possessions, not even monastic stuff, and satanic posters. They should kick him out." Screw Alcuin.

"Is that Nine Inch Nails?" Reginald asked. "You've got to admire the artwork on their albums, the muted blending, and surreal movement."

Novice Reginald was only five years older than Paul and soon to be a full-fledged monk. Nine Inch Nails was a heavy metal band with albums entitled "Pretty Hate Machine" and songs titled "Head like a Hole."

"They aren't bad, but I like KISS too," Paul said.

Reginald smiled. "KISS is a little over the top. I think I've a concert tee-shirt that might fit you."

Paul stared at the poster of the heavy metal band, KISS, with their black-and-white makeup and extreme poses. They appeared menacing. But anything would look startling next to the doe-eyed icon of St. Teresa that hung next to them.

"Thanks, I didn't think anyone here listened to NIN, not since Brother Dominic gave me his collection," Paul said, glaring at the boxes Reginald had set on his desk. "I'm not packing, because I'm not going anywhere."

"They told me you would say that."

"What else did they say?" Paul asked, crossing his arms.

"Pack what you want and what's left the monastery we'll give to charity."

"They can't do that."

Reginald stepped back. "The Rule tells us not to presume to keep anything unless ordered by the Abbot."

"Don't tell me what the Rule says. If Abbot Gordon were here, this wouldn't be happening."

Reginald stood at the door, his arms anchored to his sides as if he wanted to say something more. He turned to leave but stopped. "I heard it was Abbot Gordon's kindness and vision that let you stay here. But he is dead. I don't think it is proper of you to use his memory as a personal weapon whenever you don't get your way. The former abbot, may he rest in peace, liked you. Is this how you repay his hospitality?"

Paul noticed the neatly stacked boxes, and he felt his cheeks redden as he trembled with rage.

Reginald lowered his eyes with a sad smile. "I shouldn't linger, and I've said too much. I'm sorry."

Liar.

The door closed. Paul shoved the cartons into a corner of his cell before climbing into bed. Nobody is sorry.

The ache of Gordon's death shook him. The man was just

gone. He felt his eyes fill up with moisture. He wiped the wetness with his sleeve.

The crucifix bored into him.

Why did God kill off those he loved? Cut it out, okay?

PAUL WOKE TO A KNOCK. Brother Moses carried a tray of food. "Here's your dinner. Fried chicken, spuds, green beans, and baked beans. I got you salad because you must have green food and cheesy bread. Also, two desserts, apple pie, and a brownie."

"Thank you," Paul said, sitting up, disoriented from the nap. The smell caused Paul's stomach to rumble as he climbed out of bed, tossing his twisted blanket to one side.

Brother Moses took a step closer to Paul and peered at him.

"What?" Paul asked.

Brother Moses shook his head. "You don't look possessed. Don't stay in here too long. We'll have a big party with lots of wonderful food when we invest our new abbot. Oh, I like the sound of that. The entire Crow Nation will probably attend, and we'll have fry bread. You don't want to miss that."

"That isn't happening," Paul said, watching the face of Moses move from calm to turbulent.

"Oh, guess they forgot to tell you. We elected Father Jacob. I like him. He's gentle and wise. He used to cry a lot, but not so much anymore. He's always been fair and kind to me, even when I didn't deserve it."

The election was over. Paul knew that. But Jacob sent him to this cell, like a child. He had to protest. Paul didn't believe that Moses could be anything but nice.

"He isn't the abbot, not as far as I'm concerned."

Brother Moses smiled and backed out, mumbling something about being on a timer. With a mighty kick, Paul toppled the stack of empty boxes, causing them to blend into the already messy room. Paul ignored the cartons and ate dinner, then climbed into bed, reaching for his copy of *Oliver Twist*, and read until sleep overtook him.

Morning bells rang. Paul checked his floor, hoping for a note. But there was nothing except dust bunnies chasing each other in the warm light.

He missed prayers and wondered where Father Joannicus was, reckoning that he didn't care either.

He could at least say he thinks Jacob being the abbot is a good idea.

Guilt rose as he remembered shouting at Joannicus. He hadn't meant to. He was tired of funerals. They had three community members die before Abbot Gordon. The words rang in Paul's mind. "Stop talking about the dead and death."

Grounded. His friends had talked about being grounded and losing their freedom to go out. He never went out. Paul's entire life consisted of religious things, school, farm, and an occasional a trip down the hill to the college. He knew this banishment was more about isolation than freedom. Paul picked up the towels, sniffed them, and headed to the shower. The voices of the monks drifted through the hall as they chanted the psalms of Morning Prayer, causing Paul to pause and listen.

Breakfast arrived, and so did lunch. The silence of his room mocked him. Boredom motivated. Paul sorted through his clothing. He owned five pairs of jeans, three dress slacks, and a rainbow of shirts. His sweaters, he realized, belonged to Father Joannicus.

Paul held his breath as he listened to the footsteps outside his door. Was it Joannicus? When a knock didn't come, anger welled inside of him. Mellitus had betrayed him, casting a beyond-the-grave vote, putting Jacob in the divine light. That wasn't right, Merlin.

Paul stacked his books into reading piles: fantasy, classical, mystery, and educational. At his desk, Paul read, starting with a book that Father Joannicus said a well-educated person should read, *The Crucible*. Paul watched out the window as the monks moved through their day. He observed relationships and imagined conversations. To keep busy, Paul washed the windows and swept the floor. He found six marbles, plastic cowboys and Indians, along with a glove that no longer fit his hand, and a sock without a mate.

The odor of garlic and fresh bread drifted into his room and made his mouth water. Dinner arrived, portions generous and warm. Eating alone in silence differed from eating in silence with the community. He missed the sounds of the reader droning on. They had been reading *The Confession of Brother Haluin*. A medieval whodunit, and Paul wondered if they had solved the mystery.

He marveled that his personal life fit into three boxes.

Room clean, Paul became absorbed in the novel *The Three Musketeers*.

The evening bells rang louder than usual. Paul opened his door and glanced into the silent hall. His heartbeat quickened as he walked toward the church.

Prayer is open to everyone.

Smells of incense from Mass embraced him as he entered the atrium, triggering an emotional cascade that threatened to overpower his resolve. He wanted to be with them. He blinked the wetness back, reaching for his prayer books, which were stored in a labeled slot. Cool air rushed by him as a monk walked past. The breeze sent chills through him. He ignored the novice's whispering as he stepped into the church, feeling vulnerable.

Eyes to the carpet, Paul slipped into a seat behind the second choir. Abbot Jacob's head lifted for a moment, and Paul held his breath. Prayers began. Paul exhaled.

Every psalm and word caressed his mind like the licks of a puppy. Voices united in song and prayers like the walls of a fort, comforting yet ominous. Emptiness filled Paul. Two by two, the monks filed out. One by one, the church lights clicked off. Paul braced himself. He walked to the atrium. The absence of the monks punched him in the gut, and he fought back the urge to cry out as he stumbled to his cell.

Confusion and anger danced in Paul's heart as he paced in his pristine space. Speaking the truth is dangerous. But one should speak the truth. But whose truth was it?

Unsure of what to do next, Paul picked up another novel, *Dune,* and read himself to sleep. Loneliness took up residence in his room.

Morning prayers saw monks' heads bent and eyes averted as Paul crept back to his cell. Who would bring his breakfast? Could they stay, should they speak to him? He wanted to make them linger.

He heard squeaky footsteps approach his door, and he ran to open it. Ambrose smiled.

"How are you doing in exile?" Ambrose asked, placing a tray piled high with pancakes on the desk.

"Great," Paul said with enthusiasm.

"Liar." Ambrose laughed, stabbing a pancake.

Paul frowned. Was he that transparent? "Are you supposed to be talking to me?"

"Don't worry about me. I know the rules."

"I miss you," Paul said, stunned that he was saying those words.

Ambrose's face wrinkled with pleasure as syrup glistened on the wooly beard. "Good. But are you resolved?"

"What do you mean 'resolved'?"

"Ready to accept," Ambrose said. "Your room looks exceptional. Great job."

"Why hasn't Father Jonah come?" Paul said, realizing he was ready. He wanted back into the community.

Ambrose stuffed a second steamy pancake into his mouth and said through muffled bites, "You know, Joannicus doesn't get between you and Jacob's quarrels. He doesn't pick sides."

That was true. When Paul was young and Jacob would punish him, Joannicus did not get involved. Paul took the plate before he could devour all the pancakes. "Can you stay?"

Ambrose smiled. "Nope, you're being punished by the letter of the Rule. You know, excommunication and all."

Paul slumped to a chair. "He can't keep me in here forever."

"He isn't the one keeping you in here," Ambrose said, as he ruffled Paul's hair and left.

CHAPTER 4
AWAKEN

Psalm 136: 5

If I forget you, Jerusalem, let my right hand wither!

J acob stood in his cell looking out the window at the harvest gold landscape, repeating the words, "I am the abbot."

He still couldn't quite get used to those words, although they had proven useful in the last few days. Power. Good in disarming an obnoxious teenager, bad at being able to ignore the needs of others by closing his office door. After three days, Paul emerged from his cell to attend prayers. Jacob figured it would take another day before Paul came to any realization that his actions affected others. He believed punishment should end in an epiphany, not remorseful defeat. He needed Paul to come to him on his own.

A trail of ants crawled along the windowsill. The fussing had begun, a new habit, a new office. At least his cell would remain the same. Unadorned, untouched by external change.

Too much fuss.

He leaned over his bed, tucking in the blanket with the bright colors of the Apsáalooke Nation and thought. If I were Chief on the Rez, they would come to me. But I am Chief of the Benedictines. That means meetings, and long hours of debate, and supplications of needs.

Slowly he made his way downstairs to the office, the Abbot's office, his office, where he waited impatiently for his ten o'clock appointment. He watched through the window as a shiny sedan pulled up to the monastery. Two well-dressed men stepped out, investor and executor. Jacob wondered what they would say about his plan for Paul. A knock on the door. Jacob turned to greet them.

"Gentlemen," Jacob said, extending his hand.

The pungent smell of cologne danced around the room.

Smells bad.

"You know of the money left by Sarah Warner, Paul's mother?" Smells Bad said.

"I heard she left Paul money, and that you invested it."

The men looked at each other. The second man set his briefcase on Jacob's desk. With a click, the latches on the leather case opened as the man pulled out papers and placed them in neat stacks. He stood, his legs wiggling, causing his slacks to wave, so Jacob named him Runs with Papers.

Smells Bad cleared his throat. "The money for Paul is a trust fund. He'll get significant sums when he turns eighteen."

"Paul will have just started college," Jacob said. "Giving him a considerable sum then could derail him from finishing his education. Does he have to know at eighteen?"

"Okay maybe not eighteen, but he will be a legal adult at eighteen," Runs with Papers said as his right knee bounced, a muffled thud beating the floor.

Jacob frowned. What had Sarah Warner been hoping to accomplish? They weren't miracle workers. He could see Paul going dollar-happy. The boy needed an allowance.

Smells Bad pushed the papers toward Jacob. Jacob studied the papers. He had never seen so many zeros in a row on one page.

"This column is what Paul has now," Smells Bad pointed out. The gold ring on his finger winked at Jacob. "The numbers will increase."

Jacob stopped listening. Too much money ruined good people.

"We invest as much as you see fit of the monastery's money," Runs with Papers said, his long tan finger pointing to a column.

Jacob leaned forward as the leather chair creaked. A lot of zeros there too.

Jacob recalled, from working as an accountant for his stepfather, Terence, that money was leverage. A flair of a signature and he could stomp their livelihoods.

"Why do we have so much?" Jacob asked. This was a lot of money. Possibilities swirled, central heating for the monastery, a new roof for the church.

"Abbot Gordon only spent money on health care," Smells Bad said, now perched on the edge of his seat.

"Are there strings attached? Things we cannot spend our money on?" Jacob asked, knowing Gordon was a frugal man, but he could have spared something.

"No. To get the full amount, keep Paul until he is eighteen. When that happens, the money stops, but we'll continue to invest for you," Runs with Papers said.

Jacob smirked.

Power.

Abbot Gordon was tightfisted and cautious. They are wondering if the new abbot is a spender or hoarder.

Leverage.

"Paul has a stipend."

"Stipend?" Was Paul receiving money?

"Abbot Gordon put the money in an account." Runs with Papers shoveled through the stack, producing a bank statement. "This money for spending on whatever needs Paul has, clothing, shoes, and incidentals. We have denied no expenses. But Abbot Gordon rarely charged the account."

Jacob looked through the papers. All the expenses tied to raising a child seemed missing. He noticed that a small amount was paid to Paul's godparents. Jacob assumed it was because they took Paul to events. The rest of the expenses were clothing and an occasional toy. Jacob had to admire Gordon for that. Paul was not the cash cow that most assumed. Nobody could say the monks abused the privilege of being compensated.

THE CLOCK on the wall chimed eleven times. Jacob stood and straightened his habit. He bent over the desk and signed the papers with highlighted lines, acknowledging he understood.

"If I send Paul away for a year, what happens?"

The men sat up straighter.

"You don't get your dividend for the year. You understand you can't send him to a boarding school," Runs with Papers said.

"I was hoping to send him on a vacation of sorts, a travel trip to Benedictine monasteries across the United States."

Legs wiggled, and waves traveled up his pant legs. "By himself? Are there that many monasteries?"

Jacob turned away from them and looked outside to the

private patio. A little stream of water trickled down the slate wall to a small pond, as gentle waves rippled the surface.

"Yes, there are over 120 Benedictine houses. Besides, Paul will soon be fifteen. I suspect a teen can travel alone. A monk or nun will meet him as he arrives. They may even travel with him, since we often visit each other, like a large family. They'll keep him a while, a few months. I will require him to keep a journal of his travels, so it would not be all fun and games."

Jacob turned, the icon of Benedict on the wall stared at him.

"Benedictine houses are places of education, so Paul can attend classes. He will not be idle. I wanted to send Paul on a monastic tour. The monks brought up stability and Gyrovagues, which are monks who cannot seem to..." Jacob stopped when he noticed the confused look on the two educated men's faces. They didn't care about the kinds of monks that the Rule mentioned.

The lawyers looked at each other. "Why?"

"So, he can experience the bigger world."

Lie number one.

From his perch, Smells Bad said, "Another monastery is not the world."

"True, but it is not here. We will foot the bill. I am not asking to take it from Paul's portion. I would like to give him an allowance, so he can learn to manage money."

Runs with Papers laughed. Jacob felt abashed.

"Paul won't need to. He's so rich, and he can't spend it all because there is an untouchable base that is maintained," Smells Bad said, rising and brushing away wrinkles from wool suit.

"Having money and spending it are two different things. I want him to understand money, not just spend it." Jacob could feel his anger rising. He wouldn't let Paul fall into a money trap.

Jacob looked at the men before him, with their gold watches and leather briefcases. Is that a diamond holding his collegiate black-and-gold tie in place? Jacob understood people lived beyond their means, from his parish priest days, and he'd heard stories of those who came into wealth—lottery winners who lost everything they won in a few years—but that was not the Benedictine way. Paul was Benedictine, if that at all influenced the boy.

Jacob ran his hand over the warm wood of his desk with ornate carvings and a beeswax finish that gave off a faint odor in the heat of the day. This desk was the first abbot's desk, made by Brother Cuthbert in the early 1900s.

The men's faces stared at him as if he had spoken Latin.

Paul wasn't getting all the money when he turned eighteen.

"St. Alberic's money is yours to spend as you see fit. As for sending Paul on vacation, I don't see a problem," Runs with Papers said.

Smells Bad took a deep breath. "Might we suggest you read the file we gave to Abbot Gordon? It contains information—" They paused, looking wary. "—that might prove helpful to you."

What were they not saying? Jacob narrowed his eyes, looking at them under veiled lashes, the warrior wanting to smash their heads together.

"Danger. Calm," the Elder within whispered.

"I have not seen that file. Maybe you could send me a copy."

"Sure, it might take a few days," Smells Bad said, placing the signed documents in his briefcase.

"I would like a copy of those documents," Jacob said, smiling as their faces darkened. *I know the importance of a paper trail,* thought Jacob, thankful for his stepfather's training with contracts and legal documents.

After thanking and dismissing them, Jacob stood by the window, letting the heat of the sun absorb his anger. Questions shot off like fireworks in Jacob's mind. Nobody had given him a file or mentioned it when they gave him the keys to the office, and one key was missing—the one to the desk. The one locked drawer.

He spun the dream catcher and the little prisms swirled rainbow around the room. He didn't want to send Paul away, but Joe insisted on keeping his illness a secret. There was no other solution. But he worried nobody can keep secrets here. The truth always comes out. A year is too long. What if the treatment didn't work?

A cough and the odor of tobacco alerted him he wasn't alone.

"The Lord be with you," Jacob said.

"And with you, Father Abbot," two voices answered.

Abbot Jacob turned. Father Joannicus looked ashen in the bright light. Jacob wondered how Paul could have missed that, since the boy continually pointed out inconsistencies.

What lie have you told him? What lie will I tell him? I should write the lies down and keep them in the locked drawer. My legacy: *The Book of Lies* by Abbot Jacob Mackenzie-Knows the Song, O.S.B.

"What did they want?" Joannicus asked, melting into the soft chair.

"I asked them here for a crash course on money, and they told me about Paul," Jacob said.

"What's there to discover? Paul's an orphan who'll have a lot of money someday," Ambrose said.

"A lot. That is putting it mildly," Jacob said.

"We get some money, a few million, and he gets some money. It all works out," Ambrose said, sniffing the room and wrinkling his nose. The scent of cologne lingered.

"Do either of you know about a file on Paul?"

"Why a special file on Paul? Barb gave us an excellent picture of his life before he came to us. Those documents are in the file cabinet," Joannicus said.

"He had two parents and grandparents, a history, a birth certificate," Jacob said. Had nobody inquired about Paul's past?

"No. Barb said Paul and Sarah, nobody else. Don't go digging in the past. Nothing good ever comes from disturbing sleeping facts," Joannicus said. "Don't you remember what happened to Tomas, that boy who was adopted and the psychology professor who encouraged him to find his actual parents?"

Jacob remembered. They fired the teacher after Tomas committed suicide. The fantasy of who his parents were didn't match the reality. The young man couldn't live with the truth.

"If there were relatives, Ms. Carr would have found them. Sarah didn't want her son with those people if they even exist. Is it so hard to accept a kid can be an orphan?" Ambrose said, tossing his head. "Paul's here where he belongs."

Joannicus gave Ambrose a quizzical look.

Protest heard, thought Jacob. *You don't want me to send Paul away.*

"I have a bad feeling about this missing file. Abbot Gordon did not share knowledge of it with either of you?" Jacob asked.

Father Joannicus shrugged, and Brother Ambrose shook his head.

"So, when do you start treatment?" Jacob asked, changing the subject, and staring at the locked drawer on his new desk.

Bet the file is in that drawer.

Father Joannicus shifted. "Tuesday."

"Not here for that," Ambrose said. "We were wondering when you'll release Paul from his cell."

"He has escaped several times," Jacob said, amused that these two different men stood in unison.

Wait. They are united against him.

They stared at him with a serious expression that caused Jacob to laugh.

"I will talk to him. I have something to discuss with him. You can warn him. I want an apology."

"Are you still hell-bent on sending him away?" Ambrose asked, crossing his arms, the rip on his shoulder exposing the brown-and-yellow plaid shirt beneath.

He needs a new habit more than me, Jacob observed.

Father Joannicus shook his head. "That's a rotten idea. He needs stability with us. Teens need a sense of belonging. All the experts say it's a critical time in their development."

"Yeah, we don't want him identifying with the wrong gang," Ambrose said.

"Gang is rather harsh. He will be with other Benedictines, none of which will lead him astray," Abbot Jacob said.

"He has never been away from us. Couldn't we assign him chores and duties, like we do novices to keep them occupied and feel a part of the community?" Joannicus said, his voice taking on a pleading quality.

Even though Paul was acquainted with monastic living, he wasn't one of them. Paul sat away from the community during prayers as a guest might. He didn't read or serve like the novices, and he had no chores. He was a guest in the cloister.

However, making Paul a monk didn't sit well with anyone. His living with them was not to be an experiment in conversion.

"He is not a novice, but he needs some new experiences, so I am sending him on a spiritual quest," Jacob said.

"Who'll watch over him?" Joannicus asked, leaning forward in his chair.

"Apsáalooke boys as young as twelve make spirit quests," Ambrose pointed out. "How long will his visit be?"

Visits, thought Abbot Jacob as he clenched his jaw to keep from explaining his year-long plan. Apsáalooke boys seemed more mature than Paul. Monastery living had sheltered Paul, making him unprepared to live in the world.

"What if we lose him?" Joannicus asked.

"We can't lose him. He'll come back loving us more," Ambrose said with confidence that Abbot Jacob wished he felt.

"He'll come back changed," Joannicus said, letting his head tilt back, eyes focusing on the ceiling.

"We all change. You have changed." The man feared raising Paul was now arguing to keep him close.

Frustration surged. Every decision seemed to be fraught with doubt and justifications. He wished Joannicus would tell Paul about his illness. The boy could focus on being a caregiver.

"What do you want me to do? Paul is smart. If he stays here, he will notice you are missing. Your treatment will take time, and you need to focus on you, not Paul. Sending him away will help do this. Also, the former abbot always leaves while the new abbot gets settled."

Ambrose laughed. "Emeritus Abbot Paul indeed."

"Paul is leaving Tuesday, and can you take him to the airport?" Abbot Jacob asked, turning to Joannicus. "I will meet you at the treatment center afterward."

Joannicus hung his head as if resolved by the weight of his life, heart, and vocation. Obedience was difficult. Abbot Jacob wished he could change that, make this burden easier for his friend and confrere.

"Guess he has a point," Ambrose conceded, as the two men left his office. "It is just I will miss him."

Jacob closed his eyes. He felt exhausted. The opinions of others mattered more now. Chapter 3 of the Rule reminds the abbot to hear the advice of all the brothers. So many voices to listen to.

Abbot Jacob retired to his cell. The festive planning, the new habit, the ring, and the pointy hat all had become overwhelming. Jacob stripped to his tee shirt, unbraided his hair, shaking it out as his thoughts jumped like grasshoppers. He watched the moon send slivers of light across the floor. In the dimness, he lit four candles and sat staring at the pages of the ceremony before him.

Tomorrow they would invest him as the abbot. There were questions, five of them, he would have to answer. Would his voice betray him, show his doubt? Could he say yes with the conviction? He had faith in these men, and they were his foundation. Footsteps paused in the hall outside his cell door. He cringed.

Go away.

The loud rap shattered his composure.

"Enter."

The door opened, and Paul stumbled inside. Jacob pretended not to notice the standing shadows in the hall. A quick glance made him suppress a chuckle. Paul stood with his back pressed against the wall, his eyes shut.

Jacob waited. He could hear Paul swallowing hard. He looked up, and their eyes met. Paul looked away.

Jacob brushed his hair back from his forehead. "I want to apologize. I neglected you. I hope you can forgive me?"

"No."

Jacob raised his eyebrows. "No, you will not forgive me?"

"No, I mean yes, but I came to apologize."

"So, apologize," Jacob said, enjoying the moment of Paul squirming.

Paul bit his lower lip, taking a step into the room and closer to Jacob. An arm's length away, Paul knelt on the floor.

"Abbot Jacob, I'm sorry for being a jerk."

"And?"

Paul stole a glance. "And, what?"

"What did I learn?" That was how an Apsáalooke Elder teaches the young.

"Oh, well." Paul sat down on the floor. Jacob drew in a deep breath, looking down at the boy. So much life ahead of him. "Not to piss off the Abbot?"

Jacob shook his head.

"Okay, I learned I missed you all," Paul said. "It was lonely, and I don't like that."

"You need us?"

"Yeah."

"Good, remember we need you too. I forgive you," Jacob said. "Stop. That is enough groveling. Stand up. I have some good news and some bad news. I am sending you on sabbatical. For just a year. Try it. You might have fun, new faces, new places. This is not permanent. I want you back. You need to see the world. You will not be with us forever."

Lie number three.

Jacob could not listen to the words dropping out of his mouth, and he feared Paul wouldn't either.

Paul stood and sat on the bed. "You hate me. I don't want to go away."

"I do not hate you. I love you, and I love this community. But I need your help to get my house in order."

"Am I such a distraction? You're the abbot. They'll listen to you. They have to."

"I want the monks to listen because they know I care about them. I understand you do not want to leave."

"I can protest this and take it to the council."

Jacob suddenly realized Paul thought of himself as a monk, and that he could use the Rule to make Paul obey.

"Read Chapter 5 on Obedience and then Chapter 68 Assignment of Impossible Tasks. If that is not to your liking, remember I am Apsáalooke," Jacob said.

"I'm not Crow."

"We are all Apsáalooke. Think of this as a vision quest. Boys younger than you go out and find themselves. This will help and you and me."

"You'll do it no matter what," Paul said, crossing his arms and looking like a brave warrior before battle.

"Yes," Jacob said, trying not to sound harsh. "You need to see the world. You will be a part of it someday."

"You don't know that. I might become a monk."

Jacob looked away. No way, kiddo, at least not here.

"I don't want to go. I need to be here."

"Change is scary. The day is coming when we say stay, you will leave." Jacob forced a smile. "Your old room is clean. How about selecting a new room?"

"Why? You are sending me away." Paul picked fuzz balls from the blanket on the bed. "I knew you shouldn't be abbot."

That hurt.

"Be gentle," the Elder whispered. "The boy is still grieving and needs to speak of the pain."

Jacob slid off his chair and sat on the bed next to Paul. "I miss him too."

"You should have said sorry to Abbot Gordon," Paul said, his face etched in pain.

"I know." Jacob hung his head.

Paul's eyes watered. "You hurt him by not coming back or answering his letters."

It didn't matter anymore who had begun the rift. Gordon ended it with his death, and the time to give forgiveness had passed.

A gust of air blew through the open window, scattering the papers that Jacob had been reading.

Paul picked up the papers on the floor, glancing at them before handing them to Jacob.

"Do you think I can answer yes to those questions?" Jacob asked, taking the pages.

"Will they accept four out of five?" Paul said.

Jacob's right eyebrow rose. "Which one?"

"Will you always and in all matters be loyal, obedient, and reverent to the Holy Church and our Holy Father, the Pope, and his successors?" Paul said. "You can't do that very well."

Jacob laughed and shook his head. "Smart-ass. Who said truthfulness is a virtue?"

"Father Jonah. Someone needs to be in charge of check and balance, and I assumed that was my job," Paul said, the impish smile from the past appearing on his face.

Jacob's resistance melted, and he stood and embraced Paul, feeling the stiffness dissolve between them.

"Now that you are growing up, I was hoping to assign you chores, but we can discuss that at a later date. It is time for you to go. Tomorrow is my big day. Do not open the door too quickly. Tom and Jerry might fall over," Jacob said.

"Who?"

Paul opened the door. Ambrose and Joannicus stood side by side.

"Oh, there you are," Ambrose said as Paul grinned and shook his head.

CHAPTER 5
APSÁALOOKE VILLAGE

Psalm 109:1
The Lord's revelation to my Master:
Sit on my right, your foes, I will put beneath your feet.

P aul sat in an apple tree, watching the vapors of mist rise in the pre-dawn light. He reflected on Texas. The first place Abbot Jacob wanted to send him. He had heard that it never snowed in Texas. Who wants to live in a place without snow? Yesterday's conversation with Father Joannicus drifted back to him.

"I don't want to go."

"You do. You just don't know it. It's a gift. Accept it and learn something."

A gift. Right.

Paul tried a different tactic. "What if I need you?"

"Seriously, I'm a phone call away," Father Joannicus said, but Paul had detected a note of sadness. He had expected Father Jonah to laugh and say you're too old to need me. Paul didn't feel older.

"What if you need me?" Paul finally asked.

Father Joannicus kissed the top of his head and said, "Don't worry. Trust Abbot Jacob."

Paul shook his head. They were all crazy.

The sunrise had brightened the landscape, and Paul watched Jacob emerge from the sweat lodge and shiver in the warm air of the morning. The pasture was now a makeshift Indigenous village. Teepees and trucks stood among the sheep, which didn't seem to mind the invading visitors.

Jacob spoke aloud in Apsáalooke. Paul thought he heard "run away" in what sounded like a question.

He must be praying.

Today they were going to officially make Jacob the abbot.

The monastery was like a spring hive. Decorations made, tables laid out, invitations sent, and specialty foods made Paul hoped fry bread would be on the menu. Jacob had introduced him to native foods and fry bread was still his favorite.

Paul watched the surreal activity moving around him. The tailors had been busy making a stiff new garment. Ambrose and Moses had shooed him away from the barn as they were making a crozier, a fancy shepherd's hook. Even Rebecca, Jacob's sister, had a task. The Apsáalooke tribe was contributing prayers and sage to the liturgy. Joannicus was overseeing it all and making sure it met conical standards—or something like that.

Paul walked through the camp, making his way up the hill, passing a group of girls. They giggled, and he heard the word "cute" in Crow. Who had said it? The large black eyes of the girls stared at him, and the faces blushed. One could overhear much by not telling anyone you could speak their language.

His blood raced, and he felt sweat trickle down his back as he stood next to them. He bent down and plucked a handful of daisies, then held them out to the girls. They laughed nervously and wiggled. Their shiny black hair shimmered around them. Then, like a deer in an open field, they scattered. Paul laid the daisies on the fence post as he left the pasture. Girls were silly.

He entered the church, breathing in the incense-laden air. He loved that smell, and the odor of baking day. Down the hall, he dodged monks as they straightened their chasubles. There was more excitement today than he had ever seen. He had witnessed men becoming novices, and novices becoming juniors, and then juniors making solemn vows, but never one becoming an abbot.

He now wished he had paid more attention to Joannicus when he had explained the hierarchy of the monastery. But he was only eight then.

Brother Ambrose compared the monastery to a squabble in the barnyard. The new rooster had to prove himself.

Paul made his way into the robe room, where Brother Ambrose hovered over Jacob.

"Perhaps you should eat something. You're not a young man anymore," Ambrose said, placing a firm hand on Jacob's shoulder.

Jacob frowned. "I will be fine."

"What's wrong?" Paul asked, seeing Jacob bent over as if he were ill.

"Okay, but if you pass out in the middle of the ceremony, don't expect me to give you mouth to mouth," Ambrose said. "Too much spiritual preparing, not enough physical preparation."

"It will make a believable touch. Everyone will think I am overwhelmed with ecstasy," Jacob said.

"Here, I have a candy bar," Paul said, pulling the crushed

package from his shirt pocket, worried that the passing out of the Abbot might look like what happened in June when Abbot Gordon died during evening prayers.

"Eat," ordered Ambrose as the drums began a heartbeat rhythm. The ceremony was about to start. Paul wondered how long Jacob had fasted and sweated.

Wait. Paul realized that Ambrose had taken over as master of ceremonies.

"Where's Father Jonah? I thought this was his job?" Paul asked as Ambrose shooed him out of the space.

"Not now, Little One," Ambrose said. "All is as it should be."

I don't think I believe you, thought Paul as he walked down the hall toward the church. Was Joannicus sick again? He needed to see a doctor.

Paul fought the tinge of anger that crept into his muscles. Joannicus promised to see a doctor right after today's events.

Paul knew Joannicus would keep his promise. He would ask him directly in the first letter he would write.

Paul headed into the church. He wished he was busy. They never let him help. There were warriors, painted faces, girls in jingle dresses that tinkled when they moved, buckskin, and feathers. Full regalia for this sacred ceremony.

Throughout Mass, Paul watched Jacob chew on his thumbnail.

Why was Jacob so nervous? These were the guys who elected him.

Brother Ambrose stood in front of Abbot David, his voice booming loudly.

"Most Reverend Father, in the name of our community, we present to you the Abbot Elect, Reverend Jacob Mackenzie-Knows the Song, of our monastery of the order of Saint Benedict. We ask you to bless him as our abbot."

Abbot David smiled and spoke. "Has he been duly elected?"

"We know and testify that he has."

"Thanks be to God."

And the Apsáalooke women trilled. Paul shivered at the sound.

Abbot David asked Jacob the questions that Paul saw the other night. Jacob answered, "I will," to every question.

Paul had expected to see Jacob dressed in buckskins and feathers. Had he given up his Apsáalooke spirit? A small bunch of feathers hung at the end of Jacob's braided hair. Relief washed through him. He liked the mix of Apsáalooke and Catholic.

"Take this ring, a seal of fidelity, wear it as a symbol of constancy, and maintain this community in the bonds of brotherly love."

Jacob's hand trembled, and Paul wondered if the now-deceased Brother Mellitus was hoping the ring would drop and roll away. Abbot David stood to place the mitre on Jacob's head. Paul smiled. This hat was partly Apsáalooke. The front and back lappets were beaded and embroidered with feathers. A stunning mix of war bonnet and mitre.

"Take this shepherd's staff and show loving care for the brothers God has entrusted to you, for he will demand an account of your stewardship."

Finally, Paul saw what Moses and Ambrose had created out of the cedar stick. On it hung three eagle feathers. Most croziers resembled a golden shepherd's crook. But not this one. The feathers represented wisdom, strength, and courage. Paul smiled. Those were the qualities that Abbot Gordon had said an abbot needed to lead. Abbot Gordon also said that being abbot was a balance between actions and listening. Pride swelled. They had blended both Apsáalooke with the Catholic.

Each monk then approached Jacob, knelt before him for his

blessing. Jacob looked around the church. His eyes settled on Paul. He can't mean for me to come.

Paul felt his face grow hot, and he looked away. Crap. When he looked back, Jacob's blue eyes held his gaze. Moving slowly, feeling his heart beating louder than the drums, Paul approached Jacob. Paul recalled wanting to do everything the monks did, but not today.

"What should I say? I'm not a monk."

"You are part of this community. Say as the others did, that you will obey me."

That wasn't fair. He wasn't a monk, but how can he say otherwise?

The silence hung. A heaviness filled Paul's heart. A year-long trip loomed in his future.

"You are my abbot. I will obey you," Paul said, his mouth going dry. Were Jacob's eyes watering?

Mass continued, and Jacob's hand shook while he blessed the community, his first official duty as abbot. Abbot Jacob led them from the church, the monks followed, and the jingle dancers high-stepped behind them and the drums echoed.

After the formalities, the celebration began. Paul moved his way through the people, most of whom he didn't know. Apparently, the monks did because there were black robes scattered among the crowds.

The aroma of fry bread was irresistible, and Paul stood in line to get his share. He took a bite, relishing the flavor, warm and sweet. He glanced around. There was that group of giggling girls. This time, one had a daisy pinned to her ebony hair. She had creamy brown skin, high cheekbones, and a narrow face, a combination of Apsáalooke and Lakota. Paul smiled. The girl smiled. She no longer wore the ceremonial buckskin, which made most girls look flat. This girl was not flat.

"Want a piece of my fry bread?" Paul asked, taking the few steps to be next to them. Daisy Girl blushed and nodded. The other girls drifted away.

"Cool ceremony, huh? It reminded me of a powwow."

"You've been?" Daisy Girl said as she nibbled the bread.

"Well, yeah, hasn't everyone? You've gone?"

She laughed, and Paul grinned.

"You're kind of funny," she said.

Out of nowhere, a square boy appeared and sneered at them.

"What are you doing here?"

Paul recognized him as Jacob's nephew, Holbrook.

Holbrook postured, taking the stance of a baseball player ready to bat.

"I said, what are you doing here?"

"Breaking bread with... what is your name?" Paul said, turning his back on Holbrook.

"My sister," Holbrook barked.

He lies. Natives used brother and sister, just as the monks called each other father and brother. Few were blood related. Besides, Holbrook had a reputation for telling tall tales. Paul knew Holbrook had two younger sisters. This girl stood at least a foot taller than Holbrook did. She could not be a younger sister.

"Go away, you bother me," Paul said, dismissing Holbrook.

"No, you go away, orphan reject," Holbrook said, standing on his tiptoes, leaning forward, like a cock ready to start a fight.

Paul poked a finger out, finding it hard to resist touching him. What did Jacob call it? Counting coop? Holbrook had always liked to point out that Paul had no family.

"I may be an orphan, but I belong here. Who knelt before the Abbot? You or me?"

"He's not your dad. You don't know your real dad." A small group of boys gathered.

That was true. Paul didn't know his paternity, but he had more father figures than he cared to count.

"You count your lineage through your mother, you moron. Everyone knows that. The monks are my family. Your mom, Rebecca, is sister to Abbot Jacob, so we are cousins if you must relate us."

Technically, that was incorrect because Paul wasn't Jacob's son. Rebecca and Jacob shared the same mother. Paul would not lose this pissing match.

"Bullshit," Holbrook said as he lunged forward. Paul stepped to the side, thanking Ambrose for letting him play chicken with the goat as a boy. As the boy flew by, Paul tapped his shoulder. If he was going to get pummeled, he could say he touched the enemy.

"You're not my cousin. I'm one hundred percent Indian, and you're a mutt."

That was not how genetics worked.

"Are you complaining or bragging? I'm your teasing cousin," Paul said. Jacob had told him about Crow cousins whose job it was to make sure you didn't get a swollen head over your accomplishment. They were called teasing cousins.

Holbrook snorted like an elk as Paul continued.

"You're one hundred percent stupid because your uncle has blue eyes, which means—"

Paul saw the fist and felt the breeze before his cheek ached. Time for talking was over. Paul balled his fist, jumped back, only to be grabbed by the shoulder. A meaty hand locked on Holbrook's right ear.

"Gentlemen, let's pay a visit to the Chief," Brother Ambrose said.

Holbrook protested, "Let go of me. You're not my uncle."

Paul knew better than to struggle, wondering which Chief

Ambrose would make them face. He suspected Jacob, but with Ambrose, one could never be sure.

"Today of all days," Ambrose grumbled, shaking Paul, then releasing him in front of Jacob. "These two have some apologizing to do. I thought they would go fist to cuff—a male dominance bonding thing."

"He started it," Holbrook said, a look of superiority smeared his face.

Paul recognized the Indian sneer, a fake expression of innocence. He'd watched classmates using it to get out of trouble. That would not work on Jacob.

"Paul?" Jacob said, taking a deep breath.

Paul's mouth hung open. He wasn't the instigator.

Jacob's blue eyes opened wide.

Paul crossed his arms. Fine.

"Sorry, Holbrook."

A smirk appeared on Holbrook's face.

Paul turned to Jacob. "Sorry, Abbot Jacob."

Jacob dismissed Holbrook, but commanded Paul to sit.

"Why are you punishing me for his bad behavior?"

"Jesus did not seem to mind," Jacob said as he spun the ring on his finger. The tribe had given him the silver band that had an engraved crow on a single branch of a tree.

"You are not God, and I'm not Jesus," Paul pointed out, knowing that Jacob was referring to Romans 8: 34 where the Apostle Paul writes Christ is sitting at God's right hand.

"Your punishment will be the shiner you will have tomorrow. What were you fighting about?"

"Your blue eyes," Paul said, plucking grass and making a pile of green in front of himself. "Does Holbrook have an older sister?"

"No. Two younger ones. What do my blue eyes have to do with girls?"

"Holbrook is a moron. He was claiming total Native blood, and I pointed out that you have blue eyes. That's a dead giveaway that you had a white ancestor. Are his sisters taller than him?"

"The birth order is Holbrook, Dawn, and Sabrina." Abbot Jacob chuckled. "Yes, Dawn is taller than Holbrook."

"What's so funny?"

"You were fighting over girls."

"No. Holbrook is a bully," Paul said.

"Yeah, and your point?"

"That's kind of rude. You're his uncle and all." Paul picked at the grass and then confessed. "I did egg him on."

Jacob cuffed Paul gently. "No, it is tribal culture. Uncles help a boy become a man. And stop picking on him. He is jealous of you. Perhaps you should Christian up?"

"We both can't be Christ. Fine, but I don't understand why he's jealous of me? He's your nephew, and I'm nothing to you."

"Excuse me," Jacob said, tossing a crust of bread at Paul's head.

"You know what I mean, blood related. I was just talking to Dawn, no need for him to get all warrior on me." Paul liked her name. The first beauty of the morning.

"You have a lot to learn about family. Maybe that is why he is jealous. Go. Find Dawn. She likes the first snow of the season and the color lavender," Abbot Jacob said as he stood and stretched.

Paul's search for Dawn proved unsuccessful. He headed to the tailor shop, passing the little gazebo where he saw Brother Ambrose. Smoke hung thick in the air as he approached. Abbot Jacob was with him.

"What are you doing out here? You're the guest of honor. People are leaving."

"Fresh air," Brother Ambrose said as he exhaled smoke.

Paul shook his head. Abbot Jacob leaned back, making a smoke ring, like the old Jacob, not the new abbot.

A man approached them.

"Crap," Jacob said as he handed the cigarette to Paul.

"You are too young to smoke. Put that out," Jacob said. Paul dropped the cigarette to the ground in disbelief. Ambrose crushed it with his sandaled foot.

Terence, Jacob's stepfather, looked suspiciously at Paul, and then at Jacob. "We're going to be heading out. Your mother has a headache. But before we leave, we have something for you." Terence handed Jacob a beautifully carved box.

Jacob looked at his stepfather. "This is Grandma Tiama's box. Thank you."

Paul had seen that box at the Mackenzie farmhouse. He had also heard the story of the blue-eyed Frenchmen, who the tribe had named Cold Feet. The man was ill and near death. An Apsáalooke woman, Sings in the Night, found him. She nursed him back to health and married him. Paul remembered that Cold Feet had carved the box, and it smelled faintly of sweet grass.

"Well, open it," Terence said.

Jacob slowly opened the box. Inside was a cross with a star at its center. Not your average pectoral cross, but Oglala Lakota design. Paul recognized it was a medicine wheel with a silver braided circle that glistened in the sunlight. The pendant had four inlaid stones, in the traditional colors of black, red, smoky white, and sandstone yellow. The design reminded Paul of the stain glass windows in the church.

"Oh," Jacob said, his voice cracking. "This is a Lakota design, did Todd...?"

"Yes, Rebecca, Todd, and myself."

"But not Basahke."

Sadness deepened the wrinkles that were etching themselves

across Terence's face. "Your mother, well, she is who she is. All we can do is love her. Please accept this gift."

Jacob shifted from side to side as he stood in front of his stepfather.

Paul felt the uneasy tension between the two men, not quite understanding what caused it.

"May it heal the past between us," Terence said in Apsáalooke.

Jacob stepped forward and embraced the man, choking out his thanks.

Terence left. Paul knew Todd was Holbrook's father. Todd was Lakota, he had married Rebecca, and she was Apsáalooke. Maybe Holbrook hadn't reconciled his Apsáalooke nature with his Lakota spirit. Paul was grateful he had one religion because understanding that what hard enough.

Paul turned to Jacob. "That was unkind."

"My mother does not care for me, never really did. It was not a gift from her. My father deserved the credit for his thoughtfulness, not her."

This family relationship stuff baffled Paul.

"It's really a cool cross. Do you think they will let you wear it?"

Jacob laughed.

"I am the abbot. Who is going to stop me?" Jacob said as he pocketed the abbot's large golden cross and replaced it with the brilliantly colored one.

CHAPTER 6
SINS OF THE FATHERS

Psalm 52: 4
All have left the right path, depraved, everyone.
There is not a good man left. No, not even one.

The office of the Abbot was ancient, as was the furniture that decorated it. Icons, glass cabinets, Victorian chairs. Jacob had safely tucked Paul in Texas and Joannicus in the hospital, recovering from surgery. He now needed to embrace being an abbot. He pressed his hands firmly on the desk, feeling its coolness. Jacob closed his eyes, saying a quick prayer. When he opened his eyes, he focused on a picture of Paul and the community, both whispering a threat to his peace.

The leather chair seemed large as he stared at the ornate wooden door, rubbing the edge of the skeleton key Ambrose had handed him with chagrin. Nothing good was behind drawer number one. Jacob was sure of that.

Abbot Jacob glanced at the clock. Two hours and a locked drawer. He inserted the key. The lock protested. Inside were neatly stacked pages, one file folder, and several unopened official looking pieces of mail.

Jacob pulled out the handwritten pages containing information about individual monks and read. The conclusions drawn from the histories appeared logical. Father Michael had alcoholic tendencies because every male in his family from generation to generation had become alcoholics all the way back to Europe, a pattern of premature deaths, and business losses all because of drinking. A blessing that he was a monk. He spared others suffering. Michael had never been sacristan. The temptation of unlimited access to the wine. Gordon was wise in this choice.

As Jacob sipped his lukewarm coffee, he recalled Ambrose curbing Michael's drinking at celebrations by taking the liquid away. Jacob wondered if Michael asked Ambrose to stop him.

Four hours later, Jacob locked the door to his office and closed the drapes. The room become shrouded in secrecy. Gordon had complied a file of every member of the monastery. The kind face of Brother Moses caused Jacob to sigh.

His father and mother were uncle and niece, so his grandparents were his great grandparents on one side and his paternal grandparent was a cousin. When most family trees were expanding with each generation, this tree grew smaller. Jacob tried to draw a family tree, but his head swirled in lines too closely connected. Moses was unaware of this. Who needed to know this history?

Jacob pulled out his file. As he read, he found it was incomplete. Missing was Jacob's eldest brother, Jimmy, who had followed in the footsteps of their biological father and fell into the white man's brown bottle. Another victim of oppression and genocide. The assumptions Gordon made concerning him, his fitness to be alone with the child. Jacob's jaw clenched.

Gordon saw everyone as a demon. That was clear. The troubling aspect was that the research lacked a dose of faith that one could grow and change. Where was the Benedictine ideal?

A new file, Father Pius James Carrington, who was abandoned by his father, raised by a strict mother. That explains Pius, but it didn't predict that he would be the one to hurt Paul.

Past influences didn't forecast the future. Conversion was possible.

Jacob thought about adding his name to the list of monks on antidepressants.

The papers left Jacob recoiling in disgust and shame. An abbot should love his monks. Jacob ran his fingers through his hair, wishing that Ambrose had never given him the key. What to do with the material? These evaluations gave Jacob knowledge that he had no right to. Why had Gordon done this? Why did he feel compelled to read them? Anyone reading this information would think of them as misfits and riffraff. And worse, he was part of this group. These files should be burned.

What was normal? Jacob had read the one-page synopsis of whom Gordon viewed as normal, Brother Barnabas, Father Damien, Brother Cletus, a dozen or so. Was Joannicus? With trembling fingers, he flipped open the file. Father Joannicus Brookes, Collin Brookes, a convert to Catholicism, entering at eighteen. There was a note in Gordon's handwriting, "I'm concerned whether this man could parent with no worldly experience. He has the greatest access to the child. I trust the Lord wouldn't be so cruel."

Anger washed anew. Gordon was crazy. Predicting what a man would do? The logic behind the system made sense.

Ambrose's words rang in his memory... Nope, wouldn't put Paul and Brother Donald together, too much like raw meat and wasps... Jacob had thought Ambrose had misplaced his metaphors, but now he saw differently. Donald liked adolescent boys. Donald worked in the mailroom that left him opportunities. Jacob jotted a note to himself that Donald needed a new position away from the college.

Even though Gordon had many monks evaluated psychologically, he still couldn't predict that Pius would be the one to harm Paul. All his precautions and worries amounted to nothing when protecting Paul.

Jacob sat back and squeezed his temples. The chimes on the clock rang once, twice, three, four, five. Hours wasted in the brain of a dead, paranoid abbot.

He picked an envelope that was large and sealed, marked "Paul."

Crap.

All this investigating and Gordon failed to open the most important envelope, one that had Paul's name on it.

The lock to his office door snapped. Jacob gasped, startled by the sound. He scrambled to cover the files as Brother Ambrose and Father Hilary entered. Bacon and freshly brewed coffee filled the air, reminding Jacob that he hadn't eaten since lunch the day before.

"Told you he was lost," Ambrose said, pouring a hot cup of coffee.

Jacob looked at Hilary St. Ours, alias, Cameron Morgan, an orphan from birth. His file read like a fairy tale. Everyone was aware of Hilary and his orphan status, but not the details of his mother or father. The nun and the mayor, a great novel title.

Jacob smothered the pancakes in syrup as he ate in silence,

stealing a glance at Ambrose, whose gigantic hands cupped a steaming mug.

Ambrose the felon, living the life of the man who died on his watch. The knowledge changes nothing. He's still loveable.

Breakfast tumbled.

Jacob drew a deep breath. End the silence. "Did you know about these files?"

"If you're referring to my felony, a prison sentence keeps one from doing more than just getting a decent job," Brother Ambrose said. "Abbot Jacob, our former abbot, had some odd habits and was more so near the end. Don't put stock in what you read. It's one man's opinions."

Trying not to yawn, Jacob sat up straighter in the leather chair.

They don't know the half of it. Had Gordon hired a private investigator to dig? He didn't recall seeing any special expenses, but he knew how sly a monk could be.

"You have got to stop thinking about this," the voice of his late wife Faith whispered to him.

"If the Abbot kept a file on everyone, it served a purpose," Father Hilary said.

"I see no purpose other than fear. I feel it is wrong. Gordon harshly judged us. I did not need this information," Jacob said, gripping his coffee mug. He scanned Ambrose. This news was no surprise to him. It was more likely that Ambrose had broken into the drawer, read the material, and kept the knowledge to himself.

"But since you're Chief now, isn't it best to know who you are dealing with?" Ambrose said, opening a whiskey flask and pouring some into Jacob's cup.

Hilary raised an eyebrow.

"I opened these letters from Rome. There are three of them.

One from early when Paul first came to us. That one was a cease-and-desist order."

"That explains the visit from the confederation," Ambrose said.

"Yes, but the next two letters threaten dissolving our monastery and asking for Gordon's resignation. Which obviously never happened," Jacob said.

"All those trips he took to Rome, so they were inquisition trips. Poor man, he took the burden on alone to protect Paul and us. You know, everyone believed raising Paul was a death sentence. They were waiting for St. Alberic's big sex scandal to appear," Hilary said with such sadness in his voice that Jacob had to reconsider Abbot Gordon's actions.

"What should I do with them? Should I respond?"

Ambrose snorted. "Respond, hell no. I don't leave the sheep in the field without the dogs to protect them. The Church has other scandals on its doorstep. We are doing nothing wrong. Don't cry wolf when there isn't one."

Now, Jacob finally understood Gordon's reluctance to send Father Pius to jail for abusing Paul. He was living in a house of cards. One big breath, and this world could come crashing down around him.

"Good. Let us light the Easter fire with them," Jacob said, swallowing the acid liquid. "Or better yet, mix these ashes with the palms and we can then literally wear our sins on Ash Wednesday."

Jacob set down his mug and rubbed his face with his hands. "There is a file on Paul. Gordon did not open it. Should I open it? What if it is information Paul might need someday?"

"We have time," Ambrose said, pouring himself a mug full of booze.

Jacob frowned as his head spun from the early morning cocktail. "Am I doing the right thing? Procrastinating?"

"Not opening hasn't harmed us," Ambrose said in a husky voice.

"Leave well enough alone."

Hilary sipped his coffee; a thoughtful expression pursed his lips.

"If Paul has questions about his past, we need to tell him the facts. His mother loved him, and we love him. The knowledge of the past is history. What matters is today," Ambrose said, forgoing the glass and gulping the remains of the flask.

Abbot Jacob shook his head. "Your advice is to wait?"

Hilary grinned. "There is prudence in time. Abbot Gordon knew that. Most problems like acne clear up given time. If there's a question we can't answer, then open it."

Or maybe just avoid the truth. Who would blame him for that?

"Come, you need sleep," Ambrose said. "Make no decisions when you've stayed up all night."

And drank whiskey for breakfast, Jacob thought as he gathered the files and placed them back in the locked cabinet.

"Too bad Gordon is buried. This belongs in the coffin with him," Jacob said, pocketing the key.

CHAPTER 7
LETTERS FROM PAUL

Psalm 30:23
I am far removed from your sight.
I said in my alarm.
Yet you heard the voice of my plea.
When I cried for help.

P aul arrived at St. Scholastica's Monastery in Boerne, Texas, thinking this was in the middle of nowhere. His first visit here was with Jacob, who had brought him along while he came to visit his sister Marie.

Mother Agnes met him at the gates. She was only four feet eleven, and Paul loomed like a giant in front of her. She gave him a monastic hug, gentle and quick.

"Welcome, Mr. Warner. You will honor the cloister this time, I assume?"

Paul's cheeks burned the color of the sky over the canyon. The view was spectacular, and he didn't remember the sight. He remembered the hacienda buildings from his last visit eight years ago when he had run through the cloister, ringing the bell for morning prayers, shouting the traditional call of, "Rise up Sister, the Lord is calling." He had been so proud. Many years later, he realized that his behavior was not proper. They hadn't corrected, or scolded him, just thanked him for his efforts and suggested that perhaps a novice should have a turn.

The Benedictine rhythm of work and prayer was comforting and familiar. When the bells rang, the nuns would hasten to the church to pray. The action reminded him of Father Joannicus. They gave him a job, and he raced around from building to building in a golf cart transporting supplies and people. These nuns did not wear black habits like other Benedictines. These women wore a rainbow of pastel-colored habits.

The nuns sang an octave higher than Paul did. By the end of prayers, he smiled at having successfully blended in by keeping his voice to a near whisper. As he left to have breakfast and prepare for his day, he turned to see Mother Agnes standing at the exit of the church, her shadow casting a size that didn't fit her slight frame.

"Mr. Warner, have you given up on praying?"

"No, Reverend Mother," Paul said, looking at the woman in a pale-yellow habit.

"Then I expect to hear your voice. I heard you think we should eat meals in silence. I beg to differ. It has been almost five years since we have had a visit from Jacob." She smiled. The lines around her face softened. "I have a fondness for his community. Don't be so selfish. Tell us some tales."

Paul gulped and looked down at his feet. "Yes, Reverend Mother."

What could he tell? He had already told tales of Brother Ambrose and the barn, Father Joannicus and the college students, feast days and harvest. As he ate his breakfast, he worried he would run out of stories. Didn't she realize that talking about St. Alberic's made him want to pack his bags and return home?

THE MAIL HAD ARRIVED, with letters for him. He looked for the one from Father Joannicus. There was always one from him. Paul tucked it under his pillow.

Every evening after prayers, before retiring, Paul would take a swim in the pool. He would float on his back and stare up at the stars, remembering when Jacob taught him the names of the constellations.

Each letter told him a slightly different tale of an event. Each monk had a unique perspective. He longed to hear what really happened. Bones were the physical evidence that something had existed. They intrigued Paul, but he sought the who and how. When he was a student at the Native American school, he discovered conflicting facts. He recalled the stories of the saints and once believed those tales, but now he questioned the stories. He wondered who decided what was true.

He could hear his friend Charlie telling him to find the truth. She relished a quest. They shared an interest in the past and how it affected the present. Of all the letters he received from non-monastics, hers were the most captivating. Her tomes were filled with stories of school and history and lore. She also said she missed him and hoped they would go to classes together next year. *At least she misses me.*

Abbot Jacob's sister, called Sister Marie, looked a lot like Jacob and Father Vincent. Dark-skinned, black hair, high cheekbones. Unlike the brothers, she was short. Sister Marie's personality was nothing like her brothers or her other sisters. She was obedient and meek. She spoke of God's blessings, and Paul could see a little of Joannicus in her.

He wondered whose faith was stronger. Marie applied the Rule and scriptures to everything she did. Paul picked up his pen and wrote.

Dear Abbot Jacob,

Today, I learned about the land and the monastery. This used to be the Kronkosky family's home. They were 'chili powder' heirs, and they sold to the sisters for less than it was worth.

I like your sister. She is not like you, or Father Vincent. Are you sure that she's a sibling? Just kidding.

As for Mother Agnes, you should have warned me about nuns and mortification. I tell stories of the monastery, and I'm running out of them. I hope she will continue to tell tales of you and your siblings at St. George's in Montana. Father Vincent has a collection of bibles. Do you think your sister Rebecca ever made a deck of saint playing cards? Sister Marie must have a collection of rosaries, for I noticed she had a different one every day. Mother Agnes claims she was the principal, and you spent a lot of time visiting her.

I miss you. When I can return home?

Love, Paul.

It seemed odd saying I miss you, but as the weeks continued to pass, memories took on new meanings. Ambrose cuffing him with his bear paws and calling him Little One. The way Abbot

Jacob would look at him when he didn't want to admit Paul's righteousness and the soft whispers of Joannicus as he said his nightly prayers.

The day before Paul would leave, Mother Agnes called him to her office and handed him the phone.

"Hello?"

"They tell me you are behaving," Jacob said.

"You asked me to be good. Didn't you?" Paul said, his voice cracked. Emotions, like a shook soda can, threatened to explode.

"Since when have you become so obedient? I received your letters. I counted the times you have said you miss me. I was curious, what exactly do you miss?" Paul felt himself blushing, and he turned away from the nun. He was not about to let his emotions overpower him.

"I miss my cell, playing checkers with Moses, arguing with the novices, and Father Jonah, Ambrose, and you," Paul said in a whisper as he felt his homesickness rising to engulf him.

"Interesting."

All his plans to be nonchalant melted. "Abbot Jacob, can I come home now? I will be the best non-monk ever. Abbot Jacob, please," Paul said, untangling the twisted olive-green phone cord. Why didn't they have a cordless? A cordless would at least allow him to talk freely and not in front of the piercing gray eyes of Mother Agnes.

"No. Consider it this way: your absence will make my heart grow fonder."

The joke did not bring laughter if it was a joke. Paul bit his lower lip and tried not to look at the little nun.

"Silence. Are you deciding if you will obey me or turn your ticket into a flight home?" Abbot Jacob asked.

His heart jumped. Could he do that? He didn't have a car or access to a phone. Maybe he could convince a novice to help.

"Paul, you cannot, so please continue to be exceptional."

Paul swallowed and clenched his free hand into a fist, allowing his nails to dig into his palm. "Can you tell Brother Ambrose not to watch the new Disney movie *Oliver and Company* until I come home?"

"Will do, I love you," Abbot Jacob said.

"What?" The words pierced something inside of him. The yearning for home drained him, leaving him weak and light-headed. He laid the phone on the desk and dazedly walked out of the office.

December 24th, St. Meinrad's, Indiana

Paul flopped onto the brightly colored quilt on his bed and stared at the ceiling. He turned to look out the window at the picturesque, peaceful landscape. In the city, sirens roared; the hilltop was a dome of peace. A Saint Icon stared at the small stack of letters from St. Alberic's on the writing desk. It seemed obvious now that Abbot Jacob had commanded every monk to write to him. He had a collection of letters, some personal and some like a greeting card. At least the letters kept him busy writing, but the dull ache of homesickness lingered with each stamp.

After sitting at the desk, he opened his notebook and crossed another day off on his calendar. He would be here at Saint Meinrad Archabbey until January. He wondered if he would be involved in the Saint Meinrad student's pilgrimage to the shrine of Our Lady of Monte Cassino. Each year around January 13th, the students would pilgrimage in the cold to the shrine on campus to commemorate and give thanks for being spared from the 1871 smallpox epidemic. There was no such celebration at St. Alberic's unless you wanted to count the barn. There were a lot of gatherings held at the barn, harvesting, and picnics. As far as Paul knew, they had no miracles attached to his monastery.

Paul pulled out a clean white piece of paper and wrote.

Dear Father Joannicus,

I miss you. I wish we could be together this Christmas so you could read me the story of Christ's birth like you have every year. I have contemplated your advent questions. Jesus had humble beginnings, a smelly barn, as a helpless infant. Are you aware that a swaddling cloth could be used as a death shroud? I wanted to be mummy Jesus for Halloween one year, but Jacob said no.

You know that Brother Ambrose read me secular versions of that story, called The Night Before Christmas and The Little Drummer Boy. He was comical in reading and acting out all the parts. I will miss watching Mister Magoo's Christmas Carol and the Grinch with him this year. The nuns watch a little TV. I understand you are busy teaching and stuff, but perhaps we could talk on the phone sometime. I am struggling to learn something from this second visit. The only thing I realize is that I miss home. Every place is interesting and prayerful. Sort of like peace leaking from the walls. That sounds kind of goofy. Miss you, write soon.

Love, Paul.

"Father Joannicus, you are mistaken, dismissing my worries by saying, what can be so bad? Everyone has to treat you like Christ," Paul said aloud to the empty room.

The nuns fussed over him, questions of food, warmth, and rest. Their attention reminded him of when he was young. Moses and Ambrose would bicker about his care. Silly things like whether a splinter should be pulled or pushed out. Paul wondered what his mother would have been like. The years had robbed him of her. He couldn't remember the color of her eyes or her frown if she ever had one.

Paul took out a piece of white paper and again wrote.

Dear Abbot Jacob,
I want to come home.
Paul.

St. Meinrad was like living in a medieval castle. There was a muffled darkness that lurked in the halls.

The buildings were old and dank. The community had a hundred members. Paul felt mostly lost in the immensity of it. Hospitality being a cornerstone in the Benedictine world, the community treated him like a privileged guest, giving him classes to attend and a monastic schedule. This Archabbey had many works aside from teaching. They made caskets and ran a press, which Paul was learning about. When a monk died at home, they put him in a simple wooden box that Brother Moses fashioned, and the tailor shop would add a woven prayer shawl created especially for the deceased. Even Abbot Gordon's casket was plain and unadorned.

The monks of St Meinrad had taken him to the Sisters of St. Benedict at the Immaculate Conception Monastery and the contrast of buildings was like stepping from darkness into light. Paul noticed that there were angels everywhere, and he counted them. He found eighty-nine angels but suspected there were more. Both places were impressive. Paul decided he liked the simplicity of his monastery, the wood, and the plain stained glass over the marble and huge glass images of saints.

Paul returned to his desk, crumpled up the letter to Abbot Jacob, and opened his mail. There were more letters than usual. Christmas cards from monks and friends of monks. Ambrose's card was secular, held a picture of a Santa Claus warning him about the naughty list and note that said, "If they are treating you like Christ, you best be acting like him."

How could he get into trouble when it was him alone?

His hands trembled when he saw a letter addressed to him from Abbot Jacob. Those letters ended with a coziness that left Paul aching to be home: As always A.J.

Indiana is close to Montana—they should let me visit home.

The snow fell in large flakes, and the radiator in his room sighed. A melancholy settled as the sky grew a soft gray. Bells beckoned Paul to community prayer, and he made his way to the church. Newer monks brushed by him in a hurry.

"Have you seen him yet?" whispered one.

Honestly, the birth of Jesus is a memory, not an actual event. The excitement of Midnight Mass preparation did not fill Paul with joy.

He missed his monks, the joy, the decorations, and the caroling. A vision of Ambrose eating a powdered sugar treat that left a dusting of white on his black scapular filled Paul's mind. His monks had always let him help. Now, as a perpetual guest, he found himself a spectator of another liturgical event.

Ten seminarians crossed to the monastic side of the church in the shadowy dimness of the winter light as Paul sat. The church had two sides, the secular and monastic side. A low rail marked the secular side, reminding one that there was a difference between monastic and worldly. The monastic seats paralleled the sides of the church, making a grand entry to the altar. At home, the altar was central, and everyone circled it. Flipping his breviary to the page with the evening antiphon, he glanced at the rows of monks hidden by the intricate wooden panels. All that was visible when they sat were their arms and black habits.

That made them seem mysterious, almost holy. They are just people dressed in black. Their abbot rose, and the choir chanted. Each monastery had a different range of voices.

Paul's head rose sharply. Someone had a powerful tenor voice that reminded Paul of Abbot Jacob. Searching the faces, he thought his heart would explode when he spied Abbot Jacob. He glanced to see if Joannicus was with him. Prayer was lost. The silence between psalms hung like a broken pendulum. This was taking too long.

As the last monk exited the church, Paul sprang to his feet and raced to Jacob. Excitement bubbled, filling his mouth with a million words.

"How long are you here? Are you taking me home? Where is Father Joannicus?"

Jacob smiled, pulled him into an embrace, and shushed him. Placing his hands on Paul's shoulders, the Abbot looked at him. "You look well. Need a haircut, but well enough. Sorry, no Father Joannicus."

Paul wasn't sure if it was the disappointment or just the shock of seeing someone from the community he missed so much, but tears pooled in his eyes, and he struggled to keep them contained.

No, don't cry, only little kids cry.

Jacob put his arm around Paul, ushering him into the monastery's dimly lit hall.

"Lie to me and say those are tears of joy," whispered Jacob as they entered a cell. "This is a brief visit. Let us make the most of it."

Paul looked around at the comfortable yet meager surroundings. This cell looked like the one they put him in. Empty but clean. Jacob was an abbot; shouldn't he have something better? Paul shrugged. He wasn't sure his heart could take this meeting and the departure.

A thought flickered in his mind. *If I pray hard enough, God will send a blizzard and Abbot Jacob will have to stay. God did it for St. Scholastica. She asked her brother, St. Benedict, to stay and visit. The holy man refused, so she prayed to God, and a storm prevented his departure.* Paul paused. *Wait. The Abbot should be home for Midnight Mass.* It was a big deal. The late Abbot Gordon liked Christmas more than Easter, and Paul had to agree with him staying until midnight was far better than rising hours before dawn.

"Why aren't you home?"

"Flight delays and I was close enough to here to detour, besides spending Christmas alone in a hotel is no fun."

"So where were you?" Paul asked as Jacob unzipped his habit and hung it up.

"I had to attend another abbot meeting at St. Vincent's. I bet you did not know that abbots have meetings, a lot of them."

He was lying. Paul remembered the drive to St Meinrad. It had been a two-hour drive from Evansville. This wasn't a trip to make from St. Vincent's monastery in Pennsylvania. Paul knew Indiana was not on any route from Pennsylvania. Besides, monks didn't spend time in hotels.

Jacob opened the closet door, and Paul saw a small suitcase. A monk needed little to travel, a habit and a change of clothes.

"Latrobe is like six hours from here. Your flight didn't detour to Evansville," Paul said as a nagging thought prickled his mind.

Jacob chuckled and stretched out on the bed, crossing his blue-jean-clad legs. "So instead of joy at my visit, you are going to argue with me? Maybe I should fly home."

Paul frowned.

"St. Vincent's is not on my list to visit. How come you didn't send me to the house that began it all?" Paul asked, thinking that it was the oldest monastery and first Benedictine house in the United States. I wonder if it is cold and dank like this place.

"I dislike the abbot," Jacob said, crossing his arms.

"Does he like you?"

"Not particularly. This visit was not a social call. I had an abbot meeting."

"Who picked the places I'm visiting?"

"I sent you to Texas because I like Mother Agnes and my sister is there. You are here because the community liked this abbey. St. Procopius, which is next, because of Brother Moses, he thinks the name is funny. And Father Joannicus is fond of the gals at Fort Smith, Arkansas, probably because they have a hermitage. You will like it because it has an underground pool. By underground, I mean in the basement."

"If you're gone all the time, why can't I be home?"

"I am not gone all the time. I fear if I left you home with my monks, I would return home to find them corrupted and mutinous. I have been told that you have gained a taste for heavy metal music."

Paul moved across the room. "They are monks, not pirates. Don't you have to be home? This is your first Christmas?" Paul was surprised that Jacob wasn't home.

"I chose to be here." Jacob smiled. "I came to see you."

"I don't think you get the office of Abbot."

"Is that so? When you return home, you can teach me all you know. I look forward to your guidance."

Paul stood at the little window, watching the snow dance around the sconces that hung on the outside of the brick building. "Can I come home now?"

"No. I read your letters, I note your sadness, but I need more time."

"For what?" Paul turned and crossed his arms. He still didn't understand why his presence at the monastery caused an issue, or how his absence helped.

"I have business to deal with and with you away. I am not torn. And you have lessons to learn." Jacob sat up, swinging his legs to the right side of the bed.

Paul felt his anger rise. How could he learn a lesson when he didn't even know what they sent him to learn? This is stupid. Obedience is stupid.

Jacob opened the nightstand drawer and pulled out a tin and a candle, then reached into his shirt pocket and produced a matchbook. "Let us pick another topic. Of all the Benedictine houses you have visited, which ones do you like?"

The match sputtered to life. Sulfur wafted through the air. The candle was lit, and shadows shimmered around the ancient room.

"St. Alberic's," Paul said, partly out of spite, but mostly because it was true.

"Excellent. One goal done," Jacob said, extinguishing the match and flipping off the light. A soft glow filled the room.

"This is a dumb way to make me like home."

"It is working," Jacob said, his blue eyes piercing Paul.

Paul's jaw jutted out and, in his mind, he could hear Joannicus scolding him to trust. The job of abbot is difficult. Give Abbot Jacob a break.

"Why are you torn?"

"It is complicated, but once, when you were young, I vowed to keep you safe," Jacob said.

"Ah, I think you failed," Paul said with a smirk.

"I ultimately succeeded. Father Pius got caught. You are safe.

Now, I have vowed to guide the souls of the monks in my care. I need time to learn how."

Jacob's candor took Paul's breath away. Never had an adult talked to him like he was an adult. Uncrossing his arms, Paul sat on the chair next to the small desk.

"Monasteries all the same, with minor differences. It helps that every place is familiar. There is peace and beauty at each house," Paul said, thinking about the moth-infested monastery. They didn't complain, they just continued with life. Paul recalled the old monk, Brother Clement, who seemed to spend his day gathering them, and then putting them back outside, and yet whenever the door opened, they would fly back in. The activity struck Paul as futile, yet nobody stopped the old monk. Staying away was hard, and Paul hated the yearning for home he felt at bedtime.

The candle wavered in the cell's draftiness. "Have you ever been to a hermitage? I visited a hermitage. It was quiet."

"I sometimes thought of St. Clare's as a hermitage." Jacob leaned forward. "Did you like being a hermit?"

Paul remembered the silence, the morning's brilliance and splendor, the distant sounds of the monks praying, and the birds singing. "No. I know Father Joannicus would have thought he died and gone to heaven, but really, it's lonely."

Jacob nodded. "Do you like nuns or monks better?"

"Nuns are, well, they are busy, fussy, and I don't know, cleaner?"

A grin appeared on Jacob's face. "The word is feminine, and I am glad to see that you are noticing the difference. What do you want for Christmas?"

"To come home," Paul said, regretting the sadness it caused on Jacob's face.

"Cute, you remind me of someone who is still very stubborn,"

Jacob said, rising and retrieving a brightly wrapped package from the closet.

If he has a present for me, then he planned this. Panic rose inside him. What news required the Abbot to deliver it?

"What's wrong? Who died? Is Father Joannicus dying?" Paul watched Jacob's face for signs of a lie.

"What? No." Jacob turned away and stood tall before turning back. "Nothing is wrong. Nobody has died. Joannicus is alive and kicking. I just missed you."

Jacob fluffed up the bow on the package as he set it on the bed.

"I don't believe you. Father Joannicus still has a cough. He needs to see a doctor. You're the abbot. Make him go."

Jacob walked to the little window. "I will do that. Remember, people get sick."

"What do you mean by that?"

"Father Joannicus does not do winters well. You know his nose runs all winter long."

Paul knew that was partly right. "But if he gets sicker, will you let me come home?"

Jacob tapped on the glass, causing the stacked-up snowflakes to cascade down. Paul could feel anger rising inside of him, and he struggled to contain himself.

"If things get worse, I will bring you home," Jacob said slowly.

Paul felt as if the lights on his Christmas tree had shorted out. Why wasn't he doing that now? What if Father Joannicus was deathly ill?

"Promise me," Paul said sternly.

"I promise," Jacob said, placing his hand on the cold frozen window.

CHAPTER 8
RETURN TO EGYPT

Psalm 22:6
Surely goodness and kindness shall follow me
all the days of my life.
In the Lord's own house shall I dwell for ever and ever.

J oannicus cranked up the heater and the air under the desk billowed around him. Although summer had arrived, he still felt cold and empty, like a spent seedpod. He wished he could suffer with Christ, but the six months of chemo and radiation left him thirty pounds lighter and bald. The poison chemical's side effects seemed to be exaggerated in him. His joints ached, and his stomach threw back everything he put in it. Three months had passed, and he was still tired. His foggy mind prevented him from teaching and preaching.

Joannicus gritted his teeth as the memory of his first community Mass returned to him. There he stood, and the words jumbled on the page. Chemo head. Someone pointed out his place in the book. His name still appeared on the Mass roster. When he questioned the schedule, the Abbot said, "Do not worry about the words. We know what is in your heart."

What was in his heart?

He had always fancied himself becoming a hermit. Weeks in the recovery unit, praying alone, reciting the psalms to the ceiling with no second choir response left him wanting and prayer fleeting. Sometimes his Psalter sat silently, a holder for the vomit tray. He missed them, his confreres, during those times. Community. The word echoed in his soul like a pebble in a metal drum.

Christ was with him and so was his community.

What more could he ask for? Joannicus reached for the quart container, popped off the lid and drank the warm water. Flush out the chemicals, drink. Oh, how he had tried. The water burned and licked his open sores from his lips to his stomach. Every drop felt like what he imagined rolling in brambles would be. Today, the water slipped down with ease.

Rejoice.

Once he had embraced his cancer, he was free to embrace others. They all needed a hand to hold, a prayer whispered, a tear wiped. He could do that.

One testicle was all that was gone. Not a leg, not an arm.

A conversion, a detachment from self, always leads to new zeal, a renewed commitment to God's will. Then a desire to give back. He had life, and he had watched the mother of two—the boy barely ten—surrender their lives. He would embrace life.

The lines from Psalm 114 came to mind, and he spoke to them aloud, "Turn back, my soul, to your rest for the Lord has been good, he has kept my soul from death, my eyes from tears."

You are alive.

The boards in the hall creaked. The custodian had been through hours ago. He was afraid of falling back into fear. Remission, relapse, any of the tests in the coming months could be grim news.

Be gone, Satan.

Joannicus thought of his twin brother, Conner. The eight-year-old boy was just a shadow now. All he recalled was what he saw in photos and stories. What does Paul remember about his mother? Does her death affect him now? The lingering effects of deaths that echo to remember. He didn't remember Conner. He knew Paul didn't remember his mother. But Paul remembers Brother Mellitus. The monk was such a character, not easily forgotten. Will I become a name in a list of deceased confreres, an etching on a concrete stone? Have I lost my purpose?

The soft knock on the door pulled Joannicus from his thoughts. Abbot Jacob entered the office and Joe's spirit rose.

"The Lord be with you, Father Joannicus," Jacob said.

"And with you, Father Abbot, are you checking up on me?" Joannicus asked.

Abbot Jacob fanned himself. "Well, it would be like you to not bother us and die alone with your savior."

"It seems I'm destined to live despite myself." Joannicus noticed the sweat on Abbot Jacob's brow. "Sorry about the heat. Seriously, I'm cold all the time, now."

Joannicus stood and turned off the portable heater. "Who'd a thought that hair served such an important function? I wonder what color it will be. Will it still be curly?"

"You might use it to your advantage. Struck by God," Jacob said with a grin.

"Let's try touched by God," Joannicus said, thinking it could be an advantage in teaching what it means to convert your will to God. Give up your desire to conquer cancer and embrace the disease. Cancer and Paul were blessings. Both were opportunities for him to move closer to the divine. That child, the one who disrupts my life, is Christ. Joannicus wondered if Mary wanted to scream and run away. She excelled at acceptance. He was much slower to utter the words. Thy will be done.

"Do not worry, Barb knows how to dye hair."

Joannicus smiled, worried that any relationship with a female was like a Mobius strip, doomed to go nowhere. Ms. Carr was non-Catholic, and she didn't understand his convictions, but she had turned out to be a helpful social worker when he had concerns about Paul. He considered her a friend and was honored when she asked him to witness her marriage.

Jacob cleared a chair of papers.

"Do you believe in divine interference?" Joannicus asked, dumping the half-empty glass of water on a small jade planet.

Jacob sat down and let the air slide through his teeth. "Interference or intervention, I would call it something else besides divine because I do not think God has that much spare time to curse or bless us. I trust in choice and embracing that choice. Sometimes there is no good choice."

Joannicus slipped on his wool gloves. "I know you want me to tell Paul about my cancer, but seriously, it would have ruined his faith. He would have prayed to God, and what if I died? Then what?"

Jacob fanned himself with a pamphlet entitled, "So you want to become a monk?"

"What if you lived? As you have? That would have strengthened his faith, been a cause for immense joy. I see your point, but the community would have been able to help him through your death."

"It's all in the past now, so let's move on," Joannicus said.

Jacob scowled. "You cannot be the boy's savior. Protecting him from life does not work. Life is to be lived, not observed."

"I'm not playing martyr," Joannicus said, dusting the shelf with his gloved hand, not quite convinced of his own words. How many times had he pursued sympathy for his condition rather than joy? Had he turned away rather than show compassion? He now had a second chance. He would keep himself focused on the will of God, realizing that change did not mean defeat. God wanted him free from attachments. Cancer was a wake-up call, a sharp kick in the butt to get his attention refocused.

Jacob realigned a stack of books, building a stable tower. "When Paul returns, he will ask questions. How long before someone slips up and discloses the cancer? Then what?"

Joannicus dumped half-filled glasses of water onto thirsty plants. "I'll make something up."

"Just remember what happened the last time we lied," Jacob said as he unzipped his habit and flung the scapular over his shoulder. Dark stains formed on his white tee shirt.

Was the room that hot?

The lie had been a misunderstanding. Paul assumed that the resurrection of the body was soon after the burial of his mother.

"Paul kicked Moses in the shins. He tried to unearth his mother."

Joannicus shivered from the harrowing memory of a little boy clawing at the mud to get to his dead mother.

"Be with him. Tell him the truth. Life is acknowledging what you have lost. Without that realization, are you really living?"

Joannicus shook his head.

"You didn't sit with him every night as he cried himself to sleep. When we told him Brother Mellitus was dying, and that didn't make it any easier. I think my way is less harmful." Joannicus rubbed his arms. His way was better. The deaths of Jacob's family, his wife and children, had affected him for two years. Jacob grieved and, like a man missing limb, stumbled and reached for what was not there. Paul had suffered enough loss. Joe was not willing to reopen those wounds.

"It pains me to read his longing to return. Let me bring him home."

"Seriously, how is my lack of disclosure any different from you not telling him about his money?" Joannicus snapped as the image of a muddy boy faded.

That was an unfair comparison. Abbot Jacob rose, zipped up his habit, and straighten his scapular and pectoral cross.

"I do not want to fight. The truth about your health differs from money. It is a gamble I wish you would not take. I think you are being selfish. Paul deserves the only thing you have to give— time with you. Paul loves you, trusts you. Do not betray that because you fear attachment and detachment. Do not let your zeal for God consume all."

Joannicus leaned against the bookshelf. The truth left bruises on his heart.

"I have a clean bill of health. If the cancer returns then, maybe."

Would he come clean? He had prayed for the recovery of his brother Conner. He had trusted that God would answer his prayer. His brother died. As a child, and teen, he didn't understand how God let that happen. Not until he was an adult witnessing Jacob's loss had he fully grasped the power of faith.

God tested a man's faith, not Joannicus.

Father Joe's stomach twisted. There was sadness and an ache etched Jacob's face. A look Joannicus had not seen since Paul's arrival. That's when Jacob changed. A healing. A slow opening of his heart to love again, which occurred when Paul arrived.

Abbot Jacob handed Joannicus a heavy overcoat. "Come, it is time for bed. I fear this is going to backfire on you, but I hope I am wrong."

Joannicus said, "This is only August and Paul will return in October. Perhaps by then I won't be bald."

CHAPTER 9
HOME

Paul squirmed in the back seat of the cab as St. Alberic's came into sight, the hills dark and the golden land and the brick monastery looming above the college. He paid the driver, then hauled his suitcases into the monastery. Who to see first? Where to go? His room, the community room, the Abbot's office? He dropped his suitcases by the angels, listened and heard nothing. No soft conversation drifted into the hall. He moved to the community room. It was empty. The clock read noon, so Paul ran down the hall to the church. The smells of candle wax and incense caused him to slow down. He was home. In the atrium, he could see that the church was dark, silent. A panic rose. What if they moved and the letter telling me was still in the mail? He had heard that some communities folded.

"Can I help you?" a voice said.

Paul whirled around and faced a young man dressed in black who looked barely eighteen. Neither recognized the other.

"Ah, where are the monks?" Paul asked.

The young man, like a Dickens ghost, pointed to the note.

Harvest.

Paul dashed out of the church without saying a word, heading to the barn.

Joannicus sat in the shade with the older monks, boxing the produce.

"Paul?" Brother Moses called, squinting in the noonday sun. Father Joannicus lifted the straw hat from his face and looked in the direction that Moses was pointing.

"Get some water, Moses," Brother Ambrose said, from the shade where he was resting. "Next, you'll be having a Medjugorje event. I know you miss him. We all do. Don't fret, my friend. He'll be here soon. Besides, if it were Paul, the first words out of his mouth would be—"

"Where's Father Jonah?" Paul said.

Brother Ambrose sprang up, hit his head on a low branch, and then cursed. The community gathered and greeted Paul. Joannicus waited, thankful that he was only tired today.

Paul had grown. Gone was the pudgy awkwardness, where arms and legs move with minds of their own. Paul approached him and they embraced, the straw hat falling to the ground.

"Just couldn't be obedient, could you?" Father Joannicus said.

Paul stepped back and scrutinized Joe. "What's wrong with you? What happened to your hair?"

"Oh, this," Joannicus laughed, rubbing his hand over his bald head. "Barb is always challenging me about worldly contributions, so I shaved it off to support cancer patients."

Paul shook his head. "No eyebrows, that's a little extreme."

Joannicus fished out his sunglasses to hide his lack of lashes. "It will grow back, come let's drive this harvest to the kitchen. I want stories of your adventure."

"You really don't seem well."

A fly buzzed and landed on the crates. Silence hung as monks looked everywhere but at Joannicus.

Brother Ambrose laughed. "Nothing's wrong. You're home and all grown up and at least six inches taller. We've all changed, some more than others. It has been a long a year."

Joannicus breathed a sigh of relief.

Paul seemed placated for the moment with the big man's explanation. Joannicus said a silent prayer of thanks.

Energized, Joannicus stepped quickly for the first time since his treatments had ended. He listened as Paul chattered. When Paul was younger, his incessant talking was an annoyance, but now, they lulled him into a state of blissfulness. Although Paul paused and looked worried, the boy didn't question him again, confirming that he had made the right choice.

When they arrived at the kitchen, the fuss and "welcome homes" allowed Joannicus to carry one box of harvest and quietly take a seat in the refectory. Brother Barnabas brought in tea and a snack. Joe watched Paul and the younger monks move the rest of the boxes.

The boy had grown muscles. Paul plopped down on in the chair. Was that facial hair or dirt on the boy's upper lip?

"Are you sure you are, okay?"

"Seriously, that's all you can say? Do you want me to be ill?"

"No, of course not, but you've lost weight and I don't like the bald thing," Paul said, pouring the tea.

"My hair will grow back. Let's focus on today. Abbot Jacob and your early arrival?"

Paul laughed. "He probably already knows. I don't think secrets stay secret in monasteries. I bet the nuns called him the moment my plane took off."

Joannicus hoped that was not true, for he didn't need monks talking about his treatment. Half listening to Paul, he reflected on the almost man before him. He had experience with young adults.

"What are you grinning at?"

"Nothing. I'm just enjoying the moments before the community arrives and takes you away."

"I'm here to stay," Paul said.

The community arrived, and Joannicus slipped away to his cell. In his chair, he pulled the blankets around him and fell asleep.

Joannicus felt cool air on his cheek and shivered. He opened one eye. Paul sat by the open window as a fan osculated.

"You lied to me," Paul said, crossing his arms.

Joannicus let out a low breath and then shook his head.

"What is wrong with you?"

"Seriously, nothing."

"Not true. It's eighty-nine degrees outside, and your room is sealed like a jelly jar."

Joannicus shook off the blankets and stood. "Fine, something is wrong. I'm anemic."

"What?"

"Low iron, so I'm a little cold and tired."

Paul turned off the fan as the bells rang for evening prayers.

"Come now, the Lord is calling," Joannicus said, feeling guilty about the half-truth he told Paul. He was anemic, bald, and in remission, but alive.

At the end of evening prayer, Abbot Jacob stood up and faced the community. Joannicus wondered what was happening. He had missed many council meetings.

"I would like to welcome Paul back to his community and make his return official by asking him to join us in name and spirit by making him an official oblate."

A sound of joy and agreement murmured among the monks as Paul gasped and turned, looking questioningly at Joannicus. Clever move, inclusion into the community, officially.

"Do you know what an oblate is?" Abbot Jacob asked.

"Laypeople who follow the Rule," Paul said with a creased brow as some monks chuckled.

"And you are a layperson who follows the Rule. Let us make it legitimate."

Joannicus agreed with the sentiment. Paul already led the life of a monk, prayers, and recreation. What was left?

"Come up here."

"But don't I get to think about it?" Paul asked hesitantly.

"What's to think about?" Ambrose asked. "You've been living as one for years."

"I need more information." Paul paused. "What is going to change?"

Pride surged within Joannicus as he shook his head in disbelief. Paul understood commitment. Damn, those other communities had changed him.

Jacob smiled. "Nothing much. It just makes me officially your abbot. Also, it will tell me you know what it means to live our life."

Family ties. Paul needed that. Everyone needed to belong. Sadness crept up into Joannicus. Guilt followed. He hadn't known how to be that kind of a father. Did Paul still feel like an orphan?

"But I know that stuff already. I know I belong here," Paul said.

There were nods and mumbles of agreement among the monks.

"I am glad you recognize the importance of this. A few things will change. You will sit with us in choir, lead prayers just as the novices do, be assigned chores and given a small stipend."

Money for what, thought Joannicus. They took care of all his needs. Was this to prepare Paul for his inheritance? Jacob was a clever man, if that was his plan. Learn mistakes from small spending errors to avoid blowing his inheritance when the time came for him to oversee it. A great admiration rose in Joannicus. This was his abbot.

"I'll think about it," Paul said, with maturity in his voice. Maturity that Joannicus was sure was more bravado than real. How much had Paul changed?

Jacob's eyebrows knitted together, his mouth opened and then closed. No words fell out. Joannicus laughed and thought, a silent abbot, a superior quality in any monk.

CHAPTER 10
TRAPPIST

Psalm 126:2

In vain is your earlier rising, your going later to rest,
You who toil for the bread you eat,
when he pours gifts on his beloved while they slumber.

Paul's alarm rang at three in the morning. He yawned and rubbed his eyes. Paul dressed, made his way downstairs, and started the coffee in the community room.

He shivered as he slipped outside. Although October hadn't quite settled in, the predawn air was sharp in contrast to his warm bed. He entered the tailor shop through the basement door, flipped on the light. The glare from the single bulb overhead sent a mouse running for a crack and triggered Gandalf, the large gray cat, into action, arching from the cutting table to the hindquarters of the mouse just as it squeezed into the opening. A muffled meow announced his success and made Paul wince. Life was not fair. Brother Alcuin's favorite saying.

He had lived the Benedictine life longer than Brother Alcuin. He had accepted the invitation to be an oblate, promising to live the Rule as he lived his life. Father Joannicus had been an oblate before he had entered the monastery. Paul didn't think he would be a monk. The world intrigued him, lured him.

This odd assortment of men was his family, though it looked nothing like the families of his classmates and friends.

Gandalf coiled his body around Paul's legs, the mouse protesting. Paul pushed the gray cat out the door with his foot. The linen needed washing. The wheeled canvas cart overflowed with white sheets and white towels, so sorting was not essential. He laughed that he even knew this.

See, I know more than some monks here, he thought, recalling the pinkish socks and tee shirts of monks who hadn't realized colors needed to be washed separately.

"Thank you, Sister Leonessa," Paul said, for she was the one who had prevented him from turning the linen into a sixties art project when he had put the red vestments in with the white altar cloth.

Laundry started, Paul headed down the hill, walking briskly on the trail to the farm. He pulled open the door the smell of hay and animals greeted him. The protesting hinges made the sheep bleat. He liked the sound of the sheep.

Paul picked up the oval basket. St. Benedict didn't say one needed the best and newest. Yet on his travels, he saw both the poor communities rich in joy and the rich communities divided in loyalty.

He attended a county fair with four monks, astonished to see the amount of money they had. Here one asked for money and explained why it was needed. Sometimes one didn't get the money. A monk at the fair bought a sizeable amount of art and a poster of KISS for Paul. Not sure if he should decline the kindness, Paul had accepted the gift, noticing that the man used a credit card that had his name on it, minus the title Father or Reverend.

"Do you all have your own cards?" Paul asked.

The monk laughed, "Oh no, this is mine." Paul winced at the word. Joannicus would not like that word. "My friend pays the bill. That way, I get things I want."

"Does the Abbot know?" Paul asked, knowing the answer to the question. Monks didn't have accounts, monks receiving gifts asked the Abbot if they could keep them. Personal possessions weren't something monks had. Paul wondered if Abbot Jacob would have found out if that monk lived here.

Why did that monk have to lie? His monks were always good at raising money. Brother Moses would wander the campus gathering glass bottles and cans so he could request a tool and money to buy it. Barnabas made glazed donuts and sold them to the students, and he baked breads he sold to those who came to Mass on Sundays. With his cash, he requested and got permission to buy several serving carts for the kitchen.

Paul stuck his hand under the warm hen and gathered the eggs. She clucked in protest.

Memories of secrets he had uncovered at other monasteries flooded back to him. old Sister Phoebe, a soft-spoken, thin woman, with large thick glasses hanging from the tip of her nose. She had died suddenly during his stay with the sisters at Fort Smith. She was the librarian and was strict about her domain. During her funeral vigil, loud barking and whining echoed through the convent. The perplexed community sent him and a novice to find the problem. When he and novice entered the library office, a large black dog raced past them, obviously tired of being confined. With nose to the ground, he followed a scent.

ALL FOR ONE CHILD

Both Paul and the novice trailed after him. The dog ran to the church and leap to the coffin to be with his deceased mistress and the community sat stunned. Sister Phoebe had more than books in the library.

Paul jumped when the hen struck. He put his bleeding hand to his mouth. "Not ready to share?"

He learned that being in charge doesn't mean you know what is happening. Paul wondered how many monks had secrets.

The thought intrigued him as he cleaned the stall, laid fresh straw, and fed the cow, sheep, and chickens. With a basket of eggs, Paul climbed the trail back up to the monastery.

Paul got to the kitchen and changed the radio station to hard rock. The recent music didn't eliminate his other listening choices, just added enough loudness and passionate lyrics that were missing from his choir boy selection.

There is only so much Jesus music one can listen to.

Paul recalled once when he was in the classroom with Father Joannicus, a young man used the word fuck repeatedly in sentence after sentence. Joannicus responded with, "With so many descriptive words in the English language, try a few others along with fuck." What Paul remembered most was that when Father Joannicus spoke that word, it sent the faces of the students into shock.

He checked the breakfast menu while putting the eggs away. Bacon, sausage, pancakes, and the usual variety.

Paul looked at the clock. An hour left to mix the batter and start the bacon and sausages. He turned on the urns for coffee and then mixed the jugs of juice.

He ate as he cooked.

Brother Daniel came into the kitchen.

"Paul, that is loud..."

"Oops sorry. I was hoping someone would show up. I gotta

get going. The meat's in the oven." Paul disappeared before Daniel could get a question out.

THE SUN PEEKED BRIGHTLY on the horizon. Lights glowed softly from rooms as monks rose. Paul slipped his headphones on, feeling energized and excited to see the reactions of the monks to a lighter workload. The heavy metal band, Nine Inch Nails, screamed in his ears as he danced his way to the side entrance of the abbey. He did a jump and air guitar as he continued dancing down the dimly lit hall to the church, smiling and bowing at those he passed on his way to the church. It was good to be home.

He was feeling generous and might even say hi to Father Pius. Almost eight years had passed since the man had hit him hard enough to leave bruises. Paul couldn't stand the man, but if Pius kept his distance, the state was big enough for them both.

Paul sat down in his seat in the front row with the novices, his new place within the community. He'd have preferred a seat with the senior monks, since he wasn't a novice.

Ambrose pointed out that the novices needed a goal and seeing someone so young, adhering to the Rule with such ease would make them better monks.

No restrictions and all the privileges. Paul could live with this change.

"Oh Lord, open my lips," announced the acolyte.

The choir responded, "And my mouth shall proclaim your praise."

On the way to breakfast, there were whispers about Paul's odd behavior. Some novices tried to explain that it was dancing. Most of the older monks were sure it was possession. Abbot Jacob and Father Gabriel waited behind instead of leading the line into breakfast. Gabriel at once felt Paul's forehead for a fever.

"You alright?"

"Sure, I'm marvelous," Paul said with a yawn.

"Please don't wear headphones to prayers in the morning," Abbot Jacob said.

"How about evening prayers?"

Jacob rolled his eyes and peered at Paul, who smiled a cheeky grin.

"Okay, okay."

They turned to go to breakfast. Paul headed the other way.

"Paul?" Abbot Jacob said.

"I forgot something, and I'll be there soon."

Paul detoured to the laundry room, took out the wash, and started another load. In his room, he gathered two boxes of music that he had color coded into liturgical seasons. On his way to catch the school bus, Paul stopped and sorted the mail.

"Hey, what are you doing in here?" asked Brother Alcuin with a frown.

Paul paused. *What does it look like?*

"You know this isn't your job? Just because the Abbot let you play monk doesn't mean you can do whatever you want."

A snarky reply was forming on Paul's lips when a scene from long ago flashed through his mind. Father Robert was scolding the then Father Jacob loudly about something that Jacob hadn't even done. Another monk had polished the brass, stripping the years of patina away. Jacob didn't argue or defend. He just stood there, letting Robert become nastier and nastier. Finally, when the man demanded a response, Jacob lifted his head and said in a soft voice, "Thank you, Father."

"Thanks Alcuin, I'll try to remember that," Paul said, picking up his school bag and heading out the door.

"That's Brother Alcuin."

Whatever.

After school, Paul went to the church to set up for Mass. Then he moved to the guesthouse to clean and do his homework. He volunteered to clean after the evening meal, sending the novices on a walk. When he was done, he wandered to the church and sat waiting for the bells to ring, calling them to evening prayer. Wolfgang was playing the church organ. The music was harmonious and gentle. Paul rested his chin on his hand and closed his eyes.

A touch startled Paul, and he woke up disoriented. Brothers Alcuin and Reginald were looking at him.

"Wake up and sleep in your cell," Alcuin said.

"Shit," Paul mumbled. He had not intended to sleep.

"Don't worry, you didn't snore," Reginald said. "Not much."

"Why didn't you wake me?"

"Not our jobs, besides you were supposed to be praying, not sleeping," Alcuin said.

"I was told sometimes horizontal prayer is acceptable, and besides, the Abbot didn't wake him, so I figured it was okay. Get some proper sleep."

"We should have just left you until morning," Alcuin said, turning off the lights leaving them in darkness.

PAUL'S ALARM rang at five thirty. He rose and walked to prayers. He sat down and opened his Psalter and there was a note.

We appreciate your kindness, signed Moo, Bah, Nay, Cluck, Meow, Woof, and Cock-a-doodle-do.

Paul recognized the large block letters that were Ambrose's unmistakable scrawl.

At breakfast, he found a note of thanks on his plate and his juice poured. After school, Paul checked his chores and found that there were none assigned to him. Paul put his bag in his room and noticed that his bed was made, and fresh sheets were on it and chocolate on his pillow. He grabbed his Walkman and wandered to the kitchen to find a plate of cookies and a glass of milk labeled "For Paul." Paul scribbled thanks on the back of the note.

At recreation, Paul played checkers with Brother Moses, and for the second time that evening, won. Moses was letting him win.

"I won again. It must be because I had you for a teacher," Paul said. Moses's face lit up in delight.

Abbot Jacob called the room to attention.

"Little Trappist, come here."

Paul stared at Abbot Jacob.

"I'm not a Trappist. I'm Benedictine," Paul said.

"Aren't they the same?" Novice William asked.

"No, Benedictines believe in moderation in all things, including moderation," Paul said, rolling his eyes. Didn't they teach anything to these newcomers?

"Trappist's are Benedictine," Alcuin said.

"They are maximizers, taking everything St. Benedict wrote to the limit. Pray, fast, and silence, twenty-four hours a day. Overkill."

Alcuin turned away.

"Glad to see you notice a difference. Now can you apply it to yourself? We all appreciate your effort to make our life easier, but doing all our jobs..." Jacob said. "I am sure you get the point. On behalf of the community, I would like to present you with this." Jacob handed Paul an envelope. Inside the envelope were three tickets to the Shakespeare festival in town.

"Wow. Thanks, everyone."

Paul headed down the hall and knocked softly on Joe's cell door.

"Enter," came the response.

"Hi, you're in bed early."

"Most Trappists are," Joannicus said from his pile of blankets.

"Very funny. They gave me tickets to Shakespeare. I would rather have tickets to the KISS concert at the MetraPark Arena in Billings," Paul said, closing the door realizing he was letting the cold air in.

"KISS? Is that the group with the black-and-white makeup and studded uniforms?"

"The makeup is based on comic-book-style characters and, well, it's just their stage personality."

Joannicus nodded. "Seriously, might I suggest you spread out your acts of kindness?"

"I know, the Abbot already told me. I just wanted to express how glad I am to be home."

Paul fanned himself as he pulled a chair over to Joe's bed.

"Why are you so cold? I looked up anemia and you're too cold."

"Perhaps I am dead," Joannicus said, pulling the wool cap down on his head.

"Funny. I think I came back to the wrong monastery," Paul said. "You are all different."

Father Joannicus peered over his reading glasses. "How so?"

"Do you know that your hair is coming in white? Ambrose complains more, mostly about help, that he has machines to do his work. Abbot Jacob has been fixing things. You know Moses is letting me win in checkers and he can barely play as it is. That makes it hard for me to let him win."

"Time for a new game. As for Ambrose, he likes to complain. Yes, Abbot Jacob has been improving things, meeting some of our neglected needs. We all got new mattresses," Joannicus said, wiggling into the bed.

"Do you think Abbot Jacob made me an oblate to keep me here

forever?" Paul asked as he stopped fanning himself and let the sweat drip.

"Forever? Are you saying you don't want to be a monk? I'm crushed, all my guidance gone to waste."

Paul scanned Joe's face, relieved that he could see merriment in the brown eyes.

When did Joannicus become funny, and when did Abbot Jacob become gentle in his guidance? They had changed.

Paul didn't like change.

CHAPTER II
PIZZA

Psalm 103:14
You bring forth bread from the earth,
and wine to cheer man's heart.

P aul stood in his old room, the one on the first floor across the alcove from Father Joe's cell. He locked the door and with trembling fingers dialed the number to Mackenzie River Pizza to place his order.

"Yes, it's been authorized. Would you like to call the Abbot?" Paul said, trying to keep his voice deep.

Paul breathed a sigh of relief as he put the receiver down. They were going to deliver the pizzas. He had at least an hour before the meal arrived. The bells for Mass rang, and he waited. The halls of the monastery were silent as he crept his way to the Abbot's office. He listened. No movement, so he opened the door and slipped inside. His hands shook as he punched the code into the safe keypad. The safe door clicked open. He extracted a single check from the checkbook and cash for the tip.

Forty pizzas for forty men, at about ten dollars each. Wow, that's a big check. Paul pulled forty dollars out of petty cash for a tip. On the ledger taped to the envelope, he wrote, "Movie money, Ambrose." He had seen Ambrose make entries when they had gone to the movies. Paul closed the safe door as he listened for any noise in the hall. Nothing, so he left the office and the monastery.

Now to stop the production of dinner.

"Brother Barnabas, it's your lucky day. You get to go to Mass. I'll take care of the meal preparation. Abbot's orders." He tried to sound confident, so the monk wouldn't suspect anything.

Barnabas smoothed his flour-coated apron. "What did you do?"

"I don't want to talk about it."

Slowly, the monk left. Sometimes monks were so easy to deceive. But it wasn't really a lie. He had done something. He was giving the monks a treat. Abbot Jacob told him to find a different way to say thank you.

"Us too?" the two juniors asked.

"Yeah, go," Paul said, and they hurried off before anyone could change their mind. Dinner was after weekday Mass; they often excused the kitchen crew from attending Mass. Brother Barnabas rarely attended since he was in charge.

Paul stopped production of the meal and began preparing salads and dessert. After that was done, he glanced at the clock. Mass would let out soon. He ran to his room and pulled out a signed permission slip. He moved to the window, slid the check over the top of the signature. Slowly and carefully, he traced the name. This is not stealing. How can you steal what is yours? St.

Benedict says each is given what they need. To some more, to others less. And we need pizza. Our money is shared.

Paul paced the walkway near the empty parking lot. He had pulled three carts from the kitchen. His heart beat wildly. Novices Thomas and Stephen appeared.

"Hi, Paul, what are you doing here?"

"I'm waiting for a delivery, isn't that what you are doing here?" Paul said as he tried to look nonchalant by leaning on the stair rail.

Thomas and Stephen shrugged.

"Where is Bother Barnabas?" Thomas asked.

"I don't know. Can you help me bring the pizzas to the refectory?" Paul's heart thumped wildly in anticipation.

"Pizza? You're joking, right?"

"No, it's the feast of Raffaele Esposito, a baker. You knew that, didn't you?"

The two novices shook their heads.

"He owned a tavern and fed King Umberto and Queen Margherita as they traveled," Paul said. Hurry pizza.

"Why is he a saint?" Stephen asked, stepping into the shade.

He would have to ask.

"Bread and cheese were food for the poor. The king and queen were royalty. Their arrival was not planned, so Raffaele prayed to God to give him inspiration. He used bread, red sauce, basil, and cheese and basically made pizza, impressing the queen," Paul said with as much authority that he could muster.

Shut up. They're going to get suspicious about this babbling.

"That's why a margarita pizza is plain."

"That's a lame miracle," Stephen said as he kicked a pebble with his foot. "Did the Abbot approve of this?"

"He didn't disapprove. Didn't he ask you to be here and wait? I think an oblate is responsible for the celebration," Paul said, thankful that novices didn't know one monk's handwriting from another. Paul had enough "come see me" notes to fake Abbot Jacob's mixture of cursive and capitals.

"Who?" Stephen asked. "You?"

"Do I look like I have money? No, Mrs. Van Horn. You've met her, old and classy. She's always giving us special foods for our big holidays, sweet bread at Easter, baklava at Christmas." That was true. Her name appeared next to dishes on holidays.

Come on pizza.

Both Stephen and Thomas shrugged their shoulders. Novices were easy to fool. An older monk might have recognized the name.

Paul could see two cars coming up the hill from the road.

Thank you, Jesus.

Paul raced to the driver with the check in hand.

"You know, I have been dreaming about pizza. I sure miss it," Thomas said, loading the boxes on to the carts.

Paul and the novices waited inside the refectory for the monks to arrive from recreation. The smell was making Paul's mouth water.

"What the heck is going on?" Brother Barnabas whispered to Brother Ambrose, seeing his kitchen transformed into a pizzeria.

"Who cares," Ambrose said. "This is wonderful."

The delight of the monks made Paul's heart dance. He could feel Brother Mellitus smiling down from heaven for pulling this caper off with no one the wiser. They would forgive him for the money, especially after tasting the pizzas.

"This is not healthy," Barnabas hissed.

"Is too. Hits all the food groups: dairy, meat, grain, veggie, and pineapple. That's a fruit. All one bite, the perfect food," Ambrose said, cutting in line in front of the juniors, using his rank as a professed monk to keep them from protesting.

Paul was grateful that the meal would be eaten in silence. He sat back and enjoyed the smiling faces of his family, ignoring the stare of Abbot Jacob.

Paul hoped to avoid questions by staying to help with cleanup. He overheard many thanking Abbot Jacob for the feast. Once again, he was grateful for the set routine, evening prayer, then silence until morning. Who could question an act of kindness? They all shared the money, and they really needed pizza. Just this once, an extravagance.

The bells rang. Paul walked to the church, taking the outside path at a determined pace.

"You did it, didn't you," Brother Alcuin said, his nasal voice stopping Paul's movement.

"I don't have access to the money," Paul said, thinking he should have signed Alcuin's name on the check.

"I should just tell," Alcuin said, blocking Paul's path to the church. "I know it was you. I don't think the Abbot would have done this. The cost alone is we don't waste money."

"There was no waste."

"You're a liar and a thief," Alcuin said gleefully.

"Why don't you focus on your own faults rather than mine," Paul said, stepping around the monk. "I've a list of them if you would like a copy."

"You're so full of yourself. You are an oblate, a step above the ordinary person and you have no vote or say in monastic matters."

"If I'm so low, why bother with me?" Paul asked as he moved down the path to the church.

News flash: no monk material here. *Jerk. You are the most negative man here.* Sometimes it baffled Paul how some men made it to monkhood. Why hadn't anyone pointed out to Alcuin that he was a dick? They have four years to tell him before he makes his solemn profession. Benedictines were too patient.

Prayers were uneventful, except for Psalm 33, which mentioned evil and lips that spoke deceit, which caused Paul's conscience to itch.

Belly full, Paul made his way to his cell, where he said his bedtime prayers, and fell asleep in the glow of Brother Mellitus, cheering from heaven. Operation Pizza Delivery, checked off as a success.

Twenty-four hours passed and the wonderful meal of pizza was still being discussed, to Paul's delight. Finally, he had given back to the community. He wondered when Abbot Jacob would question him, and he hoped not at all. One should be humble enough to accept the kindness of others.

Paul went about his chores. Everything seemed normal. Night came and Paul found sleep troublesome.

"I did nothing wrong," he said aloud to the poster of KISS on his wall.

Morning arrived, the bells rang, and Paul's eyes snapped open.

His first time being an acolyte, and he was late. He sprang out of bed, threw on yesterday's clothes, grabbed his sandals, and ran down the hall barefoot.

Tossing his sandals to the side in the atrium, they sounded like a gunshot as they hit the floor. Paul skidded to a stop. The church was dark. Why were the lights off? Was this some kind of test? No, this was prayers, God's time.

Taking a deep breath, Paul turned on the lights. The community was there in silence, waiting. Paul moved to light the candles, fumbling with the matches, flame to wick that would not catch. Paul dropped the burned stick.

Damn. Just start the prayer. The hymn is next, the choirmaster will lead that.

"Oh, Lord, open my lips," Paul said. The wick caught, and the flame sparked.

Thank God.

Paul made his way to his place in the front row. The hymn began. Crap, crap, what week was it? Two or three? Just last week, a novice started the psalms using the previous week, and Paul had pointed out which week it was. But the novice wasn't helping him in return.

Brother Alcuin cleared his throat. Yet another annoying habit. He should help me. Isn't that what the Rule says? To help each other? Paul looked up. Abbot Jacob stood in front of him and handed Paul his own Psalter, which was covered in a soft hide. The Abbot took Paul's Psalter. Was there anything in his Psalter that would make the Abbot cringe? Too late now. He wasn't going to grab the book back.

"Week one, Saturday morning, you know how to use this?" Abbot Jacob said before returning to his place. Paul felt his face become hot. He knew how to work the breviary. Of course, he knew how to use the breviary. He had used this book three times a day for the past ten years.

The order of the psalms for each season only changed sightly. There are only four seasons, Advent, Lent, Easter, and Ordinary times.

Piece of cake.

Paul started the psalm.

"Alleluia, I love the Lord for his has heard—"

"Paul," came the voice of the Abbot, interrupting him. "Louder, not even the Lord can hear you."

Behind him, Brother Alcuin snickered. Paul stiffened, thinking, *I wouldn't do that if you were making mistakes. Well, maybe I would.*

The shroud of humility weighed heavy. Paul took a deep

breath and started again. There was a quiet time between each psalm for meditation. Paul caught Mellitus whispering in his mind.

It's a trick. The Abbot knows nothing. He can't read minds. Don't give in. But it was too late. Confessing after prayers loomed around him.

Ambrose cleared his throat loudly, and Paul realized he had been lost in thought instead of beginning the next psalm.

"Save me, oh God." The words were appropriate.

"That can only happen if he hears you," Abbot Jacob said with a sigh.

Crap, crap, crap. Paul wished the floor would open and swallow him whole. He hung his head and bit his lip in horror. Brother Simon leaned forward and whispered in his ear.

"You can do this. Sit up straight, hold the book in front of you, take two deep breaths, and slowly say each word."

Paul sat up and glanced around. Nobody was really staring. He took two breaths and started. During the meditative silence, Paul chewed his thumbnail. How long was the pause between psalms? The Abbot was probably regretting the day he allowed Paul to be an acolyte.

Were the monks fidgeting or nodding off? He could see nothing but calm, heads bowed, and still monks. This should be enough time.

"Have mercy on me, God—" Paul said in a clear voice.

"Not yet," Abbot Jacob said as someone behind Paul snickered.

What the hell? Why is Abbot Jacob doing this?

He hadn't corrected the novice who messed up in the last week.

Paul waited, holding his breath.

"Start now please." The words were clipped and sharp.

Paul started in a loud but wavering voice and then closed his eyes. Alex reached over and patted his arm in a gesture of comfort. When the psalm ended, Abbot Jacob said, "Paul, to yourself, count to thirty-two and then introduce the next psalm."

Paul hung his head and swallowed.

He had an entire week of this.

All thoughts of a confession retreated to the shadows.

CHAPTER 12
BALES OF HAY

Psalm 126:3
Truly sons are a gift from the Lord,
A blessing, the fruit of the womb.

Procrastination ticked away like a pendulum on a wind-up clock. Paul figured if he ignored payment, so would the community. Hungry and tired, Paul dropped his backpack off on the chair in the community room. He had finished helping Ambrose to the farm and was seeking a snack and shower. He passed the mail slots and noticed he had mail. That was odd, for it wasn't his birthday and too early for Easter cards.

Picking up the envelope and walking to the refrigerator, he opened the door and saw nothing worth eating but fruit. Checking the cabinet, he saw that someone had cleaned out the stash of cookies. Abbot Jacob was taking this Lent fasting thing to an extreme. No worry, he had cookies in his room.

He grabbed an apple and opened the envelope. The high-lighted interest on the bill mocked him. The debt wasn't going away.

"Why the long face?" Ambrose asked, entering the room smelling of deodorant, soap, and tobacco.

"Abbot Jacob sent me a bill. Doesn't he know how hard it is to find a job? It's not like I haven't looked," Paul said.

Looked was really all he had done. Nothing on campus interested him. He didn't want to work serving food to snotty college students, and he did not want to pull weeds or haul trash.

"Have you checked with student work study?" Brother Ambrose said, taking the apple out of Paul's hand and biting into it before handing it back. "Try being an assistant to a professor? You know, a go-fetch boy."

"Talk to the Abbot. He's the one making this difficult," Paul said, taking a bite out of the apple.

"He's being an abbot," Ambrose said, opening a cabinet and taking a lid off a pot and extracting a napkin wrapped doughnut. Paul tried to grab the stale treat from Ambrose's hand.

Brothers Reginald and Alcuin arrived to restock the little kitchenette.

"It's still Lent in case you have forgotten," Alcuin said, and Ambrose stopped chewing and swallowed.

"I'm not a monk, in case you forgot," Paul said. "And Brother Ambrose needs more than most. The Rule states we each get what we need."

Alcuin sneered as he put the filters away. "Okay, not a monk, but you're Catholic, aren't you? Fasting is for everyone, not just monks."

"He's got you there," Ambrose said, handing Paul his half-eaten doughnut.

"Well, I've decided I want to be like Jesus, so I'm converting to Judaism."

Brother Reginald laughed. "Heard you were looking for work. Try bucking bales."

"What's that?" Paul said, thinking too much work.

"No, Little One, that is arduous work. Carrying hay, scorching sun, long hours, sore back, blistered hands," Ambrose said.

Paul cringed at the boyhood endearment, wishing Ambrose hadn't used it in front of Alcuin.

"Yeah, stick to a desk job," Alcuin said, "Wouldn't want you hurting yourself. You're not built for that work."

A spark of indignation made Paul stand taller. He was already taller than Alcuin, who reminded Paul of a bulldog in stature.

"I've worked the harvest every year. I can do demanding work. I've stacked the hay."

"And you do a superb job," Brother Ambrose said. "But farm work is not field work."

Paul frowned. "How much does it pay?"

"More than flipping burgers or washing dishes," Reginald said. "There is an ad on the student bulletin board.

Ambrose glowered at Reginald.

"What?" Brother Reginald said. "Paul can buck hay."

"He has never done it before. Most of those kids have been bucking hay since they were twelve. They got upper body builds now," Ambrose said, crossing his massive arms. Ambrose was the farmer of the community, and built like a sumo wrestler, with huge biceps that could pin an uncooperative sheep or unruly little boy.

"I will do push-ups until then. I have muscles," Paul said, stalking out of the room. As soon as he was out of sight, he ran down the hill to the college and ripped the ad from the board, lessening his competition. He knew the experienced could be hired before him. He stuffed the paper into his pocket, and ran up the hill to join the community for Mass.

No sooner had Mass finished, the monks heading to recreation, than Paul hastily rushed down the hall to the Abbot's office. Empty. He headed to the community room.

No time like the present.

"Abbot Jacob, what do you think?" Paul asked, shoving the wrinkled paper in front of the man.

The conversation paused. Jacob ironed the paper with his hand as Father Joannicus leaned over to read the printed material.

"Thanks, but I already have a job," Abbot Jacob said.

"Hilarious, but I meant for me," Paul said as he watched Joannicus slowly shake his head and look pleadingly at Jacob.

Brother Ambrose leaned over, groaned, and then snatched the paper from the Abbot, balled it, and shot the controversial announcement across the room into the wastepaper can.

Why was everyone so opposed to him getting this job?

"Brother Ambrose, you can't do that. This is between me and Abbot Jacob."

"No, this is a community matter," Ambrose said, shaking his wooly head.

Paul stood up straight so that he was eye to eye with the man. "How so?"

"I would have to dig your grave when you fell over dead."

Was the man serious?

"I am asking Abbot Jacob," Paul turned, knowing that when Ambrose decided there was little one could do to sway him. "This is the perfect job. Nobody has to take me. They pick you up and drop you off, and you get paid for what you work. Can I sign up?" Paul held his breath.

"May I sign up," mumbled Father Joannicus.

An odd smile appeared on Abbot Jacob's face. "You want the job, go for it."

Father Joannicus shook his head more vigorously.

"No, Abbot Jacob," Brother Ambrose said. "This is wrong. Bucking hay is dangerous. You're in the blistering sun lifting one-hundred-pound bales, tossing them on a moving truck. And then there's baler's lung."

"Baler's lung?" the question echoed around the room. Was Ambrose inventing diseases?

"Nasty cough from the spores," Ambrose explained, crossing his arms, daring anyone to challenge his knowledge.

"Brother Ambrose, this is a farming state. Everyone bucks hay for a summer and then decides on college," Abbot Jacob said.

"Not everyone," Ambrose grumbled, trudging out of the office.

Paul crossed the room and retrieved the ad.

They are exaggerating. It can't be that hard. Why do they dislike changes? They had fussed when he was sent traveling and nothing bad had happened to him. What were they afraid of? He heard nothing about anyone losing an arm or suffocating in a rolled-up bale of hay.

On June 12TH, in the early morning, Paul stood in the fading darkness on the side of St. Xavier Highway. A bus pulled up and Paul climbed aboard. He took a seat up front, noting the boys sprawled out, attempting to get a few extra minutes of sleep.

The morning began with crew assignments, four to a crew, and each leader called a name. Most of the crew leaders were young. That was a surprise. Paul had expected them to be at least college age. Paul felt like the runt of the litter as he stood waiting for his name to be called. By the end of the selection, Paul knew he was a leftover.

"We're going to Macdonald's farm first. He's got about twenty-seven acres and we'll be stacking in the hay shed, then on to the primary fields. This afternoon, we have the north end," said the boy who called himself Lucas.

The other boys nodded and piled on to a truck bed. Lucas was Paul's age.

"Hey, princess, are you waiting for a personal invite?" called a voice from the truck bed.

"Warner," yelled Lucas. "Get up here."

Paul felt himself blush as he quickly climbed on to the truck bed before it sped off down the road. Ambrose would disapprove of driving down the highway in the truck bed. MacDonald's farm, funny. He decided not to make a lame joke. He wanted to be liked.

When they unloaded, the boys got to work lining up next to bales. Paul had counted twenty-one rows with twenty bales in each row as they passed the field. That made for 420 bales of hay to buck.

By ten in the morning, Paul's stomach rumbled. His shirt was wet, and his hair clung to his head as endless rows of hay taunted him. His throat was parched and scratchy. Had he gotten baler's lung so quickly? Someone handed him a red bandana. He observed others looked as uncomfortable as he did, yet nobody complained. At noon, Paul flopped down to the ground. His arms refused to lift his sandwich. The smooth movement of lift, hoist, and toss he had not mastered. Paul noticed he was the slowest boy on the crew and feared they would fire him on his first day.

When Paul boarded the bus to go home, it reeked of sweat and hay. Every bump in the road jarred his bones as he thought about soaking in a hot tub for a week.

Paul trudged up the hill, every muscle in his body protesting.

Muscles refused to move, and his back ached. He had never had a backache before. His hands pulsed like a fresh burn.

He headed to the showers, hoping the hot water would relieve the sting of the day. Paul cringed at the memory of Lucas's voice pointing out all his mistakes. The massaging water helped ease the soreness but did nothing for the bruised ego. This wasn't farm work. He could hear the community saying, I told you so.

Paul slowly limped to the community room and eased himself into a soft chair, feeling older than Brother Mellitus and praying that he could rise when the bells rang for prayers. The clock mocked the time as he wished he could just go to bed. This day is too long.

The squeaking of sandals forced Paul to lift his head from his chest. Ambrose paused and frowned.

"Damn, didn't you think to cover up? You're the color of a cooked lobster. Come with me."

Paul rose, and in an unsteady gait, followed Ambrose to the infirmary. He wasn't sunburned, for he had covered up.

I need a real hat and boots, thought Paul, reflecting on the blue jeans, large belt buckles, pointy-toed boots, and cowboy hats of the crew. The Wild West minus the gun, horses, and Natives. He had originally thought Lucas was Native American, but soon found out that wasn't the case when someone on the crew called Lucas "Cochise." The reference was to an Apache Chief who killed whites. Paul wasn't sure they were being worked to death, or the boy hated Indians. Lucas set the kid straight with one punch to the chest, sending the boy to the dirt and a clarification for his dark skin. "Mexican you, Tonto." Paul had heard that "Tonto" was a Spanish slur meaning idiot. The exchange was sadly comical. Paul laughed. Ambrose gave him a worried look.

Upon seeing Paul's hands, Ambrose huffed.

"That's it. You will not work tomorrow. This isn't the job for you. You should have listened to the Abbot and gotten a job these past months. This job is going to kill you."

"Ambrose, no, I just need good gloves," Paul said. "Leather or something. My hands will be fine. I want to work."

Ambrose grunted as Brother Michael poured a solution that jolted Paul awake as it stung. Now his hands hurt more than his muscles.

"I will get better," Paul said through gritted teeth as Brother Michael applied a wrap to his hands. "I'm so tired. I just want to eat and go to bed."

"Excellent idea," Ambrose said.

"Don't tell the Abbot. I want to do this."

"Little One, this isn't working." Ambrose said, pressing his forehead to Paul's. "Fine. One week. If you die, so help me."

The aroma of hay, which once was comforting, suddenly drained Paul.

"I'll be fine," Paul said, placing a bandaged hand on Ambrose's forearm.

"Hard is right," Ambrose muttered with a scowl.

Together, they headed to the refectory, and then downstairs. The smells of roasted chicken made Paul's head spin. Paul ignored the quizzical looks over his bandaged hands. Father Joannicus and Brother Ambrose sat across from each other, gesturing, and scowling and pointing to the Abbot's table.

Paul giggled. I must be feverish, Paul thought, watching them plot as to when they could approach the Abbot and stop him from returning to the fields.

He ate a whole chicken, pasta, green beans, salad, and two desserts, an apple cobbler and peach pie. As he headed out of the refectory, he noticed Abbot Jacob giving him the once-over.

Crap. He was acolyte, no skipping prayers. Double crap.

Paul walked to the church. Evening prayers were shorter than morning prayers by fifteen minutes.

Thank you, Jesus.

Paul lit the candles and turned on the lights in the church. The bells rang, monks filed in. Paul stood.

"Lord, come to my assistance."

The community responded, "Lord, make haste to help me."

He sat in the hard chair reading the first lines of the Psalms. During the meditative silence between psalms, Paul fell asleep. Silence always accompanied evening prayer. The familiar sounds of movement, the groan of creaking joints and tinkling of holy metals and relics, which hung around necks, did not disturb Paul's slumber.

"Wake up, sleepy head," Father Joannicus said. "Come, it's bedtime."

"What happened to prayers?" Paul asked, yawning.

"You slept through them."

Paul sat up straight and then groaned. His body did not like the quick movement.

"Oh, no, how could I? I was awake when we started. Is Abbot Jacob upset?" Paul asked.

"He didn't sound angry. He makes a good acolyte."

Joannicus put an arm around Paul's shoulder and the weight was like a beam of wood. Paul didn't complain. They walked to the third floor. The smell of sweat and grain filled Paul's nose as he entered his cell.

"I suck. I'll be surprised if they let me work tomorrow. I'm the weakest worker there. I'm not quitting, but I'm never doing that kind of work again, as long as I live," Paul said, peeling off his socks and leaving them on the floor. "Pay my debt and be done with it."

"I see," Joannicus said, picking up the discarded clothes scattered around the room.

"Oh, my stomach hurts," Paul said.

"Yes. You ate like there was no tomorrow."

Paul climbed into bed. "I was hungry."

"Moderation, Paul," Father Joannicus said. His voice held more humor than condemnation.

"What if I fail at this?"

"What if? Seriously, you will try again. Begin again," Joannicus said, putting clean clothing out on the desktop.

"Is my alarm set?" Paul asked, as Joannicus pulled the covers up. Paul hadn't been tucked into bed since he was a little boy. The gesture, coupled with exhaustion, made him nostalgic.

Joannicus looked at the clock. "It is. Now get some rest." Paul felt Joe's thumb making a cross on his forehead. He was being blessed.

"I will say your prayers for your," Father Joannicus said.

"Pray that I survive this," Paul muttered, his eyes heavy with exhaustion.

"You will," Joannicus said.

CHAPTER 13
IN THE MORNING

Psalm 112:7
From the dust, he lifts up the lowly,
from the dung heap, he raises the poor
to set him in the company of princes.

Crisp and familiar, the bells rang. Five minutes to get to the church before prayers started. Paul rolled over.

The room glowed with sunlight. Paul opened his eyes.

Crap, it is six thirty.

Jumping out of bed, he hit his head on the shelf, causing books to cascade to the floor. His alarm lay unplugged among them.

Double crap.

Paul threw on clothes, opened his cell door, and tripped over a box of work gloves and hats that lay in front of his path. Thankful and cursing, he grabbed a pair of leather gloves and a Montana Grizzlies cap, then raced through the hall to the stairs, down to the first floor. Someone would be in the community room.

He needed a ride. Nobody was there. Damn.

He raced down the hall to the church, passing two monks on their way to prayers. They clicked their tongues as he dashed by.

Paul skidded to a stop. Prayers had begun. Inside the church, he tried to catch someone's eye.

Abbot Jacob raised a finger, pointing at Paul's head. Paul removed his hat as he walked into the church.

"I need a ride," Paul whispered.

"After prayers," Jacob said.

"That will be too late," Paul said. "Can't Father Joannicus take me now?"

"No, we are praying. Go sit."

Paul plopped to the floor, wishing he could throw a fit complete with kicking and screaming.

Prayers dragged on as Paul sat on the floor at the feet of the Abbot, fuming and thinking, *if I was bleeding, would he wait until after prayers?* He wants to see me fired.

His second day, and it would be his last. The minute the Abbot rose to lead the monks out of the church. Paul walked as fast as he could without running out of the church, beating Abbot Jacob to the atrium. Brother Barnabas was startled as Paul burst through the refectory doors.

"Paul, what the heck are you doing?"

"Later, gotta go. Thanks," Paul said, as he grabbed his lunch. Monks filed into the refectory as Paul exited with a one muffin stuffed in his mouth and two in his hands. In the Abbot's office, he signed out a set of car keys and turned, almost crashing into Brother Alcuin.

"Paul, what are you up to?" Alcuin called. Paul left him in the hall, ducking into Joe's cell.

Wallet, wallet, where are you? Paul moved papers and opened a desk drawer.

Alcuin stood in the doorway with his arms crossed. "What are you doing in Father Joannicus's cell? You have no business in here."

The brown, thin wallet lay peacefully in an abandoned flower-pot. Paul grabbed it and moved to the doorway.

"This doesn't concern you. Move."

Alcuin didn't move, so Paul pushed him aside and dashed out of the room. In the hallway outside of the refectory, Paul found Father Joannicus and Abbot Jacob.

"You sure you are up to this?" Jacob asked Joannicus.

Come on, we have to go. Paul jiggled the car keys. Abbot Jacob frowned.

"All is fine," Joannicus said as he turned to Paul. "I have to get my wallet."

"Got it," Paul said, handing the billfold to Joannicus.

Paul checked the speedometer. Joannicus was going the speed limit. Paul glanced at his watch. He would not arrive until eight. Would they let him work?

"What should I say about being late?" Paul asked.

"The truth is a desirable choice. But I would say nothing and just start working."

The truth. No way.

Even if it was a virtuous trait, he would not risk being laughed at.

As they arrived at the field, the car barely came to a stop as Paul jumped.

Lucas, the crew boss, approached Paul.

Oh, crap.

"You're late, you surprised me, Warner. I just figured you quit. Well, why are you standing around? Get to work."

Thank you, Jesus.

The day wore on. Exhaustion came in waves like the heat, but Paul was determined to prove himself. His hands burned despite the new gloves.

Finally, the engines of the trucks and the clanging of the gears fell silent. Lunch time had arrived. Paul wiped his face clean of the grain dust with a red bandana. Lucas moved among the crew. Lucas wasn't a huge boy. He was just lean and tall. He worked alongside of them, sweating and grunting. I bet he plays sports. He looks like a jock.

"You, Davis, my mother works faster than you. It's grab, lift, and toss. Really simple."

Tim snickered. Lucas spun around and glared. "What are you laughing at? You miss the truck half the time, which means we have to go down the row twice to pick up your misses."

Lucas kicked Mark's foot. "You're on the line. Warner is driving."

"What no way," Mark said.

"Maybe he can drive the truck in a slow and straight line. This isn't Friday night."

The other boys chuckled at the reference to drunk driving. Paul had no license. However, he was on private land. Ambrose taught him how to drive and occasionally he drove up the hill from the farm to the monastery. Abbot Jacob refused to allow Paul a driver's permit, even though he was now sixteen. Lunch churned in Paul's stomach.

"Did you hear me, Warner?" Lucas said.

"Yes, sir," Paul said, squinting as he looked over in Lucas's direction.

Davis snickered.

"I have a quota. It'll be met, or pay will be docked," Lucas said. A shadow darkened Paul's lunch. Paul glanced up to see Lucas standing over him.

"What did you call me, Warner?" Lucas asked, his voice deep with challenge, his dark hair shadowing his face, brown eyes boring into Paul.

Oh crap. Paul's ham sandwich balled in his throat as he tried to swallow it.

"Sir?" Paul said in an unsteady voice. What else should he call him?

"Shit." Lucas spat on the ground, shaking his head.

Lucas's brown eyes stared out from the tanned face as a smirk played on his lips. Paul felt his face grow hot. Crap, now what?

"How come you're calling me that?"

Paul held his breath. "You're the boss, right?"

"Yes."

Paul glanced around at the other boys. He knew some boys called Lucas slave driver, boss man, but Paul would not use those words.

"Do you want to be called something else?"

"No, sir will do. Now come with me."

Paul rose and followed Lucas, convinced he was about to be fired.

As they got a distance away from the group, Paul could hear Mark complaining. Mark was a wrestler built like a tank. Paul recognized him from school, and he was thankful that Mark did not recognize him. They approached a weathered pickup truck. The sides stained with rust and the bed dented and beaten. Lucas stopped.

"Hands, Warner. Let me see those hands."

"I'm alright," Paul said, wishing he had more gaze and ointment. The popped blisters burned and throbbed.

"I'll be the judge of that. Let me see," Lucas said.

Paul held out his hands. Lucas whistled through his teeth. "Baby butt hands."

Lucas climbed into the bed of the truck and opened a metal box. "Who's the fucking asshole who sent you to me? I'm so blessed. You need moleskin. Don't you know anything? You need a pair of cowboy boots. Don't you own a pair? Those are plowing boots. New boots or don't come to work tomorrow," Lucas ranted. "Let me see your hands."

Lucas pulled out a jug labeled "not H2O" and splashed soapy water over Paul's hands. The sting made Paul grimace and draw in his breath, closing his eyes to the pain.

"Sorry. But you're not getting an infection if you're on my crew."

Calloused fingers applied ointment and cut moleskin, bandaging Paul's hands.

"Thank you, sir." Paul said. "I have boots."

"Good." Lucas handed Paul a pair of thick, worn gloves. "Take these gloves."

The box clunked close, and Lucas hopped out of the truck bed. He marched toward the others. "Come on, Warner, you're wasting daylight."

Driving a truck was simple work. His hands were grateful. Guilt and shame sat with Paul in the cab. He wondered if Lucas was sparing his feelings. No, Lucas could say that and more. Paul was sure of that. Lucas fascinated Paul. Like a spinning top, roughness to kindness, Paul wasn't sure what side would show itself.

Paul made his way to the bus. He needed cowboy boots by tomorrow. Where was he going to get them? Monks did not wear cowboy boots under their habits. He envisioned the community in boots and large belt buckles, for all the boys on the crew had large belt buckles. Monks wore black cloth belts under their scapular that was part of the habit. If they had big belted buckles with the medal of Saint Benedict embossed on them, would they wear their belt in plain sight? I must have sun stroke because I think those additions might fit.

Paul leaned his head against the window. The fields of hay, yet to be mowed, sweep by on his way home.

CHAPTER 14
GIRLS

Psalm 107: 2-3
I will sing, sing your praise. Awake my soul.
Awake, lyre and harp. I will awake the dawn.

Cowboy boots appeared that evening, and Paul was grateful for the added protection. The days reminded Paul of monastic life, work, eat, and rest. Summer plowed on, Paul grew stronger, and the crew worked more efficiently. Paul saw his lunches were getting bigger and bigger. Brother Barnabas must have thought his exhaustion was food related, for inside his cooler stood meat sandwiches and a peanut butter and banana sandwich. Nestled on top and bottom were carrots, grapes, an apple, tomatoes, and three oatmeal cookies. Paul noticed the crew had bags of chips, candy, and soda pop.

"You gonna eat all of your lunch?" Kevin asked, eyeing a roast beef sandwich.

"No, I have too much. You can have some," Paul said.

"Hold it," Lucas said. "That's the runt's. I mean Warner's lunch, and he eats first. You, beggar, pilfer after he's done."

Paul recognized that there was a hungry pack of wolves around him as he ate his fill and let the crew devour the rest.

"What kind of bread is this? It is very thick," Kevin said with his mouth stuffed full.

"Homemade, probably wheat," Paul said.

"It ain't white bread, that's for sure," Kevin laughed, swatting at the flies. "Your momma must love you."

Paul did not correct the assumption. He already felt like a crab on the beach at low tide.

"What are you doing out here?" Lucas asked one day after lunch.

"Working, earning money," Paul said cautiously.

"Why?"

"I have a debt I have to pay off."

Lucas nodded. "Punishment. You got one mean son of a bitch of a father."

Paul smiled. No point in correcting the assumption. He would probably not run into these guys again. Even if they went to the same school, they ran in different crowds.

Rest time was a welcomed break. Most slept, but Paul sat and wondered about the land. How many lost civilizations lay hidden under this dirt?

Sometimes he would close his eyes and listen to the surrounding conversations.

"Are you going out for football?" Mark asked.

"Of course. I'm hoping to draw the attention of the University of Montana," Lucas said. "Are you continuing with wrestling?"

"No, basketball," snorted Mark.

"Don't be a jerk," Lucas said. "It's too hot to be funny."

"She's hot," Kevin said. "There was a group of chicks in town Saturday night. They were trouble."

"So, you got in trouble?" Lucas said.

"This story is true," Mark said. "He was with two girls."

"They put out. You lucky dog," Richie said.

Many of the conversations were about girls, conquests, and reputations. Paul listened with keen interest, reflecting on a conversation he had with Ambrose.

Paul was sitting on the patio bench outside of the community room thinking about boys and girls. The sky glistened with stars and the night was muggy. The slider opened and Paul moved over on the bench as he heard the heavy steps of Ambrose.

"Keeping company with Orion?" Ambrose asked.

"Waiting for Venus," Paul said.

"Venus, danger."

"Are all girls dangerous?" Paul asked, thinking about the only girl he knew. Charlie.

Ambrose bumped Paul's shoulder. "Nah, the right one is fun."

"Charlie is fun," Paul said wistfully, thinking about the adventures they had skipping assemblies.

"That's not a girl," Ambrose grunted.

"Am I missing something? How do you find the right one?"

"She comes when she is ready and when you are." Ambrose stuck a match, lighting up the darkness, the air filled with sulfur.

"That is not helpful. I need to figure them out."

"Talk to Abbot Jacob. He understands them."

That would not happen. He didn't want Jacob's cautionary tales.

"The guys talk about the girls, putting out."

Ambrose blew out a breath of smoke. The cigar scented the

air. "The ones who say they are, are not. The ones who are not bragging are."

"You're not making any sense," Paul said, thinking about Kevin and Elisa, or was it Lizzie?

"Listen and watch, you'll learn who is shooting at the stars," Ambrose said.

"Should I be chasing after girls?"

"Chase, no, look, yes. You're too young to be thinking about a mate for life."

"I don't wish to marry them. I just want to..." Paul felt like his face was glowing.

"Yes?"

"Put the tailgate down and watch the corn grow."

Ambrose laughed. Paul had heard all about sex, hormones, and desire. Joannicus cautioned him about straying thoughts. You can control those. He had no success in that department.

"Don't worry. Love will come," Ambrose said, crushing his cigar on the brick wall.

"And joy," Paul added, hoping that was true.

August came and soft muscles turned defined. Skin glowed with the kiss of the sun and Paul's curls lightened. Physical labor changed a boy into a man. Paul was no longer sore or as tired. On a sweltering day, as everything melted and dripped, the crew sat in the barn's shade, listening to the country and western tunes blaring on the radio. An old rusty pickup truck rumbled down the road, a dust cloud drifting behind it.

"Holy shit," Mark said, "It's them."

Lucas looked up from the bale of hay he was resting on.

"Damn," Kevin said, "What was her name, the blonde one,

Lizzie, Lisa? Shit." Kevin wiped his hands on his jeans and then raked a hand through his hair as hay dust floated away.

Paul opened an eye and peeked out to see glistening bronze legs and blue-jean fringed shorts stepping over the tailgate onto the bumper. Hot pants, which is what Charlie, Paul's friend, called them.

"Well, howdy, Lucas," the blonde-haired girl with a ponytail said. "I wasn't aware you lowered yourself to this in the summer."

"Elsie, muscles need a workout," Lucas said. Paul noticed how taut his muscles became as he spoke, turning the heads of the girls.

"Hi, you all," Kevin stammered.

A short-haired girl stomped her way over to Kevin, the tassels on her boots swinging as she walked.

Four other girls with spaghetti-strapped, tight tops that seemed to defy gravity posed with a cooler between them.

A girl bent over to brush a nonexistent stray straw from her boot. Mark grinned and rose, moving toward her. Paul forced himself to study a trail of ants. Don't stare, he scolded himself as his cheeks flush.

Paul sat up from his reclined position to accept a soda. He was not fond of the bubbly drink, but Joannicus said one should never decline kindness.

"Thank you," Paul said, giving her a smile. I don't have to open it. The coolness soothed his damp skin.

"You're new around here," the petite brown-haired girl said.

Paul shrugged his shoulders as Lucas and Elise danced.

"Oh, and shy," the redhead said, turning away from Kevin.

"Hey, baby, you got one of those drinks for me?" Kevin said, trying to grab her arm.

Mark wrapped his arm around the tall girl as they headed to the barn.

"Hey, where are you going?" Lucas said, unwrapping himself from Elsie.

Mark gave him the finger before continuing his way.

"Don't be smoking in there."

Paul watched Lucas and Elsie. She slithered up his leg and raked her fingers across his bare chest. Paul was sure that any thoughts of Mark were gone. They were for Paul.

The snap of the pop top made Lucas's head turn. He untangled himself from Elsie's snare and strode over to the two girls, handing out drinks, and took the beer can from Ritchie.

"Hey, that's mine," the boy complained.

"Drink it and you're done for the day. That includes pay," Lucas said.

Paul stared in amazement as Richie grabbed the beer and drank it in a guzzling manner, the girls cheering him on.

Lucas scowled, and the others declined the offers of alcohol. Paul was sure that nobody was of drinking age.

"What's your name, handsome?" the redhead asked.

"Paul." Sweat dripped down his neck, pooling at his collarbone. Suddenly, Paul felt parched.

The moment dissolved. Lucas announced back to work.

"Take Richie with you. Mark, pull your pants up and get out of here," Lucas said.

Grumbling, they headed to the truck and bales.

Mark came out of the barn grinning, picking straw from his hair, giving the guys a thumbs-up.

Paul took his place next to Kevin, who turned, scowled, and gave him a shove. Paul stumbled forward.

"Hey, what the hell?"

"Like you don't know, runt," Kevin snarled, testosterone flaring. "What's the big idea hitting on my girl? Go find one of your own."

"Which one was she?" Paul asked, as Kevin shoved him again. Kevin took a step forward, fists balled. Paul backed up.

Lucas stepped in.

"Look, moron, if you can't control your women, it's not Warner's problem. Settle this some other time."

"Stay away from my girl," Kevin shouted, straightening his shoulder, and stomping the ground like a bull in the chute. Dust billowed around him.

"Don't mind him," Lucas said. "He's paranoid. This is his fifth girlfriend this summer. He's good at roping, but not so good at hog tying."

Paul found the comparison of girls to rodeo events odd. He knew females were peculiar. Then there was Charlie. She was unusual. He had known her for years in school. They always seemed to end up partners for trips and projects. However, these alien creatures were vastly different and the stirring they cause inside and out was puzzling. Had he heard right?

He attracted them, but how?

CHAPTER 15
PAYMENT

Psalm 95:10
Proclaim to the nations God is king.
The world he made firm in its place.
He will judge the peoples in fairness.

M ass had ended. People filled the atrium, lingering and chatting. Paul squeezed his way through the crowd, past monks, past children. The din of conversation faded as he made his way down the hall toward the monastery. He didn't particularly care for the meet-and-greet after services. The churchgoers just wanted to rub elbows with the monks. As if being near them, they could become holy.

Ha, if they only knew. Entering the monastery hall, the silence greeted him, like a mother's embrace.

"Hey, Warner, wait up," called a voice.

Paul stopped and whirled around to see Lucas, the boss from his summer job, walking down the hall.

Crap.

"What's the hurry?" Lucas asked, catching up with Paul.

"You can't be in here," Paul whispered as he headed to the closest exit.

"Why not?" Lucas asked, following Paul.

"It's private," Paul said, trying to come up with an understandable explanation of cloister. The girl's locker room.

Once outside the cloister, Paul glanced around, hoping that no one had seen their exit.

"You were in there," Lucas said.

Paul had successfully hidden his living arrangements all summer long. He didn't have an hour to explain. He led Lucas toward the church.

"What are you doing here?"

"I bet you thought you'd seen the last of me," Lucas said.

"Well, I had prayed," Paul said, realizing he had spoken the words aloud when Lucas laughed.

"Yeah, I bet you're good at that. I brought your last paycheck. We got a bonus. I thought I would deliver it and say thanks for all your hard work."

Was he joking?

Paul scanned Lucas's face for deception as he opened the door to the outside.

"How did you find me?"

"Well, it wasn't easy." Lucas laughed. "I saw you at St. George's at Mass and thought the old couple were your folks. They said I could find you here."

"No, the Hoffmans aren't my parents, they're my godparents."

Lucas handed Paul the check. "What are you doing here? Are

you some kind of monk in training? They talked about vocations at youth group, but you're a little young to have been accepted."

Just lie.

"I live here."

Lucas's face scrunched, as if he had bitten into something sour.

Should have lied.

"Okay. Does that mean your dad is here? Was he like widowed, but they wouldn't accept him unless he took care of you first?"

"No." Paul shoved his hands into his pockets and walked toward the parking lot.

Lucas took a step back. "Why else would you be here, then? Unless one of them is, but PJ says don't look at the worse plausible reason. Look for the other reason."

Why does everyone assume indiscretion? Why did people want to know? What difference could it make? He was Paul. His family, or lack thereof, didn't change that.

"Look, they are monks. I'm not, and I don't want to be. I'm not blood related to any of them. I just live here," Paul said, his voice cracking.

The September breeze swirled the dry leaves into a little tornado that died as quickly as it started.

"You've got to admit, living here is a little odd," Lucas said.

Paul pushed the dying leaves on the ground with his foot.

Go away.

Who was this bossy boy now turned curious toddler? Why did he care?

"I was only asking. PJ says there are no stupid questions. You are a little weird, Warner. You were not my average field worker. There were rumors about you. I was curious. Sorry."

Guilt smacked Paul, and his gut churned. He wiped his sweaty palms on his jeans.

"My, aren't you the epitome of Benedictine ideals? Rude, sullen, and hostile. Seriously." The voice of Father Joannicus echoed in Paul's mind.

He doesn't understand, Paul argued.

Lucas crossed his arms. "I didn't mean to embarrass you. You are different. Now I see why."

The muscles in Paul's neck tightened, and his fists clinched. A freak. He hadn't thought of himself as odd until he entered middle school. Then, he realized he was the only white man at a powwow. Brother Ambrose had told him after you finish with schooling, none of that matters. That advice didn't help. Keeping to himself and his mouth shut worked mostly until now.

Several monks walked by on their way to lunch.

"If you aren't a monk, you're free to leave, right?"

"Right," Paul said, cautiously

"I just got a truck. Shall we go for a ride?"

The invitation pulled at Paul's spirit. It was Sunday, a day of rest. Would he be missed? No, they would figure he was sleeping.

Paul looked at the monastery, the red brick, black stains, and white patches.

"Ah, come on. PJ says it is better to ask forgiveness than permission," Lucas said, grabbing Paul's arm.

The prized truck was green, with a red door on the driver's side. The seats in the cab squeaked as Paul slid in. Most of the dashboard was missing dials.

"She's all mine," Lucas said. "From tailpipe to crank shaft. Ain't she a beauty?"

The gun rack blocked the back window of the truck bed. Rust flakes bounced on the floorboard and Paul could see the road seep by through the hole at his feet.

Paul wondered if they hit a bump, would the back just break off? They drove west and then south. A little too fast, Paul thought as he glanced at the speedometer, which waved erratically between zero and ninety-three. Did that speedometer even work?

An hour later, Lucas asked, "You hungry? You like pizza, don't you?"

The word pizza reminded Paul of the check in his pocket and the fact he had no cash.

"Sure, but I don't have any money," Paul said.

"Not a problem," Lucas said as he walked down the wooden sidewalk, his boots tapping out a confident, steady beat. Paul followed.

The plastic checkered table coverings felt sticky as they sat down near a window.

"Hi, Lucas," the server said. "The usual?"

"Hey, Karen. You got a favorite pizza?" Lucas asked Paul.

Paul's stomach growled. All pizza was good.

"Coke?"

"Water," Paul said as the woman laughed.

"Are you a health food freak?" Lucas asked.

"No, I don't like the bubbles."

"So, you live with the monks. What happened to your parents? If you don't mind me asking."

Paul's stomach jumped and his palms felt sweaty.

"My mom died when I was four," Paul said, flipping through the menu.

"Wow, that's rough, no mom. I have a mom, but my dad, well, he's probably dead."

Paul shrugged his shoulders. His mother was a faint memory. Apart from a photograph of her, his recollection of the dark-haired, smiling woman was fuzzy. He asked about her, and Father Joannicus talked about a woman who loved him. Paul placed her in the category of guardian angel, a constant presence supplying protection. Brother Ambrose had painted her as a hero of courage, a saint who had blessed them with the gift of him. Paul did not feel like a blessing, but a saintly mother was comforting.

"You don't know if he is dead?"

"I don't remember him much. He was Mexican—probably illegal. He tried to take me back to Mexico with him. He wasn't nice to my mom, and he drank. That is all I remember about him. PJ said, probably better that way. Guess he knew him well."

Drinks, plates, and napkins arrived.

"I don't even know if I have a dad," Paul said, sipping his water.

"Everyone has a dad. What did they tell you?"

Paul remembered asking about a biological father. They had told him about his heavenly father. A faint memory of the social worker Barb Carr came to mind.

"A lady once told me he wasn't in the picture, something about he gave up his rights. I didn't know what that meant." Paul folded his napkin.

"Means he didn't want you," Lucas said, sucking down his drink. "You are probably better off without him. Besides, you have fathers to spare at the monastery."

Paul unfolding his napkin. Did this man ever think about him?

"Who is your favorite?" Lucas asked. "I used to think PJ would be a wonderful dad."

"I like Father Joannicus. Brother Ambrose is like my big brother letting me hang at the farm."

"Is he the one who sent you to me? Were you whining about farm work?"

Paul laughed. "Not exactly. Abbot Jacob told me I had to get a summer job. So, I picked bucking hay, figuring I could make more money in a shorter time than at a fast-food joint all year."

Lucas laughed. "You know you figured wrong."

"It wasn't that bad. I earned more in a few weeks than a year flipping burgers," Paul said, pouring more water.

What would PJ say about that? If he mentions PJ again, water might spill on him.

"The Abbot, that's the guy in charge. Bet you didn't know that I knew that. I went to elementary school at St. George's. The pastor is from the monastery."

Father Pius. Right.

The pizza arrived, hot and greasy.

"Where did you go to elementary school?"

"Chet Huntley for kindergarten and then St. Charles," Paul said, closing his eyes and savoring the smell of hot cheese.

"Indian school? You an Indian lover," Lucas asked, biting into a slice of pizza, grease dripping down his hand.

"They're just people," Paul said, keenly aware that this might end the friendship that had barely begun.

Lucas shrugged. "People think I'm Indian, but I'm half Mexican. I don't understand why the whites and Mexicans think I'm Indian."

"What do the Indians see?"

"A white boy."

"Is that why you were such a tool in the field?"

"Did you just call me a tool?"

Paul nodded, shoving pizza into his mouth.

Lucas laughed.

"You're alright, Warner. PJ said if you're in charge, establish yourself. Just like in a barnyard. The rooster lets everyone know he's top dog. But I wasn't a tool."

Paul envisioned himself gagging at the mention of PJ as a group of girls walked by, in a pack, shoulder to shoulder, arms locked around each other, making them seem like a three-headed person.

"Hi, Lucas," they chorused, blonde hair swaying.

"Hello, ladies," Lucas said, giving them a grin and sending them into a moment of twittering giggles.

"We're on squad this year," they said in unison.

"We will lose for sure. Nobody will watch me."

The girls glowed and wiggled onto the bench next to them. Paul wiped his sweating hands on his jeans. One turned and asked Paul, "You on the team?"

"The debate team," Paul said as he watched a cloud cover the pretty face before him.

"But you do like football," Lucas said, wiping his greasy hands on his jeans.

"Yeah," Paul said. It was a lie. He had no intention of telling Lucas that he enjoyed unearthing buried treasure and building skeletons in his room.

Paul knew he could get the monks to teach him about the game.

"Good, I'll give you our schedule and then you can come and watch. This year should be great."

"I'm Susan and she's Sandy, and that's Sierra. You new?" Susan asked, her mascara-caked eyelashes blinked rapidly as if something bothered them.

"No, I wasn't here last year."

"Where were you?" Sandy asked, leaning closer.

"I was visiting family around the country."

Lucas gave him a quizzical look but didn't challenge him.

Thank God.

The girls listened to Lucas in the same dreamy daze that Paul had seen in college girls taking a class from Father Joannicus.

Paul watched Lucas with keen interest. How did he hold their attention?

They finished the meat lover's pizza, paid, and hung with the girls. When it came time to leave, the girls trailed behind. Paul got the distinct impression that they wouldn't have minded squeezing into the cab with them.

They drove until the sun dropped low on the flat horizon as the hill where the monastery stood came into sight.

"You want to stay for dinner?" Paul asked. "I owe you since you bought me lunch."

Lucas parked the truck. "Sure thing. Can I use your phone to call home?" Lucas looked at his watch he said, "Guess I'll call PJ, since mom's at work."

Paul gathered that Lucas's mom worked the swing shift, and that PJ monitored Lucas in her absence. Paul waited as Lucas called from the parlor and wondered if he should tell someone he was bringing a guest to dinner.

It's not like we don't have enough.

"We eat in silence," Paul said, as they walked from the monastery parlor to the refectory.

"Okay. Weird. PJ says, when in Rome, do as the Romans," Lucas said.

Paul was impressed by how well Lucas adapted to the silence of the meal. Monks looked at Lucas and nodded in his direction. Reginald sat across from them at the table, grinning.

What?

Chairs scraped, and monks left in silence. Reginald and Ambrose elbowed each other as they headed out of the refectory.

What is the big deal? Paul thought, realizing the last guest he had was when he was six.

Charlie came, and they had a sleepover in the guesthouse. Paul smiled because most of the monk's thought Charlie was a boy. He at six he didn't bother to correct them. Why were they making this visit a big deal? Paul waited until Lucas finished eating so they could head out together. As soon as they stepped into the hallway, they found Jacob and Joannicus.

"Where have you been? We missed you," Joannicus said. "Do I need to remind you about getting permission?"

"A heads-up would have been courteous," Abbot Jacob said.

Lucas stood tall and extended his hand. "I'm Lucas."

Crap. Hospitality, introductions.

"I am Abbot Jacob, and this is Father Joannicus."

"Paul has mentioned you two," Lucas said.

Paul held his breath. Double crap. What had he told Lucas about them?

"All lies, I assure you," Jacob said with a smile, shaking the boy's hand.

"You're the S.O.B?"

Abbot Jacob smirked. Shock graced Joe's face.

"The term is O.S.B. not S.O.B."

Lucas smiled. "Funny man, O.S.B, Order of St. Benedict. I have heard about that, too. I think you are kind of harsh sending a farm boy to do field-hand work."

"I did not send him. And if you noticed, he survived," Jacob said, crossing his arms.

Paul's heart pounded. Don't poke the Indian. Lucas ignored Paul's feeble attempt to silence him. A sly grin appeared on Abbot Jacob's lips.

"What did he do? Take twenty bucks from your wallet?" Lucas said with a toss of his head.

"More like hundreds on a forged check."

Lucas clapped Paul on the back. "Wow, really? That's honorable."

"Honorable." Jacob stepped closer to Lucas.

"Yeah, if you're going to steal, steal something of value. Twenty bucks is nothing."

This needed to end.

Paul produced a wrinkled check from his pocket and handed it to Abbot Jacob.

"Thank you." Jacob accepted the check. "By the way, what have you learned?"

"Money needs permission too," Paul said, hoping that was the answer Jacob expected.

Lucas grabbed Paul's arm, attempting to stop Paul from losing his money.

"It is more than what you owe," Lucas said.

"I don't need it. Put the rest in the poor box."

Abbot Jacob smiled, winking at Joannicus, who glowed with pride, as Lucas shook his head in disbelief.

"Warner, you need some guidance," Lucas said.

"I don't need the money." Paul crossed his arms, and Lucas took a step back.

"So," Lucas said, "We have a football game next Friday. Paul can come home with me after school. You can pick him up after the game. That's alright with you guys, right?"

Paul held his breath. Lucas had balls.

"Football. Are you asking permission to go?"

"Yeah, he wants to go," Lucas said, head held high. He looked Jacob in the eye, challenging him to say no. "Whoa, you're Crow. But you have blue eyes. So, you are white."

"Not enough to matter."

Lucas stood so close to Jacob that one touch could be counted as coop.

"Right, that's not what the blue eyes say," Lucas continued baiting.

"I go by Apsáalooke."

Paul watched Abbot Jacob's face become stony. Warrior gaze. Crap.

"And your ancestors?" Jacob asked, their breaths mingling.

"I'm not Crow. I'm Mexican."

"Same thing, Native, just a little more south," Jacob said, clearly taking a victory hit as Lucas ponder that connection. Lucas stepped a half step back.

"Paul doesn't like football."

"He does now," Lucas said.

"He needs to ask permission."

"He's not a monk." Lucas leaned in, as if challenging Jacob to touch him.

Shut up Lucas.

Paul shot a pleading glance at Joannicus.

"We can arrange that," Joannicus said. "It's this Friday. It will be fine."

"Great," Lucas said, turning and pulling Paul away from the monks, grinning proudly.

Lucas and Paul walked outside. What had just happened? Anticipation and dread filled Paul. What if Jacob didn't like Lucas?

CHAPTER 16
CHARLIE

Psalm 44: 11-12
Listen, O daughter, give ear to my words.
Forget your own people and your father's house.
So will the king desire your beauty.
He is your lord. Pay homage to him.

Girls had never looked twice at Paul. Now suddenly, that changed. Girls at school sang, "Hello, Paul."

Paul grinned. They moved as one, swallowed up by another group. The three S's. Sandy, Susan, and Sierra, like gossamer willows, moved down the hall. Paul watched them with fascination.

"You've got to be kidding me, Warner," Charlie said as she slammed her locker closed. "Don't talk to them."

"To who?"

"Sleazy, Snarky, and Stupid," Charlie said. "The slut sisters."

Paul shook his head. Her name was Charlemagne, but she preferred Charlie. She was different, preferring black lace and spikes to cowboy boots and tight jeans. He heard she had a tattoo. Charlie and he had been in kindergarten together before he switched schools. They reunited during homeroom because her last name was Winters and his was Warner. They both were outcasts. Only Charlie called attention to herself, and Paul preferred to go unnoticed. She had always spoken freely. Joannicus would have called it unfiltered. Paul liked that about her, and her obsession with mysteries and artifacts. Monthly she had strong-armed him to be her escort as she perused sales looking for antiques. She also wrote to him the year Jacob sent him away. She wrote epic letters that smelled heavily of sandalwood incense and told of things she had found, combing through attics and garage sales. He marveled and wondered at stories she attached to the items.

"That's a pretty harsh judgment," Paul said, grabbing his textbook and a book on archeology.

"You're a means to an end. They want Jockstrap Lucas, and you hang with him. Don't flatter yourself."

Well, that doesn't make me feel great, thought Paul.

They made their way to class. A girl darted up to Paul and shoved a flyer in his face, a notice for the next school social and dance. Paul folded it and placed it in his pocket.

"You're killing me, Warner," Charlie croaked.

"What? It's a dance, not a lifelong commitment," Paul said.

Charlie opened wide her heavily caked eyes. She had purple swirls running from her outer eye on to her cheekbones. "Can you dance?"

"I know how to waltz and do the Charleston," Paul quipped.

Charlie balled her right hand. "Charleston?"

"It's a dance that was popular in 1920. Sort of like tap dancing, lots of footwork," Paul said, taking a step back.

She punched his arm, then snorted. "Waltzing, I don't even know what that looks like. I can tap dance, we can go together, and be the cheap entertainment."

"Waltzing is sort of ballet-ish."

"Do I look like a ballerina? Can you moon walk? We could moon walk together and do some Jackson moves."

Paul felt his ear getting warm. Jackson moves with hands over his crotch.

No.

Paul held the door open for her. Charlie reached up and pinched Paul's right cheek, hard. "Sometimes I think you were raised by nuns. You're the boy girls want to bring home to daddy."

That wasn't far from the truth. His parentage was not an issue in grade school. Only as he got older, rumors and attempts to embarrass him about his odd living arrangement flew around the school. When asked where he lived, Paul would say, "Wherever they put me, I'm an orphan, after all." If they mentioned the monastery, he would shrug and say orphans must live somewhere.

Paul followed Charlie into the classroom. Today, she wore a black velvet top with a red ribbon drawstring and flowing sleeves. Her black skirt had the same-colored ribbons woven into the lacey material. She wore three-inch platform boots with buckles and sounded like a Clydesdale horse as she clonked her way down the aisle to her seat. The girls stared at her.

"Punk," Susan hissed under her breath.

"That is so 80s. Get your subcultures right," Charlie said.

"She's Goth, dark magic," someone next to her whispered.

Susan eyed Paul. Charlie smiled as she sat down. Paul tried hard not to laugh as he took a seat.

Paul stepped off the school bus and saw the green truck with its red tailgate and door. Lucas.

"I could have given you a ride," Lucas said.

"No problem. I finished my history paper on the bus ride home," Paul said, knowing that Abbot Jacob preferred him to travel on the school bus.

"Is it due Monday?"

"No, more like a week from Monday," Paul said, patting the black leather satchel that hung with a strap over his shoulder.

"Why?" Lucas said, shaking his head. "You're an alien. I'm convinced of that."

Even though it was a weeknight, Abbot Jacob had given permission for Lucas to spend the night after Paul had explained they had a diorama to complete for science class.

"I'm taking you to school in the morning, so don't even protest," Lucas said.

As long as transportation wasn't mentioned, Abbot Jacob would assume that he had taken the bus, no permission needed. He had learned during his year away what the Abbot didn't ask about, he didn't need to know.

Paul climbed into the truck, and it rumbled up the hill, passing the farm. Paul searched the land.

"Something wrong?" Lucas asked.

"I usually help after school."

The truck swerved and turned toward the farm, parking next to a pile of wood.

"Good, you brought help," Brother Reginald said, tossing the chunks of pine.

Lucas dropped his backpack and donned gloves. Alcuin paused in his chopping, wiping sweat from his forehead.

"Thought you had some enormous project to finish, but here you are."

"No, Paul finished that weeks ago," Reginald said, tossing the split wood into the pile.

Paul winced. He had finished it.

Lucas paused. "You finished the diorama?"

"Well, not completely."

Lucas returned to stacking wood. Reginald grimaced.

An hour passed, then they were all ready to head up to the monastery. Alcuin opted to walk.

Reginald climbed inside the cab, and they headed up the hill.

Paul and Lucas passed through the guardian angel gates into the dimly lit hallway of the monastery. The cowboy boots tapped loudly on the highly polished floor. Lucas's blue jeans rubbed as he walked. Paul winced at the noise.

They headed up to the third floor. Paul moved swiftly to the third door on the right.

Lucas looked up and down the hall. "All the doors looked the same. How does anyone find you?" Lucas asked, his voice sounding like thunder.

"Years of practice?" Paul whispered. He had heard Ambrose say those words many times, and today he understood the meaning. Paul opened the door to his room.

"No lock?"

Paul closed the door quickly. Voices carried in quiet halls. "Why would I need a lock?" Paul set his satchel down. Lucas glanced around the room. What did he see? The whiteness of a half-finished skeleton lay on his desk. A chicken, but still it screamed, "You're a weirdo," as Paul moved to drape a dirty tee shirt over it.

Lucas nodded. "You like KISS?"

"Yeah, I like Nine Inch Nails too."

"That's very Catholic of you," Lucas said, hammering his palm. Paul held his breath at the irreverence.

"Do you listen to any cool music? And I don't mean Bach or Beethoven."

"Do the Grateful Dead count?" Paul assumed that cool music for Lucas was country. He was not sure if the Grateful Dead were folk or country.

Lucas stepped toward a curtained alcove. "What's behind those curtains?"

"My un-made bed," Paul said as he kicked his misshapen stuffed tiger under the bed.

"Why curtains? Is this what monastic rooms look like?"

"Old buildings get cold at night. Curtains keep the heat in. Yes, most cells look like this."

"Cells? You a prisoner?"

Depends on who you talked to. They might say prisoner of God. That would not go over. "It's what a monastic room is called, a cell. No bars or locks and no warden."

"Where's all your stuff?" Lucas said, looking at the nearly empty shelves.

"We had a give away," Paul said.

Lucas's eyebrows knitted together.

"We put things we aren't using in the community room, and. It's like a big garage sale with no money."

"That's a little weird."

"How so?" Paul asked. He had always liked the give away. A second Christmas, only you got things you wanted, like new books and sweaters. He still had an enormous collection of roseries, tucked away in the bottom dresser drawer.

"Don't get pissed. You're weird. But hey, you live here. That explains a lot."

Lucas turned and noticed the table with the nearly completed solar system diorama. He frowned.

"You finished it. Why would you do that? I thought we were working on this together?"

"Well, I," Paul stammered, seeing the displeasure on his friend's face.

"I don't need you to do my work for me. I'm not stupid."

Paul felt his friendship and potential dates with girls wither on the table.

The bells rang, drowning the conversation.

"Those ring every hour?"

Paul took a step toward the door. "No, just four times a day calling us to prayers and Mass." Maybe he should have said *them* instead of *us*.

Lucas set down his backpack. "So, do you have to go?"

The urge to pray weighed heavily, but Paul said, "No, not really. Do you want to go to Mass?"

A crooked smile appeared on Lucas's face. "Sure."

THROUGHOUT MASS, Paul tried to think of a way for Lucas to contribute. He could disassemble the diorama, or Lucas could add something to it. He would not mention that he had finished the report and wrote the presentation.

"Now what happens?" Lucas asked after Mass.

"We can go work on our project. The monks are socializing."

"Let's socialize."

Odd, why does he want to socialize? Is he here to spy and report to his jock friends? Would there be snickers in the halls at school tomorrow?

Paul noticed how at ease Lucas was among these strangers. Ambrose invited him to play chess. Ambrose won.

Paul's appetite waned as his envy of Lucas grew, and the truth of the science project loomed closer.

After dinner, they returned to Paul's room. Lucas examined the diorama.

"You did an excellent job. What are we going to say?"

Paul sat at his desk, shoved the cue cards under his books, and took out clean paper.

"You know I have a three-point grade average. I assume you have a four-point. I can read, write, and catch a football."

"That makes you one up on me. I can't catch a ball, a round one or a prolate spheroid."

Lucas laughed. Paul breathed a sigh of relief.

They worked together on the presentation until the bells rang for evening prayers.

"Shall we?" Lucas asked, putting down the papers. They went to the church and Paul handing Lucas the books for the day.

"Just follow from this page. I'm going to sit in my place."

Paul sat in his place in the front row. Was he a liar or, worse, a freak? He wasn't a monk and yet he was sitting with them.

Halfway through prayers, Paul noticed that Abbot Jacob was not in his usual place. A glance around the church caused Paul to pray that the floor would swallow him. Abbot Jacob was sitting in the back next to Lucas.

Crap, hospitality to guests. Prayers ended. Paul exited the church. He found Lucas standing next to the Abbot, who was frowning.

"Paul, it's customary for one to be with his guest at prayers."

"Yes, Father Abbot," Paul mumbled, feeling the heat radiate up his neck to his cheeks.

Lucas spoke, but Paul quickly pulled him outside. "After prayers, the monks observe silence."

"He just spoke out loud. And he shouldn't criticize you in front of your friends."

Paul shrugged. Maybe that didn't matter.

"He's the abbot, and he is right. I made a mistake. I should have sat with you."

Lucas kicked a small rock. "I can sit alone. But you seem on a roll for mistakes."

"Sorry about the project," Paul said.

"Don't do that again or I'll have to pulverize you."

"Okay, I'll try to forget you're a jock," Paul said.

Lucas stopped and grinned. "And I'll try to remember you don't want to be a monk."

Reentering Paul's room, they discovered a care box of munchies and soda.

"Room service. Do you get this every night?"

"No," Paul said, his muscle tensing in defense. "They think we'll be working all night."

"They're nice, and I'm starving," Lucas said as he rummaged through the box and pulled out some beef jerky. "Are you sure that you will not become a monk?"

"Yes," Paul said, as he shoved Lucas from the box.

Lucas regained his balance and stood, waving the jerky. "It's just you know all the stuff."

"There's more to it than that," Paul said, kicking off his shoes. Funny what people assume about monastic living. It always amazed him the reverence and awe monks inspired, not just college students, but ordinary people who came to visit. He remembered overhearing two visitors talking about having seen the Abbot sewing a button on a shirt. What was amazing to them, that the Abbot could sew, or he would sew? They would probably be stunned to know that the monks who taught as professors also mucked out stalls and picked fruit during harvest season. Lucas didn't seem mesmerized by monks. Paul liked that. Lucas spoke his mind with confidence, and Paul liked that, too.

"You going to the dance?"

Lucas laughed. "I always go. I have to, you know, being the quarterback, got to show school spirit. You're going right?"

Paul wrinkled his nose. "I don't know. Dancing?"

Lucas kicked off his shoes and plopped on Paul's bed. "You don't dance at a dance. You go to hang with the guys. They let us shoot hoop, there's food and music."

That was odd. Paul thought a dance meant dancing.

Paul grabbed a bag of chips and pushed Lucas over to sit beside him on the bed. "Would you if a girl asked?"

Lucas sat up. "Like she asked me on a date? No way. Girls don't ask. Guys ask and mostly get turned down. Not me, of course. I have a selection of girls wanting to be asked. Once I took two girls."

Paul opened the bag of chips. "Weren't they jealous?"

"Hell, no. They were grateful to be with me."

This social thing was confusing. He was sure that Charlie asked him to the dance. Did that mean he shouldn't accept? This information was different. The monks told him to stick with the person he came with and dance. Lucas's idea of a dance was something altogether different.

"You should come," Lucas said, breaking a jerky stick in half and handing half to Paul. "You gonna ask a girl?"

"You think I should?" Paul said, not wanting to tell Lucas about Charlie. "Who do you think I should ask?"

"Guess it depends on what you like?"

"Girls," Paul said, chewing on the spicy meat.

"Well, duh, but invite one with a rack," Lucas said, grabbing the chip bag away from Paul.

A rack? Did he mean a girl who could hunt?

ALL FOR ONE CHILD

"A pair, Cheech and Chongs, Simon and Garfunkels, Sonny and Chers?"

Paul shook his head.

"A set of melons," Lucas said, laughing as he gestured with his hands in front of his chest.

Oh breasts.

Paul felt himself blush. Breasts? Size? The person to ask would be Charlie. She had breasts. If he asked about them, he was sure he'd have a black eye.

"How do you ask out a girl?" Paul said.

Lucas sat up and crossed his legs.

"I would say, 'hey baby, I'll pick you up at seven on Friday.' But, in your case you should double date with me for a while. Who are you gonna ask?"

"Don't need to ask. I already have a date. Charlie Winters," Paul said, figuring she already asked him, but he didn't need to add that information.

"That punk girl?"

"She is Goth, and yes her," Paul said.

Lucas froze. Was he stunned? Paul smiled. He had made an impression.

CHAPTER 17
WE BEGIN AGAIN

Psalm 87: 12
Will your love be told in the grave
or your faithfulness among the dead?

Joannicus flattened the crumpled paper from his trash, smoothing it on the desktop, then reread the letter. Dr. Cole wanted him back at the treatment center. Like one looking at the aftermath of a tornado, weakness and fear overwhelmed him.

He turned to the crucifix on his wall. He made the sign of the cross and prayed, *Dear Lord, give me strength to endure the endless days of suffering after they pump my body full of chemicals.*

Mouth sores, nausea, aching bones, and constant cold. He shook himself to dispel the dread. This was his garden of Gethsemane.

Simple facts muddled in his brain and words often stayed hidden from his tongue.

Joannicus walked down the corridor to the church. Hidden away in a corner was a small statue of Saint Joseph. Poor Joseph, he was insignificant, a passing thought, the father to someone else's son.

How did Jesus take the news that Joseph wasn't his 'real' dad?

Paul had asked once about his father. Joannicus had perpetuated the myth, emphasizing Paul had a community rather than what he lacked, which was a parental unit. The day was coming when Paul would ask the direct question, "Is my father dead?" Then what would his answer be? Paul had wondered about many things, but a biological father didn't loom in the forefront of Paul's curiosity. Joannicus presumed the kid had too many father figures to want to add another.

Father Joannicus moved around the perimeter of the church, touching the icon of Mary on the wall. She was a woman of strength and his source of inspiration. His hand slipped into his pocket, the beads of his rosary gliding through his fingers. He breathed deeply. The sweet smell of incense imbedded in the fibers of the carpet flooded his senses. He listened to the bubbling of the fount in the atrium as the candles flickered, drinking up the beeswax.

Joannicus shook his head for he could sit quietly for the rest of his life bathed in the glow of God's love. He was not a hermit. He had chosen a community.

Reality slithered onto Joe's path as he stopped and watched the sun fade and reappear through the stained-glass windows, putting a rainbow across his feet and path. A promise. He had promised to take care of Paul, physically and spiritually, even if it meant keeping this cancer a secret. For years when Paul was younger and anyone became ill, Paul would ask, "Is it cancer?" This time, the answer would be yes.

Father Joannicus continued his pacing. Movement helped clear his mind. Stopping in the Blessed Sacrament chapel, tucked into a small alcove to the right side of the altar, he stopped again and let his fingers trace the Hebrew letters on the tabernacle, Exodus 25:8, "... make a sanctuary for me, and I will dwell among them." Joannicus sighed. God had made this monastery a sanctuary for him. Had he made a sanctuary for Paul? Had he built Paul a firm foundation?

Did Paul worry about cancer?

Kneeling before the altar, he prayed. Images of funerals played out in his mind. He wrestled with his deep desire to be with God, his desire and God's will wobbling like a teeter-totter. The monks would heal if he died. They understood the yearning to join with the Almighty. Joannicus feared Paul would not understand or accept his death. His dying would destroy Paul's faith, and he didn't want to be responsible for that.

He will be afraid to love because everything he loves dies. Don't let that happen.

Would he survive? A tiny trickle of doubt tried to take hold of his faith. No, not going there. Believe in God's plan.

JOANNICUS LEANED over as he heard feet moving quickly into the church. There was no black robe, so he knew it was Paul. He watched the boy hurry, a tray with cruets of wine and water for Mass. The soft tinkling of glass bumping together as Paul made his way to the side table.

Slow down.

Paul raced back with three chalices, oblivious to the fact that he wasn't alone. Sadness crept into Joannicus. Where had the time gone? Joannicus could remember when he had complained that Paul was blocking his journey to God, interfering with his relationship. Fearful that Paul had replaced God, because he devoted all his time to taking care of a child. Lately, there was a growing distance.

Where had all the questions gone?

Now there was Lucas. The two of them, so dissimilar, had become friends. Jealousy splashed into his sadness.

Abbot Jacob and he had discussed Lucas. Was this a safe friendship? Jacob's advice was to wait and see. Joannicus did not like the uncertainty. Should they allow Paul the freedom to associate unsupervised with girls? That kind of freedom frightened him. Paul had asked about them, and Joe avoided a direct answer. His only experience was in the emotional pitfalls of romance. He could not bring himself to share such weakness, and he could not share the indiscretions of others. Some mistakes youths made were fatal. He had seen college students make choices that changed their lives forever.

Joannicus shivered. Panic danced inside of him. Stop being a coward. Step be the guide.

Treatment would only take six months.

At first, the truth was easy to hide from Paul. Abbot Jacob sent the boy to tour other monastic communities. This time would be different. He would be without his community. Would he be able to endure this trial?

All he needed to do was convince Abbot Jacob this was the best way.

Joannicus blessed himself and rose and walked to the Abbot's office. The door was open. Father Joannicus willed himself to walk in. Abbot Jacob sat at the desk and looked up as he entered.

"The Lord be with you," Abbot Jacob said.

Amen, thought Father Joannicus as he softly closed the door behind him and said, "And also with you, Father Abbot."

Abbot Jacob walked to the small velveteen sofa and chairs midway in the room. Joannicus followed him from the other direction. They met in the middle and sat. The two men looked at each other. Jacob's blue eyes filled Joannicus with peace. Abbotship agreed with the man.

"So, what is up?" Jacob asked.

Father Joannicus pulled out the wrinkled paper from his pocket and handed it to Abbot Jacob. The clock on the wall ticked in the silence. Joannicus picked at his thumbnail. When he looked up, Jacob rose and stepped forward, bent down, and embraced him.

"Thank you."

"For what?" Joannicus asked, his throat constricting.

"For letting us support you," Jacob said. "For letting me help you. This tumor could be benign."

"Chemo isn't benign. We both know I don't manage that well," Joannicus said, remembering the weeks of vomiting, chills, and yearning for soft, freshly baked bread. Twelve rounds with the chemo-devil had almost conquered him.

"Do you have a plan? What do you need from us?"

"You can't send Paul away this time, so I was thinking I would stay at St. Vincent's treatment center for the six weeks or however long it takes. We can afford that, right?"

Jacob folded his hands. The silver raven ring glistened on his finger.

"Money, my friend, is not the issue. What is best for you?"

The year of treatment flipped quickly through Joe's mind. Memories of decades of rosaries, fifty Hail Marys, five Our Fathers, times that by four for each of the mysteries associated with the prayer form, when sleep eluded him as he sat in the community room in front of the fireplace to get warm. Joannicus shivered. Surgery was the simple part. He anticipated waking up and seeing the worried face of Jacob. Treatment was the hard part. Two weeks of hell and then one week of peace, only to be thrown back into the chemical bath, which drank his energy, fogged his brain, and left every joint inflamed and aching. Several times while recovering at home, between treatments, he had fallen to the floor from exhaustion. Abbot Jacob assigned him a constant silent companion, not unlike a guardian angel. Someone beside him to make sure his dignity stayed intact.

"This isn't about me," Joannicus said, knowing that wasn't entirely true.

Jacob shook his head. "Please do not close us off."

"I'm not," Joannicus said, eyes darting around the room. "I don't want to be burdensome."

"You are not a burden."

"That's not true. Many helped me with time, transportation. Clean up after me. I was a burden."

"Fine, I will give you the humble monk award. You keep forgetting we are a community, and we all need to share this burden. You deny others and Paul an opportunity to grow."

A humble monk award. There was no such award, thought Joannicus. He clearly saw the faces of the living as he lay in the infirmary. The palpable sadness in their eyes and the tears he shed at night as he prayed. Joannicus cringed as the devil in his mind hissed, "What has death done for any of one but to leave us cracked open like calm shells on a vacant beach?"

"Are you aware of how hard it was to endure the pity and fear?"

Jacob's eyes narrowed. "You did so with such grace. If only we could all do that."

"I'm tired, I'm spent."

And ashamed.

"Then let us carry you. Even Jesus did not die alone."

Jacob leaned forward. Joannicus could detect the musky odor of sweet grass.

"Do not continue with this deception."

Joannicus shifted in his chair. "I'm not deceiving. I'm protecting Paul. You know the word cancer would crush him. It would convince him I'm dying."

"But you could," Jacob said.

His eyes held that look, the one between hopelessness and helplessness, the look that Joe despised.

"No, I'll be fine," Joannicus said with more confidence than he possessed. "So, I will tell him I'm giving a few retreats. Besides, Paul is busy with friends, and school, he won't notice my absence. He doesn't need me that much anymore."

"Yes, he does. As Ambrose puts it, he is at the age of stupidity."

"He has all of you. A short break away is no big deal," Joannicus said. The words hurt as he spoke to them.

"You are just making excuses. Some of them are good. Protecting Paul is good, but he is not a baby. He has experienced death. Why not let him experience suffering? We both know that it is something none of us escape from."

Joannicus winced as he looked at the crucifix that hung on the wall. He needed to make Jacob understand. This choice hurt. The dark night of his soul consumed him, and he feared he would fail like he had the first time.

Confess to them.

"Jacob, I'm not a saint or a martyr. Last time, I prayed to die."

There he had said it. His weakness lay exposed. He had not successfully offered his suffering. He just silently seethed, wishing for the end.

Jacob stood frozen. Then his fingers stretched, and he waved the air in front of him before covering his face.

Is he praying, or are those wise elders speaking to him?

This man was an odd blend of Crow and Catholic.

Jacob lowered his hands and sat tall, running his fingers over his black shiny braid.

"I am thankful that the Lord was not listening. I forgive you for being human."

"You give me too much credit."

Jacob rose and walked to the window. His frame blocked the sunlight.

"I know you struggle. It took forever for you to love with Paul. However, you got there. Do not deny that you love him. He needs to know you are flawed, that you struggle, and still have faith."

Was that true? Did he love Paul? He folded and unfolded his stiff hands in his lap.

"Let Paul in on the journey."

"No, I can't," Joannicus whispered, envisioning Paul's face. The pity there would kill him.

He knew Jacob disapproved. In desperation, Joannicus said, "Swear to me, by your ancestors, that you will honor my request and not tell Paul."

The devil smiled.

Abbot Jacob walked to the edge of the desk and sat.

"Fine, I will honor this, but I have to ask you, is this request your desire or God's? Do you think yourself so humble, or special, that you must suffer for the Lord alone?"

Joannicus attempted to swallow, but his mouth was dry.

"Maybe you need to stop trying to control what is beyond you. I think you forget Paul needs you now, not in six months when you are in remission. He will notice and if he comes to me, I might not deny him."

"I don't want to hurt him," Joannicus said, feeling like a child.

"Really? Whenever you die, we will grieve and weep. You cannot deny us our mourning. We will suffer. Only with the fellowship of community, our shared memories of you, will we be able to heal. Do not take that away from Paul. Let him have memories, even if they are hard. Do I need to remind you that Jesus let his mother witness his demise?"

Joannicus stared at his folded hands and shuddered. He didn't deserve the comparison, not after the manipulation he had just pulled.

"I can't, I'm not ready."

Jacob stood and walked to the chair behind the desk. It creaked with his weight as he sat.

"Get ready."

CHAPTER 18

CLOISTER

Psalm 114:5
How gracious is the Lord and just.
Our God has compassion.
The Lord protects the simple hearts.
I was helpless, so he saved me.

The truck was a tight squeeze for four, and Paul was pretty sure Abbot Jacob would disprove of the lack of seat belts, but he was not calling home at eleven p.m. to ask for a ride.

As they pulled up to the monastery, Lucas said, "Shall I take you home, Charlie?"

"Nope, I'm good," Charlie said, as she hopped out of the cab. Paul waved to Lucas, who grinned mischievously and drove off into the night.

What to do? The monastery windows were dark, but that did not assure him that Abbot Jacob wasn't waiting in the dark.

"Do you want to call your folks to come pick you up?"

"No, not going home tonight."

They had filled up at a gas station across from a liquor store, and Charlie told Lucas to drive Paul home first.

Charlie shivered. A snowflake skated on the frigid air. She arrived at the dance, not dressed up in glitter and satin. She had worn lace, but it was black lace. Paul noticed she had boobs. Who wouldn't have noticed them smashed firmly and puffing out of the corset bodice? The top part of the dress was red and detached from the sleeves, which were velvet, glove-like with handkerchiefs trimmed in lace hanging from them. The skirt bunched out with scratchy black fabric that hung unevenly, giving the appearance that it had gone through a shredder before being pieced back together. This was her design. Paul knew Charlie had designed and sewn it because she had complained that her home economics teacher was upset because she had refused to buy a Simplicity pattern. She wore fishnet stockings and army boots. He wore his Sunday best. They had stood out, but as Charlie said, "Isn't that why you came?"

The snowflakes competed for space as they fell. Charlie's teeth chattered as she spoke. "It has been a while, ten years."

Paul sighed.

"Come on and keep quiet."

He grabbed her hand, avoiding the spiked bracelet, and pulled her through the garden to the church's side entrance. The door was unlocked. The halls were empty and silent as they headed into the monastery.

Avoid the community room and the elevator; use the back stairs.

Up the stairs, they climbed, and Paul listened with every step

ALL FOR ONE CHILD

and noticed how the stairwell echoed even as they moved slowly and carefully. He stepped into the third-floor hallway. All was dark. Paul eased the fire door closed. Standing in the hall, listening, snoring echoed, so with Charlie in tow, he headed toward his room. One door, two doors. Paul pushed Charlie against the wall because of the sound of running water. The nightlight three steps away illuminated their shoes. The door to the restroom opened, out shuffled a monk. Paul was grateful the man wore pajamas. The man mumbled, walking past them to his room. Don't turn around. The door to the monk's cell closed with a click. Paul hurried to his room, shoving Charlie through the door. Closing it ever so slowly and leaning against it, he let out a loud sigh.

"Are you allowed in here?" Charlie said in the dark.

"Yes," Paul said, turning on the light. "This is my room. But lower your voice. We don't want to wake them up."

"Oh, you mean the dead?" She snickered. "So do you have something I can change into, jeans, a tee shirt?" Charlie looked around the room.

Paul pulled out some clothes from the drawer and stood there holding them like a well-mannered valet.

"Jesus, Warner, we danced. Not got hitched. Turn around."

Paul turned his back to her and closed his eyes.

Idiot and a dead one if we get caught. But who's going to do that?

Father Joannicus was gone again. They should make him the official Retreat Master for the Benedictine world, since he seemed to give more retreats than teaching. Retreats were mostly in the summer for communities, and this was winter. It all seemed odd, yet he had little reason to question Father Joannicus.

"So, I imagined you lived in an orphanage?" Charlie said.

Paul opened his eyes. She had put on his clothes, and they fit her relatively well. "What? No. This is a monastery. I live here."

She laughed. "You're shitting me, right?"

Paul shook his head. Perhaps he should have taken her to the guesthouse. He wasn't sure how many guests were visiting. He couldn't be opening doors to find a vacant room.

She had looked so sad, shaken, and adamant that she was not going home. He didn't know why. If she wanted, she would tell him.

"I remember this place. This was a castle, and you were a secret prince. Later, I thought I had invented an orphan fantasy since I saw you with the Hoffmans. Today I want the truth."

"I'm not a monk. They're my guardians. The Hoffmans are my godparents. Why would I make things up?"

"Cuz we all do. We want our families to look perfect. So, you're really an orphan?"

"Yeah, I guess."

"Mom is dead?"

"Yeah."

"Dad is dead?"

"I guess. I don't really know if I had a dad."

Charlie rolled her eyes as if he grew a second head.

"Everyone has a dad. If he is alive, don't you want to find him?"

Paul pondered that for a second, another male role model. "Not particularly. Things have been good so far."

"Sometimes that is for the best. So how did you end up here?"

"My mom left me here when she died. I guess because she liked this place."

A funny smile appeared on Charlie's face, softening her features. "Ultimate Goth. I bet you one of these guys is your dad."

"No." Paul had often wanted one of them to be his father. But nobody had claimed him as a son. He wondered if he should ask about his biological father. Would the monks even know? Paul shook the idea from his mind. The man was probably dead. Why else would his mother leave him here?

"You always dismiss things so quickly. Everyone has a past. The past is full of mystery and discoveries."

Paul had to agree. He and Charlie both were fascinated with the ancient items. St. Alberic's had tons of old things, treasures found in the attic and basement closets.

"Are you hungry, thirsty?"

"Vodka?"

Paul shook his head. He had a bottle of beer hidden in his underwear drawer. Ambrose had allowed him sips of beer from time to time.

"Stay here, I'll be right back." Grabbing a pair of jeans and shirt, Paul exited the room, feeling excited. Standing in the hall, he changed out of his dress clothes and into his jeans. He could hear Lucas bragging on Monday. Paul took a girl home. The knowing and nodding that would follow from his classmates. She was his friend. They discuss what happened to the dinosaurs or where the First Nation originate. They would need snacks. Quickly, Paul ran down the stairs to the community room. He grabbed a bag of chips, cookies, pausing at the bowl of fruit and deciding against it, and headed back to his room.

Paul opened the door, half expecting Charlie to have wandered off. She never stayed focused on one thing for very long. She had pulled the mattress to the floor so that the moonlight bathed it. Paul grimaced, worried about the noise. He listened but heard nobody stirring. She stood next to his completed skeleton of a cat. Paul froze.

"Cool," Charlie said. "Should I be concerned?"

"Thanks," Paul said, grateful that she hadn't run screaming out of his room. "No, I was curious. There were no cadavers lying around."

Charlie rolled her eyes. "So, you're an orphan? I like the story that some religious cult kidnapped you, but the state made them send you to school. The story Lucas tells is that you are a rich brat who lives in a castle with servants."

Paul sighed and set the food down. "Why didn't you believe me? And Lucas has been here, he knows."

"It seems over the top, monks raising an orphan kid." She set the photo of Paul and his mother back on the shelf. "You look like your mom. I don't see a dad photo, so I can't really be sure."

"I don't have a photo of my dad. I don't even have a name." Paul tried to recall if his mother had ever spoken of him. The monks never volunteered information, and Paul had assumed the man was dead.

"How do you know he is dead?" Charlie asked.

Paul stared at her. Was she reading his mind?

"You're not being very scientific. The facts, Warner, you need the facts to make statements like I'm an orphan."

One school project, a family tree, had prompted him to ask who his father was, and they had charted Father Joannicus's family. "I asked about him, but the monks never really gave me a straightforward answer."

"And that didn't pique your curiosity? There's a mystery here. You have a birth certificate. Everyone has a birth certificate, even the adopted. It will be on that. We should go adventuring."

Why was she, after all these years of knowing him, interested in his parentage? Paul figured it was because she was upset with her own.

Charlie plopped cross-legged on to the bed and opened the chips. Paul rinsed out two cups and popped open the beer bottle.

"I can't believe you're not on this. If I had the slightest hint that my parents weren't my own, I would be researching."

"Why?"

"Because it's a mystery. Aren't you the least bit curious?"

It had crossed his mind, but somehow it seemed wrong to pursue that truth. Wouldn't Joannicus be hurt if Paul searched to replace him? Joe wasn't a terrible father. Ambrose was more fun because they spent Sunday afternoons watching Disney movies. Jacob was sometimes hard to understand, like not allowing him to take drivers' education. What would he want from a biological father that he didn't already have?

"He hasn't been in my life. Maybe he isn't a good guy. What if he's in prison? What if he's like Charles Manson?"

"You're not old enough to be a Manson son. You would recognize that if you read *Helter Skelter*. What a magnificent study of a psycho."

"No, I don't need to know." Wondering if she was a little psycho in her obsession with the dark side of humanity. "You really like that kind of stuff?"

"Yea, I love the true crime writer Ann Rule," Charlie said as she sipped on the beer.

Murder, sociopaths. Paul felt a little squeamish. Time to change the subject. Perhaps the discussion of his parentage wasn't such an uncomfortable topic after all.

THE BELLS RANG for morning prayers, waking Paul. He untangled himself from Charlie, her arm and leg flung over him as if he were an oversize pillow. They had shared a blanket and pillow. Her scent, like sweet peas, had lingered between words as they fought to continue conversing all night. Apparently, sleep had overtaken them.

He should get Charlie out now. The monks were praying. Where would she go? How would she get there? Outside, he noticed the layer of snow. Damn, he couldn't have her standing around outside for thirty minutes, nor could he act all surprised that she was here. He could wake her up and bring her with him to prayers. Not in his clothes, and the outfit she had worn would raise eyebrows. He would think up a plan during prayers.

"Don't go anywhere, I'll be back," Paul whispered to a snoring Charlie as he pulled the covers over her shoulders. The night had been enjoyable. The closeness, the wide range of conversations. A warmth filled him as he made his way to the church.

"Oh Lord, open my lips," Novice Craig said, breaking the silence.

"And my mouth shall sing your praise," Paul said with the rest of the monks. They stood, they sat, and they chanted the psalms. Paul's thoughts muffled the words of the monks. Should he have woken her? How would he get her to the guesthouse without being seen?

Paul shuddered and turned when he heard a sound of footsteps in the atrium. Was it Charlie? He could see her wandering the empty halls. Paul let out a sigh, seeing that it was the hyper holy group from the campus. His mind flickered from plan to possibilities like a hummingbird.

Mindlessly, he bowed, sat, and rose like a well-oiled gear and yet he was stunned as the monks headed out of the church to breakfast.

He now had to choose a plan and act. He dashed to his room and held his breath as he opened the door and quickly glanced around the room. The mattress was gone, as were the wrappers and bottle.

"Boo," Charlie said as she peeked out behind the door. Paul jumped. Charlie laughed. She was back in her corset and tutu-like thing.

"We don't have time for games," Paul said tersely as he opened his closet doors, pulling out a black habit. He had taken

174

one from the tailor shop and sometimes wore it in the privacy of his cell.

"I used the restroom." Charlie said. "This place is disturbingly deserted."

"Crap. Did anyone see you?"

"No. The room next door is really sparse."

"What?" Paul said, his voice higher than normal. She had entered the Abbot's room.

"Yeah, numbers on the doors would really help."

"You touched nothing, right?"

"Well, I stopped and smoked some sweet grass and used the talking stick."

"You did what?" Paul said. "You can't be taking a tour."

"You're stupid, Warner. I opened the door and saw it wasn't your room. What is that room? Is that where secret rituals are held? I didn't see a pentagram on the floor."

"If you didn't stay long, how do you know?"

"Some people are observant."

It was time to get her out.

"We have to sneak out. So, you can wear this."

"Oh, a creepy black robe. I love it." Charlie put the robe on. Her stiff skirt material made the middle of the habit billow out.

"You can wear my jeans until we get to the guesthouse." Paul grabbed his backpack, dumped the contents on to the floor, and waited for the skirt. Now the traveling monk would have luggage. Paul was grateful that she wore army boots rather than high heels.

"Way cool," Charlie said as she lowered her voice. "*Quid novi?*"

Paul shook his head. Nobody speaks Latin, and he was sure they didn't say, what's up?

"Keep your hood up and don't talk. Just follow me."

At a quick pace, they walked down the dimly lit hallway of the third floor, then down the back stairs. They passed the juniors in the alcove between the church hallway and the monastery. Paul glanced back, and the juniors didn't even look his way. So far, so good, Paul thought. They turned the corner and collided with Brother Moses.

"Where's the fire?" Moses said.

"Sorry," Paul said.

"All's good," Moses said, peering at Paul and the shrouded monk next to him. Moses stepped closer and to see the face hidden by the hood. Charlie turned away, sidestepping them both and heading to the exit.

"Who is that?" Moses asked.

"Brother Charlie," Paul said as Charlie opened the church doors, the cold air rushed in. Paul could see the guesthouse front door.

"Brother Charlie, we don't have a Charlie, do we?" Moses asked, scratching his head.

"Yea, we do. He's a new postulant. I had him try on a robe to get the feel of walking in one," Paul said, moving to the church exit.

"Oh," Moses said, "I don't remember him. But he smells nice."

Paul raced to Charlie, who had made her way halfway across the courtyard.

"This way." Monks emerged from the refectory. Fortunately, the snow and cold kept everyone on a brisk walk from building to building.

They reached the guesthouse door. Paul punched the code, the lock clicked open, and they rushed inside.

They stood in the parlor. Paul handed Charlie the backpack, and she went behind the sofa and ducked down to change her clothing.

"What are you doing?" Brother Alcuin said, appearing in the doorway.

Paul jumped.

Crap. *Hurry, Charlie.*

Paul glanced over his shoulder.

Where was Charlie?

Alcuin pushed past to the center of the room and glanced around the space. "I asked you what you're doing in here?"

Paul's mouth was dry. His tongue lay heavy, lifeless.

Charlie stood up, her black and red bodice contrasted with the blue mantel of Virgin Mary painting behind her.

"What the heck," Alcuin exclaimed. "Who are you?"

"NOYB," Charlie said. This meant none of your business, only Alcuin wasn't aware of that.

"What?" Alcuin said, licking his lips as he rubbed his hands together. "You are in so much trouble."

Paul could not believe the delight he heard in Alcuin's voice. Alcuin tossed his head and turned to leave the room.

"Alcuin, no. Wait."

"For what? Some lame excuse. What are you doing with a college girl in the guesthouse? A college girl who will be expelled from school."

"You can't expel college students," Charlie said as Paul wondered if he ran now, could he reach the Abbot before Alcuin?

Alcuin reentered the space to confront Charlie.

"Yes, we can," he said, noticing the discarded monk's habit laying crumpled at her feet. His eyes grew large, and his face took on a crimson hue.

"The two of you are disgusting," Alcuin hissed and moved to pick up the black material.

Charlie laughed. "I think you should remove that plank in your own eye before hanging us from your holy poplar." Charlie waved her hand as if she were fanning the air and pointed a finger at Alcuin. "*Satan recedemus.*"

Oh God, Paul thought, turning and running down the hall to the stairwell. He stood at the refectory door, with a trembling hand opened it. Alcuin appeared at the end of the hall.

The dining room silence made Paul feel as if he had entered a secret ceremony that Charlie had invented. Abbot Jacob looked up and then returned to his meal. I can't approach him now. Paul slid into the first empty chair, ignoring breakfast. Ambrose gave Paul a quizzical look as he licked the jam off his fingers.

Alcuin did not enter the room.

Crap. Crap.

Before he could form a plan, Abbot Jacob rose and headed out of the refectory. Paul jumped up, his chair scraping on the floor like screeching brakes before an accident. He moved to the exit and opened the door. He saw what he knew he would see, Alcuin talking to the Abbot, black habit draped over his arm.

Run. No, walk casually away.

Abbot Jacob looked over Brother Alcuin's head, and Paul could not ignore the piercing blue eyes. Taking a deep breath, Paul walked with exterior calmness as his insides imploded.

The Abbot raised a hand to Alcuin's discourse, causing the excited monk to stop.

Paul held his breath.

Jacob said, "Where is our guest?"

Words hid behind Paul's teeth as he pointed upward to the floor above.

"St. Benedict says that guests are to be treated as Christ. Who is attending to Christ's needs?" Jacob asked.

"She is certainly not Christ," Alcuin said. "She evoked evil using gestures and foreign words."

"Charlie's not evil," Paul said. Finally, his voice had arrived.

"Please. Popping up in a scantily clad get up, muttering curses at me."

"That's Latin. She speaks Latin."

"Right. What were you doing behind the sofa, on top of a black robe? Sewing lessons?"

Paul could feel his face getting hot. He turned to Abbot Jacob; all of his words jumbled as he stammered, "Father Abbot, we, I, nothing."

Jacob cleared his throat, placed his hand on Paul's shoulder, and gave him a gentle nudge. Paul took his cue and ran down the hall to the stairwell, pausing for a moment to hear Alcuin continue his nasal dissertation. This wasn't over, he knew that.

CHAPTER 19
SEVENTY TIMES SEVEN

Psalm 50: 3-4
Have mercy on me, God, in your kindness.
In your compassion, blot out my offence.
Oh, wash me more and more from my guilt
and cleanse from my sin.

Paul trudged to the guesthouse. As he opened the door, he heard voices and found Brother Reginald with Charlie.

"Hey," Charlie said, "My mom is coming to pick me up. She should be here soon."

"She's coming here?" Paul asked.

"Yeah, where else would she come?"

"Didn't you tell your parents you were at a friend's house?"

"I did. She trusts me," Charlie said. She crossed her arms, indicating the conversation was over. "You're in trouble, aren't you?"

"Kind of," Paul said.

"Yeah, he has some explaining to do, but they will let him keep his birthday," Brother Reginald said.

"So punishment will be involved? Flagellation? Mortification?" Her eyes lit up. She looked pretty without all her makeup, pale but pretty.

Brother Reginald laughed as Paul cringed. He had to stop her before she started talking about Satan and zombies.

"Do you want breakfast?" Paul asked, not waiting for an answer. He grabbed her arm and pulled her to the stairs.

Paul led Charlie into the refectory, which was half-empty by now. Alcuin sat a table with a smirk. Heads turned and looked. Paul was thankful that the meal was silent.

He had forgotten to tell Charlie that she needed to remain quiet. She ate little. She twisted around, taking in monks, the religious artwork that adorned the walls, and the life-size crucifix that hung large and looming near the Abbot's table. A pack of wolves and prey. Paul picked at his food, knowing this day was going too long. Brother Reginald entered and smiled at Charlie.

"Your mom is here," he whispered to her.

She rose from the table and Paul stood, meaning to go with her, but she placed a firm hand on his shoulder.

"Thanks for everything," Charlie said, as she turned and kissed him lightly on the cheek.

A quick thrill of excitement rushed through him, followed by an overwhelming panic, as Paul watched her leave. What did that mean? No time to ponder the gesture. The Abbot was waiting for him.

"He doesn't know a thing," Paul chanted to himself as his heart thundered in his ears. He plodded to the monastery. Puffs of freezing air created a fog as he went. Once inside, before the gates of angels, he heard the juniors whispering.

"Alcuin said they were in the guesthouse with a girl."

"She is a little odd."

"She is vampire-ish. What was he thinking?"

"She is dangerous news. What if she accused us of stuff?"

Stuff? Novices were really naïve, thought Paul. Charlie is harmless. She wasn't dangerous. He was sure her voodoo incantation was made up.

St. Benedict was right. Wagging tongues in the monastery were dangerous. He'd done nothing wrong and yet here he was standing convicted. Paul saw that the door to the Abbot's office remained closed. The juniors dispersed as Paul approached. The door to the office opened. Ambrose lumbered out, stopped, and gave Paul a bear hug.

Dread filled Paul as he entered the office. Abbot Jacob looked up.

"Good morning, Paul. The Lord be with you."

"And also with you, Father Abbot," Paul mumbled, head down, noticing his untied shoe.

"How was the dance?"

"Good," Paul said as he ran his finger over the shiny desktop edge.

"You got in at the appointed time, I presume?"

"Yeah," Paul said, wondering if the half-asleep monk had seen him arriving last night with Charlie.

Jacob leaned forward and pushed a book toward Paul. He put a finger on a word in the book. "Read, please."

"Cloister. A monastic establishment. A covered walkway. A house of persons living under religious vows, connotes seclusion from the world."

"Can you tell me what that means to the monks at Saint Alberic's?"

Paul shook his head, sitting down in the chair in front of the desk.

Jacob leaned back in his chair. "Tell me again. What is a cloister?"

"A private dwelling place for the religious."

The chair creaked as Jacob moved side to side. "Who is allowed in the cloister?"

This is a trick. How would Joannicus answer?

"Religious persons of the same sex if invited."

"What was the gender of the person who spent the night?" There was an icy coldness in Jacob's voice.

"Female," Paul said, rubbing his shoe over the dangling shoe-string. He doesn't know she was in my room.

"Where do we host guests?" Jacob asked, crossing his arms.

"The guesthouse."

"Where was your guest last night?"

It's a bluff. Paul's mind raced. The silence loomed. Paul looked up. Jacob's eyes beckoned an answer.

"The guesthouse, I was going to tell you." Paul felt his face grow hot as he picked at the threads of his worn jeans.

The clock on the wall ticked. The wooden chair creaked as Jacob shifted.

"Damn it, Paul, that is not the truth."

"Why don't you ever trust me? Charlie's parents believe her."

Jacob closed his eyes and sighed.

"Where did Charlie spend the night? You need to think before you speak. So far, this is not going well."

"Here. Where else would she spend the night?"

Jacob frowned and shook his head as he folded his hands, as if preparing to pray.

"Lies make me rather upset. She was in your cell."

"If you know that, why keep asking me?" Paul said, regretting the words that flew out of his mouth without restraint. "How do you know that?"

Jacob stood and strolled around the large desk. He stopped in front of Paul.

Resolve, along with conviction, ran and hid. Confession time.

"Nothing happened. We had our clothes on." Paul's mouth was dry. "We were just talking. She didn't want to go home. She wanted to talk. I can't tell you what we talked about. So don't ask. It was private, personal."

Jacob crossed his arms. "Okay, but I need to ask, is someone hurting her?"

They had seen her father coming out of the liquor store last night when they had stopped for gas. Paul could tell by his gait that he was drunk. She hadn't said he was a violent drunk. She said that she didn't want to listen to the fighting. "No, nobody is hurting her."

"Good." Jacob sat on the edge of the desk. "Alright, then let me define the parameters of guests. They belong in the guesthouse and most certainly if they are female. One other thing, you must first clear it with me."

Paul studied the picture on the wall. Guilt, like a morning glory, wrapped around Paul's mind, making him groan softly. Why did he need permission when the monks didn't ask permission for visitors? A protest formed in his mind, but before he could speak, Jacob continued, "It's my monastery. What goes on within its walls is my business. I don't want Charlie on my doorstep nine months from now making allegations."

Oh my God, he assumes we were having sex.

Paul stood up. He liked Charlie, but this was his first real date. Was it an actual date? Confusion competed for center stage. She had just kissed him, hadn't she?

"Why do you assume the worst? I wouldn't do that. She doesn't do that. We talked, we fell asleep, and then she went home. What did you want me to do? Wake you up in the middle of the night to ask permission."

Okay, he should have taken her to the guesthouse. He knew that now. Jacob rocked in his chair, his fingers poised over his lips as if holding back what he really wanted to say.

"That is one option. You mention to me after prayers that we had a guest, in the guesthouse."

Paul's heart pounded. Permission, rules that seemed designed for him alone.

"I'm not a monk."

Jacob folded his hands. "Monk or no monk, you share a house. You have an obligation to tell us who is visiting. You need to respect our privacy."

A realization dawned. That noise he had heard before prayers. It wasn't the radiator clicking. It was the door. "You came into my room, didn't you? How respectful is that? You had no right."

"Don't change the subject. Do you want to be allowed to have friends visit?" Jacob said, his voice restricted and calculating.

Paul looked at the floor, at the frayed hem of Jacob's habit, struggling to keep his own voice low and controlled. "You let Lucas spend the night in the monastery."

The hem danced. "Lucas is male. That was a onetime decision based on my knowledge of Lucas. This is our home. Its sanctity is important. I need assurance that you understand this."

"I understand you were spying on me." Paul's voice was high, close to a shout.

"I was not spying on you." Jacob said, his voice growled.

"Did you have permission to come to my cell? I think not."

Jacob gripped the desk, his knuckles grew white, and then he stood pushing off the desk, flexing his fingers. The Abbot walked to the window behind the desk. The sun peaked and the virgin snow on the patio glistened. He turned and glared at Paul, his voice now low and hissing. "I knocked and you didn't answer. Guess you were asleep."

The sarcasm inflamed Paul. "You talk about the monk's privacy. What about my privacy?"

Jacob's face turned serious, almost cold and threatening, as he returned to sit behind the desk. "You seem to forget the cell belongs to Saint Alberic's Monastery, not to Paul Warner."

"You are being unfair. You let me have a lock once. Maybe I need one now."

Jacob leaned forward on the desk. "Stop."

"No," Paul said. "I want to know why?"

"Are you four? Stop being so pigheaded. You know why. Because I'm the abbot, you're my ward, and I'm responsible for you," Jacob said, rubbing his jaw as if the conversation were painful.

Paul felt his lower lip protruding as his jaw tightened. "So, I am a burden. You really don't trust me, do you?"

"Should I trust you?" Abbot Jacob's voice boomed.

Paul realized he had pushed too far.

"You have never trusted me." Paul slouched in the chair.

Jacob stood, turning his back to Paul. He stood for a long time. His head shook slightly, as if he were responding to a private conversation. His braid snaked its way free from his hood. He turned, his face and eyes softened. "I'm not at this moment ready to stop my checking in on you. I didn't check on you last night to violate your privacy. None of us who enter your room at night have done so to violate your privacy."

Paul sat up. "What us? Who else enters my room at night?"

"Brother Ambrose, Father Joannicus, to name a few."

Standing up, Paul paced the few feet in front of the desk.

"Why would they do that?"

"We don't do things to piss you off. Father Joannicus enters your room to take the books from your face and turn out your lights."

"How do you know he does that?"

"He told me. As for Ambrose, I think he thinks you might wonder off into the night."

"I'm not a sheep." Paul cocked his head, trying to remember if his lights were on come dawn more often now that Joannicus was not home. The truth glared at him like a naked bulb.

"You? Why do you do it?" Paul asked, curiosity squelching his anger.

"Because Abbot Gordon told me to remember that you are a good boy. When I see you asleep and quiet, not arguing with me, I remember you are a good boy. It reminds me that when I have to listen to you defend the indefensible to be merciful and kind."

Paul sat, silenced, touched that Jacob cared.

"Do not pull this crap again."

Some of Paul's indignation had melted away.

"I don't plan to bring anyone into the cloister."

And I am getting a lock for my door, thought Paul.

Jacob placed a sheet of paper on the desk and pushed it toward Paul.

"Good, now for your punishment. You will apologize to each monk. Ask his forgiveness for violating the cloister."

Paul looked at the list. Everyone was on it, even the parish priests. "There are at least seventy names on this list. I have to ask forgiveness seventy times?"

"There are fifty-four names on the list. Be thankful it's not seventy times seven. Come back when you have finished, and we shall talk."

Paul envisioned the task. Sorry, please forgive me, sure thing kid, then on to the next monk.

Snatching the page, Paul headed out of the office.

This is really a stupid punishment.

CHAPTER 20

FORGIVENESS

Psalm 87: 9
You have taken away my friends
and made me hateful in their sight.
Imprisoned, I cannot escape.
My eyes are sunken with grief.

T he sooner I knock this out, the sooner I can catch up on my *sleep*, thought Paul. Girls can really wear you out with all their talking. He had enjoyed staying up all night chatting. Paul smiled to himself as he went to the kitchen. The crew was working, and the mixer was loud.

"I need to talk to you all," Paul shouted over the din.

"So, talk," Daniel said, cutting carrots with a chop, chop, chop.

"No, individually."

"Paul, we don't have time for interviews. Speak or be on your way," Brother Barnabas said, turning off the mixer.

"But you don't understand. I need to apologize individually."

Barnabas said, "Oh, an Abbot Jacob kind of penance."

"Sort of."

"Okay, you have twelve seconds." They all turned and looked at Paul. It was rather intimidating. Paul took a deep breath and blurted out, "I violated the cloister last night, and I'm sorry. I hope you can forgive me."

"You did what?" Brother Godfrey said.

"Don't repeat it, Paul," Barnabas said. "And don't repeat the action in the future."

"I won't," Paul said as Barnabas turned away.

"That girl, you and she, in the cloister," Brother Daniel said as he sent his knife down on a bunch of carrots, the sound crunched like dry kindling. "I'm disappointed and angry."

"I'm sorry. I won't do it again," Paul said, curling and uncurling his toes in his shoes.

As the day progressed, Paul found his apologies getting longer and longer with each monk he encountered, and nobody said that they had forgiven him. Weren't monks supposed to be kind and forgiving? Perhaps he had misjudged them. He could name them, and he was aware of where they sat in choir, but if questioned what their job was, he didn't have a clue.

Paul counted the names left on his list. Forty-four.

Father James entered and sorted through his mail. Father James taught in the College. Paul tried to remember what subject. Physics or Biology?

"Father James?"

The man turned. "Yes, Paul."

Wow, he has really gray eyes. "I need to apologize for violating the sanctity of the cloister. I'm sorry and ..."

"Try that in English," James said, shaking his head.

"I violated—"

Father James peered over his glasses. "Clarify, be specific, boy."

"I had a friend without permission in my cell."

"A friend? A female?"

"Yes."

The glasses came off, and James pinched the bridge of his nose. "I told them this would happen."

"I'm sorry," Paul said, feeling like a seven-year-old. Apparently unknown to him, he was a topic of discussion.

"That was stupid of you."

I'm aware of that, thought Paul, thankful that he hadn't blurted out his thoughts.

"I need to apologize and ask forgiveness."

"Then do it," Father James growled. His patience appeared to be wearing thin.

"I thought I was," Paul said. Oops, that was stupid.

The priest glared. "No, you're telling me."

"Father, I brought a female to my cell and I'm sorry. I shouldn't have done that and I'm sorry. I hope you'll be able to forgive me."

"I see. I suggest you go to confession, for that is where forgiveness is. How did you get her in here? Oh, never mind. You're what, fourteen now. Terrible choice, young man," James lectured.

Sixteen in a few days. Why doesn't he know that? Paul penitently lowered his head. Remorse settled around him. The choice to bring her home was the right one, but where they ended up was the problem.

His mind wandered as he made his way to the church for noon prayers. She had kissed him on the cheek. Was it a proper kiss, and what did that mean? Nobody had said anything. Reginald had seen it. Paul smiled and then blushed. He had liked the kiss.

He made his way to the refectory with Charlie on his mind.

Brother Ambrose came up to him and punched his arm playfully.

"Missed you this morning at the farm. You plan to come down this afternoon, or is it a holiday?"

"I'm sorry, but after the Abbot finished chewing me out, I had little time left."

"I accept that excuse. I think the Abbot should chew you out regularly," Ambrose said, a grin spread across his face, showing his tobacco-stained teeth.

"Even if I've done nothing wrong? How fair is that?"

They entered the hallway outside of the refectory.

"You bet because you're bound to get into trouble, eventually. So, what did you do this time?"

Paul pulled the large man aside in the hall.

"I violated the cloister," Paul said in a quiet voice.

"You did what?" Ambrose's eyebrow formed a single brow, and monks who were standing in the hallway turned to look at them.

"I had a friend overnight in my cell, and that was violating your privacy. I'm sorry, and I ask for your forgiveness."

Ambrose grinned and then wiped his face with his hand, causing his smile to turn serious. "Your date? You took her to your cell overnight. You're walking around, and the Abbot just chewed you out. Our Abbot just chewed you out. Damn, he should have whipped your ass or something."

"Brother, I'm sixteen. I'm a little big to be turned over his knee."

Brother Ambrose laughed as if Paul said something preposterous.

He can't be serious.

"You're not too smart if you got caught." The big man shook his head slowly. His shoulders rose and dropped as he let out an enormous sigh. "You've made more work for us. We now have to re-bless everything. We might have to move out until everything is made holy again."

"What are you talking about?" He was joking, wasn't he?

"Oh Lordy. The cloister is sacred and needs to be blessed. Why else would we have gates at the entrance of the cloister? Honestly, I thought you were aware of this stuff. The novices are," Ambrose continued, his head wagging from side to side. Paul could not make out a grin.

The line moved forward into the refectory. Dread filled Paul. Crap, what had he done?

"I wonder if we'll get new furniture because we'll have to burn the old stuff," Ambrose whispered. "Just like worn out old habits, you can't turn them over to the thrift shop, must burn holy things. Well, next time be smart, save us some money and hassle, and take the girl to the guesthouse, where girls belong."

Paul swallowed hard. "It will never happen again. I promise."

"Oh. Okay. Well, good." Ambrose nodded and headed into the refectory, chuckling to himself.

Paul understood blessed things were sacred. He even remembered that you didn't sell blessed objects. As a little boy, he had taken solace in the power of a blessing. The monks blessed him frequently. He felt loved when they blessed him, even when Ambrose would bellow in anger that he was going to sell Paul to the Indians. Why hadn't he made the connection between that and the monastery itself? A re-blessing ceremony, that was probably why the Abbot wanted to see him. Double crap.

That evening, Paul headed to the community room and sat

down next to Brother Moses and Abbot Jacob. He pulled out his list, counting the names left.

"You don't have to accomplish that in one day," Abbot Jacob said.

"Yeah, I know," Paul said as Jacob rose and left the table.

"Hey, Little One, why so glum?" Moses asked.

"Can we talk?"

"Okay, shoot," Brother Moses said, smiling expectantly. Paul almost hated to erase that smile.

"I brought a girl home, and she spent the night in my room. It was wrong, and so I'm sorry. Will you forgive me?"

"Well," Moses said thoughtfully, scratching his head.

"Well?" Paul sat, squeezing his hands together in the silence.

"Don't make a habit of it. Not the end of the world. We all make mistakes. I forgive you."

For the first time, Paul's spirit lifted, his burden lightened.

"Thank you, I won't do it again."

"I know you won't."

Paul wished every monk would respond like Moses. They did not, making every apology seem like a mirror to his poor judgment. As Paul sat for evening prayers, the words of the psalmist resonated in his heart:

"You have laid me in the depths of the tomb. In places that are dark in the depths. Your anger weighs down upon me. I am drowned beneath your waves."

He now understood what the monks meant by the living words of the psalms. His community was displeased with him. Paul headed in silence to his cell, the isolation of his actions profoundly haunting him.

Sleep came, but it was a troubled sleep. Sunday dawned and

Paul went late to breakfast. In the nearly empty refectory, he spied Brother Reginald and figured he needed to start the next round of apologies sooner than later.

Brother Reginald held up his one free hand. "I don't have time, Paul, but I think you were really dumb. You need to see the big picture. What if she says she was in a house full of men? Kid, the accusations she could make, that put us all in danger."

"She wouldn't do that," Paul said.

"People do strange things. I like her. I think she's interesting with her outlandish dress and the things she says, but don't take a risk like that."

"I don't think she would lie," Paul said as worry crept into his mind.

"I hope for all our sakes you are right."

Paul nodded and Brother Reginald smiled a crooked smile. "Okay, I'll tell the Abbot you apologized if he asks, and he won't. Hold on," Reginald raised his hand, making the sign of the cross. "I forgive you. Go. Sin no more. I have always wanted to say that."

Reginald turned to leave.

"Hey, wait," Paul said. "What's your favorite season?"

"Liturgically I like ordinary time, that's when the best songs are sung. Earth-wise I like fall because change is in the air and the colors are vibrant and everyone is busy."

At two, Paul knocked on the open door of the Abbot's office.

Jacob looked up from his desk.

"The Lord be with you, Paul."

"And also with you, Father Abbot. I have a question," Paul said, moving into the room.

"Yes."

"What about the ones not here?"

The Abbot looked at the list of monks that he had given Paul. The paper was in a shabby shape, having been refolded several times.

"The parish priests. You can do it by phone," Jacob said, handing Paul a sheet of paper with the phone numbers to the parishes.

"But they weren't even here."

"This is their home too," Jacob said. "You can use my phone. I need a break anyway." Abbot Jacob rose, stretched, and poured himself a cup of coffee before making his way to the outside patio. Paul sat in the warm leather seat and dialed the first number. The phone conversations were just as difficult.

Paul dialed the number for Father Joannicus.

"Hi, Father, this is Paul."

"Yes, Abbot Jacob told me you would call," Joannicus said.

Paul opened the desk drawer and took out paper and a pen.

"So, you know?"

"I would rather hear it from you."

"Charlie, she's a girl, spent the night in my cell. We just talked." Paul looked over his shoulder to see if the Abbot was listening. "We drank a beer, one. We weren't drunk. She didn't want to go home. Her dad was drinking, and she doesn't like him when he drinks. He acts all mad and bossy. So, I let her stay. Was that so wrong?" Paul made little crosses on the paper in front of him.

"What do you think?" Joannicus asked.

Paul heard announcements in the background noise of the phone. "Are you in a hospital?"

"Yes, I'm visiting the sick," Joannicus said.

"I thought you were giving a retreat," Paul said.

"What, I can't do both? I talked to the Abbot this morning."

"I messed up. Everyone is mad at me. Do you think I should be here?"

"Seriously? You belong. Those mad at you will forgive you. Monks are good at that. We practice it a lot."

Paul drew loops around his crosses. "I hope so, because right now, it feels like I'm alone."

Paul looked at his list. Only Father Pius at St. George's and Brother Alcuin remained. Both men were mean. They won't forgive him.

Paul dialed the number and then hung up before it rang twice. He got up from the desk and poured himself a cup of coffee. He didn't normally drink the stuff, so he added spoonful after spoonful of sugar. Paul sat in the oversized chair at the desk. He dialed the number again.

The first ring barely finished.

"Hello?"

"This is Paul Warner. Can we talk?" Say no, please say no.

"Sure, what can I do for you?" Pius asked.

Hang up on me.

"I'm apologizing for violating the cloister and your privacy."

There was a pause. Had he hung up?

"You had sex in the monastery?"

"No, Father, I violated the cloister."

"What does that mean, exactly?"

"I had a non-religious person in my cell overnight," Paul said, hoping Pius wouldn't ask any more questions.

"Male?"

"No, Father."

"And you claim you didn't have sex?"

"Yes, that's right, Father." Paul took a sip of the hot coffee.

"Why?"

Swallowing quickly and burning his throat, Paul coughed, almost choking. "Why? What? Why didn't I have sex with her?"

"No, why did you bring a girl to your cell?"

The hot liquid hit his stomach, making him feel queasy. "It was late. Too late to ask permission and she didn't want to go home."

"That was stupid."

"Yes, I know."

"So, the Abbot is having you call me?"

"Yes, he is."

"Well, good for him. I'm glad to see he's making you responsible for your poor choices."

"Oh, he is," Paul said, hoping his voice didn't sound sarcastic.

Pius's voice took on the quality of a lecture. Paul watched the seconds tick off on the clock. The man droned on. Paul spun in the chair as he watched Abbot Jacob in the little garden outside the office. How many monks visited him and complained? Paul wondered. This task has placed a burden on the Abbot. Paul suddenly realized that his behavior affected others. Abbot Jacob picked off the dead blossoms from a bush. He gently retied the wandering branch to the trellis. A curious bird hopped from the chair to the table and onto the rim of the coffee cup. Jacob watched with amusement on his face as the bird used the cup for a private caffeine-filled bath, then boldly fluffed and puffed on the papers that Jacob had been reading. Flying to a branch above the Abbot's head, the bird scolded and chirped as if protesting the contents of the bath. Jacob emptied the cup and gathered his spotted-brown papers.

"Paul?"

"Yes Father, I was listening."

Jacob entered the office.

"You forgive me? Thanks."

Jacob narrowed his eyes and Paul smiled weakly, shrugging his shoulders before hanging up. That was unexpected.

"You finished?" Jacob asked.

Paul shook his head. He wished he was.

Together they walked to the community room, which was crowded with monks because it was Sunday. Most were engaged in holy leisure, reading the paper or working on the jigsaw puzzle.

Paul approached Brother Alcuin.

"Brother Alcuin, can you spare a moment?" Paul didn't wait for an answer. "Last Friday night I had a female friend in my cell for a visit and I—"

"Excuse me, I don't want to hear any more."

"I'm sorry, I violated—"

"No," Alcuin said in a stern voice. "You're a disgrace to this monastery and to anyone who wears a robe. You repeatedly make a mockery of what we stand for. I don't know why the Abbot tolerates it. He should've had that chapter meeting and voted you out of here. He should have never allowed you back."

What the hell? The Abbot hadn't sent him away as a punishment. He had sent him away so he could establish his abbotship without distraction. The man himself had told Paul that. The gossip had mixed with the truth. Paul looked over at Abbot Jacob. The man studied his coffee cup in silence.

"But, Brother," Paul said, feeling the entire room's focus on him. "I need to tell you I'm sorry and I understand I made a mistake and that..." Paul paused. Brother Alcuin rose. Paul chased after him.

"Brother, please stop."

Alcuin stopped, and Paul almost ran into him. He turned and looked at Paul.

"You have done your duty for the Abbot. Please do not follow me."

"I'm not doing this for the Abbot. He didn't force me to do this. I'm sorry because I am sorry. I messed up. Don't walk away." Alcuin was out of the door. "I wanted your forgiveness, would have liked your forgiveness. I'm sorry," Paul said in a whisper.

JACOB SAT at the oval table as Ambrose glared at him. He didn't blame Ambrose for the scathing look, for he had witnessed too many unforgiving monks. Sadness filled him. The lesson to Paul seemed insignificant compared to what he learned about his community. Had everyone forgotten that correction was to reconcile the sinner back to the community? His community had forgotten that Paul was a member who needed compassion and guidance, too. Paul's face made him realize maybe he had corrected too harshly.

He watched Paul walk over to the table where he and Ambrose sat. The pace was not the usual flash of movement. Paul sat down in the chair and leaned his head on Ambrose's shoulder.

You shouldn't have tried to do this in one weekend, thought Jacob.

"Abbot Jacob," Paul said. "I'm sorry I violated the cloister. The cloister means different things to different people. I didn't know it meant anything. I also learned that forgiveness isn't a given."

Ambrose growled.

"You are forgiven," Jacob said.

"I didn't ask," Paul said.

"Well, perhaps you shouldn't have to ask. I know you understand and respect us. We all make poor choices. But together we have to realize our mistakes and practice compassion," Jacob said in a loud voice, hoping that the monk-filled room heard him.

"I'll help with the re-blessing and cleaning," Paul said.

Jacob shot a fixed stare at Ambrose, who shrugged his shoulders.

"Do you think I should live here?" Paul asked.

Ambrose harrumphed. Silence, as if time paused. Jacob felt the weight of the surrounding souls.

"Yes, you belong. The matter is closed. Tomorrow we begin again."

CHAPTER 21

THE ABBOT WHO DIDN'T PRAY

Psalm 17:27
With the sincere you show yourself sincere
but the cunning, you outdo in cunning.

Paul attempted to comb his hair over his face. His left eye was still puffy and swollen. Standing at his closet door, he opened and closed it. No way could he say he hit the closet door. Nothing was eye level anymore.

The bells rang for Mass. He hesitated, wondering if he would be less noticeable if he sat with the people rather than the community. The turnout for daily Mass was sparse. It would be impossible to hide. Brother Ambrose scowled and squinted at him as if he was not sure that Paul was sporting a black eye. He nudged others to get a second opinion. Paul tried to keep his head down.

Brother Alcuin turned and gave him a sneer. Paul shot back with a wide-eyed stare. The sharp stabs from the swollen orb made him wince, ruining any effect he had hoped to make.

After Mass, Paul took his time leaving the church, knowing that the monks would pepper him with questions and a trip to the infirmary. Why can't they just pretend that a black eye is no big thing?

Paul left the church slowly. Brother Reginald was in the sacristy washing and drying the chalices. He smiled and nodded. Paul stopped in the restroom, checking to see if a miracle had occurred. The eye was still puffy and now turning a purplish green.

Damn Charlie.

Moving to his cell, Paul hoped to avoid any encounters that would lead to questions.

Damn Ambrose. It was his advice that had gotten him into this mess. Charlie had a mean right jab. He had to make it through dinner and evening prayers. After that, the grand silence would leave him hassle free until morning.

Dinner proceeded without issue. Although there were stares, nobody said anything directly to him. After dinner, he ducked out, using the entrance to the mudroom. He had a good hour and a half before vespers. He did not want to talk to anyone, and especially not Brother Ambrose. That would be a challenging because he knew all of Paul's hiding spots. He walked back to the church. He moved to the ancient confessional box. This space was rarely used. He entered the dark space and was careful not to sit on the kneeler, because that triggered a little red light outside, a sign someone was inside. The confessional sat opposite the sacristy in the church's atrium.

He flicked on his flashlight and pulled out a paperback novel. An hour later, he noticed how voices carried and wondered who was in the atrium, so he listened with his ear pressed to the vent.

"Did you see that shiner? I bet he gets suspended from school," Brother Alcuin said.

"That's if he fought back. If he didn't throw a punch, how can they kick him out?" Brother Reginald asked.

"Why are you always defending him? You sound like Father Joannicus. The boy is not a saint. If he were here, he'd see that's not the case."

Paul turned off his flashlight.

"I don't defend him. He deserves a fair hearing. Must be difficult to live here when it wasn't your choice."

Alcuin's nasal whine continued, "I don't understand what he is doing here. Is he going to be a monk?"

"No, don't think so."

He liked Reginald even more for his consideration of every angle. I should have asked him about girls.

"Why does he get privileges when other guests don't?"

Paul stifled a snort. Privileges? What privileges? Praying, having to be quiet after eight p.m.?

The voices were louder as they moved closer to the church.

"He isn't a guest. This is the only home he has."

He had a home, a fading memory, a bedroom and cookie crumbs.

"Do you wonder if he's someone's indiscretion?"

"No, I heard he was dropped off like the baby Moses."

No. They had it all wrong. He had two parents, just like everyone. A mother and a father. Charlie was looking into that. Probably not anymore. He would ask her if she ever talked to him again.

"You have to agree that he's in the Abbot's office more than any monk."

Paul leaned closer to the vent, holding his breath.

"That doesn't mean he's in trouble."

"Thank you, Father Joannicus. He has no balls when it comes to seeing Paul for what he is, a charlatan."

"He has one," Reginald said. "At least for a while longer."

"I don't see what the big secret is."

"That doesn't matter. You're bound by obedience. Besides, Father Joannicus asked us to keep that knowledge to ourselves, not to make it public knowledge. As for Paul, you came here knowing he lived at the monastery. That was no secret. I don't get why he bugs you so much."

"He doesn't believe half the time and challenges all our values."

Reginald laughed. "He's a teenager. He's supposed to do that."

Paul's mind swirled. He was right. Something was up with Joannicus. He was privy to Father Martin's hemorrhoids, that professor Rice had a baby girl, and named her Genesis. He even knew who dented the brown car. The Abbot didn't even know that. Monks weren't that good at keeping secrets. *Why don't I know what is wrong with Joannicus?*

The bells rang for evening prayers. Paul emerged from the dark confessional and hurried into the church.

Throughout prayers, Paul tried to piece together the clues. He came up short. Joannicus was on retreat, or was it a sabbatical? The last monk to take a sabbatical never returned, leaving all his belongings. Paul had learned he had fallen in love and married a college student.

Crap. Was the secret that Joannicus was leaving? Stop. That made no sense. A woman? Joannicus always acted uncomfortable around the female students he taught. Did he have any women friends besides Gracie and Barb? Double crap. Ms. Carr, the social worker who had dropped Paul off as a child and remained involved in all their lives. When was her last visit? In a daze, Paul headed to his cell. No, not Joannicus.

As he brushed his teeth, his one eye glared at him. Damn Ambrose, your advice sucked.

"Go for it," Ambrose had said.

Paul crawled into bed, turned off his light. The conversation he had overheard echoed in his mind. He wanted to pick up the phone and talk to Charlie. She'd be able to help him sort out the facts. Can't call her now, not after what happened. A veil of sadness cuddled with sleep. Joannicus gone, Charlie most definitely gone.

MORNING CAME. Paul ate breakfast, wishing he didn't have to go to school. He made his way down the hill to the bus stop. A monk appeared by his side. Paul turned around seeing Abbot Jacob, who had been absent from prayers. Paul had assumed that Abbot Jacob was at another abbot meeting.

"I don't want to talk about it," Paul stated. "You weren't at prayers. Why?"

"I do not want to talk about it either," Jacob said, pulling his coat tighter around himself. Was Abbot Jacob ill? Crap, his life was suddenly unraveling.

"Brother Ambrose is concerned," Abbot Jacob said.

"He should be. He's the idiot who got me into this mess."

Was that a smirk? Together, they walked toward the bus stop.

"He told me to go for it..." Paul's voice trailed off. Kissing Charlie was a mistake. She didn't like him like that. Did he? Not to worry, she would never talk to him again.

"Today is going to suck," Paul said.

"How so?"

"Really, look at my eye. People are going to ask questions."

"So, what happened?"

"I don't want to talk about it."

Abbot Jacob nodded. Paul watched as the man wrinkled his nose and his eyes wandered the flat landscape.

"Tell them the truth."

Paul shook his head. "Are you crazy?"

"Well, there is always my favorite. I was goofing around with my sister and her knee..." Jacob said, his voice trailing off.

"I don't have a sister," Paul said. Paul had heard that Jacob's stepfather, Terence, beat Jacob when he was a kid. That was hard to envision and even harder to believe. Terence McKenzie had always been nice to Paul. Confusion filled Paul's mind. He really didn't know the monks.

"Then say you were moving boxes around, piled things too high, and they crashed down on you and pow a black eye."

"Guess that could work," Paul said. "But what do I do with Charlie?"

"Apologize," Jacob said. "Or you can pretend that it did not happen."

"That's all you got? I'll figure something out," Paul said, as the yellow bus approached.

"Good. I wanted to bring up confirmation at St. George's. Are you sure?"

"I guess. He isn't the teacher, is he?"

Association with Pius would be insufferable, but time with Lucas was his goal.

"No. But he will be involved. He is the parish priest."

The sacrament of confirmation involved a slap to the cheek. Paul knew that even if they practiced the ceremony as they had when he received First Communion, the man wouldn't dream of actually slapping him. Paul realized he could take Pius, for he wasn't a little boy anymore. Pius could no longer physically harm him. That didn't stop his stomach from clinching whenever he thought of the man.

Jacob chuckled, as if reading Paul's unspoken words. "They do not slap you. I thought that you could have confirmation at the monastery. Just like you had your baptism here, I can administer the rite."

"Really? Cool." One good thing to balance the anticipated worse.

The bus approached and red lights flashed. Paul boarded, keeping his head down.

Students looked with morbid curiosity, but nobody said anything until lunchtime. Paul sat a table near the door at his usual table, but Charlie did not join him. He had seen Charlie, but when he had approached, she had slammed her locker and stomped off. Lucas muscled his way in between Gwen and Steven, who were at the table.

"Nice shiner," Lucas said. "Is the other guy still standing?"

Paul took a bite of his sandwich.

"Heard you could use a few pointers," Gwen said.

"From whom?" Paul asked, wondering what rumor-filled story was floating around now.

Gwen stood up and glared at Paul. "Rumor has it the guy deserved what he got."

What guy? Him?

"That's what Charlie said," Steven muttered.

Lucas moved closer to Paul, filling in the empty space.

"They say you were defending a girl's honor," Lucas said, punching Paul's arm. "So which girl?"

Charlie. Leave it to her to start a rumor and save him.

"This Saturday is the first confirmation class. Why don't you spend the night?" Lucas said, crushing his milk carton with one hand.

"Sure," Paul said, wondering if he could.

STANDING IN THE KITCHENETTE, in the community room, Abbot Jacob pinched the bridge of his nose as he waited for the coffee to brew. Heaviness pulled at his eyelids. He longed to go to bed, but he had been absent from prayers too often. That wasn't a good example, the abbot who didn't pray. He had watched the community avoid Paul's glaring black eye and had expected a phone call from the school. The call never came. Jacob poured himself a large mug of coffee. Maybe the jolt would keep him stay awake through evening prayers. Stirring three teaspoons of sugar into his mug, he sat down at a table, propping his head on his hand.

The chair next to him creaked. Abbot Jacob opened his eyes, but he knew from the musky smell that either a buffalo or Ambrose had just sat down next to him.

"The boy won't even speak to me," Ambrose muttered.

"Do you blame him?" Jacob asked. "What were you thinking, telling him to kiss her?"

"I did no such thing. I just told him to let her know he liked her. You can't get anywhere if you stand and watch. She hit him. I'll teach him how to give a right hook," Ambrose said, cupping his right hand with his left.

"How about ducking? We want a lover, not a fighter," Jacob said.

"He isn't Franciscan. Some critters need a firm hand."

"Girls are not critters," Jacob said, watching Ambrose's eyebrows bounce and knit together.

"That girl is wild."

Jacob shook his head and that hurt. What was Brother Ambrose thinking, giving advice on girls? Paul was late with being interested in girls. This incident could make his approaching them come to a stop. Father Joannicus would be pleased. He didn't think Paul needed a love interest. Jacob knew there was no stopping love.

"Rose, the boy's sixteen. Let him figure this out for himself," Jacob said, watching Paul playing checkers with Brother Moses.

"But Joannicus asked me to keep an out," Ambrose said, lowering his voice and leaning closer to Jacob. "How is he?"

Jacob had spent last night at the hospital with Joannicus.

"He survived the operation. Tomorrow treatment," Jacob said in a low voice.

"And how are you?" Ambrose asked.

"What's wrong with you?" Paul asked, startling them with his sudden presence.

Abbot Jacob's eyes narrowed as he looked at Brother Ambrose.

"I have a migraine," Jacob said.

"Oh. Can I spend Friday night at Lucas's house?"

"Will his mom be home?"

"Yeah, I think so."

Jacob inhaled deeply and cleared his throat. *If not, come home.*

But he couldn't bring himself to say that. He could only trust Paul's choices.

"Fine, have a fun time."

Paul's hasty exit gave Jacob a slight chill.

"Get some rest," Ambrose said, and then lowered his voice. "He's never spent the night at friends, unsupervised."

"Not tonight, Rose," Jacob said, his head pounding.

CHAPTER 22
MILK CARTON BOY

Psalm 68: 14-15

This is my prayer to you.

My prayer for your favor.

In your great love, answer me, Oh God.

With your help, that never fails.

Rescue me from sinking in the mud.

Save me from my foes.

Football. Ambrose had explained the idea, but it wasn't until Brother Reginald had explained the probability and statistics that the game became interesting. There was a psychological aspect to the game that Paul found fascinating. He had watched both teams warming up. He had stats on the players and predicted the outcome of the game. By game's end, he had discovered that there was some dumb luck involved. Lucas and his team had won.

After the game, they ate pizza, which seemed to be a staple in Lucas's diet. The team was boisterous, having won. After eleven, Paul and Lucas made their way to Lucas's home. The apartment was dark when they entered. The space was small and sparsely furnished. A sunken sofa with a floral pattern with a water-stained coffee table, and no room for a kitchen table.

Paul followed Lucas down the narrow hall, where two doors stood opposite each other. Lucas knocked on a door. When there was no response, he opened the door slowly, letting the hallway light laminate the space.

"Guess she's not here," Lucas said, closing the door.

They entered the second bedroom, that was smaller than Paul's cell at home. Two twin beds. A closet, no doors. Boxes, labeled with clothing contents. A small desk, no chair crammed into a corner. A bare bulb hung overhead. Paul gazed at the many sports posters that decorated the walls.

"Mom's probably at work. Can you still stay?"

Abbot Jacob's voice resounded in Paul's head. He should not stay without an adult in the house. Only he wasn't eight, so that rule didn't apply now.

"When will she be home?"

Lucas shrugged his shoulders. He moved to the kitchen and opened the refrigerator door. Paul could not believe he was hungry.

"I was right. She's at work. The graveyard shift so in the morning probably around eight or nine," Lucas said as he peeled a note taped to a milk carton. "Tomorrow morning."

Paul bit his lower lip, trying not to make a joke about taping a note over the face of a missing child that appeared on the milk carton.

"You can't stay?"

No, would mean he risked Lucas thinking of him as a wimp. Yes, could get him in big trouble. He didn't intend to tell Abbot Jacob.

"I can."

"We can go to PJ's. He won't mind. I do that all the time. Get your stuff."

PJ couldn't be that bad if he let Lucas call after midnight.

"It's kind of late," Paul said.

"Nah, no big thing," Lucas said, leaving a note for his mother on the milk carton, which was now empty.

Paul wondered if he should call the monastery. Everyone would be asleep, and he would get the monk on telephone duty. Would they even remember in the morning to inform the Abbot of his change of plans?

PJ's wasn't far from the apartments where Lucas lived. Paul thought it was close to St. George's church because he could see the tall brick entrance. Paul was grateful Lucas knew where he was going. The temperature was dropping, and snowflakes fell. *Don't worry*, he thought, trying to calm his conscience. *You're not breaking any rules since now there will be an adult present.*

They clomped up the steps onto the porch of a small cottage. The porch light was off, and the house was dark. Apprehension filled Paul. Lucas opened the screen and banged loudly on the wooden door. A deep bark shattered the silence. They waited. Paul's fingers felt stiff in his pockets. Lucas rapped again. A light turned on inside, a warm yellowish glow spilled through the window. The porch light broke the darkness. A lock clicked, and the door opened.

A yellow lab yipped and thumped its tail against the doorjamb.

"Damn. Took you long enough," Lucas said, pushing his way past the pajama-clad man.

"It's the middle of the night. Decent people are asleep," PJ said.

Paul stood frozen. PJ. Pius James. Father Pius. He was an idiot. No, no, no. Not spending the night here.

"Mom's at work. Can we spend the night? He can't unless we have an adult. I really don't want to drive him home. I'm kind of tired from winning the game. We won twenty-one to seven."

"Yes, I was there."

Lucas dropped his backpack on the sofa, hung his coat up on the coat rack, kicked off his boots, and made his way to the kitchen, turning on lights as he went. Paul wondered how often Lucas came here to be so comfortable. The lab followed him into the kitchen and then turned, heading to Paul. The cold nose sniffed his pant leg and then his hand. Paul tentatively scratched the top of its bony head. Paul's mind raced for a graceful way out of this overnighter.

"Oh, Paul, this is PJ. PJ, this is Paul. And that is Gato," Lucas said before he disappeared into the kitchen. "Really carrot sticks? Don't you have any good snacks?"

Neither Paul nor Pius said anything. Gato licked Paul's fingers.

"Don't you think you need permission before raiding my fridge? I believe you know where the good stuff is," Pius said as he closed the front door and walked toward the kitchen. "How can you be hungry?"

"Dinner was hours ago." Lucas stuck his head out of the kitchen. "Yeah, I'm aware gato means cat. I wanted a pet. A cat, but PJ got a dog. He calls her Champ, but I named her Gato. Do you want pretzels or chips?"

Paul took his coat off and hung it up, setting his boots by the door. Crap. This was not what he expected. Gato ran circles around him as he made his way to the kitchen. Pius had a dog. One that Lucas had named. Pius got a dog apparently for Lucas.

Lucas opened two bags of chips. Pius produced a bowl. Lucas babbled on about the game. Paul watched in silence as the two talked. Gato stood, tail thumping Paul's leg. They obviously knew each other well.

"Paul, you tired? Do you want to play Nintendo or watch something on the tube?"

"I have little skill at those games," Paul said.

"No problemo, we can play Gauntlet, it's a multiplayer game, and PJ can even play."

Paul followed Lucas into a large room that held a pool table and a leather sofa. Paul rubbed his stocking foot on the Persian rug as he sat in the leather recliner.

Pius grunted. "It's late."

Lucas ignored the gentle reminder that Paul caught and grabbed the game controllers, untangling the cords and moving the chair closer to the console.

Paul's aim was off and often the game announced, "Blue Valkyrie shot the food." When his character died, Paul plotted an exit. Call for a ride home. Call Charlie, maybe she would forgive him on the spot and rescue him. No, that wouldn't work. Call my godparents. Stop being a wimp. He could hear Alcuin's nasal voice. Paul looked at Pius. There was graying around his temples. He is old. Gato licked the salty residue off Paul's fingers. Did the Abbot know about the dog?

"PJ says it's bedtime," Lucas said with a yawn. Paul followed him to the back bedroom. The room was spacious, monastic woolen blankets, that Paul recognized from their color and pattern, covered the twin beds. There was a desk and two nightstands with reading lamps.

Paul lay in the dark, listening to the soft snores of Lucas, slow and even. He listened to Pius in the kitchen cleaning up and Gato's paws clicking on the wooden floor.

The door to the bedroom opened, and Paul held his breath. The light from the hall silhouetted Pius on the wall. He stooped to pick up the discarded sweater, folding it and placing it on the desk. Paul watched as the man pulled the blanket over Lucas. When Pius turned and took a step toward his bed, Paul closed his eyes, trying to release his breath slowly and evenly as if he were asleep. Pius crack his knuckles and with each snap, Paul shivered. He hoped Pius did not see his trembling. Nothing moved, not covers or clothes. The bedroom door latch shut, and Paul opened his eyes and grabbed his aching stomach.

Sleep did not come. He reached for his backpack and fished for his jeans. He sat on the edge of the bed. Thoughts of when he was eight filled his mind. A dark nervousness danced within. Pius only hit him when he was mad or when he thought Paul was being bad. He had done nothing to piss the man off, yet his stomach churned. In the darkness, Paul struggled for air. He needed to get out.

Paul opened the door to the bedroom and stepped into the hall. No glow under any of the doors. Gato appeared from nowhere and pushed the door open. Paul caught it before it banged into the wall and hoped the ever-thumping drumbeat of the dog's tail didn't wake the others. Turning to the left, he saw a light coming from the kitchen. Crap. Paul stood frozen, listening. There were no sounds. He made his way down the hall. Gato followed him like a shadow. Once inside the kitchen, he sat and stared at the harvest gold phone on the wall. He could sit there until morning. Lucas would want breakfast here. Double crap. Pius could try to poison him. Only Pius was acting nice. That made no sense. Paul wished they had stayed at the apartments.

Paul found the phone and dialed the monastery, knowing he

was waking someone up. The ringing sounded like an alarm, and Paul pressed the earpiece to his head. Five, six, seven. A sleepy voice answered, "Hello."

"Hey, sorry to wake you," Paul said, his voice low and crackly. "This is Paul. I need to come home. Can you send someone to get me?"

The voice became clearer. "What?"

"This is Paul. I need a ride home now. I'm at St. George's."

"It's almost three in the morning. Go to bed," the nasal voice said.

Alcuin. Of all the luck. The line died. Paul redialed. One, two rings.

"No."

Before Paul could beg, he heard the distinct click. Anger washed over Paul.

Gato cocked his head, brown eyes solemn. Paul dialed a third time and received a busy signal, telling him the phone was off the hook. Now nobody could call the monastery directly. Alcuin is going to die. Paul stood in front of the sink, his body quaking inside.

One thought only consumed Paul's mind. Home. He had memorized two numbers, his own and Father Joe's. Joannicus wasn't home. He dialed it anyway and let it ring. He pulled a chair close to the phone and sat holding the receiver hard against his ear, hoping that nobody would wake up and ask him what he was doing. Gato sat next to him and then, in defeat, slumped to the floor.

PAUL SAT on the porch in the dark. His nose dripped and his fingers were numb. Snow covered his boots as it blew up onto the porch. Someone was coming. Ambrose. He had answered the phone in

Joe's room and said four words. The sweetest words ever spoken, "Hold on, I'm coming." Ambrose was coming. Paul figured the snow was hindering the travel time, but he prayed they would head home soon.

What to tell Lucas? He had left a note on the kitchen table saying he was ill and sorry before he had locked himself out of the house. Now he wished he hadn't been so hasty in his departure. The snow had stopped for now. The moon appeared luminous, making the flakes glisten with a hard crust competing with the starry sky.

As Paul shivered, a light from inside spilled across the porch. Someone was up. He scooted to the shadowy end of the bench. Even if they found the note, perhaps they would think he was already home. The porch light turned on and the front door opened. Gato yipped and trotted out to him, tail wagging furiously.

Traitor.

"Get in here before you freeze to death," Pius said, holding the door open as he stood inside pulling his bathrobe tighter around himself.

"I'm okay. Ambrose is coming," Paul said, teeth chattering.

"I don't care. You can't sit out there."

"He will be here any minute," Paul said, wishing for a car to arrive.

"No, get inside," Pius said, his voice turning cold and harsh.

Paul's stomach clinched. He rose stiff and frozen.

Headlights appeared in the street as he stepped into the open door. The warmth of the room grabbed him and his vision narrowing as he stumbled to the window. Please be Ambrose.

"What are you doing outside?" Pius asked.

"I'm sick. I want to go home," Paul said, fearful that he sounded like a whiny eight-year-old. The same whiny eight-year-old who had displeased Pius that he had an overwhelming desire to beat him.

Car doors slammed and Paul felt giddy.

Pius opened the front door. Paul heard crunching snow as Ambrose appeared, followed by Abbot Jacob.

"Morning Pius," Ambrose said.

"Ambrose, Abbot Jacob. I would have driven him home, had he asked," Pius said.

Happy to dump my body in some ravine, thought Paul.

"Do you want some coffee? Freshly brewed?"

"That would be wonderful," Jacob said, eyeing Paul.

Pius headed to the kitchen.

Paul felt his body and emotion thawing. He blinked hard, holding back tears.

Ambrose stood in front of Paul.

"Stupid boy," Ambrose said in a tender voice as he pulled Paul into a hug that smelled of barn and tobacco. "You okay?"

"I'm good."

Gato yipped for her turn, and Ambrose ruffled the dog's fur.

Paul followed Ambrose to the car and noticed that Abbot Jacob was not returning to the monastery with them.

"Why is Abbot Jacob staying here?" Paul asked. "He didn't hurt me."

"We know that," Ambrose said. "It's Church stuff."

Paul hated it when they acted as if he were a child. "I can understand adult things," he muttered, crossing his arms.

Ambrose looked at him and grunted. "Fine, Lucas is sleeping there. A priest should not be alone with a young boy. There are issues with some priest causing the rafters to shake the Holy See."

That made no sense to Paul, but he didn't ask for clarification.

"You are alone with me," Paul said, turning up the heater.

"Yeah, I have been alone with you all your life. I will not hurt you."

"Pius will not hurt Lucas. Pius likes Lucas a lot. They are friends."

"Nevertheless, to prevent scandal, Abbot Jacob is staying."

Pressing his fingers over the vents, Paul let the warm air singe his fingers. Jacob protecting Pius, that's a twist.

"What's he protecting Pius from?"

"The public, we know Pius will not hurt Lucas. We just don't want anyone making accusations about inappropriate behavior."

Does he mean sexually, like Reginald was saying about Charlie? This was making no sense. Paul yawned.

THE SUN SHONE brightly in Paul's cell as he squinted and rose from his bed. Hunger grabbed him hard, so he made his way to the community room.

Paul grabbed an apple and a muffin, then walked to the Abbot's office. As he entered, Brother Alcuin pushed past him.

"Sorry about last night," Alcuin muttered.

Paul shrugged his shoulder. Things had worked out.

"Did you yell at him?" Paul asked, hoping that at the very least scolded him.

"That is none of your business, but I spoke to him about phone duty and my expectations. Lucas called and asked if you will attend confirmation class this afternoon?"

Paul wanted to, but he felt conflicted.

"Did you see Pius has a dog?"

"Yes, I saw that."

"You're the abbot. You didn't know," Paul said, feeling a nagging confusion. Why did that bother him so much? "Why did you stay? Why are you now protecting Pius?" Paul asked, sitting in a chair. His feet now touched the floor.

"I was not protecting. I was preventing. Besides, it is my job to take care of the monks."

"Seems like everyone protects him," Paul said, biting into the apple.

Jacob stretched his arms and shoulders.

"So, what was going on last night?"

Paul swallowed. The apple chunks scrapped in his throat.

"I didn't feel good."

"You know I have a little experience in this matter. That was more than a tummy ache."

"Yeah, I heard," Paul said, remembering that Jacob and his stepfather had history and whispers of physical abuse.

"You can always go back to counseling."

"Go back?" Paul crossed his legs. "I have never gone to counseling."

The monks, Abbot Gordon, and Father Joannicus never pushed or pried, so the topic lay like a dead elephant in the yard.

Jacob stood and moved to the chair opposite of Paul. "I told Abbot Gordon to get you counseling, after I left."

"I told Abbot Gordon no thanks."

He gently kicked Paul's dangling foot. "So, what happened?"

You should have stayed here years ago, thought Paul. But he couldn't say that and risk Jacob turning away. Not with Charlie and Joannicus absent. Jacob was the only one with power on his side.

"I really don't know what happened. I don't like Father Pius. I don't understand why Lucas does."

Paul finished the apple.

Jacob leaned over and handed Paul a tissue for the core.

"Father Pius gets along better with older kids. He tolerates the younger ones."

Tolerates. Paul slumped in the chair and placed the core on the desk.

"Why be friends with Ambrose? He is loud, smelly, rude, and barely controls his opinions," Jacob said.

"That's why I like him," Paul said, peeling the paper off the muffin. "And that's not nice."

Jacob sighed heavily. "I like him too. One gets to pick their friends. You could try counseling. It might help."

Paul sat up and moved the chair back. "You want me to discuss Father Pius with a shrink? You're crazy. No. I don't want to talk about the past."

However, even as Paul spoke those words, images of Pius came back to him. The hissing, mean words uttered in his ear. The fear, the stomachaches, the burning anger when he would see Pius. Jacob might have prevented the physical abuse but not to the intimidation. Sadness crept into Paul like a mist on a gray day, soft yet soaking.

"It is better for you to remember. Do you want to spend the rest of your life avoiding Father Pius?"

"PJ," Paul corrected, with venom in his voice. "Montana is a big state."

Paul reached for the muffin on the desk and smashed it into a pancake. The smell of cinnamon and brown sugar filled his nose and left his hand sticky.

"I don't want to remember."

"You already do."

Paul gazed at the flattened muffin. He had wanted to eat that.

"I don't want to spend hours picking it apart. Let's move on."

Paul realized he didn't know how to make that happen. When

he was little, Joannicus would always explain things, making the path clear.

"To move into the future, sometimes the past needs to be relived. I will be there with you."

"Did you go to counseling?" Paul asked

"No. I should have because I carried the anger around. That is not healthy."

Paul shook his head. He was not going to a shrink.

"I am here if you need me," Jacob said.

"You won't run away like you did last time." Paul knew what he was saying was mean and spiteful. He watched the hurt tighten Jacob's face.

"That is a perfect example of bottled up anger. I should not have left that day. I confronted Pius and spilled the secret. But I was angry about my abuse that I could not see clearly. I am sorry I left you."

Paul shrugged his shoulders. "I want to talk to Father Joannicus."

Jacob stood, grabbed the trash can, and swept the muffin and core into the bin.

"Get me a cup of coffee, and I will have Joannicus on the phone."

CHAPTER 23
PJ

Psalm 4:9
I will lie down in peace and sleep comes at once
for you alone, Lord, make me dwell in safety.

Saturday afternoon came and Paul sat in the car, his palms sweaty. Snow had fallen. There were large snow-drifts along the highway creating a half tunnel for them to drive through, as he and Abbot Jacob made their way back to St. George Parish for confirmation class and youth group.

"You don't have to stay," Paul said, wondering if Joannicus had insisted that Jacob shadow him.

"I know."

"So, are you staying?"

"Yes."

"I don't need protection," Paul said, shrugging his shoulders. "But it's okay if you stay."

"You sure of that?" Jacob said, drumming his fingers on the steering wheel.

The wipers on the car squeaked as they cleared the windshield of floppy flakes. Embarrassment crept in. He should have figured out that PJ was Pius. Paul still had trouble blending Father Pius with the man Lucas loved.

Joe's advice said, "Father Pius isn't the same man you encountered when you were eight. You are not the same person. You don't have to like him, just be respectful. I understand that's hard, considering the past."

Hard hadn't even described the confusion. Joannicus had given Paul something to ponder when he reminded Paul that his friendship was with Lucas, not Pius. But could he be friends with Lucas and avoid Pius?

"Pius can't hurt me," Paul said, trying to shake the dread that had settled in his gut.

"Are you telling me or yourself?" Abbot Jacob asked.

"Father Joannicus doesn't sound well," Paul said, hoping to focus on something other than his fear.

"He is fine. It is winter, and he always gets a winter cold. We are talking about Pius and you."

Paul let his breath fog the window as he drew dots and connected them.

"Yeah, I know." But something isn't right there either.

For the second time today, they approached the parish hall. Snowballs whizzed by as snow crunched underfoot. Lucas ran past, ruddy-cheeked from the cold, and skidded to a stop.

"Sorry you got sick. You look okay now. Too much junk food. I keep forgetting that you don't eat that kind of stuff."

"I'm okay," Paul said, as his stomach churned.

Lucas and Paul found seats with those taking part in confirmation instruction. Conversation withered away as Father Pius and a woman entered the room.

Crap. He's teaching this class. Paul looked at Jacob, realizing that the Abbot knew Pius would be teaching.

A cloud of despair settled around Paul, and like the snowfall, weighed heavily upon him. Paul heard the lesson, but the words, like raindrops, just dripped around him.

"You, okay?" Lucas asked during a break.

"I don't know," Paul said, as they moved toward the snack table.

"Sometimes you're very difficult to understand, Warner, but PJ says not to give up on you. He thinks you're a beneficial influence on me," Lucas said with a laugh.

"If it makes you feel any better, I don't always understand you."

Lucas hooked his thumbs in his belt loops. "What's there to understand? I'm a pretty straight shooter."

"Why do you like PJ?" Paul said, as he took a potato chip from the yellow plastic bowl.

Lucas turned and faced Paul. "He's been there for me. Everyone needs a dad figure, kind of like the monks are dads to you."

Paul nibbled on a chip. The edges felt like glass as he swallowed. No. That's where he's mistaken. The monks, mostly, are compassionate, and treat me with fairness. The one he calls dad, did not.

"If it wasn't for him, I'd have gone to foster care. He made it so Mom and I had a place to stay until she could afford our apartment."

"How old were you?"

"About ten. That was when my dad tried to take me to Mexico. PJ helped my mom get me back. PJ made sure I wasn't alone."

The age of a young Lucas resounded like a train through Paul. This was unbelievable. Pius treating some other kid with kindness while treating him like a street urchin.

Lucas filled a plastic cup with chips. "I don't know who he talked to, but they spared me the system."

Paul figured it was Ms. Carr, the social worker who placed him, and refused to trust the monks. The aroma of the greasy chips made Paul nauseous.

"We would have been homeless if it weren't for PJ arranging places for us to stay. I owe him. I was confused and angry, but he whipped me into shape."

Paul's head was spinning. "He hurt you?"

Lucas stuffed potato chips into his mouth. "No. He's strict, sort of like that abbot guy."

The story barely made sense. Paul's body went rigid. Keep it together.

"I can tell you don't like PJ. He said as much," Lucas said, interrupting Paul's confusion.

Stop, cautioned an inner voice within Paul's head. "Did he tell you why?"

"Not really my business. He's my friend and so are you."

Paul watched Abbot Jacob and Father Pius talking from across the room. They smiled and laughed. Irritation, like a bug bite on a scorching afternoon, itched at Paul's composure. The world had gone mad. They were acting like friends. Pius and Jacob were not friends.

Paul frowned. "He isn't who you think he is."

"He is my friend. He isn't one of your monastery dwellers. He has been a parish monk. He's a good guy."

"No, he isn't," Paul said, his jaw tensing.

Lucas shook his head as if he were dealing with a little kid. "What did he tell the Abbot you were sneaking out?"

Paul stood with a half-eaten chip in his hand.

"He hurt me."

Lucas stopped smiling. "What do you mean, he hurt you? You don't mean. You had better not mean, cuz if you're not saying he's one of those priests in the back with altar boys, you are a liar. He would never do that."

"No, not that. He didn't do that."

Lucas's hands clenched and unclenched. "Then what? How did he hurt you?"

This was not going well. "Ask him."

"No, you tell me," Lucas hissed. His barbeque chip breath lingered between them. "Or are you just saying things, hoping I won't like him anymore? I don't like rumors or gossip."

Paul felt his skin getting hot.

"He didn't tell you the whole truth," Paul said, the words tumbling out of his mouth like rolled dice.

"You're pushing things. PJ doesn't lie. He is a priest, dude. A real priest."

So what? They were people, just people. What did Lucas think they were?

Lucas took a step into Paul's space. Paul backed up, and Lucas advanced until the wall held him flat. Over Lucas's shoulder, Paul watched Pius and Jacob move in tandem toward them.

"He lied to the Abbot about hurting me."

The look of disbelief on his friend's face became unbearable.

Father Pius placed a firm hand on the shoulder of Lucas. Paul could see the anger directed at him.

"Watch yourself, Warner."

Paul turned toward Abbot Jacob.

"What was that about?" Abbot Jacob asked.

"Nothing. I want to go home now."

"Class is not over—"

"I don't feel good," Paul said, interrupting Jacob and heading to the exit.

AT SCHOOL ON THURSDAY, Paul sat opposite Fred, a pimply faced boy who read a novel as he ate his lunch. Paul picked at his sandwich. Charlie slipped in next to Fred. The boy swooshed his lunch into his paper bag and left.

"What have I told you about scaring the kids?" Paul said, trying hard not to smile at her. Today she wore black lipstick and a dog collar. They had hardly spoken since the black eye incident.

Charlie rolled her eyes. "What have I told you about letting the big kids take your lunch money?" Charlie said, pointing at his nearly empty lunch tray.

Paul normally didn't buy lunch, but Lucas did. He hoped they could see each other and talk. That didn't happen, and Paul couldn't afford a full lunch with the pocket change he had. He took a seat at the table closest to the exit door. The table reserved for the misfits or outcasts. Paul realized that his so-called friends were just friends because of Lucas.

Charlie handed Paul half of her peanut butter and grape jelly sandwich.

"Say you're sorry, and then you can tell me what happened between you and Jockstrap. You know, Warner, you can't afford to offend everyone. You don't have that many friends."

Offend. Is that what he had done? Say you're sorry. Forgiveness. Was it that simple?

"Sorry," Paul said. "And thanks for the confidence building insight about my friends."

"Yeah, well, the truth hurts. I'm sorry too," Charlie said, leaning forward in a conspiratorial way. "Confess, choir boy."

The words poured out like a boiling kettle. "This guy, PJ, is his friend. But he's really a jerk. Lucas thinks the sun and moon rise and set by him. I can't stand PJ."

Charlie snorted. "Did you think he would join forces against this guy? Lucas is a team player, not a one-man band."

Paul poked his finger into the soft bread of the sandwich. "I wanted him to see the guy isn't great."

"If I told you that Jonas guy was involved with college girls, would you believe me?"

Paul shook his head. "His name is Joannicus, and no, I wouldn't."

"Whatever. I've yet to meet him, so I don't know if he's real or your fantasy dad. You are jealous."

"I am not."

"Okay fine. You don't have to hang with PJ."

"Good, I don't want to," Paul snapped, folding the sandwich.

"Geez, maybe you should figure out why PJ bugs you so much."

"I know why." Paul smashed the bread, turning it purple.

She leaned forward, waiting for him to continue.

"Fine. He abused me."

She leaned back and crossed her arms. "I don't want sordid details, but you don't just say that. Abuse is a big topic. I'm not defending him. But of course, he is pissed. It's his mentor. He has to stick up for him."

Paul found his mouth dry and took a sip of his milk. He had never said the words aloud to anyone and they seem to cling to him like woodruff seeds.

"PJ hit me, left bruises."

Charlie placed her elbows on the table and cupped her chin,

her hot-pink fingernails clashing with her black lipstick and fluo-rescent-green eye shadow.

"Perhaps if you told it like that. But if he admires the guy, then probably not. It is hard for people to see flaws in their heroes."

Paul felt drained, as if he had played a grueling soccer match and lost. The abuse still hurt. Paul looked away. He watched Lucas from across the room, shooting lunch bags into the trash, as the jocks and jockettes cheered him on. He missed Lucas.

"Sorry about the abuse..." Charlie's voice trailed off. She picked at her thumbnail. "Want a distraction? Sure, you do." She dug in her camouflage satchel, producing an official-looking document. An application for a death certificate and she had filled it out.

"I need your signature and money when you get a chance," Charlie said, as she bit her carrot with a loud crunch.

"What the heck is this?"

"We are getting your mom's death certificate, unless you think the monks have it?"

"They probably do, but where?"

"Don't they keep records?"

"Yeah, but I will not break into the Abbot's office and search," Paul said. He was sure it was in the locked cabinet.

"I thought not. We have to get one for ourselves."

"Why?" Paul flattening the form. She had everything filled in correctly. "How did you know her birth date?"

"It's carved in stone. Honestly, Warner, sometimes I question your IQ. I asked the librarian where to get records and she told me. Death certificates have parent's names and birthplaces on them. Once we have that, it leads to more information. Unless you know who your grandparents are?"

"No, I don't. How does that lead me to my father?"

Charlie rolled her eyes. "Family tree, you put families together and we will find yours. It's called genealogy. There could be a whole family just waiting to meet you."

Oh, joy, more people who wouldn't want to hang around him.

The lunchroom was nearly empty as the kitchen crew with squeaky carts came to wipe off the tables.

"Don't look so gloomy. This is fun," Charlie said.

"How long will it take?" Paul asked, wondering why this was fun.

"Probably a few weeks. The records are probably in a box in a dusty basement and some nearly blind clerk must spend hours rolling through microfiche tape to find which box they are in. God, what a job, gives me a chill just thinking about it."

Paul frowned. The idea of crawling around dusty basements did not sound like fun. A trickle of excitement splashed off her. It was a mystery. He would be with Charlie. Perhaps it would be fun. Even if he'd rather be searching for lost treasure instead of musty papers.

The football game was on Friday. Lucas had invited him before... Now Paul wasn't sure he should go. Paul wished Joannicus were home. He really needed to talk to him. This best friend thing was getting complicated.

Paul would have preferred to build his emotional brick wall higher and forget the events that involved PJ. If only those events would stay in the land of forgotten moments. They wouldn't stay buried, and haunted his dreams, making the nights short. Counseling won't help with sleep, Paul thought.

At home, Paul tried to study. Was Charlie right? Was he jealous? PJ didn't bug him until he learned it was Pius.

Paul was thankful that Charlie was speaking to him again, but she would soon deliver news about his family. Would they discover who his grandparents were? Who his biological father was? Lucas's tale of his father didn't make Paul eager to find his own.

"I'm not a baby. I can deal with this," Paul said aloud as he closed his trigonometry book with a thud. Formulas and numbers blurred in his mind. Paul climbed into bed, switched off the light, and closed his eyes.

Wrestling with the twisted bed sheets, heart thumping, Paul struggled to get out of bed.

Bad dream. Go away.

His battered white tiger sat on the desk next to the window, his green eyes looking expectantly at him.

"Fine guard you are," he said to the beloved stuffed animal from childhood. Tiger was the last gift his mother had given him. He picked up the ragged animal and put it to his nose. The smell of her was gone. He placed Tiger back on the desk and patted his floppy head. Paul searched his desk for a dream catcher. He hung up three by his bed, and more next to his window.

The pipes in the radiator hissed and popped, reminding him of knuckles snapping—Pius's knuckles. Paul turned on the light as he paced his room. Memories of Pius seemed more real tonight than the previous nights. Even with the lights on, the memories refused to retreat to their hiding places.

"Go away," Paul said as he closed the curtains to his cell. "You can't frighten me anymore."

Moments later, Paul opened the curtains. The room seemed claustrophobic. Time to go. He opened the door to his cell.

"Jesus Christ," Paul yelled, grabbing the closest thing to him: Tiger.

"Ah, no," Abbot Jacob said, standing in the doorway, looking disheveled, with his long hair hanging loose. "You going to defend yourself with that poor old thing?"

Paul dropped Tiger back on the desk, even though it felt better to hold the soft, misshapen animal.

"Cannot sleep? How about a late-night snack before you wake the entire floor with your exorcism?"

Then he was gone. Paul wondered if he was still dreaming. He stepped into the hall and jumped when loud snoring interrupted the silence. He rushed down the hall and stairs to the community room. The fireplace glowed warmly, and Jacob stood in his bathrobe.

"You alright?" Jacob asked, his voice calm but sleepy.

"Yeah, I'm fine," Paul said, moving to the sofa, grabbing a woolen blanket as he went.

"Irish coffee, cocoa?" Jacob asked.

"Coffee?" Paul pinched himself. The real Abbot Jacob would not offer him alcohol-filled coffee and coffee at this time of night would not induce sleep. The pinch hurt. He was awake.

"Cocoa. What are you doing up?"

"Brother Mellitus told me to wake up," Abbot Jacob said. "Seem we both have ghostly visitors."

Paul had to believe him, even if the idea of Brother Mellitus rising from the dead early was preposterous. Brother Mellitus, Merlin, the name Paul had called the ancient monk, had powers and influence beyond the grave. Paul was sure he had influenced the vote that made Jacob abbot.

Jacob brought two mugs to the sofa, placing them on the table before he sat down next to Paul.

"Father Pius isn't here."

"You sure? He could have arrived after prayers. I swear I saw him outside my window." Paul realized how silly that sounded because he was on the third floor of the monastery and nobody but perhaps Jesus or Mary would float outside of his window. "I woke you up, didn't I?"

"Last night, but not tonight. Mellitus did," Jacob said, sipping his coffee.

Paul stared at the fire, which danced and crackled.

"You got a lot on your mind. Want to talk about it?"

"I thought I did. Joannicus just said to give Pius a chance. I don't want to, but now Lucas is pissed at me. I didn't say that Pius is a bad person. Just that he was bad to me. Why is he mad at me? I just told the truth. Charlie wants to research my mom, so she is looking for ancestors and shit. I really don't care, but she does. I'm going to fail in trigonometry."

"I see," Jacob said.

Paul leaned back on the sofa, against Jacob's shoulder.

"I don't get this friendship stuff. Brother Ambrose is right. Animals are easier to get along with."

Jacob laughed. "I do not have answers for you."

"No, I'm not going to counseling," Paul said. He had heard the tales of sitting with a stranger, and them wanting to know your deepest, darkest secrets.

What could change talking about Pius and his mean streak? He had stopped hitting Paul eons ago. They had come to a quiet peace. Paul steered clear of him when he was at the monastery. There were other monks to hang with.

He didn't like all the monks. He didn't like Alcuin, *mostly* because he's a self-righteous idiot.

Paul inhaled. Jacob smelled faintly of sweet grass and bee's wax.

"As you wish."

"You just want a good night's sleep," Paul said with a yawn, sleep pulling his eyelid closed. "Besides, this is working for me."

Jacob chuckled, a soft chuckle, and pulled the blanket around them as the firelight bathed the room in soft shadows and Paul drifted off to sleep.

CHAPTER 24
NIGHT OUT

Psalm 87: 9
You have taken away my friends
and made me hateful in their sight

Paul didn't have the guts to tell anyone there wasn't a
reason to attend football games anymore, so Brother
Reginald had driven him to the game. Students grouped
together, climbing the bleachers. The group that Paul usually sat
with was not speaking to him. At least, that was how he perceived
their behavior. He approached them in the school hallway, the
hiss of "Watch yourself, Warner," echoed around him. The
spreading out at a nearly empty table at lunch made Paul aware
that they were never his friends, and he was not welcome without
Lucas.

That is probably what Charlie meant when she told him he

didn't have many friends. Paul found a group of kids he knew, and sat with them, wishing that Charlie attended games. She did not. The small group nodded when Paul joined them, and with note-books opened began quizzing each other on the upcoming chemistry test.

Paul pulled his hood tighter around his head and opened his novel. The band played, and the football game began. Lucas hadn't spoken to him since the discussion of PJ. Paul wondered if they would ever speak again.

Just before halftime, students started moving to the concession stands. Paul scooted to the end of the row to avoid being jostled. Someone sat down next to him and instantly wished he had not come.

"Hey, PJ," a petite blonde called. "Is it too late to volunteer for the harvest festival? I could run the cakewalk."

Paul rolled his eyes.

"Edith, that would be wonderful. Thanks for volunteering. See me tomorrow at youth group, and I'll get you signed up."

Apparently, PJ knew many kids and was popular and well liked. Paul heard he was an involved priest, one who knew his parish and parishioners, but he could not accept that the youth liked him.

"Lucas said you would be here. I figured you wouldn't show."

Fooled you.

Paul opened his book, wondering how Lucas knew he was there.

"You and Lucas are still not talking? You don't like football, so why are you here?"

"Free country," Paul muttered. Big-mouthed monks, telling Pius everything.

Paul opened his book, trying to focus on the words before him, hoping that Father Pius would see that he wasn't interested in talking. Why does anyone like this man? He is so bossy with his black-and-white approach.

"What are you reading?" Pius asked, tucking a monastic woolen blanket around his legs. Paul recognized the color and pattern, earthy browns, and berry purple.

"A book," Paul said. And he is nosey.

"I can see that. Does it have a title?"

"Yes."

Father Pius waited. The man was insufferable.

"*Remnant* by J. Ryding."

"I figured you would read something about the tombs of Coba or Sutton Hoo."

"I prefer anthropology over archeology," Paul said. This wasn't entirely true, he preferred dead civilizations. The mystery of what happened to them captured his imagination. Pius didn't need to know that.

Father Pius sighed. "What's this book about?"

"A boy who finds a key that makes it possible to travel between this world and the next. Yes, Father Joannicus knows I'm reading it. Well, he would if he were home, but Abbot Jacob knows."

Why couldn't Pius take a hint and leave?

"Fantasy," Pius said. "Are there dragons to help him?"

Oh, for crying out loud, go away.

"No, he's searching for answers about his dead mother. His uncle is a jerk, so he is on his own. He can travel to different dimensions. He just found out others can travel between places when he is on the whisper streets."

Paul looked for the sneer but found only concern. Did Pius think it was a story reflecting Paul's hidden desire to find his father? Disgusted, Paul turned away as best he could on the narrow bench. He wasn't searching for or missing his father. Charlie was.

"I prefer hardcore crime novels," Pius said.

Of course, you do. Your fantasy.

"I'm reading *The Other Side of the River* by Hal Dagart. It's about a mob boss. A guy you love to hate. A guy who seems to develop a conscience."

That's just how I feel about you. Ask me if I care? I don't, and you don't have a soft underside, thought Paul.

"I figured you were into St. Teresa of Avila or John of the Cross."

Pius laughed. Paul hadn't been trying to be funny. He had tried to pick the most sadistic religious books he could think of.

"I was conversing about reading for pleasure, not edification."

The game continued. Paul glanced up from time to time. Shouts rose and groans emitted as the team scored or fumbled.

"You don't like football, do you?"

Paul pulled his frozen hand into his sleeve. "How can you tell?"

"Be kind," Joannicus whispered in Paul's mind.

"If you don't like it, why do you keep coming to the games?"

"I came because Lucas likes the game and plays," Paul said, watching the cheerleaders bouncing in unison, pom-poms flashing color.

"That's nice of you. I'm going for refreshments. Do you want anything?"

"No, thank you." Paul said, wondering if he should leave or move so Pius would leave him alone for the second half of the game.

The third quarter started, and no Pius. The aroma of the fries and burgers made Paul's stomach growl.

"I got you something, anyway," Pius said, offering Paul a hotdog.

"Thanks," Paul said, wishing the food didn't smell so inviting and wondering if he had put ketchup or mustard on the hotdog.

"How much do I owe you? I have money." Paul took the hotdog and saw that it had cheese and onions on it. That was the way he like it. Creepy that Pius knew this.

"It's all right, it's my treat. I'm glad Lucas has a friend that isn't an athlete," Pius said, biting into his hotdog.

He was athletic. He could dribble a ball.

"He has you." Paul swallowed the ball of meat and bread, regretting the words that seemed to tumble out of his mouth.

The wooden bleachers bounced as people moved in and around them. Father Pius raised his eyes and Paul looked away.

"Are you jealous?" Pius asked, wiping his face with his napkin.

Anger seeped into Paul. He was not jealous.

"Hell no. I don't like you, and I don't understand why Lucas likes you."

The band announced the return of the teams to the field.

Father Pius wiped his face with a napkin. "Why do you like Father Joannicus?"

Paul looked at Pius. Was the man stupid? He had to be. Joannicus was loving, he listened, and was calm, prayerful, and Pius knew this.

"I don't know," Paul said. "You're nothing like Joannicus other than you are both monks."

Pius cracked his knuckle. "Why do you always make things difficult? Lucas and I just like each other."

Paul shrugged his shoulders while his spine stiffened. He took a bite of hotdog and chewed slowly.

The game continued and Paul quietly glanced at the man beside him, who cheered and groaned with the crowd.

In between the action on the field, Pius turned to Paul. "Lucas mentioned that you and he had a fight about me, and that you were avoiding him. I told him that the history is ours, not his, and that he should try to understand your feelings."

"I don't care what you told him," Paul said, thinking that Lucas obviously hadn't learned the truth. "He's free to do whatever he wants. He can be your friend. I don't really care."

Pius smiled thinly and cracked his knuckles. "No, you care. Give Lucas some time. He's a bright young man. If you want a friendship, don't shut him out."

The sound made Paul shiver and his gut hurt. Shut him out? Lucas was avoiding him.

Father Pius stood gathering his blanket and trash. Paul summoned all the courage he could muster.

"I told him the truth about you, something you seem to have forgotten. I was a kid and what you did was wrong. Very wrong."

"You're right."

Paul almost fell off the bleacher's seat. "That's it? That's your apology for hurting me?"

"Yes, I'm sorry that it happened. I didn't intend for it to go that far."

The apology was an admission of sorts. Yet, that didn't erase the ache as Paul had imagined it would.

"Okay, but I don't understand how come you didn't beat Lucas? Were you in love with his mother? Is he your kid?"

"Honestly, Paul, I don't know where you come up with these ideas. They were people who needed me. So, I helped."

He hadn't needed Pius. He had Joannicus. Was jealousy the reason for a beating? That was a lame excuse.

"That still doesn't explain why you hit me. Lucas was a kid too."

Pius didn't answer.

The silence burned like hot embers after the fire.

Finally, Father Pius said, "I found you abrasive."

Paul shoved his book into his pocket. Abrasive. What the hell did that mean?

"I was a kid." Paul blinked back his tears. Was he still abrasive? "I don't like you, and that will never change."

Father Pius smashed the trash into balls. "I'm not looking for forgiveness. I don't need that from you. Lucas likes us both. I will not make him chose between you and me. Are you?"

Before Paul could answer, the bleachers erupted with cheers. Lucas and his teammates made a final touchdown, and everyone roared. The intensity of the moment pulled Paul and Pius away from their discord. The bleachers shook with jumping spectators. Even Paul felt the overwhelming surge of excitement.

"Going to State," shouted the students. Paul could see Lucas shaking hands and slapping the backs of the losing team. Several teammates followed his example, putting aside the joy to acknowledge a game well played by both teams.

The students spilled out onto the field. Paul and Pius were swept along with the surging crowd. In the jostling and excitement, Paul turned to find himself next to Lucas.

"PJ, State, can you believe it?" Lucas shouted as he stepped forward and gave Pius a handclasp hug.

Lucas paused. A quick look of surprise crossed his face, then bloomed into a grin. "Hey, did you two talk it out? Excellent." The heavily armored Lucas pulled Paul into a hug.

"Sorry about the liar thing. It's just when anyone attacks my friends, I get a little crazy."

Paul accepted the apology, for he wanted to be a part of this glorious moment. Paul shook the hand, wondering if Lucas would be loyal to him.

"You're going to celebrate with us, right? Drive him to the pizza parlor, will you, PJ?"

Paul wanted to object, but he couldn't. The car was jammed with other students, mostly cheerleaders.

The pizza party ended; Paul and others piled into Lucas's truck and head off to the fields. When they arrived, the bonfire was high and bright. A metal keg glistened in the shadows as someone handed Paul a red plastic cup.

The truck bed party broke up some time after two, with stumbling youth driving in four directions. Lucas had been so drunk that he didn't even notice when Paul removed yet another half-filled bottle of beer from his hand.

"Buddy, I'm glad you're here. You're my best dude. PJ was a jerk. You don't have to be his friend, just be mine," Lucas laughed. "Sounds like a valentine greeting. Be mine."

"Gross," called another football player. "Lucas can now pass math. His brain boy is back on the team."

Lucas took a half-hearted swing at the boy. "He's not my brain, he just has one that he will share. Isn't that what the coach says? Use the tools you have available."

There wasn't a choice. Paul liked Lucas and had to admit he had missed him. The drinking had mellowed everyone out. The classmates that had snubbed him all week acted like friends. The girls fawned and cooed, draping arms around him, and sitting in his lap. Life in the shadow of Lucas wasn't so bad.

"Hey, are you any good in history?" another football player asked.

"Yeah, I guess," Paul said, thinking maybe that was what friendship was, collaborating for an end goal. He got popular and Lucas got better grades. He could hear Charlie snorting, "Sold your soul to the devil."

Once the keg was drained, someone began offering an array of mixed drinks, Kool-Aid and tequila.

Paul sat on a bale of hay, listening to the rehash of the game.

Ignoring Pius wouldn't be too hard, thought Paul. He wasn't jealous. He didn't like the guy. Pius was more abrasive than he was. Paul had heard rumors that Pius had issues with a controlling mother. He wondered how that colored PJ's life. Abbot Jacob reacted to things in his past. That was why he wouldn't let Paul drive. That is what Ambrose said.

The large fire had burned down, and the air had become bitter as several truckloads of joyous youth packed to leave.

"I need a ride home, got a curfew," announced a girl.

"The Lucas line is now departing Roberts, Pryor, Red Lodge, The Rez, and points in between, all aboard," called Lucas.

The buzz from the few drinks Paul had consumed was wearing off.

Lucas stood, offering a wobbly hand up to the truck bed for those wanting a ride. He fished out his keys and stumbled to the cab. Paul stopped him.

"Hey, let me drive?" Paul said.

"Nah," Lucas said.

"No, really, give me the keys."

"Are you telling me no?" Lucas stood, swaying.

Crap.

Paul stood tall in the dying bonfire light. "Yeah."

Apparently, Lucas was not so congenial when he was drunk.

"Give me the keys, Lucas," Paul said again, with all the bravado he could muster. Lucas, like a child, dangled them in front of Paul, making a game out of the request.

"If you drop the keys in the dark, we'd be stuck here."

Paul pushed Lucas against the door of the cab, intending to

pin the menacing arm in order to snatch the keys. The academic boy was no match for the athletic one. The group in the truck chanted like fourth graders, "Fight, fight." One pinning lead to one pushing, one dodge, and one ducking. Even with the impairing drug, Lucas was faster. Paul underestimated the punch.

Paul sat on the ground. His jaw hurt, but he had the keys.

"Sorry, man, sorry," Lucas said, falling to the ground next to Paul.

The taste of blood filled Paul's mouth as he ran his tongue over his teeth, checking for anything loose. Paul pocketed the keys as Lucas rolled on top of him, pinning him to the ground.

"I win, give me my keys," Lucas crowed with one arm raised.

"What keys," Paul said.

"You serious? Fuck." Lucas rolled off and began feeling the ground for keys. The darkness, tall grass, melted snow, and mud mixture made seeing impossible. Paul rubbed his jaw and got up, walking to the truck.

"Hey. Aren't you going to help me look for the keys?" Lucas called.

"Nope," Paul said as he climbed into the driver's side and locked the doors before starting up the engine. She looked like a heap of rusted parts, but she purred with precision. Lucas rose from his search and walked to the cab, attempted to open the door. He glared and walked around the front. Paul honked. Lucas tried the passenger side. When the door didn't open, he banged on the metal.

Paul shifted into drive and pushed the gas. Riders scrambled to climb into the moving bed as Paul made a large circle in the open field.

"You're an asshole, Warner," shouted Lucas, making a run for the truck. Paul sped up a bit as he watched Lucas trying to get in.

Eventually, Paul slowed down enough for Lucas to climb into the truck bed.

"Tunes, tunes," chanted Lucas as he pounded on the cab. Paul rolled down his window and headed down the highway, country tunes blaring from the radio.

CHAPTER 25
LISTEN

Psalm 72: 16
I strove to fathom this problem,
too hard for my mind to understand.

Abbot Jacob sat in his office, facing the window, watching the moonlight create shadows. The meteorologist had said it might snow, but the sky seemed clear. Weather reporters could not predict the weather any better than he could lead his community and monks. It was like praying for rain. Who knew the outcome? No, he didn't believe God bothered himself with those things. The Almighty had other concerns.

Someone should write an abbot handbook. He wished his most pressing problem was getting to the church on time for prayers.

Abbot Jacob turned in his leather chair when the lights in his office clicked on.

"Holy shit," Brother Ambrose exclaimed. "What the hell are you doing here?"

"It is my office," Jacob said, looking at his watch. It was after two in the morning. "What can I do for you?"

Ambrose walked to the vehicle sign-out board. "Need a car. Got a brief trip to take."

"Is Joannicus alright?" Jacob asked, fear rising fast inside him.

"Joe's great, nothing to worry about," Ambrose said as he turned to leave. "What are you doing up?"

"Could not sleep," Jacob said. Ambrose was up to something. "Stop."

The large man groaned.

"What is going on?" Jacob stood up.

"Nothing," Ambrose said to the exit door, his back to the Abbot.

"Try again," Jacob said, thinking that the man sounded like Paul, petulant. He had noticed that Paul wasn't home and wondered where the boy was.

Brother Ambrose said nothing. Jacob walked over to him and, with several tugs, took the car keys from Ambrose's hand.

"Let us go."

Ambrose muttered something under his breath. Jacob walked to the parking lot and got into the driver's side. The car tilted and rocked as Ambrose sat in the passenger's seat.

Jacob turned on the engine. "Well, where to?"

"St. George's. I really think you should reconsider this course of action," Ambrose said.

Really?

"No, I am good," Abbot Jacob said as he headed to the highway.

Silence hung like the moon, full and bright. St. George's, Pius, Lucas, Paul, nothing good, he was sure of that. He had wanted to tell Paul to pick other friends. Pius liked the boy, what wasn't there to like. Smart, athletic, and adventurous, Jacob would have said, smart aleck, jock, and dangerous. Pius had a set of terms for Paul that differed from his. He let Paul be with Lucas, but wondered if it was the right choice.

"Talk to me, Rose," Jacob said, thankful that he would not be administering the Last Rites to Joannicus.

"You will not like it," Ambrose said, reaching for the radio dial. "We're going to pick up Paul."

"Right, why?" Jacob asked over the blare of country tunes.

"He needs a ride home."

Jacob turned off the radio. "Why?"

"Pius called and said to come pick him up."

"Rose, cut the crap. What did he do now?"

"The right thing. Lucas and Paul and others," Ambrose said as he cracked the window, letting chilly air whistle into the car. "You know how it is with the young and celebrations."

"Alcohol, driving?" Jacob asked.

The car picked up speed.

"Yes, they were being teens, but they are all fine."

"For the time being," muttered Jacob, turning on the windshield wipers. They squealed because there was little precipitation. What wasn't Ambrose saying? Jacob grew steadily angrier, and his knuckles grew white, gripping the wheel. The wipers squeaked. How many times had he cautioned Paul about the influence of others? A million times. He had promised himself he was not losing another loved one to drinking and driving. Never again. "I am going to kill him."

Ambrose cleared his throat. "Not a good chant, Father Abbot."

"Oh," Jacob said, turning on the heater. "Did I say that out loud?"

"It escaped," Ambrose said. "Shall we practice listening when we first arrive?"

"I will not kill him," Jacob said, forcing his foot to ease up on the accelerator and turning off the wipers. "I have informed him of my distaste for field parties. I cannot believe he would do this."

"This was more of a victory cruise. They won the game. They are going to the championship. We should see it in that light."

"Rose, do not veil this incident with platitudes."

They arrived at St. George's, then parked the car. The lights were on in the refectory. As they walked to the porch, the door opened, and Pius appeared.

"They aren't here yet," Father Pius said. "A disgruntled mother called me upset about her son's condition. She was worried that they were driving in the same state. I knew Paul was with Lucas, so I called you guys. You got here quick."

Loud music filled the air long before the truck appeared on the street.

Jacob watched as the truck came to a stop. The music blared. The boys stood up and danced, singing off-key, as they jumped out of the truck bed. Lucas gave his hand to a girl. Paul stepped out of the driver's side.

Jacob blinked. He was told no driving.

Lucas pulled Paul to the makeshift line of four boys and a girl linked arm in arm. Buckles gleaming in the porch light, they walked in a staggering line, singing, "... so maybe we should all be praying for time."

Praying for something, thought Abbot Jacob. When did Paul get a belt buckle bigger than his pectoral cross? Focus.

A fifth boy tumbled out of the cab with a shotgun. Pius fell onto the wooden porch. Ambrose bellowed an "Oh shit." Jacob quickly moved forward off the porch. The gun fired a loud crack, thankfully pointed heavenward. Jacob reached the youth before he could recock and fire. He unloaded the rounds, wondering why they had a loaded gun in the cab, and killed the music. The boys didn't notice. The song continued without musical accompaniment. At the bottom of the steps, the group unlinked arms. Jacob made his way to Paul. Lucas stepped in front of him, placing his hand on Jacob's chest. The boys pressed in close as if in a huddle.

"Hey, big red, it's all right. No war path tonight."

The heavy sweetness of the boy's breath filled the narrow space between them.

They had indulged in more than beer.

"Back off, little man," Jacob said, placing his hands on the boy's shoulders.

"Wow, you really have freaky blue eyes," Lucas said, slurring his words. The boy wobbled and coughed. Jacob turned the swaying youth away from him and the huddle opened as Lucas stumbled and heaved on the shrub. A chain reaction occurred with projectile vomiting flying all around. Ambrose fanned the air, humming loudly.

Jacob glanced over and noticed Paul and the girl. She wrapped herself rather tightly around Paul, hands pawing and rubbing like an over-friendly cat. Father Pius stepped down off the porch.

"Amanda, inside and call your folks," Pius barked. Pius stepped closer and shrugged his shoulders. "Sorry, Jacob, she's a little... Let's just say she thinks her dream is to be a pole dancer."

"PAUL, don't forget you did nothing wrong," Lucas called, regaining some dignity.

Father Pius glared at him.

"Not terribly wrong," the boy muttered.

"Lucas, Dean, Mike, and Tim," Father Pius called. Tim had passed out in the truck bed. Brother Ambrose lumbered down the steps to rouse the youth.

"Gentlemen, to the porch and sit," Pius ordered.

"It's freezing out here," Lucas said.

"Then you best hope Miss Amanda's folks get here soon," Pius said in a voice as cold as the early morning air.

"Time to be going. You got this, Pius?" Ambrose said, depositing the groggy young man on the steps.

Father Pius had turned his attention to the boys. Brother Ambrose tossed his head, hinting that Paul should move in the car's direction. Abbot Jacob watched the conspiratorial pair.

"What were you boys thinking?" Pius growled. The outrage of his voice echoed in the quiet morning. A car pulled into the driveway and an unhappy man stepped out.

"Amanda, damn it, get out here."

A sullen-faced girl marched out of the house.

Jacob was glad he didn't have to deal with her. How could Paul disobey him? He clenched his fist as his heart pounded in his ears.

No.

Abbot Jacob's vision blurred. Memories of doctors, death, drinking, spun in his mind. The lives of his loved ones snuffed out in one last drink for the road. He never attended the trial. He never spoke to the man. But he knew the excuses. Hadn't we all used them when caught? Only this time, it cost the lives of his family. Despair loomed. Jacob shook his head. Beat it back. No, never again. He couldn't endure the loss of a loved one to drunk driving.

"Abbot Jacob?" Brother Ambrose called from the car.

Abbot Jacob looked at Paul. A volcanic rage bubbled inside. Damn, Joannicus, this should be you dealing with this moment.

Marching to the car, he took the front seat. His breath labored as he clinched his teeth, fearing he would scream, for the past and for now.

Ambrose waited, casting a wary glance at Jacob. Other parents arrived.

Jacob sat, working on what to say.

Ambrose pushed Jacob back into the seat and reached across to buckle his seat belt, and then he started the car. The air hung heavy with silence.

Ambrose coughed and said, "Nice song you were all singing, not country, more like rock, am I right?"

"It's by George Michael. Lucas really likes his music. The album's called 'Listen Without Prejudice.' I have the record if you want to listen to it," Paul said. "I bet it is on the radio. They play like every twenty minutes."

"That's good advice. Listen without prejudice," Brother Ambrose said, reaching to turn on the radio.

We are going to discuss music. "Do not turn that on," Jacob said, clipping his words.

"Everything is fine," Ambrose said.

"No," Jacob said. "Just because nobody died does not make this okay."

"Abbot Jacob, lighten up. Boys will be boys. All teens take risks," Ambrose said.

"Driving without a license is illegal. So is underage drinking," Jacob said.

"You don't know that he was drinking."

"I was not born yesterday. I was a teenager once," Jacob said.

Paul remained silent. That was all the answer Jacob needed.

"Teenagers make mistakes," Ambrose said, rubbing the steering wheel with his hands.

"Damn it Ambrose, it all counts," Jacob shouted. "What if something went wrong?"

"What did you want me to do?" Paul said, leaning forward and poking his head between the two monks.

"Call us," Jacob said, his voice higher than normal. "A pitcher of beer and a couple of shots doesn't make you invincible."

Paul pulled himself back. "But Lucas was going to drive, and he was wasted. I might be stupid, but I couldn't let him drive."

"But you were drinking, and you should not be driving,"

"Yes. I had a few drinks, but I wasn't drunk. I was sober. I know the difference. Besides, the State of Montana believes I can drive. Why can't you?" Paul said, flinging himself back into the seat.

"What?" Jacob hissed. No.

"I have a driver's license."

"When? How?"

"Since October," Paul said. "I got a perfect score and passed the first time."

Jacob knew he should be proud, but the fear of losing this boy he loved kept him from saying anything positive. Jacob stared at Ambrose, who was unusually silent now. You traitor.

"Stop the car."

"What?" Ambrose said, slowing down.

"Let me out," Jacob said. They pulled over.

"What are you doing?" Ambrose asked. Jacob got out of the car and started walking.

Paul rolled down his window.

"You can't walk home from here. Get in."

Jacob marched on as the car slowly shadowed him.

"I could wrestle him in the car and hold him down while you drive," Ambrose said loud enough for Jacob to hear.

How could they conspire against him? Ambrose was aware of

the consequences of drinking and driving. Alcohol had altered both of their lives. Yet he took Paul to... betrayal. The sting hurt.

"Abbot Jacob, please," Paul said.

Jacob stopped, and the car stopped. He banged on the hood of the car.

"No, no, no," Jacob shouted.

Paul opened the door, and the ding of the car alarm sang a warning.

"Get in the car, Paul," Brother Ambrose bellowed.

Jacob crossed his arms and stared at the youth. Emotions collided, a great love and a great anger.

The driver's side door opened. Ambrose's head appeared over the car, his face dark and serious.

"Get in the car, now, Paul."

"Why?" Paul asked as Jacob took a step toward him. Paul stumbled, making a dash to the other side as Ambrose opened the door. Paul dashed in.

"You did this, didn't you?" Jacob said, inches from Ambrose's face.

"We can talk when you are calmer. Let's go home," Ambrose said as he moved to reenter the car.

"He's really pissed," Paul said. "I don't understand."

The car door slammed shut.

Climbing up on to the hood of the car, he sat cross-legged. "How dare you? How dare them? I thought you were going to be helping me," he screamed, shaking his fist to the sky. Paul had disobeyed him, and Ambrose had betrayed him. He should have seen it coming. And God was once again dangling lives.

"You toyed with Joannicus and now Paul. No, you will not take him like that to test my resolve. Pick another way." The Warrior inside him stood stoic, smiling even as the Elder cautioned him against challenging the Gods.

"I have done everything to protect him from the fate you handed my wife and children. You do not play fair."

Yet here it was again, his inability to control, alter, or change fate. He felt as effective as a leaf in a river.

The sun peaked over the eastern sky. The light was blinding. Jacob hopped down from the car hood. He shook his braid loose, unlaced his shoes, and sang in his native tongue of Apsáalooke while he pounded the frozen ground with his bare feet. The car motor churned in the background. Jacob stopped. Sweat dripped even in the morning's chill. Grabbing his black shoes, he tossed them into the car and climbed in. The glow of the dome light framed his stone-faced expression reflected in the window. His feet ached. His body shivered as he tucked his hands under his armpits and leaned against the window, closing his eyes. The warmth of the car soothed his body as his mind tossed and tumbled. He snorted at the odds and memory of his white ancestor, Cold Feet and Sings in the Night, the two who started the bloodline of blue eyes. A one percent chance of ending up with blue eyes. Some might say a miracle. He didn't do any more miracles. He didn't want this child.

CHAPTER 26

SHADOWS AND SCABS

Psalm 80:12-13
But my people did not heed my voice
And Israel would not obey,
so, I left them in their stubbornness of heart
to follow their own designs.

Abbot Jacob poked his head out of his cell, listening to the silence of the hallway. He made his way downstairs to his office but paused when he heard the voices in the stairwell.

"I don't think we did anything wrong," Paul's voice said.

"Well, Abbot Jacob sees it differently," Brother Ambrose said.

"You didn't disobey, I asked you."

"That isn't quite so. I knew he wouldn't like you driving. But I figured he would warm up to the idea. Guess not. Well, don't fret too much. He will come around."

"Or not. What if he never speaks to us?"

"Now you are talking crazy," Ambrose said. Jacob detected a hint of worry in Ambrose's voice as he moved to the elevator.

Damn Ambrose. The betrayal hurt. The disobedience was a gut punch. He realized men made different choices even after consulting him. For several days now, he had avoided Paul and Ambrose. Sadly, he was not sure what he was accomplishing in doing so.

Concentration slept. He needed coffee, so he went to the community room. His mug full, he headed out the door only to find Paul standing in the narrow passageway, blocking his exit.

"Abbot Jacob, are you avoiding me?" Paul asked.

"Yes," Jacob said.

"Why?" Paul said.

"Because I can," Jacob said, and the words warmed him.

"I don't understand why you are so mad. Everyone my age drives. What if something happened at the farm and someone needed medical assistance?" Paul challenged.

"We have a house full of men who can drive. If we are going to play what-if then, what if, when you were being a hero, taking the near comatose Ambrose to the hospital, you meet a truck driver, who spills his milkshake in his lap, loses control, and crashes into you?"

"His milkshake, get real."

"I am not finished with my what-if story. They transport you to the hospital. You end up in a wheelchair for the rest of your life."

Jacob placed his hands on Paul's shoulders and moved him to one side in order to pass by.

"What about Ambrose?"

"He is dead."

Paul gasped at the harsh words.

"Then I guess you'll be stuck with me forever. I think you're being paranoid. It's more likely I'd get hit by a drunk driver."

Jacob whirled around so quickly that Paul took a step back.

"Exactly," Jacob said. His imagination formed a vivid picture as he felt his knees buckling, so he grabbed the counter for support before turning and taking an awkward step. He needed to leave, for he feared he would shake Paul like a rag doll until he listened.

Jacob headed to the patio, hoping that Ambrose was not there.

Paul followed him. "It won't happen."

Just like a puppy nipping at your heels. "Did Brother Ambrose get you guardian angel insurance? It can happen. You heard I had a family."

Paul nodded.

"Do you know what happened to them? A drunk, Mitchell Davis, killed them all. I do not want that to happen to you," Jacob said, his voice heavy. "I do not want you to be a Mitchell Davis."

Paul hung his head and picked at a hangnail. Was he getting through to the boy?

"Sorry. But I'm an excellent driver."

Jacob gripped the door handle. "I do not care. I told you no."

"Was that a forever no?"

Jacob's vision blurred. Almost Joan flashed through his mind. His little girl was born early. How he had wished she had been born alive, protected in the womb. At least his wife had seen the baby before walking on, leaving him with a hole in his heart.

Jacob blinked and squeezed the bridge of his nose.

"Paul," Brother Reginald called from inside the community

room. "Have you heard from Father Joannicus? I had something I wanted to talk to him about."

Thank you, Reginald.

Paul turned, distracted for a moment. "Not yet, but he calls on Sunday. You could wait with me..."

The dark emotion passed, replaced by a deeper burden, the lie he and Joe were telling Paul.

Jacob opened the slider to the patio.

Puffs of smoke blew in his direction as he stepped outside onto the patio. Ambrose. Jacob turned to leave.

"You can't avoid both of us forever," Ambrose said. "What's the point? Stop punishing Paul for my mistake."

Halfway across the patio, amid the scattered tables and chairs, he stopped and turned, his body trembling.

"How could you? You betrayed me."

"That's a little harsh. I taught him to drive. That's what you do with teenage boys."

"I do not care. I told him no. I told you no when you asked."

Brother Ambrose's head bobbled. "But you didn't mean it. You were just reacting to the past."

"That is a part of me. I am your abbot. If I say no, then obey me," Jacob said. The monks outside suddenly found shrubs and bugs interesting, as Paul followed Jacob outside.

"No, this is not on me. You two want to be independent. Let me see how successful you are," Jacob said.

Ambrose kicked at the pebbles on the patio. "You are being irrational. You can't protect him. Accidents happen even to the best of drivers."

"You are right. I cannot protect him. We know that from history. So, stop, just shut up," Jacob said, regretting the words that tumbled out of his mouth.

Paul gasped.

Now the boy was listening.

The sweet smell of cedar forced Jacob to sit on the bench. The past rushed in and the patio grew small and cold. He wrapped his arms around himself, remembering how their bodies grew cold in his arms as he sang to their spirits because their ears no longer heard.

He counted his breaths. One in, one out, as the heat of the day surrounded him with warmth. Paul's face, white with fear, floated in front of him, a heavy hand rested on his shoulder. He was sitting, but he didn't remember doing that.

"I'm sorry," Paul said, eyes large. "I won't disobey you again." Paul reached into his pants pocket and pulled out a wallet. He took out a rectangular card and set it on the table next to Jacob.

Ambrose made a grunting sound. "Go inside and wait for Father Joannicus to call. Go. Everything is fine, all is forgiven. Go."

Air moved into and out of Jacob's lungs, Paul reluctantly moved to the community room.

Ambrose released Jacob's shoulder. "I'm sorry too. I didn't mean to hurt you."

"One time, Rose, one thing I asked of you. Now, what do I do with you?"

"Sorry." Ambrose sat down, fishing for a cigarette.

Jacob looked at the beaming face of Paul on the plastic-coated card that lay on the table between them.

"I do not want it," Jacob said, as if handed something sinful.

"Then give it to someone who does," Ambrose said, brushing the tobacco off his scapular.

Try as he might, the pain of betrayal hurt. He thought the man was loyal and trusted him. Now he wasn't sure. Ambrose was witness to every dying second of it Jacob's pain. The forgiveness would have to wait because the pain covered him completely.

The morning sun streamed through the window as Jacob sat in the cancer recovery center next to Joannicus. On a weekday, the visitor room was nearly empty.

"You have been to the Rez," Joannicus stated.

Jacob rubbed his cheek. There was still a faint line. He had sweated and prayed, discovering that being a leader was hard. He wondered if his children would have been so challenging.

"Did it help?"

"No, not really. I went because my children keep haunting me."

Joannicus shuddered. "I thought you put them to rest."

"I guess not. The visions are upsetting."

"I think their mother is calling them. Let them go," Joannicus said sheepishly.

Jacob tried not to smile. The words comforted him. They were the same words Joannicus used when his children were alive.

A great affection filled him. Joannicus appeared healthier than his first round with cancer.

"I brought you something," Jacob said, turning away and digging in a bag. "Barnabas's raspberry muffins. We need to fatten you up before you come home."

Jacob handed one to Joannicus.

"They don't like us eating things that aren't green."

The congealed eggs on the tray next to Joannicus appeared unappetizing. Joannicus lifted the paper napkin and shrouded them as he made the sign of the cross over them.

"Too bad. You need proper food. Under the books are some chocolate bars and venison jerky."

Joannicus grinned, looking around and seeing no nurse or attendant. He took a bite of the moist muffin.

Jacob took a bite of a second one, grateful that he brought half a dozen with him.

A woman came into the room. She stood attentively to one side. Joannicus nodded, and she approached.

"Sorry to interrupt."

"No interruption. What can I help you with?"

She quickly came up to Joe and clasped his thin, ashen hand. She smelled of roses.

"Thank you. My mother appreciated every moment you spent with her. She died," the woman's voice cracked. "A smile on her face and a sense of accomplishment."

"My pleasure," Joannicus said. "Is there is anything else you need?"

She looked pained as she hesitated. "We are going to hold a small memorial, would speak on her behalf?"

"Not a problem. I would be honored," Joannicus said.

The woman left, her heels tapping pleasantly on the wooden floor.

Jacob marveled at how selflessly Joe continued to serve others.

"I think Paul thinks I am dating Ms. Carr. Seriously, when I talked to him on Sunday, he asked me questions about her. I don't think he believes I'm giving retreats."

"Where did he get that crazy idea?" Jacob said, wondering what lie Joannicus was going to tell Paul when he returned home.

"I don't know. Perhaps he is making up stuff to explain my being gone. Could be that he is working out his Charlie issues."

Jacob smiled at the thought of Joannicus meeting Charlie. The shock on his face would be a lasting memory, especially if she walked in with a spiked dog collar, torn lace and army boots.

"She is not his girlfriend. And I told you not to lie to him. He will be mad at you."

"I'll be home soon."

"He will look at you and see your lie."

"Maybe he'll be just happy I'm home."

Jacob shook his head. What was wrong with just telling Paul? At least if Paul was aware of the cancer, then he wouldn't feel helpless. He could spend time with Joe. Time not spent together was the livings biggest regret. His chest grew heavy with ache and his arms weighed down as he recalled holding a dead Elias in his arms while stroking Rosie's tear-stained cheek as she died.

Jacob raked fingers through his hair, pushing it up over the crown of his head and pulling tightly. The memories of his children dying continued to ache, a scar that never seemed to heal completely. The last words of his eldest daughter, Katie, floated back. "You will be alright, Daddy, you always are."

Joe's icy hand startled him. Jacob squeezed his eyes tight and then opened them.

"This is all going to end badly. Paul will never forgive us when he finds out you kept this from him."

"He will forgive us. Like I said, I'm done with the treatments. They will let me go home soon, then I will tell him."

"Everything?"

"No, just what he wants to know. Seriously, what good comes from him coming here? He can't do anything."

Jacob didn't agree. Paul's presence would help. When he was grieving, Ambrose's presence made him rise from the cold floor and take one small step toward living again.

"You're wrong, Joe."

"Are you going to order me to tell him?" Joannicus asked.

Ordering leads to hurt. He wasn't sure he would ever order a monk again.

"No, I am going to respect your choice, as wrong as it is. I wish Ambrose had done that."

"He was just trying to help. We can't keep Paul locked up," Joannicus said.

"Ambrose was the one who said we should brick up his doorway."

"He was just joking. Seriously, you are not mad at Paul."

Yes, he was. "Fine, I am pissed at Rose. The Rule state something about obeying me?"

Joannicus pulled his rosary from his bathrobe pocket. "Indeed, it does. Perhaps Rose tried and found it impossible. He listened to Paul's need to drive, he answered a greater calling."

"I said no. I was very clear."

The sounds of the treatment center whispered in the background. Beeps of the machines, squeaky carts, and moans of pain faintly filled the room. The odor of cleanliness made him finger the little sage packet in his pocket.

"Seriously, forgive them both," Joannicus said, rearranging the heavy wool blanket around himself.

"Why?" Jacob crossed his arms.

"Because you don't have a choice. You love them both," Joannicus said with a chuckle.

"They hurt me, going behind my back. They conspired against me."

Joannicus stretched his legs out into the sun. "Sometimes we forget the bigger picture. You fear losing Paul to some senseless accident, but that event could happen on his way to school. Paul's driving isn't the issue."

The rosary beads slipped through his fingers with a clicking sound.

"Ambrose knows my past and he's a monk because of the death of his friend. All alcohol related."

"That is why he did it. Your past is clouding your vision."

Jacob shook his head and hugged himself harder. That didn't matter. He was abbot. Didn't that stand count for something?

Jacob gripped the arms of the chair, and his legs twitched.

"Paul told me the 'what if' story. You're afraid of losing him. We know that. Don't punish Paul, or Rose because of Mitchell Davis."

The words felt like a scab ripped off a wound not quite healed. Jacob stood and walked to the window, his shadow long across the floor. The sun heated his black robe and sweat beaded on his forehead.

"I am not ready to forgive Rose. You are not ready to tell Paul the truth. We are a pair."

Joannicus winced. "Guilty as charged. I think Ambrose will wait. Do you have any more muffins?" Joannicus asked, rustling in the bag. "Now, I have a craving for fry bread. Maybe you could get your sister Rebecca to make some."

"I can make fry bread." Jacob said, a little annoyed that Joe thought him incapable of throwing dough into a pot of hot oil.

Joannicus pulled out a chocolate bar and unwrapped it.

"Oh, this is good," he said before taking a big bite.

It was hard to watch cancer attack Joannicus and not be able to do anything but sneak food to him and pray. He knew he could not sit next to Paul and watch him die. He would go crazy.

He couldn't endure it. He didn't like feeling helpless. That is what he was helpless. Nothing he could do could truly keep Joe, Paul, or any of them safe, and he knew that.

He watched Joannicus savoring the chocolate bar. Nobody ever enjoyed a bar as much as Joe was.

A nurse with a cup of water and a capful of pills entered. She looked at the muffin wrappers on the tray of untouched food and the candy bar in Joe's hand.

"That is not good for you." She glared at Jacob.

"Sorry," Joannicus said.

"It is not nice to tempt people with things they cannot have," she said, handing Joannicus his medication.

She held out her hand for the uneaten part of the candy. Joannicus handed it to her with a guilty smile.

As soon as she left, Joannicus pulled out a second muffin.

"Here's to rules. You see the irony in this, don't you?"

"Shut up," Jacob said. He wasn't breaking the rules he was helping a friend get healthy. Jacob frowned. He hated when Joannicus was right. He would have to forgive the large, loud monk.

CHAPTER 27
WHERE IN THE WORLD IS JOANNICUS?

Psalm 82:17-18
Cover their faces with shame
till they seek your name, Oh Lord.
Shame and terror be theirs forever.
Let them be disgraced, let them perish.

"Why can't I have his number?" Paul asked, leaning over the Abbot's desk. He was grateful that after a few short weeks, Jacob had stopped ignoring him. He was also sure that the community had voiced their concern that the cold shoulder punishment didn't sit well with them. Jacob was still angry with Ambrose. Paul could sense the tension between them and neither one of them had returned his license to him. Paul wondered if Jacob would ever allow him to check out a car.

"Because he is busy doing the work of God," Jacob said, closing the file on his desk.

"God's work is here. This is his monastery," Paul said. "The Rule even states as much."

Jacob shook his head. "I will have him call you."

"I have to sit by my phone, day and night?"

The pen in the Abbot's hand clicked several times.

"Stop being so petulant. If you want to be treated like an adult, act like one."

"Fine. I know something is up. Nobody gives retreats for six months. There aren't that many places. Tell me where Father Joannicus is, and I'll stop bugging you."

"First, not everything is your business," Jacob said with a wry smile. "Second, why are you asking me? This is a question you need to ask Father Joannicus."

"I have, and he doesn't give me a straight answer. Nobody does."

"Maybe that is your answer. Go do your chores or some *Lectio Divina*, which I hear you have neglected."

Paul sat, intending on staying. "What don't you hear?"

"Not much. Go find something important to do."

Jacob stood, and with a sweeping motion of his hands, he waved Paul out. "I have two billion things to do. Go, go."

Paul rose and trudged out of the Abbot's office, not satisfied with Jacob's answer. Joannicus had missed Christmas at the monastery and when Paul questioned him on the phone, the man gave Paul a lame excuse about a blizzard. He had sent Paul a Hudson Bay wool jacket. That didn't prove he was in Canada. Something wasn't right, and he was determined to figure it out.

Paul sat in his room reading the second book in the fantasy series *Dragons Walk Among Us* by Dan Rice and listening to the

Christian folk group Ellis and Lynch singing the psalms. The phone rang, causing him to jump.

"Where the hell are you?" Paul asked.

"Canada, and that's not a nice way to greet me," Father Joannicus said.

Paul coiled the phone cord around his lower arm. "When are you coming home?"

"Not for a while. I have some business to finish."

This was the same old rhetoric, vague response. "What are you doing?"

"Seriously, I am forming a new monastery."

Paul caught his breath. That was not funny. Jacob was abbot because Joannicus had declined the position. Could he form his own monastery?

"There isn't a Benedictine house in Canada," Paul said. "Is there?"

"I'm kidding," Joannicus said. "There is a house in Canada."

Paul didn't believe him. His mind skipped back two years. Joannicus had been coughing a lot then. Paul had worried that he was ill. Last year Joannicus was fine and then he ran off to give retreats. Things were not making sense.

"I don't believe you. But I would join your monastery over Abbot Jacob's. Are you alright?" Paul said, shaking the crumbs from a bag of potato chips onto a piece of notebook paper, then licked the fingers of his free hand to collect the crumbs.

"Thanks for the loyalty, and I'm fine. So, stop peppering people with questions they can't answer, okay?" Joannicus said, his voice sounding tired. "I'm glad you and Abbot Jacob made amends."

Paul licked his fingers. The salty flavor masked the staleness of the potato chips. "Yeah, well, he can't resist my charms. But I still think he's being overly sensitive. Everyone drives."

"Seriously, try to understand him."

"Are you sure everything is fine?"

"The best. Stay out of trouble. I'll call again on Sunday."

Paul set the receiver down and pushed his book onto the floor. Why wouldn't Joannicus come home? The facts were not lining up. At least that's what Charlie would say to him when he complained about Father Joe's absence. She called most nights after evening prayers. She was all about the facts. The facts lead to the truth.

Paul wiped his hands on his jeans and headed to the church. He stopped in the restroom and washed his hands. The facts about his family tickled his mind.

Charlie had studied his mother's death certificate and pointed out things he didn't know, like his mother's name was Sara Bennett-Hill, his grandfather's name was Bennett-Hill, and his grandmother was Kate Warner. Bennett-Hill was a surname. Why wasn't Paul's surname Bennett-Hill? His mother was single, or so it stated on her death certificate. So, did it mean his father's last name was Warner? Charlie proposed several scenarios: love child, widowed, kissing cousins. None of which Paul liked. Charlie insisted that Paul reexamine his birth certificate. Paul did and saw on the certificate that his father's name was listed as Bennett-Hill. Once again, no first name.

"You are Paul Bennet- Hill," Charlie had proclaimed.

Paul looked at himself in the mirror. "No, I am Paul Albert Warner."

The other shock on his birth certificate and his mother's death certificate had them both being born in North Carolina. He did not remember any mention of North Carolina. Charlie was thrilled, a new mystery to unravel. Who were these Bennett- Hill people? Excited, she went to find more evidence.

Evidence.

The bells rang for prayer. Paul made his way down the hall to the church. He needed to evaluate his theory about Joannicus.

Paul approached Abbot Jacob and tugged on his scapular.

"Father Joannicus called. Why couldn't I visit his folks? I had a winter break. I could have gone there for Christmas."

"I'm glad he called you and explained his Christmas absence," Jacob said.

No hesitation, not even a blink. Abbot Jacob was very good at lying.

I get in trouble when I tell lies, thought Paul, feeling a little annoyed.

Paul lingered as he gathered his prayer books. A squeak and heavy breathing made Paul turn and smile up at Brother Ambrose.

"Father Joannicus called," Paul said.

Ambrose paused a second. "He did? Well, that's good. Yippee, you can quit bugging everyone."

"Yeah, he said that he's really enjoying the FMA conference in Canada and he'll be home soon."

"FMA?"

"Future Monks of America," Paul said in a tone that made this fake organization sound real.

"In Canada?" Ambrose shook his head. Paul hoped he would challenge him.

"It's cold in Canada. Hope he's staying warm," Ambrose said, picking up his prayer books and moving into the church.

Paul stopped in the church's atrium. At the holy water fountain, the water bubbled and splashed. A blast of frigid air rushed in with Brother Moses.

"Father Joannicus just called me and said to tell you hi."

"Great, how is he?" Moses asked, shaking the snow from his coat and stomping his feet.

"Oh, he's enjoying his tour of Paris and said he would be home next month."

Moses's face lit up as he rubbed his hands together. "Good, it's about time he took a long vacation. Would have thought he'd go to Rome, but Paris is nice."

Really, Moses, Joannicus in Paris. If he traveled, it would be to Rome, or Subiaco, the hermitage of St. Benedict. Lourdes, if he was in France.

Paul shook his head. Anger mixed with sadness. Why were they lying to him?

Throughout prayers, Paul sat in his chair, tapping his foot and fuming. They all were liars. Near the end of prayers, Paul put his books down and stood up. Taking his chair, he set it in front of the altar facing the community. A rainbow of expressions of anger to surprise filled the faces of the monks.

"Enough with the lies. Tell me where Father Joannicus is. Everyone knows, so someone please just come out and say it."

Monks took side-glances at Abbot Jacob, who sat silent and stoic.

He had them. "Well, Abbot Jacob, he didn't go to Louisiana, nor is he in Canada or Paris."

"Paul, if you want to talk, after prayers we can talk," Abbot Jacob said as he closed his Psalter with a thud.

Paul wondered how forceful he should be. Ambrose was always warning him to not rattle the beehive.

Should he confront each one? No, he had done that already. They needed to realize that he had caught them in a lie.

Letting his anger fuel his need, Paul crossed his arms. "I want you to answer my question."

Many of the monks bowed their heads. He knew they were guilty.

Brother Ambrose turned his wooly mane and looked at Abbot Jacob.

"Okay, let's try this question. What is wrong with Father Joannicus?" Paul asked. All were silent. He had to admit they were a unified front, and that was impressive. But even walls tumble. Find the weakest link.

"Brother Moses?" Paul said, moving to stand before his victim.

Brother Moses squirmed in his chair as if the schoolteacher had just asked him to read and he wasn't paying attention.

"Perhaps you should talk to the Abbot," Moses said, in a whisper, his eyes pleading with Paul.

Ambrose grunted and stood. "Don't be a bully."

Paul turned and faced him, as boldly as he did when he was four. "Don't say another word unless you're going to answer my question."

"I can't do that, Paul," Ambrose said, and walked out.

Paul paced in front of the assembled monks. "At least he didn't lie to me. So why can't he tell me?"

"Abbot Jacob said not to," Alcuin shouted out.

Paul turned and walked to stand in front of Abbot Jacob. The Abbot shifted in his seat.

"It is lunchtime. We are hungry. If you want to talk, come to my office, and we will talk. Otherwise, quit."

Paul stood and pulled himself up tall. "I don't want to talk. I don't want a tour of the monastery. I want to know what is wrong with Father Joannicus."

"Grow up, Paul. Monastic business isn't your business," Brother Alcuin said.

"Shut up, Alcuin," Paul said. "I'm part of this community."

"I'm sick of your manipulative outbursts," Brother Alcuin said, jumping up. "For once, obey the Abbot."

Like a stinging nettle, everything about Alcuin bothered Paul.

He acted like he was the founder of the Benedictine way. Forever finding fault in everyone but himself. Ignore him, but Paul found that hard to do.

"Oh, tell me more, Brother, the great Benedictine example of obedience. Please, you can't tell obedience from stability or conversion. It is always about you. You listen and obey because you have to, because you took some silly vow that makes you a monk. I don't think that's obedience. That's just compliance. I obey because I want to obey. Sometimes disobedience is obedience."

Paul turned his back on the community, trembling. "I will obey when I'm ready." He sat, thankful his legs hadn't given out.

"So, are you ready?" Moses asked.

Paul smiled at the man's enthusiasm.

"No, Brother Moses, I'm not. I want an answer, Abbot Jacob, and I want an answer now."

Jacob stood and shook his head. "Not here, not now."

"If everyone knows but me, then what's the problem?"

"This is bigger than you think. You might not be ready."

Paul leaned forward in his chair.

"What do you mean by that?"

Jacob looked upward as if saying a quick prayer. "Everything. I can't risk you making things worse."

Paul's gut clenched as if Jacob had punched. This could not be true.

Jacob moved to toward the altar, sidestepping Paul. The community stood, following the Abbot's lead.

What did the Abbot mean? Then it hit him. Joannicus was dying or run away to be a hermit. There were other possibilities, but Paul's mind settled on the worst outcome.

"I can handle death. I can. I have."

Had he? Losing his mother at a young age, he had cried.

Losing Brother Mellitus, he had cried and felt lonely. Losing Abbot Gordon had made him depressed and angry. Was that handling death? How did one handle death?

The lack of answer was enough to send Paul into the abyss of emotions. The monks rose, stopping and bowing at the altar before leaving the church. Paul bit his lower lip to stop it from trembling and clenched his fists, trying to fight the emotions.

"If he's dying, I have the right to know. He's my monastic father. I love him more than anyone else does. He wants me to know the truth. I know he does," Paul said, the icons and statues standing as silent witnesses to the dull echo of his own words.

CHAPTER 28
EVIDENCE

Psalm142:1

Lord, listen to my prayer. Turn your ear to my appeal.

You are faithful, you are just,give answer.

Well, that didn't work.

Run after the Abbot or stand strong in his conviction? Paul felt torn. He frowned. The monks were good at talking. He was not going to let a missed meal sway him.

How many times had he been in trouble for lying? And here they were, lying to him. How grown up was that?

Paul entered his room and walked to his desk.

He wished they would cut the crap and tell him. It's not like he'd fall on the floor and have a tantrum.

His homework stared up at him. He pushed the books and papers aside. Abbot Jacob said he already knew the answer.

Damn mysteries and secrets.

In his mind, he could hear Charlie laughing. "It's not a secret if someone knows. Think this through. Use your brain."

What did he know?

Paul sat at his desk and took out a clean sheet of paper; on the top he wrote, in big block letters, "FIND JOANNICUS."

Joannicus is forming a new monastery or becoming a hermit?

He ran away and got married.

He really is doing what he said he was doing.

Paul crumpled the last one and tossed it over his shoulder as his stomach grumbled.

They were keeping him from a good meal.

He walked to the community room, picked up a pear and some cookies. The food choices were sparse, mostly meant for snacks here. On his way out, he noticed the light shining from the Abbot's office. That meant that Abbot Jacob was waiting for him. Paul headed the opposite way.

He didn't want a discussion. He wanted Joannicus.

"You said he wasn't dying. Then why can't I see him?" Paul muttered as he climbed the stairs to the third floor.

"Keep death ever before your eyes," said the little plaque in the hallway as he approached his cell.

What the hell did that even mean?

Most people he knew avoided that topic. Well, except Charlie. She seemed infatuated with death and the devil. She asked the strangest of questions, like how do you know you have died? What part is floating around out there? Is it energy or soul? What does life after death look like? Why return if it is so great? He had often wondered about the afterlife, too.

Her questions about the devil filled Paul with trepidation. He didn't want to meet the devil. He would be content with believing in his existence, but never knowing for sure.

Paul leaned against his closed cell door. Was there life after death? Would he see his mother again? He remembered her laughter, the morning, the sun in the room, her body so still. He had thought she was asleep. He knew now that wasn't the case. The police officer had come, taken him away, and fed him.

He recalled the monks inviting him to stay with them. He hadn't understood that his mother wasn't coming back. The monks told him crazy things about life in the spirit, coming back from the dead, stuff that made him believe they had buried her alive and it had terrified him. He had not been ready for her death.

Then, years later, Brother Mellitus died; the memory hurt. Paul felt lightheaded. The pear in his hand dripped juices onto the floor.

The gathering of the community, the chanting, had been oddly comforting to a child. Paul felt an absence as if he'd lost something precious, even if he believed in heaven. Those words did not bring him joy or comfort.

Moving to the sink in his room, he washed, then scooted a dirty sock over the drippings on the floor.

Is that what Jacob experienced when his family died? As if he were half of a person, with a big hole that the wind blew memories through. He missed Merlin. The wrinkly face grinning at him through a white wooly beard. Those clear blue-gray eyes winking at him. Paul remembered searching habit pockets for treasures, marbles, gum, candy, and once a mouse. He wanted the moments of life, not the memories.

In the corner stood the cane that Paul had once assumed was a magical staff. Merlin hadn't told him otherwise. Paul walked over and took it.

"I could use a little magic," Paul said, stomping it on the floor as he walked to his bed. Not that he believed in magic. Miracles maybe, Merlin had said, there wasn't a difference. He sat on the edge of his bed, letting his fingers rub the bumps on the carved cane as if there were a message hidden that needed deciphering.

"They are all misfits," Merlin had said. "Lost boys don't always follow them. Find your way."

The monks as lost boys, that wasn't how Abbot Jacob or Father Joannicus viewed them. Odd way to look at one's chosen family, yet Paul knew Mellitus loved him, but had he loved the community too?

Then there was Abbot Gordon. He was alive, praying. And dead before the next psalm. The monks talked a lot about reward and joy. The man was dead.

He still needed him. Heaviness filled his chest. Life and death didn't make sense.

He had talked to Joannicus after Abbot Gordon had died, asking why he was so joyful. Joannicus spoke of the next journey and said it was nothing to be fearful about. Paul remembered doubting him.

He had touched death. Ambrose had once let him play with a dead animal. The little rabbit was cumbersome and cold. He had never shared that with anyone. People would consider it disturbing.

He liked the journey of now and didn't want to watch anyone else die.

Death can be ugly. Paul remembered hearing snippets of the death of the Mackenzie family. The idea of that much grief and sadness terrified him. He didn't want to be sad. Death was like being in a dark cave, unable to move.

Paul stood up, and the cane thumped to the floor. The sadness came as he realized he'd done this to himself when he told Joannicus not to let him see death.

Two tears rolled down his cheeks.

He had changed my mind. He needed to find him before it was too late.

He could get a phone book and call the hospitals. He could find a bill in the Abbot's office.

"You could just ask," Charlie's voice filled his mind.

Paul shook his head. No, that didn't work before. Besides, he didn't want them stopping him. He could search while the monks were at Mass.

Paul paced his room. Finally, the bells clanged, calling the monks to the church. He had forty-five minutes. They wouldn't question his absence. They liked to wait for things to blow over, pass on, or just go away. Action was not a monastic quality. This time, it would work in Paul's favor.

The Abbot's office was unlocked. Foolish trusting monks. Paul stood in the dimness, wondering where to start. There had to be a paper trail.

If you want to hide something, put it in plain sight, Ambrose once said. Nobody ever sees the obvious. Paul looked around the room. The shelves were rather empty, only a few books. He opened the cabinets below the shelves.

Oh, look a bar. The glasses and bottles tinkled as he pulled the retractable shelf out. He lifted the stopper, he sniffed it, the odor sweetly dark. He tipped the decanter to his mouth and swallowed. The liquid burned and he coughed. Carefully, he put the bottle and stopper intact on the shelf.

His eyes moved to the safe. He punched in the code: 1909. Click.

Why hadn't they changed the combination? Foolish trusting monks. Paul shook his head to dispel the confusion clouding his mind as he began rifling through the box, only to find cash and the checkbook.

Damn.

Closing the safe door, he looked at Jacob's desk. On top of the desk were a legal pad and a folder. Paul sat in the chair. A chill ran up his back.

The clock on the wall ticked loudly. Paul opened the drawer. The correspondence on the top was from Sister Mary Germaine. He had never seen such perfectly formed letters. A request from Brother Marion, who wanted money for a computer.

Paul read the reasons to print and catalog the history and archives of the monastery. Paul snorted. It is all in boxes in the attic, labeled by year. Would it really benefit the community?

Paul tugged on the third drawer, which didn't open. Locked. Paul felt for a key, remembering the money that Jacob hid on the underside of dresser drawers. That money paid for the chalices Paul broke. They hadn't sent him away even after that disaster. Had he paid Jacob back? His fingers ran under edges. Nothing.

The old key chain. There on a hook was a large brass circle were keys. Fondly, he recalled the hours he'd spent trying to find where the keys went. As he flipped through the keys, he recognized the one to his old room. He frowned. They could have unlocked his door. He should have known. They say one thing and have a backup plan. Paul tried several keys, but none opened the drawer. What was the Abbot hiding? Gordon never had a locked drawer.

The phone rang, and Paul jumped, causing papers on the desk to scatter. Scrambling to get them all back to the desktop, Paul glanced at the clock. Time was running out. Where was the bill?

At the file cabinet, he pulled open the drawer. The metal screeched. He found a file for the automobiles, car insurance. More documents on the mortgage, repairs, the barn, and equipment. The rifling stopped when his fingers touched a file labeled "Paul." He couldn't stop himself. He flipped open the file on the desk, and there was his license, his birth certificate and several pages with legal verbiage. Was Charlie still looking for his dad? He could see her face, eyes rolling under her fake eyelashes. Right, of course, she was.

A photo of him and his mom tucked in between the documents. Paul wondered what his mother was hoping when she put only half the name of his father on his birth certificate. Was she protecting him? Why were people always protecting him? He stared at the photo. She looked so happy and alive. He wished he could talk to her.

He looked at his license. Temptation called. Take the license. You're going to need that. Paul tucked the photo in his shirt pocket.

Jacob's angry face loomed in his mind.

Yeah, but he has been lying. No. Don't mix the events. Focus.

Paul slipped the file back in the drawer and continued searching.

Finally, medical expenses, organized according to places. Paul would have preferred that the files were alphabetized. On the floor, he sorted through the data, amazed at the number of doctor bills. He read about toenails, hemorrhoids, sore throats, and warts, and that was just for this month. Crap. Glancing at the clock, he quickly stopped reading and started flipping through the papers. Time raced. Crap and double crap.

Voices in the hall caused Paul to hold his breath. It was too early.

A person in the hallway said that they needed to turn in the keys.

"Now? Everyone is at Mass. We shouldn't enter the office without the Abbot being there." The voices drifted away from the door.

Paul continued combing through papers until he found a bill

with Joe's name. Joannicus was at St. Vincent's hospital. Wow, that's expensive: $54,000.

Voices in the hall told him his time was up. He quickly stuffed the papers back into the file and slammed the file cabinet shut and darted to the patio outside of the office.

Abbot Jacob stepped into the office, followed by Brother Ambrose.

"I see you have come to your senses," Brother Ambrose said.

Paul darted past them to the door.

"Where are you going?" Abbot Jacob asked. "I need to talk to you?"

"No need, I'm good," Paul said, his heart pounding as he ran upstairs to his cell.

Ready or not, Joannicus, he was coming.

CHAPTER 29
THE RACE IS ON

Psalm 141: 6
You are my refuge, all I have in the land of the living.

In less than an hour, the old rusty truck pulled up to the orchard, leaving a slush trail like a huge snail.

Lucas leaned over and pushed open the door. Paul climbed in, hugging his backpack.

"So, where are we going?" Lucas asked.

"St. Peter's hospital," Paul said, trying to sound confident. Fear scooted into the cab with him.

Lucas shot him a confused look as they headed down Highway 212 toward Billings, the headlights of the truck making frosty tunnels through the fog. Lucas gave him a second glance, sniffing the air.

"Have you been drinking?"

"No. Well, yes. I had a drink of something. It was gross."

"Brown? And sweet?"

"Yeah, and it burned."

"Benedictine, it's an herbal liqueur. It is like hot syrup, only it lingers," Lucas said, with a snort. "From the drawer in the professor's office, right?"

"No, the Abbot's office."

"Figures. He likes sweet coffee too," Lucas said, shaking his head. "I prefer rum. Did you bring some with you? We could use something warm; my heater isn't so good."

"No. I didn't think to bring any. Thanks for picking me up."

Lucas had sampled alcohol with the monks, even though he was underage? They had let him have a glass of wine once a year at Easter. They were such hypocrites. Jealousy surged through Paul. Who had let him? Pius? Jacob?

"Who are we going to see?" Lucas asked. "I'm happy to help, since they took away your license. PJ told me that. I'm glad nobody took mine."

"They didn't take my license. I gave it to Abbot Jacob, like a peace offering, so he wouldn't be so mad."

"I don't get what the big deal was," Lucas said.

"He lost his whole family in a car accident," Paul said, surprised that PJ hadn't told Lucas that.

"Really, now that's a story I'd like to hear. A once-married monk turned celibate and now abbot."

It's not that interesting, thought Paul.

"I'm going to see Father Joannicus." The words stuck in his throat. "They have kept me from him. He's important to me."

"I know you talk a lot about him, but—" Lucas said, as Paul cut him off.

"He's like what PJ is to you. He's sick and the monks have been keeping that from me. I found out. They claim Father Joannicus doesn't want me with him. But that's just not true."

"I think it is," Lucas said.

The momentum of the words sucked the air out of Paul's chest. Even Lucas knew. His best friend knew. The betrayal stung.

"No, you're wrong," Paul said, his words clipped. Pius is a lair.

"I get it he is—well, he's kind of like your dad or something, and they shouldn't be acting like that. Even PJ thinks so. Are you certain you want to do this?"

The mention of PJ caused Paul to smolder inside of his gut as he tried not to yell at Lucas.

The world tilted and Paul's mood darkened. Lucas knew. Why hadn't he told him? Paul punched the dashboard and then Lucas's arm.

Lucas startled and swerved into the other lane, making circles down the highway like a carnival ride.

Paul gripped his seat belt as he slammed into the door. His shoulder hurt.

The truck slowed, and Lucas struggled to regain control on the snowy road. Horns of a coming car blasted as they moved back into the correct lane. Lucas let out a heavy exhale.

Paul glared at Lucas, wanting to punch him again. "What the hell. You didn't tell me?"

The car slowly edged to the side of the road. The wipers thumped.

Lucas loosened his grip on the steering wheel and turned to look at Paul.

"What the fuck? Are you trying to kill us both? I'll dump you on the side of the road if you do that again."

"Sorry," Paul said, but he wasn't. Lucas was supposed to be his friend. Anger bubbled. "I'd have told you if PJ was dying, and I don't even like him."

The truck moved back onto the highway. Paul shivered as he pressed his nose to the side window, barely making out the exit signs.

"He's not dying anymore. PJ says he will recover. They got all the cancer."

"Cancer?"

"Shit, you didn't know. Oh, God damn. I thought you knew he was sick."

Swallowing hard, Paul said, "I noticed he was sick. I figured that out. I just didn't realize it was cancer."

The word hung in the air like a shiny guillotine ready to cut hope from life.   Paul's heart pounded in his ears. That was a death sentence. His mom died of cancer. Paul rolled down the window. The frigid air blasted him.

"I'm sorry. I'm aware your mom died of cancer. PJ said it's not the same kind, Father Joe won't die from that."

Paul felt sucked back to the past. The coughing of his mother and running to get water for her, the days they spent on the bed, cuddled in blankets, watching the seasons change from that room. The car took an exit, but Paul didn't notice as his emotions skidded inside him.

The freezing fog hung from streetlamp and bare tree branches.

"You sure about this? I mean, I'm here for you, dude, but PJ said this could all go bad. So, did you tell anyone we were coming here?"

"No, why would I tell them that? They would just try to stop me." Paul wiped his face on his shirtsleeve. "Father Joannicus isn't expecting me. I'm not giving him the chance to say no."

"Good for you. It was a dirty trick not to tell you. I'd be pissed too." Lucas nodded. "Yeah, PJ said this was a bad idea."

Paul grunted.

PJ.

"No, not about me driving you to see him. He just thought it was dumb for them to keep this from you. He said it was impressive how they formed a united front for Father Joe. Maybe they elected the wrong monk to be abbot?"

"Just take me to him," Paul said, his stomach clenched.

They passed the hospital. Paul peered at the building, making out the emergency sign.

"Hey, you passed the hospital. Let me out." Panic rose inside of Paul as he gripped the door handle.

"What? No, we aren't going there."

"Let me out or I will jump."

"Dude, chill out. He isn't at St. Peter's. He's at the treatment center. I can't believe they didn't tell you," Lucas said in a near whisper.

"Treatment?"

"Cancer treatment, chemotherapy, and radiation."

"Have you seen him?"

"Who me? No. PJ has. He said, well he said he looks sickly. Treatment makes you lose all of your hair. I mean all of it."

Pain shot through Paul. He remembered when he had returned home from touring monasteries. Joannicus was bald. And oh God, that's what it was. Crap, why didn't he question that? Stupid, stupid, stupid. Joannicus had cancer then too. Paul glanced around the nearly empty parking lot.

A brick building glowing with warm lights stood before them. Lucas cut the motor on the truck. Fog settled on the windshield, sealing them in.

"He is here?" Paul asked, a deep fear gripping him. Cancer, the sentence of death. He could handle this. After all, he wasn't four.

"PJ told me."

Paul balled his fists. PJ seemed to have all the answers. PJ and Lucas talked about him, about Joannicus, and about who should be abbot. Worse of all, PJ was giving his approval for this little adventure.

He didn't need anyone's blessing. He was going to see Joannicus.

"I need a minute," Paul said, leaning against the truck door.

Joannicus was alive. Joy. Joannicus lied to him. Anger. Joannicus has cancer. He just wanted to be with him. The swirl of emotions caused Paul's head to ache. Anger, fear, hurt, relief, all demanded a moment.

He wasn't sure if he could handle this moment. What was he supposed to do?

Uncertain of what he would find inside the treatment center, Paul opened the truck door. The cold enveloped him. He sucked in the icy air and whispered under his breath the prayer he had heard every day since his mother had died, "Oh God, come to my assistance. Oh Lord, make haste to help me." His words hung like the smoke of incense before him.

CHAPTER 30
DONE BEING MAD

Psalm 37:19
I confess that I am guilty.
And my sin fills me with dismay.

As Lucas and Paul entered the treatment center, Paul felt his energy leaching out of him. The entry way was cheery, walls of yellow and green, a fresh arrangement of red tulips adorning the check-in desk. As they passed by, the hushed conversations in the living room stopped. The receptionist looked up. Paul read the instructions for visitors, posted on the resident's door.

"Who are you visiting?" the woman asked.

"Joe Brookes," Paul said, knowing that many monks liked to be mistaken for ordinary people, so they often drop their titles.

She glanced warily at him. No one was going to stop him from seeing Joannicus.

"You family?" she asked, suspicion tinting her voice.

"Yeah, he's my father," Paul said. That wasn't a lie, not really. Most people called Joannicus "Father." Paul believed the man should be his father.

The woman nodded. Lucas pulled Paul toward one wing.

"Room 203, right?" Lucas asked.

The lady pointed toward the hall.

"Who are they?" the second woman asked.

"Visitors for Joe Brookes, his sons."

"What? The man's a priest. He can't have sons."

Lucas and Paul quickened their pace away from the pair. *Little do you know*, thought Paul, knowing that Abbot Jacob had several children.

Soon, security would escort them out. If they had security there. Why would this place have security?

Sounds of machines buzzed as they made their way down the hall. Carts with trays of brown congealing gravy over lumpy potatoes gave off an odor of once edible food. Damn, he should have brought some food for Joannicus. That stuff looked gross. They walked confidently past the nurse's station as if they had been here a million times.

Room 203. The door was open, but the interior was dim as Paul entered. A faint smell of antiseptic was present in the room. The light from the hallway showed a huddled figure of a man, fragile and pale against the bleached white sheets. That couldn't be Joannicus. Lucas squeezed past Paul, giving a questioning look. But it was Joannicus, for a colorful wool blanket lay draped over the foot of the bed. It was from the weave shop. The pattern was simple orange and yellow crosses set within a light blue background. Paul swallowed hard, watching the rise and fall of the breathing figure. Lucas moved a chair next to the bed, indicating that Paul should sit. Paul sat, unable to think. They said he wasn't dying. That's not true. He squeezed his eyes tight to stop the flow of water.

Lucas left the room and returned with a second chair. Paul had never seen Lucas move so stealthily.

Paul picked up the rosary that lay on the table. Muffled noises drifted into the quiet room. Neither boy spoke as the beads in Paul's hand clicked like cogs in a clock. His emotions tumbled. Hail Marys bounced in his head.

The rhythmic breathing changed. Joannicus opened his eyes. "Ah, you made it."

"We need to talk," Paul said, his voice sounding foreign as he beat his fears back.

"Who told you?" Lucas asked.

"Really? Father Pius," Paul said, knowing that meant that soon someone from the monastery would be there to remove him. That's if they could.

"Wasn't PJ, he would never rat us out," Lucas said. Paul doubted that.

Joannicus shifted in the bed. His hand reached for the controls, adjusting the back to an upright position. He smiled and gave a wave to Lucas.

"Good to see you again."

"Likewise," Lucas said. "Sorry you're sick, but Father Pius told me you're getting well."

Joannicus turned to Paul. "You need a haircut."

Lucas snickered. Paul ran his hand through his hair, which wasn't that long.

"That's it? That's all you have to say to me?" Paul said as he crossed his arms.

"You are here. Speak to me. I'm listening," Father Joannicus said.

Paul wanted to curse at him but instead he said, "What were you thinking?"

"How much I didn't want to see you suffer?" The brown eyes looked sincere.

"Well, that isn't how it worked out," Paul said.

"Yes, I'm aware of that."

Paul's voice cracked, and the words stuck in his throat. "I'm really pissed at you."

Joannicus pulled the blanket up. "I'm sorry."

Paul stood. "How could you ask the community to lie for you?"

"More amazing is that they did," Lucas muttered. Paul glared at him, wishing that he wasn't in the room.

"I was just trying to protect you. I feared what the word cancer means to you."

"No, you don't," Paul said, his voice harsher than he had expected. "I'm older. I recognize that not everyone dies from cancer."

"Good, because I'm not dying," Father Joannicus said, pulling the dark, knitted cap over his ears.

"I'm not sure I believe you," Paul said, choking on his words. Emotions like wasp stings pelted his heart. "You could have died."

"The first time. Yes, there was a first time."

Paul's chest tightened, remembering when he had returned from his tour of monasteries. "Why did you lie to me?" Why hadn't he noticed?

Joannicus rubbed his face with his hands and then folded them on his chest. "When you came to live with us, I promised God, I would protect you."

A flash of anger ripped through Paul. Abbot Jacob had promised to protect him from Pius. Funny how that didn't work.

"You guys need to try something else. None of you are good at protecting me."

Joannicus frowned. "I suppose you're right. We have failed. Why don't I just try to teach you how to live? I know this little rule. It seems to work." Joannicus said, shaky hand reaching for a cup on the nightstand.

Lucas swallowed a laugh.

The rule of St. Benedict, the monk's answer to everything, only it had never provided him with all the answers.

"I'll get it," Paul said as he handed Joe a plastic cup of water, then sat in the chair by the bed. He put his head in his hands. Cancer, the word, sent chills through his bones. The confession of guilt by Joannicus did not lift the heavy weight from his heart. He felt cheated of time with Joannicus. Many times, Paul wanted to talk to Joannicus.

Joannicus looked directly at Paul. "Seriously, I'm sorry. I made a mess of this. I didn't want to be a burden to others. That's why I went away. I was a burden the year you were gone."

Paul could not imagine the community complaining about helping a fellow monk. They just didn't do that.

"You're not a burden."

A nurse stuck her head in, surveyed the boys, and looked at Joannicus.

"Everything alright?" she asked.

Paul held his breath.

"All is good. Thanks for checking," Father Joannicus said, giving her a smile before she left. "So you're mad at me?"

"I want to be," Paul said, looking at Lucas, who shook his head slightly. "He lied to me. I have a right to be angry."

Lucas shrugged his shoulders.

"Then be angry," Joannicus said.

Paul stood. He paced the side of the bed. Anger bubbled, and it ached. "I don't want to be angry with you. I just want to be with you. Why won't you let me be with you?"

Joannicus reached his hand out. Paul stopped pacing and took a seat, clasping the cold, bony fingers. His grip was firm, and that gave Paul a sense of relief. Maybe he was telling the truth.

Paul held the cold hand to his cheek. "I don't want you to die."

"I'm going to be okay."

They stared at each other. Thankfulness threatened to smother Paul's anger.

"This is my fault, isn't it?" Paul said. "I know I said I didn't want to be around death when Abbot Gordon died. I'm sorry, I didn't mean it."

"It's not your fault. You didn't give me cancer," Joannicus said, his voice stern.

"I know that, but I did say don't talk to me about death. I was just upset. Confused, tired of the people I care about dropping dead."

"I know," Father Joannicus said, squeezing Paul's hand. "Seriously, you should be upset. This is on me. I knew you didn't mean what you were saying. But I really didn't want to see you hurting and worried about me."

"He still worried," Lucas said.

Paul glared at Lucas. Shut up, Lucas. He could manage this.

Joe squeezed Paul's hand. How could he be mad at Joannicus when he confessed his wrongdoing? As water poured into a hand cannot be held, Paul felt his anger trickle away.

"Please tell me that you're done being stupid," Paul said.

"Excuse me," boomed a feminine voice from the doorway. A girl stood in baggy sweats, holding onto a metal pole that clicked a soft rhythm of medicine into the skeleton of a girl. Her eyes were huge under the mop of thick purple knitted braids.

"Who are you anyway? Did you wash your hands? You

shouldn't be that close to Joe. He's sick and you, obviously, are the stupid one."

Lucas sat, eyes wide with amusement at the bossy girl. She looked sixteen, thin as a twig, and pale as dandelion seed.

"Brittney," Joannicus said gently

"No problem, Joe, I got this. Back off, boy," Brittney said, banging her monitor as the medicine bag swung wildly on the pole.

How can you be mean to someone dying? Clearly, she was ill. She seated herself on the edge of the bed. A surge of jealousy flashed in Paul when Joannicus took her hand. What the hell?

"Brit, be kind. This is Paul," Joannicus said.

The girl's face softened. "Oh, that Paul, I remember. Where the hell have you been? The man suffers."

Lucas snorted. Britney glowered at him. Joannicus tugged her arm, and she turned, her face softened.

"*The Wonder Years* is about to start. Are you coming?" Britney asked.

A shock jolted through Paul. Joannicus watches TV? Joannicus did not watch television at home, the exception of maybe an occasional movie. He read the paper for news, and books were his source of entertainment. She must be joking.

"I'm sorry, I've some catching up to do," Joannicus said, not letting go of either of them.

Brittney's face fell. Paul felt a mixture of sadness at her disappointment and joy at being chosen.

"Is that the show with the horse-girl?" Lucas asked.

"No, her name is Whinny. She's not a horse. You know nothing," Brittney said as she rolled her large brown eyes.

"Can I watch with you?" Lucas asked, putting on the hopeful pout that seemed to mesmerize girls.

"Sure," Brittney said, patting Joe's hand and rising from the bed. She shook her finger at the door. "Don't tire him out."

Another girl appeared in the doorway. She was tall and tan; she looked out of place, healthy. Paul stood up. She moved so gracefully, her long, dark hair shiny in the florescent lights.

"The nurse is looking for you, Brittney," the girl said.

"Like that's a good thing? Let her look. She needs the exercise. Can't go far with this pole." Brittney laughed and then coughed. It took a few moments for her to catch her breath as the other girl moved to help her. Lucas followed them, but paused at the door.

"Warner, put your eyes back in your head. You got a girl-friend," Lucas said as he trailed after the girls.

"So do you," Paul said, but Lucas was gone.

Joannicus spoke, "That was Brittney. Don't be jealous. She is fierce, but you would be too if you were dying. The other girl was her twin sister, Bethany."

Twins.

Bethany. Her presence hung in the air like the scent of honey-suckle on a hot day. Bethany. Paul stared at the space she had occupied. Such a contrast, one so worn and one so alive.

"I can introduce you to Bethany," Joannicus said.

"I can talk to girls on my own," Paul said, staring at the empty doorway.

"Seriously, do you have a girlfriend?"

Paul shook his head. "Charlie's not my girlfriend. We just go to dances together."

"When do I get to meet Charlie?"

"As soon as you come home," Paul said.

"I'll come home when you forgive me," Joannicus said, holding out a hand.

Paul looked at him, remembering all the times that he had stood before Joannicus with those words on his lips. I'm sorry I ate all the hosts. I'm sorry I drew on the test papers. I'm sorry, I don't like brussels sprouts. Every time Paul had apologized, Joannicus, with little hesitation, had said, "You're forgiven."

He grabbed the thin, cold hand in his.

"I forgive you."

"And the community?" Joannicus asked, placing a second hand in the clasp.

"Fine, the community too."

"Lucas?"

"Let's not go crazy," Paul said with a smile. "So, when do you think Abbot Jacob will arrive?"

"Soon, he called me yesterday and told me he was going to confess all."

Paul frowned. Was Jacob ready to confess? Had his protest worked? Joannicus released his grip and fumbled for the blanket. The cancer had weakened the man he used to chase after.

"I'm all right," Joannicus said.

"I'm not sure I believe you," Paul said, wishing he could.

"I believed you when you told me you didn't eat all the candy corn, and that you wouldn't read until midnight, and all those other times," Joannicus said.

"Fine," Paul said. It didn't matter; he was here now. He found a second blanket and tucked it around Joannicus before pulling a chair close to the bed.

"It's time for me to rest. If you like, you can read me Chapter 7 of the Rule."

Paul found himself feeling tired and oddly peaceful. Finally, he was allowed to do something for Joannicus instead of Joannicus always doing for him. He picked up the worn booklet with curling edges, opened it to Chapter 7: On Humility, and read.

CHAPTER 31
WHO AM I?

Psalm 1:1-2
Happy indeed is the man
who follows not the counsel of the wicked
nor lingers in the way of sinners
nor sits in the company of scorners
but whose delight is the law of the Lord
and who ponders his law day and night.

Paul walked into the community room, and he could not believe his eyes. Joannicus was outside, in the pollen-polluted sun, and Ambrose was with him. Not good. Brother Ambrose spent his day with the animals, dirt, slop, and germs.

Joannicus had on a woolen sweater and cap, but Paul grabbed

a blanket as he rushed outside to the patio. The sweet aroma of roses filled his nose as he noticed the bush covered in blooms.

"What are you doing? You could catch a cold," Paul said, sniffing the air, ladened with burning hay.

"I'm breathing in the fresh air and noticing the intricate folds of these roses, not to mention the color. Can you imagine being a rose and unfolding to the warm tickles of the sun? What an existence, and all for the glory of God," Joannicus said.

Brother Ambrose fanned the air with his scapular.

The man was talking weird again. He had been talking like that ever since Paul brought him home. Now they were both acting strange. Ignoring the poetic nonsense, Paul handed Joannicus the blanket and perched himself on a table like an owl waiting for the grass to move.

"Seriously, I can't get a cold from the fresh air," Joannicus said.

"He's right, germs come from people," Ambrose said, wiping something off his fingers onto the underside of his scapular.

"You're making me nervous, all this worry and bother," Father Joannicus said, spreading the blanket over his knees. "I'm not going to fall over dead. Go. Live. Then come back and talk to me about your adventures."

"I would, if I didn't have to worry about you all the time," Paul said, placing his elbows on his knees. "You could get sick at any moment."

"I'm not dying."

"You have cancer. That kills you."

Joannicus closed his eyes. "I had cancer and I'm alive."

Ambrose snorted, lighting what looked like a hand-rolled cigarette, only he held it funny between his thumb and first finger. Breathing in smoke would not improve Joe's health, and his health was improving. Joannicus wanted to teach and take part in community activities. Joe's lack of cooperation forced Paul to be vigilant to prevent the man from overdoing it.

"Don't you have some place to be," Ambrose said.

"No. Why? What's going on here? And what is the funny smell?" Paul asked.

That was when Paul noticed a plastic bag with what looked like herbs and Jacob's ceremonial smoking pipe.

The Indian artifact was worn and longer than most pipes. The bowl had symbols carved into it and painted bands of blue and red triangles. Tied with leather, midway on the shaft, hung one black feather and a yellow bead.

"What smell? You mean the roses," Brother Ambrose said.

He was never good at acting innocent.

"No," Paul said, becoming suspicious. "Why are these artifacts out here?"

"We are using them," Ambrose said, stuffing the baggie into his habit pocket.

Paul sniffed. He recognized the odor. It was not hay.

"Why are you using weed?" Paul asked.

"Seriously, this is for med- dis- in- ol purposes," Joannicus said.

"Okay," Paul said, not entirely believing, but willing to accept it might be the truth.

"Besides, I love the new perspective it is giving me. Have you ever noticed the lights at prayers? They seem so soft, almost caressing. And the silence between the psalms, I swear I can hear the monk's blink."

Paul ignored Joe's babbling and turned to Ambrose.

"You're not sick, Rose," Paul said.

"Lighten up. I'm teaching him how to smoke," Brother Ambrose said. "How do you know about marijuana?"

"Oh no, don't turn this on me. I'm not the one being bad. You two should not be doing this. I'm going to tell Abbot Jacob."

"We aren't sharing with him, are we Joe?" Ambrose said as Paul rolled his eyes and shook his head.

They can't be serious. They shouldn't be doing this. Paul doubted that Abbot Jacob knew.

"Fine, I'll put the pipe back," Ambrose said as he lit the hand-rolled smoke. The aroma of the sweet weed filled in the air.

Joannicus sniffed the air. "Do you have any potato chips? Seriously, I saw Jesus in one of those grease patterns. I swear it looked just like him."

Paul was sure that Joannicus was already stoned. He had heard rumors that smoking weed helped cancer patients. A vision of staff and patients at the treatment center high and mellow passed through Paul's head.

No wonder they seem so casual about cancer.

"Is it just me, or do I draw mother hens?" Joannicus said, his eyes large and round, stared up at Ambrose.

Abbot Jacob appeared at the sliding glass door with a stack of messages, and he handed them to Paul. Brother Ambrose quickly crushed the smelly herb and quickly lit a tobacco one. Abbot Jacob looked at Ambrose and Father Joannicus and then at the pipe as he turned to Paul.

"Did you give Charlie my office number?"

"No," Paul answered, shocked that Charlie was calling the monastery.

"Tell her to stop calling me," Abbot Jacob said.

Why is she calling the Abbot? She doesn't even know him.

"As I recall, Charlie was a force to be reckoned with," Joannicus said.

"She doesn't like you guys. She finds you a little creepy," Paul said.

Ambrose laughed. "The feeling is mutual."

"What's wrong with her?" Joannicus asked, looking from Paul to Jacob to Ambrose.

"Can I go to the library?" Paul said, changing the subject.

"Sure," Jacob said.

Paul looked at them, waiting for the edict. They were silent.

"The library. I suspect that's code for meeting a girl," Ambrose said. "What's her name? Bethany?"

Paul looked at Joannicus in disbelief. Marijuana not only made Joannicus a philosopher, but someone who said unfiltered words.

"Charlie, I'm meeting Charlie," Paul said, feeling his face getting red.

DOWN THE HILL, he found Charlie inside the college library at a big table, alone. Students looked at her as she sat in her black jumper and pink-and-black striped tights.

She beckoned Paul over with an excited hand wave.

"Okay, the birth certificate of your mother states she was born in North Carolina, and she was a twin. In fact, you got twin genes running throughout your family. Your grandmother was a twin and great grandmother, too."

Paul's head was spinning. "Whoa, you've lost me. I'm not a twin. My birth certificate doesn't say twin."

But Bethany is a twin. Her sister, Brittney, had just died, and Joannicus was intent on attending the funeral. Paul and Lucas had visited the sisters many times since Joannicus had returned home. Paul found it surprising that Lucas was interested in a dying girl. But it fit his short-term relationships with girls, for he had many girlfriends in a year's time. Paul was far more interested in Brittney's sister, Bethany. Whatever the spell the girls cast on them seemed to work. Paul agreed with Bethany, and Lucas with Brittney, on matters that when they weren't with the girls, they asked themselves what they had agreed to.

"Your mom's a twin, fraternal and your name is messed up. You should be a Bennett-Hill."

No, he was Paul Albert Warner.

"Are you even listening to me?" Charlie said, her voice rose above the hum of the lights.

"Yeah, it's just confusing," Paul said, remembering that Lucas was going to the funeral. He could attend Brittney's funeral and see Bethany, and nobody would be the wiser. Paul wanted to see Bethany again.

A library attendant came by and shushed them.

"How did you get this information?"

A smile grew on Charlie's black lips. "I wrote letters to the genealogical society, and used the newsgroups on the computer, and asked questions. These are the nineties. Get involved in the new technology or at least familiarize yourself with the how it works."

Paul's heart thumped.

"Did you use my name?"

Charlie looked at him. "I had to use some name. You can't start without names. What are you worried about?"

That was a valid question. Whenever Paul thought about finding his family, a weight, like an anchor, caused his stomach to hollow out. There were too many what-ifs.

He shrugged. "It makes me nervous."

"Nervous?"

Paul picked up the papers and stacked them. "Well, my mom didn't want me to live with them. I should just accept that."

"We should find out why before accepting it. There might be

an entirely reasonable explanation for keeping things hush-hush. It might not be sinister."

"Reasonable? If it's hidden, maybe it needs to be kept that way."

"Where's your sense of adventure? Maybe it was an affair, and daddy wasn't able to marry. Perhaps they didn't have time to because he died. Or they planned to marry, but they drafted him."

"Or worse, it was rape, and the dude's in jail," Paul said bleakly.

Charlie smacked his arm. "Stop being gloomy. Perhaps your dad is rich and just waiting to find the son he wasn't aware he had."

"I don't need money."

"Everyone needs money," Charlie said, as she scribbled on a piece of notebook paper.

She handed Paul the paper. In bold print it said, "I, Paul Bennett-Hill, also known as Paul Warner, bequeath half my inheritance to Charlemagne Scout Winters. Once it is discovered that I am filthy rich."

"Really?" Paul said.

"You two—" came a voice behind them.

Paul and Charlie jumped.

"—need to shush." They hadn't noticed the librarian.

"Sorry, Mrs. Miner," Charlie said.

"Just keep it down," Mrs. Miner said as she leaned over them. "That needs a notary for it to be legal. I'll be right back."

As silently as she had approached, she returned with a notary stamp.

Paul signed, hesitating which name to jot down. Mrs. Miner stamped, and Charlie smiled.

"Thank you, Mrs. Miner."

"Anytime, Charlemagne, just keep it down. We don't want

people to think libraries are cool hangouts," Mrs. Miner said as she left them, gathering runaway books off tables.

"Did you know her first name is Cymbeline?"

Paul wrinkled his nose.

"Oh, never mind, you're uneducated as to who that is, let alone the significance," Charlie said. She put the signed and stamped document in her backpack and fished out two letters, handing them to Paul.

"Well, open them," Charlie said. "I have been dying to see what is inside."

Paul wiped his sweaty palms on his jeans. There were four documents. A birth certificate for Sarah Warner and one for David Warner and a death certificate for both of them. Three of the dates matched Paul's birth date, October 1975.

"Wow, your mom must be the only person on the planet to have two death certificates," Charlie said, producing a Montana death certificate and placing it next to the North Carolina one.

"That doesn't make sense," Paul said. Knowing his mother died when he was four. The second letter was from Ms. Nellie Bennett-Hill. The handwriting was elegant. Two words covered Charlie's letter: not related.

"Yes, it does," Charlie said. "Look who the informant on the North Carolina documents was. Nellie Bennett-Hill. She lied."

"People don't lie on legal documents," Paul said.

"Wake up, Warner, this isn't the monastery, this is real life. People lie."

They opened the letter from Bernice Warner. Charlie leaned her head close to Paul's. Her scent was pleasant. Paul turned and took a quick glance at her. She was pretty, even with hot-pink-streaked hair.

Charlie frowned. "Stop looking at me like that, or I will sock you."

Paul concentrated on the family tree before him.

"Bernice said Sarah died with her infant son."

"You mean I had a twin brother?"

"Let's not jump to conclusions. Don't you think one of you is enough?" She smiled, the little diamond stud in her nose twinkled.

That wasn't an answer. As Paul looked over the charts. He didn't like the idea of a duplicate of himself. Did he have a brother?

"My mom never mentioned him," Paul said. "We got the wrong family."

Charlie groaned. "Don't be daft. Why would you talk to a kid about the death of his brother?"

Paul tapped the page with the tip of a pencil. "This is the wrong family. Do you have my birth certificate?"

She handed them to Paul.

"Charlie, this makes no sense. How can I have been born in Montana and my brother in North Carolina?"

As he pushed the paper, Paul said, "None of this tells me who my dad is. My birth certificate has the name Bennett-Hill listed as my father."

"That's true. Your mom was telling us he was one of the Bennett-Hills. Bernice is telling us that Sarah had two babies. The baby David's birth and death certificate, match your birthday and it says the father is Sean Bennett-Hill. I conclude Sean is your dad."

Charlie chewed on the end of her pencil and studied the family tree.

"That is odd," Charlie said. "I have the right family. Someone is lying. My money is on that Nellie person."

Charlie shrugged and studied the pages again, spreading two photos on the table. Paul stared at the faces. Did he look like a

Warner or a Bennett-Hill? Paul's head hurt. Charlie picked up a photo and held it up to Paul's face.

"Yea, I think they look like you."

Paul pushed her hand away.

"There is a mystery here. Aren't you the least bit curious? Let's not forget Nellie. She has something to hide with that 'not related' edict."

"Why would Nellie lie?" Paul said, wishing for a distraction from the uncomfortable possibilities that lay scattered before him. "I think I owe you a lot of money for all these documents."

"We'll sort this out. As for the money, don't worry, I'll collect. In the meantime, my mom's just happy I'm taking an interest in family history."

Paul sighed. He didn't think he wanted to have this family.

"You don't care about where you came from, do you?"

"No, not really," Paul said. "I don't want to change things. I like things the way they are. Having forty dads is okay with me."

Charlie glared at him. He had blown it again.

"Then why the hell did I waste all my time doing this?"

"It made your mom happy," Paul said, grasping for something to keep her from stomping off in a huff. He only let her continue searching because it meant they could spend time together. She would probably hit him if he said that.

"True, it gave us something to talk about on those nights that dad was off doing whatever."

"Can you name your ancestor?" Paul asked.

Charlie leaned back in her chair. "Yes. Everyone can."

Paul wasn't sure he believed that; the bells for evening prayers rang.

Charlie gathered the various piles of papers and her black knee-length sweater.

"Want to go to prayers?" Paul asked.

Charlie was a little hesitant but rose to follow him.

They walked up the hill at a quick pace and entered the church just as the novice said, "Oh Lord, come to my assistance."

Abbot Jacob turned, and he and Charlie exchanged a nod. Paul thought that was odd. Paul frowned. Joannicus was at prayers. Paul wished he wasn't. Not because Charlie was with him, but simple colds often ran amuck through the monastery, and he feared Joe would be the first one to catch it. Paul was losing the battle, for Joannicus wasn't staying isolated.

Paul prayed. Charlie sat and listened, shifted, and watched. Heads turned and looked as they sat behind the community.

Father Joannicus rose and walked to the podium to deliver the evening reading. Paul fumed. He shouldn't be reading. He should be in bed, resting. Paul had set up a baby monitor so that Joannicus could listen to prayers from his cell. The man was just too stubborn.

Joannicus looked up halfway through the reading, staring at Paul and Charlie. Then, clearing his throat, he continued.

Charlie leaned over. "That's your Joe, isn't it? I think I scared him."

Paul almost laughed. If she only knew how correct she was.

When prayers ended, they made their way out of the church toward the atrium.

"I won't do that again," Charlie said. She stopped at the floral arrangement by the icon of Mary. A pussy willow branch arched over three red tulips. "Nice ikebana."

"What are you talking about?"

"The flowers, but I was first talking about prayers. It's a little creepy, all those black robes, the chanting, and that fragrance."

Paul stopped and looked at her. "Incense, it lingers. I thought you were Catholic, familiar with priests in black robes."

"It's a little too much Catholic."

Paul laughed. "This is the ultimate Goth. I thought you'd believe that you had died and went to Goth heaven."

Three monks, Brother Ambrose, Abbot Jacob, and Father Joannicus, stood in the atrium waiting for them. Another nod was exchanged between Jacob and Charlie. That was now more than suspicious.

"Hello, I'm Father Joannicus," Joannicus said, stepping forward with a hand extended.

Charlie stepped up and shook his hand. "Sorry. I didn't mean to frighten you," she said, in an apology that Paul had never expected would come from her lips.

"You've gotten taller," Joannicus said, looking the girl up and down. "Stunning color combination you have put together."

"Thanks, I like black, but my mom says I need to add some color. So, I use splashes of color to keep her happy."

"I like black too. Basic, simple and goes with every season."

"She looks like a burnt zebra," Ambrose muttered.

Paul cringed.

Charlie's eyes narrowed. "You're a laugh a minute. You know zebras bite."

"I'm not scared, little girl. I work with all kinds of wild animals," Ambrose said in a menacing tone.

This was rapidly deteriorating.

"So, did you knit that sweater yourself? You know we have homespun yarn at the monastery store," Joannicus said.

"Yes, it is Llama yarn. And no, I didn't know you had a yarn shop," Charlie said, turning and scowling at Paul. "Do you have a spinning wheel?"

"Yes, several, Saxony wheels," Joannicus said.

Paul shook his head. Charlie knits? Joannicus knows about spinning wheels? Had he stepped into an alternate reality?

"I like the Castle wheel," Charlie said.

"Have Paul show you our textiles. We make great weaves and use natural dyes," Joannicus said.

"I will do that. Nice to have finally met you, but I must get home," Charlie said, as she headed to the church door.

Paul watched her go.

"Don't you think you should go with her?" Jacob said.

"Hell, nobody is going to mess with her," Ambrose said.

"Paul, go escort you friend to her car," Jacob said, and it wasn't a request, even though Paul agreed with Ambrose. Nobody messed with Charlie.

Paul headed out the door and jogged to catch up with her.

"Hey," Paul said. "How do you know Abbot Jacob?"

"The Crow? He answers the phones a lot. So, we talk."

"That's cuz you call his office, and not my room," Paul said.

"Well, you are never in your room. So why would I call your room?"

"I don't know," Paul said with a shrug as they approached her car.

Talk? What did a seventeen-year-old Goth girl have to say to a Benedictine abbot?

"What do you talk about?" Paul asked, not sure he liked the idea of them conversing.

"Get over yourself, Warner. It's not always about you," Charlie said.

Paul stared at her, and she laughed.

"You really want to know? Okay, we talked about sex." Her face was now serious.

Paul felt horrified as Charlie climbed into her car and drove away.

He didn't think he'd ever understand girls.

CHAPTER 32

SUFFERING

Psalm 138:23

O search me, God, and know my heart.

O test me and know my thoughts.

T he afternoon sun warmed Paul as he sat with Joannicus on the patio outside of the community room.

"Now, seriously, guys," Joannicus said, scolding the flock of birds. "There is plenty for all." Joannicus broke the bread into small pieces and scattered them to the squabbling birds. The braver birds charged up. One bird landed on his knee and feasted upon the crumbs that had settled in his scapular that lay folded in his lap.

"You haven't commented on Charlie," Paul said.

"Do you like her? Is she a good friend?"

"Yes, the best."

"Then what is there to say?"

"Ah, she's a little over the top in dress and makeup," Paul said.

Joannicus laughed. "I heard she speaks Latin. Abbot Jacob told me she is wicked smart."

Paul rolled his eyes. "How does he know that?"

"Apparently, she calls him frequently."

"I told her to stop." Why was she still calling the Abbot? A twinge of jealousy pricked Paul's mind. They were his family, not hers. She called him every night after evening prayers.

"Perhaps she wants to join our community," Joannicus said.

"She can't. She's a girl," Paul said. Maybe she wanted a community. Charlie had no siblings or friends that he was aware of. Lately, she had mentioned that home was a bummer. Paul didn't understand what that meant, but figured that her folks were harassing her.

He was lucky the monks didn't hassle him.

"Perhaps she wants to join a female community," Joannicus said, tossing more bread on the patio as the visiting bird flock grew.

Charlie a nun. That was absurd. Almost as bizarre as the things she sometimes hypothesized about his family. Paul had spent the week haunted with dreams and not all of them good. What if it turned out that he was related to Father Pius? Lucas had said that Pius had a family in North Carolina. Is there a code of blood? He had overheard people say, "their family."

"Do you know who your ancestors are, your cousins, grand-parents, and great-grandparents?" Paul asked.

"Yes. Cajun on my mother's side. They've lived in Louisiana a long time. My dad's side has a lengthy line of preachers. I've met a small group of them. It's not like Abbot Jacob, who knows his linage back to that French trapper."

Paul recalled the tales of Cold Feet and his Crow wife, Sings in the Night, the myth of the one with the blue eyes. Paul wondered if he had any grand stories in his family.

"Do I have ancestors?"

Joannicus turned and looked at him. "Seriously, you aren't Superman. We didn't get you in an abandoned pod or a basket. Why the sudden interest?"

Paul shrugged his shoulders. "Charlie and I have investigated it. My mother was a twin. I was wondering who my father was. All I have is his surname Bennett-Hill, but I'm a Warner."

Paul couldn't help but notice the cloud of sadness that covered Joe's face.

He shouldn't have brought it up.

"Seriously, everyone has a father. I don't recall seeing any information about him. He might be alive," Joannicus said, brushing the crumbs from his scapular.

Paul looked away. The pain was too visible on Joe's face. The birds protested when a squirrel came down the wall.

"Do you want this knowledge?" Joannicus asked, sounding tense.

"Charlie wants it. She thinks the man is waiting to find me. That my mom didn't tell him," Paul said. "She wouldn't do that, would she?"

Joannicus shrugged his shoulders and folded his hands into his lap. "I know that sometimes the results of the search are disappointing."

"Yeah, that's what Lucas said. Don't look for a man who hasn't looked for you. He didn't want you or care about you."

"That's one possibility." Joannicus said as he pulled a woolen cap out of his pocket and fumbled to place it on his head. "There are papers, which Abbot Gordon had, but I never actually looked through them. We could look together."

Paul looked at Joannicus. This man was his father. In his heart, a lack of biological connection did not change that. He was such an idiot. Change the subject. He's so kind. If cancer doesn't kill him, his doing this would.

"No, I'm good," Paul said, reaching over and grasping Joe's hand. "You were a twin, right? Just like Bethany and Brittney."

"They were fraternal. Conner and I were identical," Joannicus said, patting Paul's hand.

"Do you remember your twin?"

"Yes, he died when I was eight. I have lots of memories."

"Did he have cancer?" Paul said, regretting the words as they tumbled out.

"No, Conner developed Reye's Syndrome. We had been ill, and my mother had given us aspirin for our fever and, well, he didn't recover. I remember his funeral. In my family, it was customary to have the person in the house. To this day, I can't stand the smell of camphor. I thought the wake went on for weeks. I was able to peek into the coffin one night. It gave me nightmares."

Now Paul understood why Joannicus had tried to keep him from Merlin. He was afraid that the death of Brother Mellitus would have given Paul nightmares. A wave of nostalgia embraced Paul. It would be weird to see yourself in a coffin as a child. Charlie would probably think it was cool.

Bethany's sad face haunted Paul's memory. "Do you miss him? Do you think she'll get over it? She seemed broken."

"Time heals all. Even my mother has recovered. She blamed herself for a long time."

Brilliant, Warner, go from one depressing subject to another.

"I miss my brother, usually on our birthday. Twins are closer than most siblings are. There will always be a missing part inside of Bethany. That doesn't mean she can't love others."

"She said she's half a person. I don't understand what that means."

Joannicus squeezed Paul's hand. "It means she is grieving. Give her time."

"That's it. I want to help," Paul said, feeling helpless.

"You can't fix this. Losing someone you love hurts. Be there and listen."

The patio door opened, and the birds scattered, tweeting their annoyance from the safety of tree and wall. The squirrel froze and then darted under the table.

"Ah, there you two are," Pius said, entering the yard. "Nice comments at Brittney's funeral. I didn't know she was a twin."

"Thanks. Brittney was a sweet young lady," Joannicus said.

"Speaking of that," Pius said, turning his attention to Paul. "You and Lucas need to rein in the testosterone. That kind of stuff is not proper at a funeral. A word of advice: when someone like Bethany loses her sister, a twin, she needs time and healing, not romance and jealousy."

Paul felt his spine stiffen. Joannicus hadn't said his behavior was out of line. Lucas was hitting on Bethany, not him. Lucas had his arm around her as if she was Britt, the one who had died. The worst part was that Lucas was aware Paul liked Bethany. The gesture was a ruse.

"I don't think I need your advice about girls," Paul said as Joannicus put his hand on Paul's arm, causing Paul's fist to unclench.

"Suit yourself, but the flare of tempers... Don't you think so, Father Joannicus?" Pius asked, oblivious to Paul's fury.

"Emotions were raw for all," Father Joannicus said. "A life cut short is hard to understand."

Pius shook his head slightly, and Paul waited to hear, "You let him get away with too much." But Pius asked, "Are you planning on confirmation at Easter?"

"Paul was wondering why the man asked.

"You've missed a lot of the classes."

"No. I have done all the assignments. I have logged my hours and talked to both my godparents and others as was required," Paul said. Pius was aware he was taking care of Father Joannicus.

"But your presence in class is lacking," Pius said, cracking his knuckles.

That's it. Paul couldn't hold back his indignation.

"Why are you making this so hard? I'm not receiving with the class, so what difference does it make if I attend?"

Pius looked at Father Joannicus, who was oddly silent.

"Get your folder and give it to Father Pius," Joannicus said.

Paul left and went to retrieve his folder from his cell. Father Pius had no right to be handing out relationship advice. Father Pius was aware Abbot Jacob was going to confirm Paul, so why did he care about stupid essays? In his room, Paul found the papers and shook off the cracker crumbs. Paul noticed he hadn't filled out the questionnaire. Digging for a pen, he quickly filled in the page.

As for Lucas, they had words, but that was because Lucas was hogging Bethany. She had sat next to him, not Lucas, and yet Lucas swooped in and spirited her away. His actions angered Paul.

Paul had never experienced a funeral outside of the monastery. Bethany cried. Paul wasn't sure what to do. Charlie never cried. She always got angry when she hurt. The monks didn't wail when a community member died. They didn't look so sad that you could almost feel it. At Brittany's funeral, Paul felt as if he could touch the grief. The sadness covered everyone like a mist over a once beautiful lake. He even saw Joannicus wiping tears from his face. Paul had never seen the man cry. He had seen Jacob weep, and that was just as disturbing.

"I didn't mean to argue with Lucas," Paul said to his white tiger, who lay stuffed on his bookshelf between two novels, *Remnant* and *The Other Side of the River*.

A book Pius had been reading, and Paul had borrowed it, without asking. He was curious about what he read. Paul scowled at the tiger. "Fine, it was good a book. I took it, I will return it. Even though he has good books, I don't like him."

Maybe Joannicus was right. Emotions were raw that day.

Paul walked down the hall past the Abbot's office. The door was open, and he heard Jacob and Joannicus. Paul paused, but then continued into the community room. Father Pius was at a table, and Brother Ambrose was in the kitchenette pouring coffee. Paul approached, holding out the folder.

Pius scowled but didn't take the folder.

"I thought you wanted this. You made a big deal about it."

"Apparently you'll be confirmed with or without my opinion," Pius said, crossing his arms under his scapular.

Paul shook his head. "Why wouldn't I be confirmed? Why are you against me?"

"I have nothing against you. I just don't think you grasp fully the duties to which you are committing yourself."

He wasn't a monk candidate, and he had done the work.

"You're mistaken. I know what it means to be a Catholic." Paul picked up the folder. He held up the paper in front of Pius. "Read my stuff before you judge me. You don't know me... or what I believe."

Pius pushed the folder away. "Why is everything a challenge with you? I just asked for your work. We expect all candidates to do this. Just because Catholicism is your life doesn't give you an exemption. That is not how the Church works."

"I'm not asking for special treatment," Paul said through gritted teeth. "I'm not challenging you. I'm a reasonable person. Why can't you see that?"

"I could say the same thing."

"You're just picking a fight. Stop," Paul said, the loudness of his voice rattled the silence of the monastery.

Pius cracked his knuckles. Paul threw the folder onto the table, and the pages of Paul's faith flew and scattered.

"Little One," Ambrose said, his eyes looking at the mess.

"No, don't yell at me. I didn't do anything," Paul said, shoving the chair away from the table.

Rapid footsteps echoed in the hallway as Jacob, followed by Joannicus, appeared in the doorway to the community room. Brother Ambrose moved to stand behind Pius. Jacob placed a hand on Paul's shoulder. Paul shrugged it off.

"I didn't do anything wrong. Why are you taking me away?" Paul asked as Jacob ushered him into the office.

"Sit," Jacob ordered, letting go of his arm. Paul sat and crossed his arms, rubbing where Jacob had clamped a hand.

"We need to talk. You need to get control of your emotions," Jacob said, his voice solid and cold.

Paul shifted, eyeing the doorway until Jacob stepped in front of him. The Abbot's blue eyes pinned Paul to the chair.

"Paul, don't." Jacob's voice sounded more like a whisper inside of Paul's head.

"Don't what? Don't tell him he is a jerk and is ruining my life?" Paul yelled.

Pius always seemed to be a menacing force in his life and often in his dreams, giving him nightmares. The man was like cancer, eating away at Paul's happiness. "He's the one making life difficult, meddling in my affairs, trying to make it impossible for me to be confirmed. Why does he even care?"

"I'm sorry," Jacob said.

"You didn't do anything to me. You tried to protect me. Pius should be sorry. He should say that, not you."

"If he did, would it change anything?"

"No, I wouldn't forgive him, so let's just drop it."

CHAPTER 33
STUBBORN BOY

Psalm 118:9

How shall the young remain sinless?

The conversation was not going well. Stubborn boy.

"Paul, stop," Jacob said. The boy paused and looked at him with venom. "This is not a contest. You will be confirmed. Father Pius does not need to approve it."

"He thinks he does, and he will not stop me because of a technicality. I'll be going to Mass and doing everything that candidates must do."

"You are not listening. Leave Pius out of this. I will confirm you at the monastery."

"I know," Paul said, waving his arms.

Like an unexpected slap to the face, Jacob realized this wasn't about confirmation. It was about Pius. Why hadn't Abbot Gordon dealt with the physical abuse? Jacob knew Gordon had made Pius seek counseling, but why not Paul? The answer was simple: the monks had adopted a "wait and see" attitude.

"That never actually works," chanted the Elders in Jacob's mind.

Paul headed out the door just as Brother Ambrose and Father Joannicus entered.

"We done with the attitude?" Ambrose asked Paul.

"Get out of my way," Paul snarled, pushing his way out.

"Teenagers are such emotional roller coasters. One minute they're happy and the next they think the world is ending," Ambrose said, shaking his wooly head.

"Didn't you tell him he was going to be confirmed here?" Joannicus asked.

Jacob wanted to knock both of their heads together. This was not about confirmation. It was about Pius and the abuse that happened.

"That's water under the bridge. Pius isn't abusing him now," Ambrose said.

"Abuse leaves scars," Jacob said, rubbing his upper arm where a scar was. A failed attempt by his mother to kill him with a gunshot, and the mental pain still stung, though the physical had long since healed. There was no love lost between mother and son. He had known that all his life. The total acceptance of that reality still ached.

He should have stayed, not run away. He was to blame as well.

"Paul acts this way because he is hurting."

The faces before him clouded with dismay.

"You absolved and forgave Pius. Paul was expected just to ignore it ever happened. You do not forget abuse. You eventually put it aside, but hell, that has taken me years. I have not forgotten that my stepfather, Terrence, hurt me, or that my mom wishes I would die. I just..." Jacob paused and swallowed. The ache inside throbbed. His past was a series of anguished memories. "I just chose to dwell on pleasant thoughts."

Joannicus folded his hands and closed his eyes for a moment. Then he stood up and walked over to where Jacob sat. Placing a hand on his shoulder, he said, "I didn't know. I'm sorry. What can I do?"

Jacob reached up and patted Joe's hand.

"I am taking Paul to counseling this week," Abbot Jacob said.

Father Joannicus and Brother Ambrose looked at each other. Jacob could see a protest forming on their lips.

"He is going to counseling before we lose him," Jacob said, giving them a piercing look.

"He doesn't need counseling. You didn't need professional help. You're healed," Ambrose grumbled.

"Healed? Are you healed?" the Elders in his mind asked. A tickle of fear glanced in his direction. The line between abused and abuser wavered. Jacob shook his head.

The physical abuse was nowhere near the caliber of what Jacob had survived, yet Paul held on to the anger and picked at it. Jacob understood that, for he had many times poked the evil. Jacob remembered the dagger of pain he shoved into people's hearts when he would boldly show a bruise or welt to the powerless adult. Oh, they had wanted to help, but for whatever twisted reason, they couldn't prevent the abuse. He had stopped the violence toward Paul, but the monks had quickly spun a protective cocoon of denial around Paul, which only kept Paul's anger at a slow burn.

"I still have scars, both mentally and physically. The fact that you focused on Pius and not Paul was naïve and foolishly wrong."

"But Pius was the sinner. His soul was in danger," Joannicus said, standing now next to Ambrose, who was snorting like a buffalo.

"We cannot wait any longer," Jacob said.

"Paul will not grow up to be an abuser," Ambrose said, crossing his arms, allowing the rip at his shoulder to expose the red undershirt, which stood out against the black of his habit. "They provoke each other. Paul is unkind to Father Pius."

"No," Joannicus said.

Jacob wanted to hug the man for finally loving Paul.

"Father Pius is not any better. He does the same to Paul. They cannot resist being nasty," Jacob said.

"Seriously, can't we fix Paul ourselves?" Joannicus asked.

Jacob frowned. The monks were outsiders when they had helped in Jacob's healing.

"We are too close to the issues. Paul needs someone from the outside, someone who can point out his self-destructive actions."

Ambrose grunted, and Jacob wasn't sure if he was agreeing or disagreeing. Jacob locked eyes with the solemn-faced man.

"Yes, Father Abbot," Joannicus said, tugging on Brother Ambrose's sleeve. Ambrose harrumphed, turned, and walked out of the office.

Jacob hurried down the hall to the sacristy to dress for Mass. He put on his chasuble and alb and caught the tail end of the procession into the church. Looking for Paul, he spied him sitting with his arms crossed tightly across his chest.

Stubborn boy.

Behind Paul sat Rebecca, Jacob's sister, and her husband, Todd, along with other family members from the Crow reservation. That was when Jacob remembered. He was going out with them to celebrate Rebecca's birthday.

Good, he needed a distraction.

As Mass continued, Jacob said the words and performed the

gestures, but his mind raced with thoughts other than the divine. Frustration rose inside of him. The monks should have addressed the issues long ago. Maybe Paul wouldn't be angry. Paul wasn't living with the past very well these days. Lucas had caused a chink in Paul's protective armor—a coating that all abused kids wore. He heard the nightmares through the silent halls at night. He knew the shouts coming from Paul's room were about Pius.

Jacob stood at the altar offering the cup of consecrated wine to those before him. He glanced over to see Paul in line for communion, face pinched, his eyes hard, focused. He had seen that look before. A look of fierce determination that followed a sharp clicking of the tongue before his mother acted upon him in a blind rage. A slap or something would fly in his direction when she narrowed her eyes. He had gotten good at provoking and ducking and watching her suffer when she missed her mark. Him.

Jacob mentally willed Paul to come to the right side, to him.

But the stubborn boy stepped to the left, to Father Pius.

Damn. Why does the evil always tempt us?

The hairs on Jacob's arm prickled as if lightning were about to strike. Jacob placed his chalice on the altar. The next recipient stood, confused. Jacob moved around the table, dodging those receiving communion, hoping to get between Father Pius and Paul.

"The blood of Christ, Paul," Father Pius said.

Paul stared fixated on Pius through narrowed eyes and tight lips. The world grew small, and sounds faded. Time seemed too slow. Over the music, and the people, Jacob could hear Paul.

"You shouldn't be serving. You're a sinner, not yet forgiven. How dare you stand before me and offer the cup of compassion?"

"Excuse me?" Pius said, jerking his head back.

"You heard me. Say you're sorry," Paul hissed.

"Enough," Pius said, attempting to turn away from Paul. Jacob watched in horror as Paul pushed the cup, spilling the contents onto Father Pius.

Everything stopped. As it should have, for pausing was an appropriate response. A respectful acknowledgment of the presence that the wine represented. There was more shock than respect. Consecrated wine dripped off Father Pius. The robes were washed in the sacrarium. A special sink not connected to the regular plumbing, but directly to the ground. Monks used the sacrarium to wash the chalices and other sacred vessels that contained trace elements of the consecrated wine or host.

Would Pius's head fit under the faucet of the sink?

Time resumed in a rush of sound, gasps, and exclamations. Monks moved to help Pius disrobe. Mass was over. Jacob ushered Paul out of the church, followed by a trail of monks.

"What were you thinking?" Joannicus said.

Paul's face was void of emotion. This was not the time to explain.

"He shouldn't be allowed in the church, he shouldn't, he's evil, and he's bad," Paul said, his voice childlike, filled with confusion and anguish.

"The Church is for saints and sinners alike," Jacob said as his voice cracked. He had waited too long.

"He held Jesus in his hands, hands that are evil," Paul said, his eyes full and wild.

"Ambrose's voice boomed over the voices in the hallway.

"It was an accident," Father Joannicus said. "Seriously, they collided."

"No, he did it on purpose," Brother Alcuin said. "I saw the whole thing."

Father Pius appeared in his black habit, hair wet and dripping.

Brother Alcuin turned toward him. "What should you do with Paul?"

Monks rallied around Pius, his face red. "I'm all right," Father Pius said. "Paul, we need to talk."

Abbot Jacob pulled Paul closer to him as Pius approached. Several Crow Indians who had been attending Mass moved to stand next to Jacob.

"I have nothing to say to you," Paul croaked over Jacob's right shoulder.

A senior monk spoke. "Nothing short of excommunication will suffice since that was sacrilege, a gross irreverence of what is sacred."

"No," Brother Moses said, "We can't send him away. He's just a kid."

"He's almost an adult," Alcuin said. "We have been allowing him to break the rules for years."

"That was a shameful disregard for everything we stand for, everything the Church stands for," another monk said. "Send him away."

"If we excommunicate him, then we have to reinstate him. Canon Law states, I quote, 'A person who habitually lacks the use of reason is considered incapable of an offense, even if they have violated a law or a precept while appearing to be sane.' That's Paul. He habitually lacks the use of reason and seems rational," stated a novice. Everyone turned a looked at him.

Impressive, thought Abbot Jacob. This one has priestly tendencies.

"Abbot Jacob, what should we do?"

Paul pushed closer on Jacob's back and a hand gripped Jacob's arm.

"Will you have to destroy the church?" Rebecca, Jacob's sister, whispered into his left ear.

Jacob glowered at her. Accident or on purpose, defacing the consecrated wine was sacrilegious and not a joke.

"We will take him. I know he can't stay here right now," Rebecca said, her voice lost to the protests of the community arguing among themselves.

"Go with Rebecca," Jacob ordered.

"But I didn't mean it," Paul said, his face still frozen in anguish.

Jacob placed his hands on Paul's shoulders. "It will be okay. Trust me."

Jacob's sister and family enclosed Paul and escorted him out of the church through the protesting monks.

"Canon Law states we can extract just punishment," Alcuin said.

"That is true," Pius said, in a soft and dangerous voice.

The voices blended and rose around Jacob. He wanted to go with Paul.

"Abbot Jacob, what should we do?" Brother Ryan asked, standing on Jacob's right side.

What to do with the blessing of Paul? Today, he was a challenge. He looked at the expectant faces before him. Jacob felt torn. Listen to the voices around him or to the one in his heart.

He had done what the Church demands, removed Paul. Nothing else needs to happen today.

"Brothers, enough. We will continue the evening in silence and ponder our sin," Jacob said.

"What?" Pius said, his voice soft with disbelief. "This is what I was concerned about. He wants confirmation, but he acts like this. I don't think he is ready."

"This has nothing to do with confirmation. Paul was showing us his scars, his emotional ones that are still there because we have been supporting the wrong person. Paul cannot let go of the past until all of us acknowledge Father Pius's sin toward Paul."

"What sin?" the newer monk whispered.

"He physically abused Paul years ago," Brother Ryan whispered to the newer monk.

"I wasn't here for that," Alcuin murmured smugly.

Jacob watched the shock and confusion dance across the faces of the newer members, followed by the slow steps of relief as it sank in that the abuse was in the past. The sins of one were the sins of the entire community.

Monks shook their heads. Jacob felt his ire rise. He was the abbot; they would listen.   "You have forgiven Father Pius his offenses, and that is wonderful, but what about Paul? We are guilty of pushing Paul aside. We are sinful by our complacency," Jacob said, looking from one monk to the next. Monks hung their heads in silence. Pius's face hardened.

"What shall we do?" Father Joannicus asked.

Jacob's anger drained at Joe's needs to unite them.

"Acknowledge our sin and ask Paul for forgiveness," Jacob said, looking directly at Father Pius. The man's face was unreadable.

CHAPTER 34

THREE CROWS

Psalm 50:15
That I may teach transgressors your ways
and sinners may return to you.

P aul woke up, and his mouth was dry. Had he been drugged? All he could remember was that two Crow men and Jacob's sister, Rebecca, escorted him out of the church and pushed into him the back of a service truck, a windowless box that smelled faintly of dirty linen. He had been enraged as he lay in the dark, the engine rumbling, attempting to sort out the events. Pius had hurt him as a child, and the priest had never said he was sorry, nor had he treated Paul with kindness. He was kind to Lucas. When Pius offered the blood of Christ to Paul, he thought of how wrong it was. The sacrifice of a life done by the least compassionate man he knew.

The rage and confusion had left him exhausted, draining his senses and will. The fight within him dissipated when the back door of the van opened. He felt ill and barely aware of his surroundings. He just wanted to sleep.

Strong arms pulled him out and apparently placed him in this location. But where was he?

Paul sat and looked around. Nothing was clearly visible in the dim light. The ground was cold and damp. The conical shape told him he was in a teepee.

"Hello?" Panic rose in the darkness. "Hello?"

The flap to the entrance opened. A small flashlight shone on a pair of old, faded turquoise cowboy boots. The design looked familiar. Where had he seen that feather and thorn?

"What am I doing here?" Paul asked.

This was crazy. Irritation filled Paul. He was in no mood for games.

Paul realized he knew he couldn't go home. He had offended the Church, and the monastery was part of the Church. Paul hadn't violated the cloister this time. He couldn't just say sorry. Paul stood. The man was tall and muscular. His hair hung loosely past his shoulders.

He wasn't staying here. Surely Abbot Jacob was outside. He'll be mad, but he always tried to understand and forgive. Paul made a dash toward the opening, but the man stuck out his foot. Paul stumbled, crashing into the tent wall.

"Do not go. There is no place to go."

"I'll be the judge of that," Paul snapped, rubbing his elbow.

The man held out a rock. Paul took it. The cold stone looked like a polished lump of coal with ragged edges.

"You keep that in your hand at all times. When I come, if you have your stone in your hand, you may ask me one question."

"What if I don't?"

The man looked slightly amused. "Is that your question?"

"No. What am I doing here?"

"Listening," the man said, leaving the teepee.

Crap. This was stupid. Paul pocketed the rock, stuck his head out of the flap, and encountered two legs in faded, frayed blue jeans and cowboy boots. He looked up and saw they belonged to another Crow Indian.

He thought he must be on the Crow Reservation. Paul crawled out, but didn't recognize this place.

The sun was rising over the distant mountains, washing the sky in pink. The air was chilled, and the light hadn't yet touched the ground. The man looked at him.

"I have to use the restroom," Paul said. He had to pee. The man pointed toward a wooded area. Paul could barely make out a path through the mist.

No restroom. How barbaric.

He remembered how, as a kid, he loved to take a leak outside and that Brother Ambrose let him. Standing at the edge of the woods, Paul glanced around. The teepee was a standard stick and canvas, not tourist white but cream colored with a purple loop design, and crows perched on a purple line, all but one looking in the same direction. A man is sitting on a carved tree-stump chair. This place appeared to be remote. They didn't just materialize. Where was the car? Paul moved into the woods. He ran after the campground was out of sight.

He listened but heard no pursuing footsteps. As Paul wandered, he soon became confused which direction he was going. It didn't matter if he knew which direction was east. East from where?

Crap and double crap.

The trees and underbrush looked the same. The sun rose. Paul sat down on a log. A nicely smoothed one, flat on one side. Paul ran his fingers over the initials of lovers. This was a hiking trail. How far from people was he? He hoped he would run into campers rather than hunters. They would only laugh at him if he said, "Help, Indians have kidnapped me."

He thought of the first map where he'd placed St. Alberic's Monastery in the center of the state, with the Crow Nation to the east, and heaven, where Canada sat.

Damn you, Abbot Jacob. All your fault. If he hadn't been needling him about Pius, he wouldn't have lost his brain. The voice of Joannicus nudged his conscience. "I think you did this to yourself." Okay, so what if he had? Why did Pius befriend Lucas? Why couldn't Pius leave him alone?

He should have grabbed a jacket. Come nightfall, he'd freeze to death.

He envisioned the newspaper headlines. *Dead white boy found on the Reservation.* They would probably bury him in a shallow grave.

Paul walked, and the trail became narrow and then vanished. Wait, was he following an animal trail rather than a human one? A twig snapped. Paul jumped.

Great. A bear or cougar was about to eat him. A false bravado. In Montana, the threat was real. Paul kept moving. He got to his feet and headed in the direction away from the noise. The wet smell of rot and growth filled Paul's nose, reminding him of the spring plowing when Ambrose would dump manure on the fields.

He wished he could just go home. A feeling of defeat filled Paul. He would not be making confirmation. Damn Pius.

Suddenly, light filtered through the pines, and then an opening in the trees, but as he exited the woods, he found he was nowhere near the camp. He looked about the meadow. The grass shone bright green, bent with dew. A mist hung low as the sun drank the water. He took in his surroundings as he sat on a large rock. A flock of geese honking flew overhead.

Do birds always fly south? This is spring, not the winter. Who would come looking for him? Nobody. He messed this up. Damn, why did he let Pius get to him?

He wasn't the only one around. He sat on a large stone as the sun warmed him. His emotions bounced around like little pinballs, seeking to make points.

He had committed sacrilege, but was it his fault? His stomach growled. A small group of deer tentatively entered the meadow, warily nibbling and then nervously glancing. He realized if he made any sound or movement, they would bolt. He wasn't in Yellowstone where the deer would come to him for handouts. Montana plains were hunting country, population controlled with a rifle.

A shadow was the only thing that alerted him to company. From the shape, Paul was 80 percent sure it wasn't a bear. The deer hadn't even noticed the approach of the Crow Indian. Maybe this one's name was Silent Deer. Silent Deer squatted next to Paul and offered him an apple.

Paul accepted the food. A crisp crunch caused the deer to look around, tails twitching.

After a while, Silent Deer stood up. "You done sightseeing?"

"I was running away," Paul said.

The Apsáalooke man laughed. "More like running in circles. I'm going back."

Stubbornness poked the nagging worry that once evening came, they wouldn't lead him back to camp. Reluctantly, Paul followed through the woods back to the teepee on the ridge. Paul was grateful he hadn't run blindly in the early morning light. A fall off the cliff would've been unpleasant.

Two Legs nodded to them as they entered the camp. Paul sat

on a stump. Two Legs filled a bowl from a pot on the fire pit. Paul's stomach growled, and even though he could not identify what was inside, he filled his bowl. He longed for bacon and eggs or even a bowl of lumpy oatmeal.

"You two my guards? Why have you kidnapped me?"

The two looked at each other. Amusement graced tanned faces.

"Kidnapping, what do we want with a bratty white boy?" Two Legs said.

"You are not a kid. You are free to leave. We only removed you from harm's way as a favor to the Chief." Silent Deer said.

Chief? Did they mean Abbot Jacob? Of course, they did.

"I wasn't going to harm Abbot Jacob," Paul said.

"But you did. Your entire tribe is pissed at you. Some things are sacred," Two Legs said.

"If you aren't keeping me here, then what are you doing?"

"You ask too many questions," Two Legs said, handing Paul his dirty plate.

Great, a prisoner and a slave. Paul would have protested, but he knew dirty dishes attracted wild animals and he wasn't sure these two would protect him.

He figured they would sit and watch as a bear devoured him.

A large plastic container of water sat on the edge of a platform. Paul rinsed the blue speckled tins and startled when he looked up to see the crazy stone man. He stared at Paul.

"In my pocket."

"In your hand," Crazy Stone said.

"That's insane. How can I clean the plates with a rock?"

The man strode away. He was serious about not answering questions.

"Your possessions are inside," Silent Deer said, causing Paul to jump at the sound of his voice.

Damn, that one was creepy quiet.

"The river is in that direction." The man pointed. "Don't forget to fill up the jug sometime today. Yes, you will get wet, so do it before nightfall."

"I thought I was free to leave," Paul said.

"You are."

"I don't know which direction?"

"Go west," the two said in unison, and then laughed. Paul glared at them.

Two Legs threw his drink on the fire. A loud hiss and smoke filled the air.

"Perhaps you should stay and find your path," Silent Deer said.

Paul entered the teepee after cleaning up. His backpack was there. Inside was a change of clothes, his jacket, and schoolwork. No note.

They had abandoned him. He wished he had someone to talk to, someone like Charlie. She would tell him what to do after she stopped laughing.

Paul didn't feel like doing schoolwork, so he curled up in the sleeping bag and went to sleep. Laughter woke him, and he searched for the rock. Had Crazy Stone returned? With his rock in hand, he crawled out of the teepee. Only two Indians sat together as they glanced his way and then returned to their conversation. Two Legs and Silent Deer spoke in Apsáalooke. Paul caught a word or two, something about thunder. His Crow language skills were rusty. Jacob never used his native tongue around the monks.

Great, a storm on the horizon. He despised the seasonal thunderstorms. Inside of a building, they were tolerable, but out here, in a skin teepee with wooden poles sticking up, taunting the lightning to strike... Were they just hoping that God would strike him dead? God should have. Paul knew he had disrespected the Mass, and all it meant to the monks.

"Stupid, stupid, stupid," he could hear Charlie scolding him. Paul shivered and looked at the sky. He saw only white puffy clouds on a clear blue backdrop. The winter snows were still on the mountain ridges. Weather fluctuated wildly in the spring. The temperature could soar to seventy and then plummet to freezing. Paul rubbed his arms.

"If you want warmth, chop," Two Legs said to Paul.

"Me?"

"You will never succeed in life if you remain petulant," Silent Deer said.

"He is not a man. He is still cikyake," Two Legs said.

Why were they calling him a little boy? Were they trying to provoke him? They didn't know him. The words were just mildly irritating, like a mosquito. If Pius had said that... The man haunted Paul. Damn Pius. Paul knew his actions had landed him here. The worst part was that Lucas would now make his move on Bethany. Lucas always got the girls. In one moment, one stupid act, he had ruined his future. They had talked, and he was just about to ask her out.

Damn, he was an idiot. He turned the rock over in his palm. He looked up, noticing he was alone. The silent brothers had left. Would they return? The woodpile lay un-chopped. There must be a cabin nearby. Paul scanned the treetops and the horizon for signs of smoke. A melancholy settled in around Paul. If he wanted a fire this evening, he would have to chop wood.

He was tempted to set his rock aside but worried that Crazy Stone would return, and he would miss his opportunity for a question. The rock bit into his hand every time he swung the ax. The sun crept downward.

Paul started a fire, thankful that Ambrose had let him make

fires as a kid. Soon the wood was snapping, and fiery flames warmed the evening air. He entered the teepee, knowing that there would be food from the times he had spent with Abbot Jacob exploring the reservation. He spied a red cooler and a wooden box, several blankets, jugs of water, and a lantern. The camping cooler held raw meat.

He searched for a grill and tongs and settled on meat on a stick. Paul cut the meat into strips with a pocket knife.

The flames burned the stick, and some of the meat fell into the ash. Paul fished them out and wiped it on his jeans. The outside was crunchy and crisp, and the inside was soft and underdone. Paul now wished he had spent more time with Brother Barnabas, learning to cook rather than just eating.

The sky grew dark. The stars filled the heavens. He remembered when he and Jacob would climb to the barn roof and watch the night sky.

Would the monks ever take him back? They would. Even when they had sent him away, they kept in contact with him. He would hear from them soon. Paul reflected on Silent Deer's words about a path. Abbot Jacob wanted him to figure something out. Might have helped if he left instructions. He knew it had to do with Pius, his repressed anger. That's what Jacob called it. Maybe he should have spoken to a counselor.

An owl hooted, and another answered. Twigs snapped and bushes rustled. Paul grew nervous. Paul lit a lantern before entering the teepee. There wasn't very much protection in skin walls, but at least he wasn't totally exposed. His guards, protectors, whoever they were supposed to be, had not returned. This fear was similar to the fear he had as a boy.

He was not a kid. He could handle this. Pius was not here. It is just him and mother nature. Paul crawled into the teepee. Didn't they believe in air mattresses? Grumbling to himself, he gathered all the blankets into a pile, rolling one into a makeshift pillow before placing the sleeping bag on top. Paul lit a single candle before extinguishing the lantern. The candle, a thin taper in cupcake-like tin, reminded him of the Easter vigil candles that they lit during the three-hour vigil before dawn. Placing the candle a small distance from his bed, he settled into the sleeping bag and watched the tiny flame flicker. Paul tried to recall the prayer to Mother Earth that Jacob used when they had been camping in a teepee years ago. The night's sounds were not comforting. The distant coyotes calling did not feel nearly as endearing as they did from the third floor of his monastic cell. Paul wished for his soft, warm bed. Saying his prayers, he asked God to keep him from freezing during the night and added thanks for all that Mother Earth had provided. He had offended enough people in the last twenty-four hours and didn't need her wrath upon him. He thought of the monks sleeping peacefully somewhere on a hilltop. They would come tomorrow.

CHAPTER 35
ROCKS AND STONES

Psalm 81:3
Do justice for the weak and the orphan,
defend the afflicted and the needy.

P aul woke to the aroma of bacon. He fished around for the miserable rock, which he found stabbing his left shoulder. He needed to find another way to hold the stone.

Both Silent Deer and Two Legs were well rested. Paul found himself envious but grateful they were here. Neither of them talked much and brought only black coffee.

"So, where is your campground?" Paul asked, nibbling on a thick slice of bacon.

"Motel 6," Two Legs said, scrambling eggs over the fire pit. "You didn't think we were camping, did you?"

Paul shook his head. He was done talking to them. They got

too much pleasure in watching him suffer. He figured Jacob wanted him to suffer. After all, he had upset the community. Paul knew he should reflect on his actions, but every time he did, anger and sadness filled him. Anger at Pius, what he had done, and that Pius never really acknowledged his wrongdoing. He let things get out of hand.

He wanted to be an Indian like Jacob. Abbot Jacob had told him of the quests and spending days alone and the appearance of an animal guide.

If this was a spirit quest, it is not working. He was all alone, talking to a rock. He needed a sacred pouch like the one that Jacob carried in his habit pocket.

Once Paul had looked inside the bag and found a feather, a piece of bone, two small soft squares of brightly colored fabric, several ribbons, and an earring. Paul assumed the stuff had significance to Jacob. He had nothing that is important here. Everything he cared about was at the monastery.

To pass the time, Paul ventured out in a different direction each day, deliberately counting his steps, marking his way. He figured Two Legs and Silent Deer would not rescue him if he got lost again. On his first day out, he had met a group of wild horses. For several days, he worked up the courage to get closer to them. They were aware, but didn't seem to mind his presence. The black stallion was defiantly in charge, for the others parted and made space for him. The horses smelled musty and like freshly plowed earth. The herd had a few foals. One was chestnut brown with a white diamond on his head. Paul felt gifted when one horse gave him permission to share the grass meadow by grazing next to where he sat.

Paul spent many hours watching them, discovering that each was an individual, yet a member of the group. Personalities appeared, as did disputes and moments of what appeared to be tenderness. Tails swatted. Heads nodded as some galloped and played a lively game of tag. Yesterday, the gray mare was not happy with the brown yearling. She snorted and stomped the ground. Dust clouds rose from her hooves. Heads tossed, and manes waved until the chestnut horse with the half-eaten ear nudged the gray one away as if to say, "Leave that one alone." Paul recalled the Apsáalooke legend about the boy left by his mother and raised by the buffalos. His teacher had said it was a story about adoption. Paul had never understood it. Why would buffalo raise a boy? Why would monks raise him?

In the late afternoon, when Crazy Stone appeared, the rock was in his hand.

The man nodded.

"How long will I be here?" Paul asked, having lost track of what day into his exile this was.

"How long do you wish to stay?"

"That is not an answer."

Crazy Stone turned his head. "Does it matter?"

"I don't know what I'm supposed to be doing here."

"That is the lie you keep telling yourself so you can hold on to the rock."

Crazy Stone walked away. Paul fought the urge to throw the stone at the man.

He wanted to say, "I didn't know what I was doing." But he knew that was not true. Paul hated Pius at that moment. He interfered with his life and his relationships. He figured Joannicus and others were very disappointed in him, for he had I've scoffed at all his beliefs.

He missed the monks. Would they be so mad at him they might vote him out? Was there ever a vote?

The days passed slowly. Paul worked on his homework with only the chatter of the squirrels and the soft buzzing of bees as they visited the blossoms. The peaceful setting fought with his roaring mind and his yearnings to be home. He wondered what excuse they gave to the school.

The rock left a bruise in his palms and often fell out of his hand when he slept, so Paul had taken a cloth and fashioned a wrap for it. It was cumbersome, but at least it brought him a few moments of conversation.

"Hey," Paul said when he saw the silent two walking toward the woods. "You guys coming back?"

"Do we look like babysitters?" Two Legs asked.

"Can I come with you?"

"Sure," Silent Deer said as they walked in different directions.

"Fine, I see how it is," Paul shouted to them. Jerks. Envious of the soft bed and warm rooms, he was sure they had.

With nothing else to do in the wilderness, Paul wondered if the monks missed him, or if they were celebrating his departure. Had Charlie demanded his whereabouts and was she searching for him? Lucas probably heard from Pius about what had happened. Paul tried to imagine Lucas taking his side against Pius, but that vision wasn't coming, only the realization that Lucas was with Bethany. How could he have been so stupid?

Time blended with the sunrise and sunset as bookends to his day. Rise, pray, eat, wonder, watch, listen, eat, pray, and sleep. Memories of good times and bad paraded through his mind. Dreams of the future called him to change his current situation. The herd entertained him, keeping him away from the campsite for hours. Missing Crazy Stone meant missing a question, but that didn't matter so much because nobody was giving him any answers.

Today was warm, and Paul stretched out in the meadow. The heat felt good as he watched the eagles floating over the trees.

He wanted to go home. What if Joannicus became ill? Would they tell him?

Paul woke up to darkness. The day had slipped into night. Crap. He patted the ground for his clothing and that rock. He was missing his sock and the rock. Double crap. Shivering, he fought panic. His markers were not visible at night.

He was in the dark without food, water, or a blanket. He was unprepared. The cold embraced him. Determination, but no destination, pushed Paul to move.

His fingers ached and his teeth chattered. Paul knew he had to keep moving. He had to get back. Where was the tree? His foot caught, and he tripped, crashing to the ground. He pushed himself to a sitting position. He sensed something soft and stiff. He jerked his hand away. Whatever it was, it hadn't moved. Think. He touched the mystery thing, which was damp and stiff from the cold. His wool sock. He slipped the sock on before fumbling with his shoe. The side of his face felt wet and warm to his stiff fingers. Was he bleeding? He licked fingers, tasted the blood. Wolf bait. Cut it out. He wasn't dead, but he needed to get up and move. If he found his sock, perhaps he was walking in circles. Panic rose, which way was the campground. Exhaustion came like a wave over him. He laid back down and the earth seemed warm. Things were not making sense as he curled up to rest.

Paul opened his eyes and quickly closed them against the brightness. Sunrise, oh thank God. His senses awoke to the sound of snorting and whinnying. The horses' musty odor filled the air. He remembered falling. He opened one eye. He saw hooves as they circled him. The ground thudded with each step. A deep sense of awe filled him. They hadn't trampled him to death.

Gradually sitting upright, he recognized the herd he had been watching. Chestnut leaned close to his mother. From this vantage point, the colt seemed frail and skinny. His mother stood next to him, her muzzle gently touching him, stroking his neck. Paul knew that Chestnut was not well. The little foal took a faltering step and wobbled before he folded onto the ground. Paul gasped, then held his breath. Get up, get up. You can't die. Spring is almost here. Paul tried to stand and make his way to the pair. But he couldn't. Something anchored him to the ground.

The little pony lifted his head once to his mother. The herd ambled around them. The mother whinnied mournfully. Paul shivered as tears stained his face. No, no. It's almost springtime. The black mare approached and laid his head across the filly's back. She tossed her head to the sky and neighed again. The herd echoed her call. Paul experienced a profound sense of loss.

"FOUND HIM," called a voice that sounded familiar.

This is odd, horses don't talk, thought Paul. Arms pulled him up from the ground.

"Where are the horses?" Paul asked Two Legs, recognizing his musky balsamic odor.

"No, horses. Just frozen white boy," Two Legs said.

A heavy wool blanket warmed Paul's body. A fire blazed, as did the sun.

"Drink," Crazy Stone said, holding out a thermos. Paul drank the warm, sweet tea.

"Where are the horses? I know there were horses." Paul said, glancing around and finding himself in the campground.

"The Pryor Mountains wild horses?"

"The little foal died," Paul said, his voice rough. Had he witnessed or dreamed the death of Chestnut? He needed to see Joannicus.

"She is gone," Crazy Stone said. "Few survive to celebrate a year."

Energy drained from his body, and an odd clarity filled him. He touched his head, a bandage. Pain.

"How do you know? I just saw it." But it had been light and warm. Confusion made him take in a ragged breath and shiver.

"She passed yesterday. The herd moved on this morning."

"I heard them cry," Paul said, remembering the sound of the herd's sorrowful calling.

Crazy Stone nodded.

Had it been real? Had they granted him a vision? The herd left and the filly would be consumed by the earth. The cruelty of nature struck Paul hard. What did it mean? Was he the filly or the herd? Jacob had wanted him to move on.

Paul stood up, as wobbly as the Chestnut filly. His hands were cold and stiff, so he stuck them in his jeans pocket only to discover the rock he had thought he'd lost. He moved to sit next to the fire and Crazy Stone. "I don't have a question. I know what I need to do." Paul said. He looked at his hand. Without the weight, his hand felt vacant. Paul handed the rock to Crazy Stone.

"So, how does your hand feel?"

"Empty."

"Is that good or bad?"

"It isn't either, it just is," Paul said with a shrug.

"The stone has a name. Do you know the name?"

Paul was familiar with the tales of the Crow tribe from childhood. His teachers in elementary school often told the class stories. There are two interpretations of every story, the obvious one and the lesson.

"It's called Pius."

"Ah, I see Little Thunder is more than just noise." Crazy Stone pocketed the rock, retrieved a stout stick, and flicked open his pocketknife.

Little Thunder was better than Runs with Scissors. Paul would have preferred Fly with Eagles or Runs with the Herd, instead of Little Thunder, which sounded like a name for someone who wasn't quite strong enough to be the actual storm.

"You are right. You have grown accustomed to thinking one way toward this Pius. You have bound yourself to him and you can function relatively well. However, your emotions of anger and fear are keeping you from accomplishing other things. Like maintaining a friendship, obeying the gods, and your Elders."

Anger crept into Paul's voice. "I have a right to be angry."

"What happened was unfortunate, so why are you holding on to it? That is not very Apsáalooke. If we spend all our time saying they have abused us, what would we ever accomplish?"

Small pieces of wood curled as the knife made smooth the rough stick.

"It's not that easy. Father Pius is friends with my friends, my tribe. Even Abbot Jacob is kind to him. Pius isn't going away. What does everyone expect me to do, be his friend?"

Crazy Stone leaned back and scanned the sky. "I would rather have power over evil than give it power over me. You give him power. Set yourself free."

Paul frowned. "Just like that. Just say the past is the past."

"It is the past. You cannot change it. I am baffled that you want to keep that sadness with you. Does it bring you comfort?"

"What? No, he hurt me."

They stared at each other. Crazy Stone cupped Paul's empty hand, and he pulled out a pouch and poured the contents of the bag into Paul's opened hand. When Paul's hand could hold no more, the sand spilled onto the ground. Crazy Stone gently closed the fingers around the slipping grains.

"Carry that around for a while."

Paul watched the sand escape his grasp. The tighter he closed his fist, the quicker the sand fell. "I can't. It will spill, and then I'll have nothing."

"Exactly. So, is something better than nothing? Anger shadows the other emotions."

What might he learn if he didn't hate Pius? Sympathy? Pity? Paul shook his head. Would Paul end up liking the man? No, no. He didn't want to forgive.

"Could you care for someone who beat you?" Paul asked, realizing that Pius didn't care if Paul forgave him. Pius had moved on.

"Possibly. I heard of one who did that," Crazy Stone said. He pushed the wood shavings into a small pile and lit them. Wisps of smoke rose.

"What is he, a saint?"

Crazy Stone dropped his carving he had been working on into the flames. "No, Crows do not have saints. We have only those who persevere."

"I didn't cause this, Pius did. He hurt me first." Paul looked away to the mountains. Even he could hear how idiotic that sounded.

"You took the sacred and threw it away. That hurt many people who love you. The whys of your actions are incidental to the event. Why did Father Pius choose you to beat? Is there an answer that would satisfy you? You handle your actions, not his. Why did you act without kindness?"

"I can't be kind to him," Paul said. The sound of Pius's knuckles cracking in his mind caused him to shudder.

Crazy Stone took Paul's sand-filled hand and poured the rest of the grains into the dying flames. Smoke filled the air.

"It is more like you won't. You are a spring colt who has survived the winter."

Stirring the embers with his boot, Crazy Stone pulled out his carving, and with an oily cloth, he rubbed the carving until the blackness shone like a polished stone.

"You're wrong. Sometime after forgiveness, you grow closer to the person. But I am going home, anyway."

Crazy Stone laughed, and the sound echoed. "I don't think you need to worry about that."

He handed Paul the carving of a horse's head

"Get your gear. It is time to go home," Crazy Stone said, standing up.

CHAPTER 36
OBSIDIAN

Psalm 77: 38
Yet he who is full of compassion forgave
their sin and spared them.

J acob knew Paul would come home today. Thank goodness, because he wasn't sure he could take the scathing looks of the Joannicus. The man questioned him daily, accusing him of keeping secrets. There was no secret. His twin cousins had not consulted him on where to take Paul. He suspected it was on the Rez, but they could have taken him to the wilderness of Wyoming.

Jacob looked up from his dinner of beef stew as the door opened. His brother-in-law, Todd, entered. The tall Lakota man gave Jacob a slight bow and proceeded to the food. Jacob's cousins, Marcus and Marco, followed Todd, and then Paul appeared. The young man looked contrite. The refectory reader stopped reading, and the room grew silent. Too quiet. Jacob glanced at the reader. The young monk resumed reading from a book about the extraordinary women of the Middle Ages called the Beguines.

Jacob watched. Paul had a bandage on his head and an over-filled plate. Had they starved him into compliance? Paul had been gone a week, enough time to complete a spirit quest. Jacob was pleased when Paul took his usual place at a table with Ambrose and Joannicus.

Jacob didn't like the results of his spirit quest as a youth. He favored a wolf because of its devotion to the pack. Yet, he feared it would be a lumbering elephant, the symbol for remembering. His guide was a mosquito, thirsty and annoying. Jacob stirred his food around in his bowl and waited for his relatives to finish eating. Once they had finished, he followed his guests out of the refectory.

Outside in the icy evening air, he turned to the men.

"Thank you for taking care of Paul," Jacob said.

"Interesting kid," Marco said.

"Yes, he's like you," Marcus said. "You've influenced him well."

"I do not have to be correct all the time."

They paused, giving him a sideways glance, then slapped him on the back before chuckling.

"We have a chess date with the big one," Marcus said once they entered the monastery.

"We shouldn't be long," Marco added with a chuckle.

Todd and Jacob entered the office as the twins headed into the monastery to challenge Brother Ambrose in chess.

"Here's your stone," Todd said, laying the rough stone on the desk.

Jacob had noticed it was missing. His ugly rock from child-hood given to him by his friend Tiny.

"This was the physical manifestation of Paul's burden. He was to carry it all the time."

Jacob was impressed with the concrete way in which the stone represented emotions.

"Did he give up his anger toward Pius?"

Todd smiled. "Does that kind of hurt ever leave us? All we can do is hang it out of reach."

"Thank you for dealing with this." Jacob sat behind his desk.

Todd had been at Mass that memorable afternoon. He had seen and known the story of Paul and Pius, from his wife and Jacob's sister, Rebecca.

"No, thanks necessary. It was what needed to be done. Paul is your heart-son. I am his uncle."

That was the Apsáalooke tradition. Male relatives shared the honor and duty of converting a boy into a man.

"Was the carrying of the stone an old rite of passage I missed?"

Todd smiled one of his knowing smiles as he ran his finger across the shiny surface of the desk. "No. I made it up."

"Would you consider being abbot?" Jacob said, wishing he had that talent for such clever conversions in those around him.

"Little brother, you are shortsighted. I have watched you. This job of leading warriors suits you."

Monks as warriors. He nearly laughed. These monks were his new tribe, his clan. Warriors of God. He could get behind that vision.

"Rebecca chose well when she married you."

This time Todd laughed. "About time you recognized that."

There was a knock on the door.

"Enter," Jacob said. Paul stepped into the room. "The Lord be with you, Paul."

"And with you, Father Abbot, and you too, Crazy Stone."

Todd and Jacob laughed in unison

"It's a good name, Little Thunder. I accept it." Todd gave Jacob a wink before he exited the office.

"His name is Todd. He is my brother-in-law," Abbot Jacob said as he moved from behind the desk to the sofa.

"He isn't Apsáalooke, is he?" Paul asked.

"Correct. He is Lakota, but my cousins are Apsáalooke." Impressed that Paul knew the difference.

Paul sat on a chair opposite of Jacob. A painting of White Buffalo Woman stared at Jacob over Paul's left shoulder.

"I want to come home. If that's possible. I'm sorry for what I did."

Jacob smiled. Thankful that he had a house full of monks well versed in Church law. The consensus had come after they had read Paul's assignments—the ones that Pius had given all the confirmation candidates.

"We have decided to allow you to return, as long as you recognize the seriousness of your actions. Confirmation will be a fresh start if you wish to go ahead with this next step in your Catholic journey."

Paul nodded. "I'm ready. I have an apology to give to the community after evening prayers."

That's a good time, thought Jacob. In the morning, perhaps forgiveness and acceptance, after prayers, was silence and overnight contemplation. Not everyone believed Paul should reenter the fold.

Paul shifted in the chair and grabbed a pillow. "Can I ask you a personal question?"

"Sure."

"How come you don't hate Father Pius? You treat him as if he's a good man and his past sins don't matter."

Jacob hadn't expected that. "Hate is an unyielding word. It colors the present. To live with what he did to you, I had to separate Pius from his actions. Pius is a good person. You and I will never be best friends with Pius, but I am his abbot. What he did was wrong. I wanted him to go to jail, Abbot Gordon said no. He did not want me to confront Father Pius."

"Yet you did," Paul said, hugging the pillow.

"Yes, we are both prodigal sons. The abuse had to stop. I am sorry I had not stopped it sooner."

"I'm still not sure I can forgive him."

"Then don't."

"I thought you sent me to the hills to figure out how to forgive him."

"No, you needed to see your choices have consequence. You should see a counselor."

Paul threw the pillow at Jacob. "I talked, to God, to Crazy—I mean Todd. I don't need to talk about the past anymore because I carried a stone. I need to let it go."

Damn, he wished he had figured that out before he was an adult. Jacob reflected, the past made him, but didn't define the future. Paul's epiphany caused Jacob to swell with pride.

"How are you going to do that?"

"I will speak with Father Pius. Will he be here this weekend?"

Jacob mashed the pillow.

"I will go to confession. The Church expects that of me. It is the right thing to do. I figured going to Father Pius might help him see that I'm not a total idiot."

"Why do you care what he thinks about you?" Jacob said, regretting his words as he tried to reshape the pillow. He knew why. Everyone wanted to be loved, even if they couldn't love back.

"I don't care. Not really. I wish he would see me as others see me."

Jacob swallowed hard and gently placed the pillow on the sofa. That would not happen.

"This is not a promising idea."

"Yes, it is. I want Father Pius to..." Paul paused, and Jacob fought the urge to say that you hate him.

"I want him to know that I'm not holding on to the past. I'm not afraid of him and that he can't ruin my future."

"You do not need to tell him that. Your actions will speak for themselves." Jacob flattened the pillow with his hands.

This could go wrong. But perhaps Paul needs to see that Pius is a cold-hearted, unforgiving man. He needed to trust them both. Father Pius would perform his priestly duty even when faced with something emotionally distasteful to him. He remembered that he had heard things in the confessional that made him angry.

"You do not have to do this. I can absolve you from your sin, here now."

"I know. I need to do it my way."

Jacob's stomach spun, and the misshaped pillow would not return to its former self. He wanted to stop Paul, but he realized that would not happen. He was powerless to protect Paul from discovering the dark side of men.

THE RECONCILIATION ROOM was in the hallway between the monastery and church. The little space used for personal confessions. Today, it felt cramped and stuffy. Father Pius entered and sat opposite of Paul.

"What do you want from me?"

"Bless me, Father, for I have sinned." The words stuck in Paul's throat. "It has been two months since my last confession."

Paul took several deep breaths to calm his racing heart. He'd rehearsed the words a hundred times. "I sinned against the Church misused the sacraments. I should've said that then, but I was stubborn and stupid. I blamed others for my actions."

Paul paused, bit his lower lip, and looked around the room. The small table between them held an unlit candle and alb. Pius didn't move to join in the sacrament of confession.

He should have warned him. Paul looked into the gray eyes of his confessor. The eyes stared impassively at him.

He was confessing; didn't he recognize the sacrament?

Paul swallowed, but his mouth was dry. "I want absolution. I'm sorry for spilling the blood of Christ you."

Pius's eyebrows rose. He shook his head. "Spilling? It was more than that. If you hurt someone by your actions, apologize to them. You are aware of this. If you think coming to confession gets you out of an apology, you are mistaken."

Paul clenched his teeth. His eyes darted away. He hung his head as he picked at a thread on his shirt. He studied the floor, searching for one imperfection on the priest's shiny black shoes, as if salvation came from the ground up.

"What do you want, Paul?" Pius said, his voice soft, but to Paul, it sounded like the squeaking of the hamster's wheel, prickling his already weak resolve.

Paul looked up at the stern face. "I want forgiveness for my sins."

"From whom, the Church, God, me?"

"I'm not confessing to you. I'm confessing to God through you. Is that some kind of trick question?" Paul asked, leaning slightly forward.

Father Pius blinked. "Is this a real confession? You can do better than this."

Paul's conscience stung. He looked away. Anger bubbled slow

and thick. Hold on to the rock and nothing changes. Crazy Stone was right. He needed to let go.

"Yes, Father," Paul said, glad his voice did not show his churning emotions.

Pius picked up the alb and placed it over his shoulders and lit the candle. Paul was relieved. The priest acted like a priest.

Father Pius cleared his throat. "Misuse of the blood of Christ is a severe sin. A mockery of everything that the Church teaches and of what your family believes. Everyone is aware of the circumstance that brought you to that moment. It's hard to accept the words of compassion from a man you distrust."

Paul concentrated on the shiny shoes. Forcing himself to listen.

"Our family understands. I understand. The Church may not. The key here is that you understand."

Paul inhaled and exhaled before he spoke. "I was out of line and should've dealt with my feelings...like leave the church or talked to someone." Paul felt his eyes fill with tears and squeezed them tight. The memory of a little boy caught with no chance of escape came back to him. Fear, confusion, and the angry face of Pius loomed in his mind. He gripped the chair, his knuckles growing white.

"Paul, are you okay?" Pius's voice shattered the silence. "I need to ask you, are you making this confession because you're sorry and want to be forgiven? Or do you just want to come home?"

Although Pius's voice came across as gentle, not quite tender, the question cut like a belt strap. Paul relaxed his hand. The air smelled heavy of cologne, a sweet yet pungent, sickly odor.

"It's hard for me to separate them. But I want forgiveness, even if it means I can't come home."

The man fell away, the priest, the conduit to the Church, asked, "When you committed this sin, what was in your heart?"

Paul shifted in his chair.

"Anger mostly."

"Under the anger?"

Bile rose into Paul's mouth and burned. He coughed and swallowed hard. "Fear and hate."

Father Pius leaned back in his chair and cracked his knuckles, and the sound sent tremors quaking inside of Paul. "Paul, in the sacrament of reconciliation, a dialogue occurs between us. I realize this discussion is hard. I need to hear what was in your heart."

The small room swirled, and the overwhelming need to run gripped Paul. Most confessions were simple. Admit you made a mistake, say sorry, and try to be better. Pius was not letting this happen.

He didn't want to discuss. He wanted absolution. Maybe he wasn't ready.

"What do you want from me?" Paul asked.

"Talk to me."

Lie. Get it over with. Tell Pius what he wants to hear. Paul stood and turned to the door. He couldn't do this.

Paul opened the door. Bright light permeated the darkness of the room. He could see a tall, slender shadow in the hall. Paul turned back to Pius, gripping the doorframe. What did Pius want to hear? That he was justified for beating Paul? That Paul understood and forgave him for being out of control? Paul furrowed his brow. No, this is not about Pius. This is about him and moving on. No more stone in hand.

"In my heart was hatred. You've always judged my actions and me. You never took the time to learn my motives. In my soul was a betrayal that someone named Father could hurt me and act as if nothing had happened. I couldn't accept the gift from you with the past hanging between us."

Father Pius exhaled, spearmint added to the overburdened air. Paul listened to the footsteps of the shadow. He recognized that rhythm, that pace. Jacob.

"What do you need from me?" Pius asked.

"I want absolution for my misuse of the blood of Christ. I want to come home." He hoped for something more. A fairy-tale ending. That would not happen. He and Pius could never be Pius and Lucas.

"That is possible, but what will you do for the man you defiled?"

The door hung half-open. One step and Paul could be free of this man. That wasn't enough. He wanted the memories of the past to stop destroying his life.

Let go. Paul stared at the balding spot on the top of the man's head.

"I'm sorry I took the blood of Christ and misused it." Paul focused on the crucifix on the wall. "I'm not sorry it was you. God loves you and sees the good in you. I can't see that. I can only say that I'm sorry for my actions. I want to come home. You are part of my family. I can't change that, but I can apologize for my mean-ness to you."

The footsteps moved in the hall, not far, not disappearing, just lingering.

"You're right. You're not ready to forgive me. I guess I can live with that. I can see that you comprehend the sin you committed and the effects of that sin. Because that is what you came to confess, I'll grant you absolution. You might consider how to become compassionate towards me. But I won't hold my breath." Pius paused, then pursed his lips as if he wanted to say more. "What penance do you think is fitting for this confession?"

In the past, Paul would select something simple, ten Hail Mary's, five Our Fathers, and a rosary, but he knew prayers were not enough. He was not a child anymore. "Father, it's not for me to decide."

"You need to serve with the approval of the Abbot. You will be acolyte at Mass for six months."

After the final blessing, Paul rose and exited the confessional. Abbot Jacob stood in the hall. Worry etched in his face. Paul tried to give him a smile. Pius had absolved him from his sins, yet the usual sense of joy was absent.

CHAPTER 37
WHITE TIGER

Psalm 31:1
Happy the man whose offense is forgiven.

Paul walked to the atrium of the church. The walls didn't groan, nor did the ground shake. The holy water trickled and bubbled in the fountain. He had always liked that sound, happy and comforting. Today, the water seemed to mock him. Never, Paul blessed himself, and his hand hung like an anchor. Never had confession been so hollow. They completed the rite, the exact words said, but Paul felt heavy.

He entered the church and sat waiting for a good feeling, resolution, joy, sadness, but even prayer slept. Maybe Abbot Jacob was right. This didn't change his feeling toward Pius, and it didn't change Pius's opinion about him. He had done it, faced his dragon.

The proud moment was replaced with irritation. Compassion? Pius thinks he needed to learn compassion. Paul shook his head, trying to recall the last time he showed compassion. Wasn't it just being nice? He was a nice person.

The church creaked as a gust of wind leaned on it. He heard a distant wind chime *clink*. Sun faded with the clouds. The sound of swishing jeans under skirts caused him to turn. He knew that noise, the heavy cloth of the skirt of a habit brushing against denim.

"Welcome home," Father Joannicus said. "Let's go for a walk. I want to discuss something."

A wind swirled around them as they walked outside.

He couldn't be in trouble. He had just gotten home.

"How did it go?" Joannicus asked as they strolled.

Paul glanced around, making sure no one overheard. "That man is an ass. Sorry."

A gust of wind, not warm but chilling, whooshed around them. A storm was coming. Paul sensed it in the air.

"You didn't think you and Father Pius would become instant friends, did you?" Joannicus said with a strange smile on his face.

"That's just it. I don't want to be PJ's friend. You're not friends with everyone."

"True. You don't have to be friends with him."

Paul sighed. It was nice to hear that Joannicus was on his side. "Do you know what he gave me for penance?"

"No, but I bet it's an action rather than a Hail Mary."

"He doesn't like me. Abbot Jacob said I didn't need to forgive Pius. But I wasn't doing that. I was seeking his forgiveness for my actions."

Another gust of wind blew, sending Joannicus's scapular flying like angel's wings unfurling.

"That was the right action. But you could've said sorry at evening prayers," Joannicus said, wrestling his scapular from the wind.

It was time to move indoors. Father Joannicus had put on some weight, but his habit hung loosely around his emaciated frame. Chemo recovery was slow. Why hadn't he noticed that before?

"You've forgiven Father Pius," Paul said, baffled at how Joannicus could do that.

"Yes. I can't help myself. It is who I am."

"Abbot Jacob hasn't, has he?"

"You should take that up with him. Seriously, Pius has good qualities. Try to find something positive about him. Everyone has one quality worthy of praise."

"He has shiny shoes," Paul said, shaking his head. "I can't be bothered. Don't tell me I need counseling. I don't want to talk about the past. I can't change the past. I want to focus on the future."

Joannicus laughed. "Shiny shoes. Seriously, lose the sad face. Happy is the man whose sin has been forgiven."

They headed to the guesthouse and to the covered patio. The thunder rumbled in the distance.

"Where does this leave you and Lucas?" Joannicus asked.

"Lucas and I are good. It's not as if we're a threesome. Besides, Lucas will get a scholarship to some school that wants a football star. I'm not going to that college."

"That is correct. You're going to St. Alberic's," Joannicus said in a dictatorial tone.

"I don't want to attend college."

"Not an option."

Paul frowned. The air was now heavy with moisture. A metallic odor filled his nostrils. The edict became an irritant, much like the sudden change in the weather.

"I'm staying in the dorms. I want to be normal."

"Well, news flash. You have never known normal."

"Fine, I want to be 'average Paul' not connected to the monastery. I don't want people knowing I was adopted. I want you all to ignore me. Treat me like a student."

The icy breeze whipped through the porch. Joannicus shivered. Paul regretted the harshness of his words. He didn't mean for them to sound like he wasn't grateful. He cared for and loved the monks most days.

"I'll get you a blanket."

"Bring me a cup of tea," Joannicus said.

Paul headed to the kitchenette, thinking tea, cookies, and fruit, and a side of beef.

He noticed part of the newspaper, the social section, ripped and tossed in the trash and heard footsteps in the hall.

The familiar fragrance of cinnamon lingered in the air. Charlie wore that scent called Cinnabar. Paul consulted the guest list from the clipboard on the wall. There was only one room occupied. Curious, Paul moved to the room. Arm poised to knock, the door opened, and there stood Charlie.

"Charlie?"

"Paul."

"What are you doing here?" Paul asked. She didn't look well. Her eyes were red and puffy.

"Guesting?"

"But I... what, who?"

"It's all kosher. The Abbot dude knows."

Paul was able to see the room. There were boxes, a suitcase, and a laundry basket. Charlie tried to block him. Paul pushed forward.

"You've moved in."

She shrugged her shoulders.

"While you were gone finding your spirit guide, things changed."

The sarcasm of her words hurt, and he retorted, "What, did you become a nun?"

"No, that's your ambition," she said. Charlie bit her lower lip. The caustic remark wilted. Something was wrong. "My mother died."

Paul stepped back. Had he heard right? He stood in front of her, lost for words.

"I found her. She killed herself, a handful of pills and a note saying she was sorry. I didn't even know she was unhappy."

"What? How? I mean, ah crap. I'm sorry."

"Yeah." Charlie sniffed, and her eyes grew watery. "This sucks, really sucks."

"Where was your dad?" Paul asked. Charlie's features hardened, and she snorted. Crap, he shouldn't have said that.

"Dad, if you want to call him that. I prefer Mr. Rat Bastard. I had to find him. He was at a bar, and he said, 'Okay, thanks for letting me know.' He didn't come home. I didn't tell the police that, of course. A 'sold' sign was in the yard when I came home from school." Charlie clenched her jaw. "I kicked the back door in. Most of the house was empty. My mom's stuff and my stuff were in trash bags in the garage. I was so pissed."

He was gone for a week and so much happened. Paul knew her dad was a realtor and so he must have used his connections. It wasn't possible for Charlie's world to fall so fast.

"I rummaged through the bags and took as much as my car would hold."

"Didn't your dad tell you he was selling the place? I mean, talk to you?"

"Talk to me? Talk to me?" her voice became shrill. "Mom died on a Sunday and by Thursday, I was homeless. And today I read in the paper he—" Charlie glanced around the hallway. "—he remarried. Mom's not even cold in her grave, and he's fucking remarried. I should have crashed his wedding or burned the house down."

She paused, eyes brimming with tears. He had never seen her cry. Paul raised his hand to hug her, but let it drop back to his side. The last time he had attempted a gesture of affection, she had given him a black eye. Wiping her eyes, she glared at him. Paul held his breath. She punched his shoulder.

"Where were you? I came here looking for you. You committed a stupid act of sacrilege and then ran away with the Indians."

Charlie's eyes narrowed and her cheeks flamed red.

Paul wanted to take a step back, but his feet rooted to the floor. Explanations loomed on his lips. He should have been here for her.

"You went to confession to PJ. You don't have to forgive the man who hurt you. You know that, right?" She grabbed his shirt, pulling him to her. A faint smell of alcohol passed between them.

"I didn't forgive him," Paul said.

"Good, don't. He doesn't deserve forgiveness." Charlie released him with a shove, and he bumped the wall as the crucifix slid to the floor with a thud.

Charlie pushed it aside with her foot. "Never mind. You couldn't have done anything but commit a crime with me."

"I'd have done that with you," Paul said. He watched her lean against the wall, strength draining from her slender frame.

"I have nothing," Charlie said in a whisper.

"Wait here," Paul said.

"Not going anywhere," Charlie muttered.

Paul raced across the courtyard, threw open the monastery door and dodged two monks who were attempting to exit. He ran up the stairs and dashed to his cell. He looked around, digging through several piles of clothing.

At last. Paul exited his room, crashing through the doors that led to the church hallway.

"Hey, where's the fire?" Brother Alcuin yelled over the loud rumble of thunder. "You're not supposed to be running."

Paul tossed a prayer to the sanctuary as he passed by. Thanks for keeping Charlie safe and for not letting her commit crimes. He could see her running her father over in her car in a fit of rage. He didn't want to be visiting her in detention.

Out of the church, large drops of rain fell from the sky. Paul splashed his way to the guesthouse. Inside the door, he stood, wet and out of breath. He looked for Charlie. The aroma of tea wafted through the hall.

Crap, he'd forgot about Joannicus. The wool blanket was gone from the sitting room. Charlie. She had saved the day again.

He followed the scent to the porch, his feet squishing, and his sneakers squeaking. A flash of light bathed Charlie and Joannicus in a purple hue.

"You guys shouldn't be making Paul forgive PJ. The man's a class act jerk."

"We didn't make him. But it's the Christian thing to do," Joannicus said.

"Well, for you and saints maybe, us humans are not that..." Charlie paused, seeing Paul in the doorway.

"Here," Paul said, holding out a damp, misshapen, off-white tiger. Joannicus coughed. White tiger's head wobbled. Years of secrets, tears, joy, and love had settled into his misshaped stuffing.

"You sure?" Charlie asked, her voice sounding rough.

The question prickled. He had been sure a moment ago. He only had a white tiger when his mother died.

"Yeah, he wants to see the world, and he is a skilled listener," Paul said, his voice catching.

"Thanks," Charlie said as she took the white tiger and squeezed him to her chest. "He smells like you. I got things to do. You know where to find me." She turned, tucking the tiger under her arm, and sniffing loudly before leaving.

Paul sat down next to Joannicus as nature roared and flashed around them. In that moment with Joannicus, he sensed God. Raindrops pelted the earth, kneading it to softness as the sun competed against the darkness, poking out from the fading clouds while steam rose like a prayer.

"Aren't we going to get in trouble, letting her stay here?"

"She will be eighteen soon enough," Joannicus said.

"No. Her birthday's April 1st. She just turned seventeen. She can't live here for a year."

"Abbot Jacob said she could stay."

"Really?"

"He's a compassionate man. Seriously, what could he do? She was sobbing in your room."

Oh God, not in his room in the monastery.

"Yes," Joannicus said, with a grin. "She was in your cell. Abbot Jacob found her and explained that his office door was always open to her. Then they negotiated, and here she is."

"Negotiated?" Paul said. One didn't negotiate with Charlie.

"Seriously, it was more like dictators saying facts or wishes. Keep the social service witches away. Ditch the Goth overkill versus I'm not becoming a nun. I won't be a charity case versus staying in school and go to college. You get the picture."

"College? Really?"

Joannicus sipped his tea, steam fogging his glasses. "There are scholarships available. She has four years of college to figure out what she wants to do."

"What about her father?"

"It appears he has decided his parental duties are finished. Seriously, I don't think he'll come looking for her. I don't think he cares. She isn't going to contact him."

"The social services will come looking."

"Sometimes I think you live in a monastery. They won't look unless someone tells them to look. Charlie doesn't want to live in foster care. A year is not a long time."

The discussion triggered the sleeping debate inside of Paul and the words tumbled out.

"I sometimes wonder about my real dad," Paul said, glancing at Joannicus. He didn't want to hurt him with his words. He didn't want to learn that all fathers eventually turned callous.

"What do you wonder?" Joannicus asked, his voice heavy with sadness.

"Who he is? Charlie was looking for him, for me. She thought a reunion was in my future."

"There is time," Joannicus said, setting his teacup down, his hand trembling slightly.

"I don't think finding a dad is a good idea."

"Perhaps you're wiser than you realize," Joannicus said, pulling out his rosary beads and sighing. Paul sensed a deep melancholy from Joannicus.

"You, okay?" Paul asked.

"Just tired," Joannicus said with a soft smile.

"What did you want to talk about?"

"Charlie being here. I wanted you to know the rules of hanging out."

This was going to change things. She was his friend. Would

she still call him on the phone and talk? Would they expect him to do homework with her? Would it be like having a sibling? The sound of Charlie blowing her nose filled the hallway.

Paul glanced down the hallway, expecting to see Charlie. But her door remained closed.

"Did I do something wrong?"

"No," Joannicus said. "Will you miss tiger?"

Paul wanted to say yes. "Charlie needs him more than me right now. Will she be alright?"

"Yes, just keep doing what you are doing."

Paul wondered what that was exactly, being her friend? That didn't seem like enough.

CHAPTER 38
BETTY WINTERS

Psalm 68:2
Save me, O God, for the waters have risen to my neck.

Abbot Jacob stood in front of the window in the church, watching a few brave birds chase each other around the garden. They didn't seem to notice that the branches were becoming bare and soon winter would turn the bird bath into a skating rink. Ah, to be so trusting and carefree.

Yesterday, the lawyers brought up Paul's trust. They admonished him for procrastinating and keeping the information from Paul. He is not ready, thought Jacob, and the Elder chuckled, whoever is.

Paul was about to start his second year of college studies in forensic anthropology. Money would be a distraction.

Jacob walked around the church, stopping at the crucifix. The longer he put it off, the more difficult it seemed to tell Paul. A year of living in the dorms had changed Paul. He adapted well to the world.

"If I tell him he has money, the greed will overpower him." The crucifix Christ answered, "He will come back to you."

Jacob shook his head. One more year wouldn't hurt. His excuses were growing thin. The argument that Paul would spend all of his money was not sound.

Jacob sat in the dabbled sunlight near the altar. "Admit you are worried that Paul will misinterpret your intentions," said the Warrior in his head. Jacob shrugged. "Even you said the child was being auctioned," reminded the Elder.

That was then. It had not turned out that way. Paul had become part of the community. His absence left a hole, his presence enriched.

The noise started softly but turned to a howl, shattering the silence careening to the rafters. A child wailing. Jacob calmed his racing heart and walked into the atrium. There he found a grinning girl running in circles around a wailing, red-faced girl and two bulky misshapen cardboard boxes. Jacob glanced around but saw no adult.

Hilarious, Lord. We're not an orphanage.

Jacob placed an arm out to stop the darting child. The screaming stopped.

"Where are your parents?" Jacob asked, guessing the dark-haired girls were ages four and six.

The older child looked at the younger one and then at Jacob. She scrunched up her face, inhaled, and exhaled several times.

"Daddy's gone." She glared at her now-silent sibling and raised a threatening fist as if to hit her. The younger child howled. The door to the church opened. A slender woman in her early thirties entered, hauling another box. She was dressed well, her shoes matching her tight skirt. Gold hooped earrings dangled, nearly touching her shoulders.

Jacob breathed a sigh of relief. They were not alone.

The woman hissed. "Andrea, stop that racket."

"May I help you?" Abbot Jacob asked over the din.

"Yea, I'm looking..." the woman paused, taking in Jacob. She took a step back, glanced menacingly at the children. The wailing Andrea stopped mid-breath and the older girl crept up and stood next to her mother. The woman's eyes narrowed, and a crease appeared on her forehead.

"I'm looking for Charlie, Charlie Winters."

"Charlie." Jacob's mind raced as fatherly protection protocols trumped politeness. "Who are you and what do you want with Charlie?" Jacob asked, realizing he sounded somewhat terse.

The woman shoved the box at Jacob and pushed her too-blonde hair away from her face, a large glistening stone on her finger.

"I'm Betty. Betty Winters, Marvin's wife," she said as if that explained everything. Her face converted from annoyance to soft and sad. Her overdone eyes made Jacob feel uncomfortable. She put out her hand, red tapered talons on thin fingers.

Jacob set the box on the stack of boxes and shook the limp hand that lingered too long in his, making him feel disturbed. He wouldn't let Charlie be her prey. He had a similar feeling when he thought about Paul's father. The appearance of that man would cause havoc in Paul's life. He thanked God daily for the young man's lack of curiosity.

"Where is Mister Winters?"

"Not yet six feet under. He died. He had last wishes. The burdens on me—" She pulled the two girls to her. "—on us. Marvin said Charlie would take care of his final arrangements. He was Catholic and wanted a proper burial. This has all been a nightmare." Betty sniffled. Andrea pouted, her lower lip sticking out exaggeratedly. Her sister batted her eyes in a creepy way. Jacob felt like a rabbit surrounded by hungry dogs.

The man had died. Jacob was relieved. He put to rest the fear that Mr. Winters would ruin Charlie's life. He wondered how Charlie would take the news. He had told her this was home.

"Well, grab a box. Charlie's in the next building," Jacob said, opening the door for her. Betty gave him a look of disbelief. Jacob looked as she picked up the box.

"So, I read it on some papers, Charlie Winters, next of kin. The address was on the yellow sticky. It's a monastery. Didn't know what I'd find, but I figured he'd want to hear that his brother had died."

So, the late Mr. Winters knew where his daughter was. He wondered what he was waiting for. The man had been a shadow lurking, unlike Paul's father, who was a dreaded event waiting to happen. Jacob believed that Paul's biological father suspected he had a son. He worried that one day the man would appear and want Paul's money. He figured Betty wanted a handout. She is in for a few surprises. Jacob fought the urge to usher Betty and her offspring back to the church.

"Marvin said Charlie was to take care of his business. Those were his last words. Get a hold of Charlie. I'm grateful for a man to straighten things out. I'm really no good with details." Betty struggled with the box, her high heels clattering on the pavement. "Is Charlie one of you? Taking a vow of poverty?" Her voice lilted in hope.

"No," Jacob said, hiding the grin that flickered on his lips. Yes, she was looking for money. He turned to open the door. "Benedictines do not vow poverty. We promise obedience, stability, and conversion of life."

Jacob opened the door as the two girls pushed through and

ran inside, trying doorknobs. Charlie stood in the hall. She was no longer a walking advertisement for anarchy. She looked relatively normal in her camouflage fatigues, with a tee shirt that said, "Don't know. Don't care." Jacob waved her to him while ushering Betty to the parlor, where she dropped the box with a thud.

"Andrea, Gale, get in here," Betty shouted. She turned and placed her red-painted nails on Jacob's arm. "Thank you so much for your help."

In a blur, the two girls darted past Jacob and circled their mother. Charlie appeared moments later.

Jacob grinned. "Mrs. Winters, this is Charlie."

A shocked expression spread across Betty's face.

"That's not a boy, Momma," Gale said. Betty's hand shot out, but the child was prepared. Gale ducked and only the air stirred.

Charlie's face darkened, and she pushed back a strand of purple hair.

"Who are you?"

"Mrs. Betty Winters, Marvin's wife. Marvin wasn't much for an extended family. So, we haven't met until now."

Charlie crossed her arms. "What do you want?"

"He's dead. Your brother's dead."

"I don't have a brother. If you mean Marvin is dead, then you mean my father is dead," Charlie said.

Jacob detected satisfaction in her statement.

Betty stiffened. The soft seductress had vanished, replaced by the harsh matron.

Two heads appeared from behind the sofa.

"Momma, I thought we were his darling daughters?"

Betty gave them a scorching glance. Charlie turned to study her half siblings.

"Okay, I brought your father's things. He's your responsibility. His body is at Richard and Sons. He wanted the Catholic stuff,"

Betty said, her voice clipped as if she were ordering from a menu. "Take care of it and we will be out of your hair. We don't have no money, so don't be asking."

After looking at Betty, Charlie pointed at the two girls.

"Those his?"

Jacob winced, but he had done the math and Gale was proof of Marvin's infidelity to Charlie's mother. Betty huffed, and snapped, "Yes, they are his. Girls, get out of there."

"That's okay," Charlie said, turning toward the girls. "There are baskets in the hall. Get them and then you can fill them with fruit."

Jacob smiled.

"Marvin passed away. How?" Charlie asked, her arms crossed, and her face held a slight smile.

Mrs. Winters rolled her eyes. "He was old, fat. He was fine one day and dead the next. They said he had a heart attack."

Bad fathers deserved nothing less. Jacob frowned and scolded himself. Not nice, Abbot.

"I brung the boxes. Just post in the paper when the funeral is, we'll come pay our respects. The girls need closure. Then you can re-vanish. We won't be needing nothing from you." Betty turned to her daughters. "Gale, Andrea, let's go." The girls quickly filled their baskets with fruit and followed their mother, leaving Charlie and Jacob alone.

The door closed with a click. Charlie kicked the box, and a puff of dust and staleness filled the room.

"I don't want this crap? I don't give a damn what they do with his body."

"Take a breath. I do not think she knew you existed until Marvin passed."

Charlie glared at him. "How the hell did she find me?"

"This is a small town. She said Marvin told her to find you."

"I bet he left a will, and she wants it all. I don't want his stupid money. She is a piece of work, made-up and talking like a country bumpkin."

Jacob pressed his lips together. Her mixed-up comparison reminded him of Brother Ambrose and his fluster. Those two had never gotten along. She called him "a windbag" and he called her "nothing but trouble." They were cut from the same bluntly honest cloth.

"She cannot take what is rightfully yours."

"I don't want nothing from them. Why did she come here?" Charlie said as she plopped on the sofa. "That's what he married. She's young, what twenty-six? Stupid bitch. Those girls, he was cheating on my mom, that bastard."

"Charlie," Jacob scolded. He understood that behind the anger was pain. "Those are your half sisters. You do not have to like their mother."

Charlie hung her head. Jacob sat next to her. Family. An invisible thread tugged at his heart.

"I didn't need this. Why is it my responsibility? He left me and now he leaves me his mess. I got to study for finals. What am I going to do?" Her voice cracked.

"My dear, put the boxes in a corner. Take a peek after finals."

"Probably bills and shit," Charlie said, squeezing her eyes tightly.

Maybe there are happy memories. Treasures, you thought you had lost forever. Jacob remembered the things packed away in the monastery's attic. Keepsakes from his former life as husband and father.

"She is his wife. She should do this. I have no money to do this."

"Do not fret. We can handle this. I have a church. Richard and

Sons know us. You will be done with him when you have a box of ashes."

Charlie looked at him, her face tight with confusion.

"Why would you do this?"

"Benedictines take care of each other. You are part of this community, our family."

She gave him an eye roll. "Brother Ambrose would object to that statement."

"Old windbag likes to hear himself grumble. And for every complaint he has, there are two compliments he gives."

"Marvin doesn't deserve this. Can't I just throw him in a lake?" Charlie said, wiping her eyes with the back of her hand, smearing mascara down her cheek.

Jacob chuckled and shook his head. "No."

Charlie sniffled.

Even if your dad is evil, losing him leaves a hole. Jacob reached over, pulling her into an embrace. It was much like hugging a rose bush.

CHAPTER 39
MONEY

Psalm 48:13
In his riches, man lacks wisdom.

J acob stood in his office and flexed his arm. Today, instead of his shoulder, the arm that he had broken as a child ached. Rubbing his forearm, he glanced at the legal papers that Charlie had brought to him. He was never good with legal documents. Plain terms suited him. When his wife, Faith, died, there was a significant settlement, court, money, and he didn't care. Life was about to change for Charlie.

He frowned. He had called the lawyers to help Charlie, but he knew they would ask him again when they could talk to Paul. A tapping sound on the window behind him made him jump. He turned to see Charlie standing on his patio. That meant she came past the "Private, do not enter" sign. He hoped nobody had seen her.

Jacob rose and opened the door for her to enter.

"We have a front door. You should become acquainted with it."

She shook her head. Her dark hair waved around her shoulders. She was an attractive young woman who wore too much makeup. He was glad her Goth days were fading into a soft rebellion.

She placed a book on his desk with a thud and stood in front of the coffeepot.

"I cannot believe you gave me this book to read. Have you read it? Do you even know what it suggests? Is Father Joannicus aware that you read this? It is not on the theology must-read list."

"Now you sound like Paul. Father Joannicus is the one who gave it to me."

Charlie looked over her shoulder. "No way"

"*Conversatio morum*," Jacob said. "Even the holiest of monks is open to change. Why do you imagine he gave me this book?"

Charlie placed two mugs on the desk and then sat down. "Abbot Jacob, it's heresy. If it were even a bit of true, the Catholic Church and its patriarchy would crumble."

Jacob smiled. "That would be fun to watch."

Charlie leaned back in the chair. "How did you ever become abbot?"

"I ask that question almost every day. If you find out, will you tell me?" Jacob said.

Charlie tilted her head to one side, her eyes narrowed. "Do you wonder if it could be true? I mean, I realize it's a book of fiction, long-lost codex hinting to a Messianic sibling..."

She trailed off.

"There you go. The idea might be distasteful, or unusual, but the intrigue and mystery. Brings up a lot of questions," Jacob said, watching the idea take hold.

Charlie jumped up and paced. "Some would be shocked by the mere mention of possibilities."

"It is all about possibilities. Did you notice who wrote it?"

She picked up the book and glanced at the name. "Why does that sound familiar?"

"You read other books by her."

"That nun, from my studies on the dessert mothers," Charlie said, taking a seat next to the desk.

A flush of fatherly pride filled Jacob. When she graduated with her degree in theology, she would be well-versed in controversy.

Someone knocked on his door.

"Enter," Jacob said, rising to greet the two lawyers. They were now older and gray. Smells Bad and Runs with Papers. He had always felt like they were jackals, hungry and pensive.

"Oh, thank God, you've come to your senses," Smells Bad said. "Paul no long needs to bother you guys for anything."

Jacob scowled.

"So, you told him. Excellent. We are happy to explain his new life to him," Runs with Papers said as he bounced on his heels.

"Gentlemen, let me introduce you to Miss Charlemagne Winters. She has money too."

The lawyer's disappointment turned to delight. Jacob exited and sat on the patio, catching a shout and squeal from inside of his office. A thud caused Jacob to turn. Paul had climbed over the wall.

"Is the front door broken?" Jacob asked.

"No, it's just," Paul's cheeks turned pink. "I came to help Charlie. I didn't expect to see you out here."

"It's a lovely day to be outside," Jacob said. He had kept the triangle of Paul, lawyers, and money away from each other.

The door to the patio opened. Charlie stuck her head out. "You can come in as long as you behave yourself."

Paul moved inside before Jacob could object.

"I got money," Charlie said, grinning. She turned to Jacob. "I'm paying you back."

"Unnecessary. You will need the money for your life after college," Jacob said.

"I can pay for college now," Charlie said.

"No. You have a full scholarship. We are sticking to the plan."

Paul's head swiveled from Jacob to Charlie, his mouth hung open like a baby hippopotamus.

"She gets a full ride and you're making me do the work-study program? How fair is that?"

"Paul, this is not your stage moment. Drop it, please," Abbot Jacob said.

"Oh, this is Paul?" Smells Bad said. Runs with Papers stood up and put his hand out. Paul shook it.

Charlie gathered her documents to her chest as Smells Bad snapped open his briefcase.

"We need to talk to you, Paul," Runs with Papers said. "Your mother left you some money."

"She did? How much money?" Paul asked, stepping closer to the lawyer.

Smells Bad handed Paul a large envelope. Paul opened it and read the top pages.

"Holy Moses. This is all my money?" Paul said.

Charlie inched her way closer to Paul and peering over his shoulder.

"Does that say 2.65 million? More like halleluiah, I have risen," Charlie said, giving Jacob a look of disbelief.

"Shouldn't I have known about this when I turned eighteen or sooner?" Paul asked, clasping to the envelope.

"Now works for me," Jacob said. Silently hoping Paul would just be grateful.

"I've had this money since my mom died," Paul said. "Why didn't you tell me?"

"Money does not concern a four-year-old," Jacob said. "We were prepared to take care of you financially."

"I didn't stay four. I could've paid for things." Paul was shaking and asked how he could get his money.

"You will have to finish college before you will be given access to the money," Abbot Jacob said, thankful for the minor power that guardianship provided him.

Paul whirled around to face Jacob. "And if I don't finish college? Then what? I don't need to finish, I have money. I can do what I want."

"You will finish college," Jacob said in a gentle, fatherly tone. "You can't be an anthropologist without a degree."

"It's my money. Charlie gets her money without stipulations," Paul said, the envelope crinkling in his hand.

"Charlie is not under my guardianship."

"Yes, she was." Paul grabbed the papers from the desk and asked, "Can he...?"

"Yes, he can, but you're entitled to an allowance," Runs with Papers said.

"I don't want an allowance. It's my money." Paul scanned the pages. His eyes narrowed. Jacob knew he read the monastery would receive money.

"Your mother stipulated that we were to ensure that you completed your education before you received the funds," Jacob said, invoking the promise of the dead, hoping that would stop Paul's greedy protest.

Paul said, his voice tight. "This is messed up. You get money for taking care of me. Is that why I'm here, why I must finish college? If I don't, you'll get nothing?"

He had expected scorn, but the accusation that they only wanted money stabbed at him.

"You must finish college. You need a degree to do anything." Charlie placed a hand on Paul's arm.

He stepped away from her. "I have money. I can go anywhere. Maybe I'll quit college and then where will that leave them?"

"Now you are just being stupid. I don't expect they need your money, you know, poverty and all," Charlie said.

"They don't do poverty here. I can't believe my mother sold me to them."

Charlie punched Paul in the arm before Jacob could stop her.

"Take that back."

"Fine, but why did she offer them money?" Paul said, rubbing his arm and stepping away from her.

Jacob didn't have an answer other than the one he had provided when they voted on the idea of raising Paul. Money entices, money gets people's attention, and the money got them considering the possibility.

"Just cuz you won the jackpot doesn't mean you run off and buy a jaguar," Charlie said, wagging a finger at Paul.

"Not a Jag, a green '97 Ford Mustang GT with a 5-speed manual transmission, a V8 engine, and power everything."

"That's not practical, a convertible in winter, in Montana. Have you lost your mind? Stop being an idiot, take the allowance, and shut up. Or do you want me to evoke the library clause?"

The library clause?

Paul frowned. "You would take half of my money? Some friend you are, especially when you have your own money."

"I'm your friend. You were not the charity case the monks took on. That was me," Charlie said, thumping her fist on her chest.

"No, I was the charity they took in for profit, their future nest egg."

Runs with Papers cleared his throat. Smells Bad ran his fingers through his thinning hair and shrugged as if to say, "Well, it looks like that."

Jacob ran his fingers over his braid. "I resent you saying we kept you for the money. After the decision to keep you, nobody revisited the money matter," Jacob's voice intoned indignation. "Ask these guys how much we spent? They have kept track of it all."

"I don't trust you. You've lied to me. I'm out of here," Paul said, slamming the papers onto the desk causing the documents to scatter.

"They spent hardly anything and have allowed us to invest it," Smells Bad said as he handed Paul an envelope. Jacob prayed it wasn't money. The notion of an angry Paul with a wad of cash caused his shoulder to throb.

"I see what you were getting at. My apologies, Abbot Jacob," Runs with Paper said. "He's not as mature as I had hoped."

Charlie stooped to pick up the fallen pages. She paused, staring at a document, her eyes wide with discovery.

Jacob pulled the paper from her grasp. She looked at him with pity. Jacob placed the birth certificate on the desk with the other papers.

PAUL EXITED THE OFFICE, muttering his way down the hill. "Not mature enough. They lied. They raised me because of the money. I assumed they loved me."

Lost in an emotional fog, Paul found himself at the farm, so he entered the barn and kicked a bale of hay.

Ambrose looked up from his work. "What's got you all hot and cocky?"

"You guys." A litter of four kittens scampered to him.

"Lumping us all together, that isn't wise. Is there someone in particular you want to yell at?"

"I already yelled at Abbot Jacob. Why did you keep me?" Paul pushed the energetic fur balls away with his foot.

"Because your mother asked," Ambrose said, scratching his head.

"Did she? I learned she offered you money to take me," Paul said, aware that he was being rude.

"He told you. Good. It's about time you learned responsibility."

"Are you crazy? You knew this?" Betrayal hit Paul hard, causing his eyes to water.

"We voted, all of us. How did you think you got here? What did you guess was going on? We weren't in the business of raising children."

"You took me in for the money." Paul stomped as he paced, and the kittens scattered and the dogs moved between Ambrose and Paul.

"You askin' me or telling me? Does it look like we are rich?" Ambrose asked. "I don't understand why you're so mad. You have money, too. Isn't it a good thing?"

Nothing at the monastery reflected wealth. The plow appeared to have been in use since the monastery was founded. If it wasn't for the money, why was he taken in?

Paul stopped pacing and crossed his arms. "Yes, I'm glad for the money. I'm mad because you lied to me. You kept it a secret."

"Lied, no. Kept you from spending it, yes. Stop your whining. You have money. Be happy. Money wasn't the issue for us. You needed a home, and we had the room."

"For money," Paul screamed, and the dogs barked.

"If you're going to be unreasonable, go kick some bales of hay because you're not listening."

"I'm not being unreasonable. I thought I belonged. I thought you cared. All my life, I believed this was my home. I was the property of St. Alberic's. You wanted me. Money helped me get here. I don't understand how my mom could do that, sell me?" The words tumbled out before he could stop. He knew she didn't sell him, but a question burned bright. Where was his family, and why couldn't she place him with them?

Ambrose dismissed the dogs with a whistle, and they moved to flank him as he took a step toward Paul and towered over him. "You'll not speak like that about your mother. She did what she thought was best. We all did. If you don't know that you're loved, then we've failed. This is your home, Dorothy, even if you run off down some yellow-brick road." Ambrose said, wagging a large finger at Paul. Ambrose heaved a sigh, tossed his straw hat to the side, and stomped away from Paul.

Even though his childhood was anything but normal, they had provided for him, respected his wishes to be orphan. At college, Paul continued to love him when he made poor choices. He could not imagine a different life. Paul raced after him. "I'm sorry. I lost my head."

Ambrose halted and turned to face Paul. "Good, cuz I didn't want to have to explain that black eye you were about to have."

"I'm sorry, I just don't get it. What's the big deal about the money? Why couldn't Abbot Jacob just tell me? He let Charlie have her money without a hesitation. We're practically the same age." Paul said as Ambrose slowed his pace.

"Typically, money brings sadness, excessive spending, and irresponsible behavior. I think Abbot Jacob was just trying to keep you from that," Ambrose said as he climbed into the rickety old Ford truck.

"I'm not that stupid. He and Charlie must think I am. She wants to evoke the library clause, all because when we were sixteen, I signed a paper saying if I was ever rich, I would give her half my money. So much for years of friendship," Paul said, climbing into the cab of the truck next to Ambrose.

"Smart girl. You're not that stupid. Only impulsive, but eventually you see reason. You gonna give her the money?"

"I don't know. I can't until I graduate from college," Paul said, thinking she probably needed it more than him. He knew he had the monks to fall back on. She was alone in the world.

Ambrose started the engine. The truck coughed and backfired.

"Smart Abbot. So, what's in the envelope?"

Paul reached into his shirt pocket and ripped open the envelope. He had a credit card in his name. The letter explained that since his eighteenth birthday, a monthly allowance of a thousand dollars was in an account.

"Whoa, Nellie, you got over ten thousand. What you gonna spend it on?"

Paul grinned.

CHAPTER 40
MARVIN WINTERS

Psalm 35:13

See how the evil-doers fall!

Flung down, they shall never arise.

Paul rubbed his elbow on the hood of his '97 Ford Mustang GT. The green hood reflected the early morning sunrise. He and Ambrose had gone to the dealership and bought the car, paid cash. He was now broke, but he had a car. Abbot Jacob had been silent. Paul took that silence to be angry disapproval. Joannicus reminded Paul that Abbot Jacob had lost his family in a car accident. "Be gentle and patient. Give him time."

The glow from the window in the guesthouse shone warmly. The bells rang for morning prayers. Charlie came out of the guesthouse carrying a bucket and a box. He helped her load it into the back seat.

"What's so important that I had to get up early?" Paul asked.

"It's liberation day, and Memorial Day all rolled into one," Charlie said. "Hey isn't it my turn to drive?"

Paul sighed. She grinned as he handed her the keys. He slid into the passenger seat as the car headed for the open highway. "So, all is kosher?"

"Yeah. Father Joannicus said he approved of us going out for the day. He also reminded me that my allowance for the month was pretty much gone."

"No worries. We have enough for what I want."

What that was, Charlie hadn't mentioned her plan. She asked if he would accompany her. How could he refuse? She had endured so much, her mom dying and then her dad, and now they had money. They had spent long hours scheming and dreaming; her building cathedrals and he unearthing lost treasures.

Charlie drummed her fingers on the steering wheel. Paul shifted in his seat. Silence sat between them.

"Where are we going?" Paul asked.

"I told you, a road trip. I must take care of Rat Bastard and we're delivering Mom to Hill Crest. Yes, I've an appointment. The stone is ready, and I need to put her ashes in the ground."

"You bought a plot?" Paul asked, knowing her mother had been in a box in her closet since her death. Charlie had been livid when she had learned that Marvin hadn't even claimed the remains of his wife.

"Yes. Stop asking so many questions."

Paul rubbed his hands on his jeans.

They arrived at Hill Crest. A small brick building stood above the graveyard. Charlie jumped out of the car and opened the hatchback. Paul stood next to the bumper, taking in the view.

"Stop looking at my ass," Charlie said.

How did she know? He guessed they always knew. He liked Charlie, sometimes he liked her more than a friend. She was pretty. Sometimes Paul could see them together forever and other times, when they argued, he could see himself saying goodbye to Charlie. Paul scanned the green grass and the rows of headstones. Charlie handed Paul a rosewood box. She then took out a cardboard box and packing tape.

"Put Mom in here," she said, "in this cardboard box."

Paul slid the glossy rosewood box into the container, surprised at how light the whole thing felt. Charlie placed a label from Richards and Sons Mortuary on the outer box and fastened it down with tape. Why was she repacking the remains?

She returned the package to Paul, pulled out a black lace handkerchief, which didn't look like it could hold a tear, then grabbed Paul's arm. What should he do if she started balling?

"How do I look?"

Seeing Charlie, dressed in tight jeans and a black shirt that hugged her breasts and flared out at her waist, he could think of nothing to say that wouldn't get him punched.

"You look normal."

"Warner, sometimes you're an idiot. Most girls want to hear pretty, but I'll take normal. I don't want to scare the dead."

They marched into the building together. The sun glistened on the highly polished floor through the tall windows, blinding those who entered. Paul found the small desk where the hawk-nosed woman sat. She was no St. Peter.

Charlie told the woman they were here for the interment. The women looked surprised and then sad as she glanced around, expecting a crowd. The woman examined the box, which Paul handed her, checking the label and her records.

"This is a double interment? Paid in full?"

Paul felt relieved. That's why she repacked. He knew she wouldn't put Marvin with her mother. His nerves clinked like the bottles in the back seat of a car.

"Yes," Charlie said, her voice rough with emotion. Paul checked to see if she was crying. There were no tears.

"All right then, everything looks in order." The woman opened the labeled box and took out the rosewood container. Charlie squeezed his arm. The woman handed a man the box.

"Jared will walk you to the site. I'm sorry for your loss."

They followed the man down a gravel path to a spot under a tree. Above a hole was a marble placard.

The epitaph read, "Best Mother Ever" and "He's Still Not Here." Charlie flashed him a smile before turning solemn. He wanted to ask her what it meant and why she squeezed his arm but figured this wasn't the time for questions.

Charlie placed the rosewood box in the ground and watched as they covered it with dirt and a plug of grass. She stood stoic and fierce.

Left alone, standing next to the headstone, Charlie kissed her fingers and then touched them to the marker. "Bye, Momma," Charlie said, her voice catching.

Please don't cry.

Paul had seen her tears when she was with Father Joannicus and Jacob. They were tears of anger and grief all rolled into one. The force of which frightened Paul.

Please don't cry.

Charlie breathed deeply, sighed, and marched down the gravel path to the car. Paul followed.

They cruised north on Highway 212 and stopped at the first gas station they came to.

"Perfect," Charlie exclaimed as she hopped out. "Supplies are needed for the party."

She grabbed two six packs of Absolution Ale, cola, chips, and jerky. Proudly, she showed her ID to purchase the alcohol. The attendant wished her a happy birthday.

Paul silently followed her out.

"It's not your birthday. And you're not twenty-one."

"This card says I am. A party isn't a party without libation."

When they got into the car, Charlie asked, "Do you want one?"

"You can't drink and drive."

"Since when did you become such a saint?" She opened the bottle of beer and drank.

This was not good. One drink will not make her drunk. She had just buried her mother. She hadn't cried. Give her time.

"Okay, now what?"

"We have a few stops to make to dispose of dear old Dad."

Paul blanched, wishing he had taken the beer. "What are you talking about? I thought we just put him in the ground?"

"Ah, no. Didn't you read the marker? I used the Turd's money to bury my mom."

"You lied to those people?" Paul said, admiring at her boldness. Why hadn't they questioned her? The weight difference of the ashes should have given them a clue.

Charlie tossed the empty beer bottle into the back seat. After several miles, they came to a construction zone. A lone blue port-a-potty stood amidst the dump trucks and cranes. Charlie parked the car. She grabbed the red bucket from the back seat and headed to the blue box. Paul's heart thumped as she strode on. He leapt from the car.

"Charlie, wait. What are you doing?"

She opened the door. The stench of chemicals and urine caused Paul to gag. Charlie opened the lid and shook some contents of the red bucket into the hole.

"What the hell? What did you do?"

"We're burying Marvin."

Oh God. Crap. That was Marvin in the bucket?

Two men with yellow hardhats came running toward them.

"You kids had better not be pouring concrete," one of them shouted.

"Run," Charlie said, tugging Paul's arm.

Oh God. Crap. Paul raced after her, barely closing the door as she tore out of the construction zone, kicking dirt and gravel behind her. Paul leaned over the front seat and looked at the gray sandy contents with white specks like seashells glaring at him.

Oh, Crap and double crap.

Charlie shoved a cola at him. "Get a backbone. This is stop one." She handed him a second beer bottle.

"No."

"Look, you can open it, or I can pull over and open it. It's time for the eulogy."

Paul opened the bottle and handed it to her, thinking, *Jacob is going to kill me.*

"I suppose words are in order. You started out as a decent dad, but somewhere along the way, you messed up. This is the best we can give you." She finished the beer in a few swallows and dropped the bottle over her shoulder and it clinked on the floor of the back seat.

"I don't think you should've done that," Paul said, as he sipped his cola.

"Did I ask your opinion? No. You're here to get me home after I'm shitfaced — so shut up because I'm doing this."

"I'm driving before you get shitfaced, so next stop you hand over the keys," Paul said as Jacob's words about drinking and driving echoed in his chest.

This was not what Paul pictured when Charlie said road trip. All he could do was hope they weren't caught. He wasn't sure if dumping someone's remains was legal, but he knew it wasn't moral. The act was the ultimate of disrespect.

Everyone has their own burial ceremony. They had discussed this point many times. Is there a heaven or hell? When burying the dead, was it for the living or dead? Did the tombs with booty get a better after life? What kind of food did the dead want on their tombstone? This was just Charlie's way. That rationalization did not soothe his conscience.

When they stopped at the Last Chance gas station next to Dry Hole liquor store, Charlie eyed the store.

"No," Paul said.

"Fine. Fill up, pay, and meet me at the restroom."

Paul wanted to wait in the car. He stood outside of the lavatory door, next to the display of sunglasses. The door opened and Charlie yanked him inside, locking the deadbolt with a click.

"You flush while I pour," Charlie said.

"Charlie, this is a bad idea."

She shot venomous daggers at him with her eyes.

The ashes filled the hole, and the water attempted to push the mass down, but they quickly lost the battle with Marvin winning.

"Oh crap," Paul said. Charlie laughed.

"Don't be difficult, Dad."

Two more flushes and water rose to the top of the bowl.

"Let's go," Paul said, grabbing Charlie and rushing out of the store.

Charlie opened another beer, drank as if she were in the desert, and laughed. She was close to being drunk. Maybe, if she passed out, they could just go home instead of finishing this gruesome task.

"I'm hungry," Paul said, thinking that food might sober her up and he could get the keys from her.

Charlie made a U-turn in the middle of Highway 212.

They pulled into the parking lot of Big Bovine Bar and Bakery. Paul wished they were going in the bakery side. Charlie strode in, a little wobbly, through the swinging doors. Hanging from her arm was the bucket of Marvin, and in her hand was her ID.

"It's my birthday, I'm twenty-one. Barkeep, serve me a tall, cold one," Charlie announced.

"Coming right up, little missy," the bartender answered while a chorus of "Happy Birthday" rang out.

"IDs," the server said as she stood at the table. Charlie handed her two cards. The woman stared at Paul and Charlie. Satisfied, she asked, "What will you have?"

"A Coke," Paul said, snatching the fake IDs from Charlie and staring at them in wonderment. They were nineteen, not twenty-one. If Jacob knew, Paul would be locked in the monastery until he was thirty-five.

Paul insisted they order food when Charlie's Long Island Iced Tea arrived.

"Here's to dear old Dad. He didn't get my money after all. I'm a rich girl now. Not as rich as you, but hell, what's a few thousand between friends?"

"Only difference is you get to spend your money and Jacob won't let me have mine until after college graduation."

"Oh, you poor little boy. You have it made, and you now get a huge allowance. Stop whining."

"You're nasty when you are drunk," Paul muttered.

"This is the best day ever. I outsmarted Marvin. He tried to get my money. But God smite—smoted—smote him. Thank you, Jesus."

She was definitely drunk.

The food arrived, and Charlie ordered a second drink.

"Don't ditz Abbot Jacob. He has been nice to me and you. You got that car, and he didn't make you take it back. He's just being a dad, a proper dad. One who cares for your well-being," Charlie said, pinkish sauce dripping down her chin. Paul handed her a napkin.

She wiped her chin and then scooted her chair close to him and lowered her voice.

"You're so lucky to have dads that care and a home to go back to anytime you feel lost." Her breath, warm on his cheek, smelled of burger and hops. He turned to face her. Sometimes she was cute. He had better not say that.

"If you ever find your bio dad, don't abandon one for the other. They worry about that. You know that, don't you? They don't want to lose you. The big guy, in particular, thinks you going to college means he won't ever see you again. You are just down the hill. They are sometimes silly. You won't abandon them, will you? No, you won't, you're a good boy."

She must be talking about Ambrose. The man had been grumpy lately. Dropping hints that he would have to watch Disney movies by himself now that Paul had moved to the dorms. A trickle of guilt filled Paul. He had insisted that the monks not acknowledge him, not make it known that they were his guardians.

"No, I won't ignore them," Paul said.

Charlie's eyes were enormous and dilated; she leaned into him and kissed him. Paul sat stunned. She patted his cheek. "Such a good boy."

Charlie stood, knocking the chair next to her over and gripping the table for support.

"Hand me the bucket. I got to go pee." She grinned at Paul.

"Charlie, no," Paul croaked. That was so wrong.

"The bucket. I really got to go. You don't want me doing it here, peeing in the bucket."

Paul picked up the bucket and handed it to her. Charlie

teetered and weaved her way to the bathroom. It was time to go home. He paid the bill and waited for her outside the restroom.

When she emerged, the bucket was empty except for a dusting of Marvin.

"Hand me the keys," Paul insisted. "I'm driving."

"Come find them." Charlie splayed herself against the wall, ready for a frisking.

Paul groaned. It was the wrong time to play. She wasn't herself. So many moments of intimacy had passed between them over the years. Paul had always felt there was a 'no trespassing' sign hanging around her neck. He knew that he, of all people, could probably ignore that warning, but chivalry trumped longing. Paul pushed himself against her and reached into her jeans pocket. The keys warmed his hand as he slipped his other arm around her waist and piloted her toward the exit.

They approached the Mustang, and Charlie retched. Burger and beer soured the air. Paul stood by, keeping her from face-planting in the dirt. The barkeeper walked toward them with two bottles of water and a towel.

"She's not driving, is she?"

"No, I have the keys," Paul said, accepting the bartender's offering. He handed both to Charlie.

Charlie wiped her face on the white cloth and stepped away from the mess.

"Thanks," Charlie said.

"No problem. Happy Birthday," the man said as he walked back to the bar.

Paul helped Charlie into the back seat of the car and handed her the bucket of Marvin dust, in case she needed to heave again.

"Don't be mad at me," Charlie said.

"I'm not."

"Don't be mad at the monks or your mom. They all just want to protect you."

Paul wasn't sure what she was babbling about.

"From biological bat rastard fathers," Charlie said. "I'm sorry you're a guy. Maybe you didn't get that gene."

Paul adjusted the mirror to view Charlie as she lay curled up in a fetal position. The next noise was a loud snore. So strong and yet so vulnerable. He stared at her for a long time, her black hair in disarray. Paul reached over and took the last bottle of beer and opened it. He drank quickly, as if to erase the events of the day. Paul gathered the bottles, placing them in the trash. He tucked his jacket around Charlie and got into the car, signaled, and turned on to Highway 78.

Not all men are rodents.

CHAPTER 41
GOODBYE CHARLIE

Psalm 93: 8
Mark this, most senseless of people.
Fools, when will you understand?

Money changed things. Once gossip had gotten out about his money, Paul acquired more friends than he needed. They were a distraction. Girls looking for husbands, guys looking for handouts. The whirlwind of fortune and ill-gotten fame wore thin. Once people learned about the waiting time. He saw Charlie in passing. She didn't come to his parties or outings. He suspected she found his behavior extravagant.

Paul walked the busy hallways of the college to his anthropology class. Someone clipped him and his books flew out of his arms. Nasty notes from Abbot Jacob fluttered to the ground.

"Charlie?" Paul said, seeing the army boots standing on his notebook. "Get off of my notebook. Don't be so high school-ish."

"You're the one looking up my skirt," Charlie said, peering at him kneeling before her. She knelt to help him gather his belongings.

"What do you want?"

"A sleepover."

Paul sighed. They had been getting together every month on the full moon, sitting in the darkness discussing dreams and worries. Paul had been faithful to the standing date since their first semester at college. However, he had missed the last few months of this private event.

"Are you going to lecture me on class attendance?"

"No, if you want to be stupid then be stupid but you'll never do what you love if you ignore your education."

Paul stood up and looked at her. Was she for real? The monks had gotten on him for neglecting his classes. Abbot Jacob had even threatened him with expulsion if he didn't raise his GPA. They will throw the whole deal away because of his grades, despite taking him in for the money. Paul decided the monks were correct after a late-night party left his room smelling of sweat and vomit. So, this week he had attended his classes and stopped midweek parties. Why hadn't she noticed?

"Hey, Charlie," three guys chanted as they walked by them. Charlie flashed them one of her winning smiles.

"Lunch?" the short boy asked.

"Yes, but make it a salad. Girlish figure preservation."

"Dinner?" the husky one with thick glasses asked.

"Absolutely, corner table, right?" Charlie said. "Ice tea."

"Oh, I remember sweet and dark, like the universe," he said, his voice dipping low.

Paul rolled his eyes. Was she falling for this?

"What about you?" Charlie asked. She turned to the only normal looking male in the trio, tall, athletic jock.

"I'll stop by for dessert," he said as his eyes roamed and lingered, causing Paul to fight his urge to beat the guy with his book.

"Since when are you interested in men?" Paul said, thinking it had been eons since they dined together. They had always eaten together in high school.

"Wow, such a sourpuss," Charlie said. "I adore men of a certain caliber."

Charlie was not girlfriend material. What were they thinking? They had better not hurt her. *Jealous?* Taunted his inner voice. *She's not your girlfriend.* He didn't want a girlfriend. She has a right to her own life.

Charlie handed him his notebook. "I didn't mean to nag, but if you want to open that society for the conservation and preservation of antiques, you need to be the best in your field. Nobody will take you seriously if you fail college."

"I know," Paul snapped and turned to head to his class, leaving her standing in the hall. She was right, even Joannicus agreed with her.

"If you don't complete your education, you'll have to get a job. Nobody can live on a thousand dollars a month. Reason this through," Joannicus had said. They would make him a monk if he didn't get a job.

Paul figured the monks couldn't do that, but he wasn't certain. But he was sure he didn't need to worry about earning a living anymore.

Paul entered the classroom and took a seat next to a willowy redhead, thankful that nobody in this class would lecture him on his life.

His studies in anthropology gave him a unique insight into the behaviors of humans. Yet he found non-human behavior easier to predict and understand.

This was his senior year. Soon he could open an institute of preservation and discovery of past treasures.

He stretched his legs and flipped open his notebook, attempting to tune into what the professor was saying, "... Understanding how people think is crucial. It is our job to listen to all the voices and viewpoints to understand..."

They haven't had a monastery of opinions over a lifetime, thought Paul. He preferred to look at silent bones and figure out the reasons for himself.

Joannicus had advised him to pick his passion when he was trying to decide what to do before he found out he had money.

His passion was for past civilizations. Charlie, with her amateur psychology degree, said he was passionate about the past because he needed to solve the mysteries of his childhood. What did her obsession with religion say about her? Was she chasing things she couldn't have? She chose a degree in theology. There were no Catholic women priests. Who would listen to a woman theologian? Yet she had a job, she wrote sermons, Charlemagne's Sermons, and the clergy paid her. If only they were aware of the actual author.

Humans are too hard to understand, Paul wrote on his paper. He punctuated it with the tap of his pencil, snapping the lead, sending it shooting across his desktop.

A blue pen waved in front of his face as the redhead girl smiled. He wondered if she'd work at his institute.

Driving his green Mustang, Paul pulled up to the old Baptist church, which was now Charlie's home. The small church, built at the turn of the century, was long and narrow, with a spiral bell tower and bright-red double doors. He wondered if the old vicar would approve of the changes. His footsteps reverberated around the few benches in the sanctuary. The floors glistened as the Christmas lights wrapped around the pillars twinkled.

"In the back," Charlie called.

"When are you going to get furniture?"

"I live here alone. How much furniture do I need?"

Paul headed to the sacristy, now converted to a kitchen. He recognized the vintage McCray icebox that Ambrose had once had in the barn. A 1930s Magic Chef Stove he played with as a child, pretending he was Brother Paul the monastic cook.

"That stove works?" Paul asked, wondering how she had gotten it from the monastery to here.

"Yes, it needed tinkering," Charlie said as she pulled two beers from the McCray. "Come, we don't want to miss the rising."

Between the headstones were two lawn chairs draped in heavy wool blankets.

They sat and watched the moon and tipped their bottles, drinking the dark ale.

"Sorry for missing. The last two, I mean," began Paul.

"Yeah, well, sometimes you're a guy," Charlie said. "I began research on the Boren family without you. I found photos of them and a living relative."

Since the time Charlie had purchased the church, her obsession with the graveyard grew. Together they had unearthed the attic and basement of the church, finding treasures and cataloging them, piecing together documents and history. Paul had to admit it was something he enjoyed doing. They researched and invented the lives of the people buried there.

Paul smiled, remembering the many hours sitting in the basements of libraries and courthouses shifting through records to find the tiniest piece of information attached to the name on a headstone. *You were lucky to be buried in Charlie's Cemetery, for you had a life beyond the grave.*

"I've missed you," Charlie said in a rare moment of sentimentality. "This is our last year together."

Was it? He could not imagine not staying in contact with Charlie.

"You're being morbid," Paul said, reaching for a second beer and handing her one.

"Really? You're sitting in a graveyard on patio furniture," she said, taking a swig of her beer. "I'm just being realistic. You're going to run off to Peruvian ruins in some wasteland."

"I could do the catacombs of Rome and you could chat up the Pope."

Charlie laughed. "What did you want to be?" Charlie asked.

"I thought of a teacher, but I don't have the patience."

"Not a monk?"

"No," Paul said. "You're kidding me, right? I live with them, but I'm sure they are not God's chosen. They are humans choosing to serve God."

"I'm aware. I adore the rhythm of their life, the poetry of the psalms. The praying is like bookends on a shelf, holding life together. It's all so peaceful."

"You're a romantic," Paul said as he thought of the grumbling and in-house squabbles.

Charlie belched. "I'm a girl, in case you forgot."

Paul looked at her shadow against the moonlight. She was exotic and sometimes intoxicating.

"No, I didn't forget." Paul bit his lower lip. He had something he wanted to ask her concerning their future. Was this that moment?

"My mom wanted me to be a designer. My dad wanted me to be an architect."

"I wonder what my parents want me to be. My mom placed me in a monastery. Maybe she wanted me to be a monk." Paul reached for another beer.

"No. I believe she had to find a place for you. She ran away from something. Sarah Warner doesn't have any records in Montana."

"You and your crazy tales," Paul said. "I think your true calling is a storyteller."

"I like a good mystery. There was this little blurb in the Fox Whole News. 'Brave woman gives birth alone on the highway.' I told you, didn't I?"

"No, you didn't."

"Your mom appeared in Montana claiming she was out visiting family. She doesn't say whom. She went into labor and delivered you. She didn't have a place in Montana, she was running away."

"Have you verified this?" Paul asked, remembering the tragic stories she weaved for the graveyard names. "Not every life is suffering."

"Okay, then why didn't she put you with family when she died?"

"I don't know. Maybe her family was dead. Why were you investigating me?"

"To see if you were marriageable material," Charlie said, tossing a potato chip at him. "Don't be stupid. She has a family."

Paul took a gulp of beer.

"Oh, come on, you realize your father is alive and lives in North Carolina," Charlie said, draining her beer.

Her nonchalant remarks caused Paul to choke on his beer.

Charlie grimaced. "You didn't know? Oh, shit."

"How do you know?" Paul asked.

"Those papers the lawyers had. Didn't you ever read them? Your father is Sean Bennett-Hill."

"The lawyers didn't tell me. What papers?"

"The papers they had when we got our money. In there was his name and a letter from your mother."

Paul jumped up, knocking the chair over and discarding the wool blanket over Jeddia Macomb's grave.

"What the hell." Paul stood shaking as if the heavens had split open, beckoning him into a new world.

"I thought Abbot Jacob talked to you."

"I'm always last to be told."

"You knew this. We had his name, but we didn't put him with your mom because he was married at the time of your birth."

"What are you saying?"

"It's not important," Charlie said, standing and moving away from him. "Who cares who our parents are? That's not who we are."

"I care," Paul said, not sure why he said it because he had never given his paternal line much thought. "I want to see that letter."

Paul headed to the house and was through the kitchen when Charlie yelled, "Stop."

"What?"

"It's one in the morning. The monks are asleep."

"So what? I need to read what my mother said."

"He doesn't have the letter," Charlie said in a whisper.

Paul stared at her.

"I have it. I took it. I read it. I was going to put it back but..." She hesitated. "The only thing that matters is that your mom loved you."

"I want to read my letter," Paul said in a slow, calculated voice.

"Promise me you will do what she asks."

What was in that letter that needed promises, sight unread? Was his dad a serial killer or rotting in jail for rape? He realized his father was married, and he recognized those things happened. What he didn't understand was why his mother left North Carolina so close to his birth.

Charlie opened a cabinet in the kitchen. On the shelf was his floppy white tiger nestled among the books of the desert mothers and collectible antiques. She grabbed a notebook covered with graffiti, the one from high school. She flipped the dividers and hesitated as she looked at the family tree. He remembered the research. They had no proof of who his father was. They had guesses. Had Charlie researched more and neglected to share her conclusions? Paul stepped closer as she handed him the letter, yellowed with age. Anger bubbled inside him. Was it sealed? He wanted to be alone. Paul walked to the main part of the church and sat in the pew. His hands trembling as he opened the envelope.

My dear son,

I love you. On the day you were born, I left my home in North Carolina. We got as far as Montana and the car died. I had planned a wonderful life for us. Things changed. So forgive me. For legal reasons, I am telling you the name of your father, Sean Bennett-Hill. Don't go looking for him. He was married. Regardless of the mistake I made, I'm blessed with you, my joy. I hope when you read this you trust I made the best choice for your future. I know this is short. I am sorry about that. I put it off too long.

I love you.

Mom.

Paul crumbled the letter in his hand. This did not explain why she had left North Carolina.

"Don't destroy that," Charlie said. "It is the only proof you have."

"What proof? I am here. That is proof enough." He stared at the raven-haired woman before him and his body trembled. He came to discuss the future, but the past pulled him back. "I thought I would ask you..."

"Ask me what?"

"Never mind. How can I trust you when you keep secrets from me? Don't I get the chance to see my father? Doesn't my father deserve to meet me?"

The look on her face confirmed his inner thoughts. Why was he defending people he didn't know?

"No. Where has he been? This family of Bennett-Hills has no scruples." She pulled out the family trees. "They split up the twins, raised them away from each other. I bet your mom wasn't aware that she was related to Sean."

"I'm not blaming her," Paul said, hoping that Charlie was wrong about the twins.

"Good, then do what she asked, run away. Don't go looking for these people. God only knows what they will do to you if they find you," Charlie said, tossing her head. Her black curls, streaked with vibrant purple, flopped over her shoulder. "Don't go. Don't do it."

"I have to."

"No, you don't. The Nellie woman said you weren't related, and we know you are. These people lie. Why do you want to hurt Father Joannicus and Abbot Jacob?" Charlie said, pushing her hair back from her face.

"They lied. Abbot Jacob lied. You lied." His stomach hurt.

"I technically didn't lie. It was none of my business."

"I'll tell you what isn't your business, me." Paul headed to the church, moonlight scattered shadows on the floor.

"I don't think Abbot Jacob knew you had a father."

Paul shot her a look of disbelief.

"Okay, everyone has a father, but I don't think anyone had a name. I guessed his name. There is proof, but if Abbot Jacob knew, he would have kept quiet. It's what your mother wanted."

Paul crossed his arms. "That's not fair."

"Life isn't fair, nothing is black and white. Let it go."

Charlie crossed her arms

"I want to know why."

"Your mother said no. Listen to your mother."

"Who are you to give advice when your dad was a dick?"

Pain shot across Charlie's face and her shoulders slumped. Why had he said that? He didn't mean it.

"You're right, he was. I'd have given anything for the fathers you have over Marvin."

She placed her hand on his arm and he flung it off. She stumbled back.

"Get the hell out of my house," Charlie said, regaining her balance and standing stiff, her fists clenched.

"Church. You live in a God damn church." Paul stomped away, leaving Charlie showered in moonlight next to where the altar should have been.

CHAPTER 42
FIRST A GIRL, THEN A BOY

Psalm 21: 12
Do not leave me alone in my distress.
Come close, there is none else to help.

P aul looked out of his window at the steeple across the street from his hotel in Boiling Springs, North Carolina. Three days ago, he had left Montana in his green Mustang, drove twenty-nine hours, booked a hotel, and crashed.

This morning, he reconsidered his rash actions. He should stop at that church and pray. God was there even if it was a Baptist church.

The street address of the Bennett-Hill in Shelby, North Carolina, lay on the table in front of him like a spider in the ceiling's corner, waiting patiently for him to move. Psalm 21 came to mind as Paul's stomach clenched.

Maybe I need them. Maybe they need me. The argument that sustained him on his drive came creeping into the room.

A loud rapping caused him to jump. He opened the door and there stood Brother Ambrose. He wore a blue plaid hunting shirt, carrying a small duffel bag with a dirty sock hanging out of the unzipped top.

"What are you doing here?" Paul asked, looking into the hallway.

"I've been waiting on the second floor." Ambrose pushed Paul aside. "I like this room. It has a refrigerator and snacks."

Ambrose flung his bag onto the bed with a thud.

"I just got here yesterday," Paul said.

"I flew in this morning. Charlie knows you well. She said you would pick this place. She was right. You should marry that girl and tame her."

Ambrose didn't know Charlie if he thought she could be tamed. He was going to propose three nights ago.

Ambrose sat on a bed and bounced. The springs sang. He patted the place next to him. "How can I help, Little One?"

The nickname hit Paul hard. Little One. That was what Ambrose called him when he first arrived at the monastery, and it had made him feel loved. Paul bit his lower lip.

He was thankful to the monks for the life they had provided him. He wanted to be with Charlie, yet he needed to understand why his mother had left North Carolina.

Ambrose scratched his beard and grabbed Paul's arm, pulling him into a chest-crushing embrace and then pushing him away.

"Enough of that," Brother Ambrose said. "We gonna meet these people or what?"

"Aren't you going to talk me out of it?"

"Do you want me to?"

"No," Paul said, but a minor part of him wished Ambrose would toss him into the car and drive him back to Montana.

"Don't you think I should go home?"

Ambrose rose. "Yes, but I know you. We will do this meet and greet, even if it's a fool's errand."

"I need to meet them."

"You already know," Ambrose said, heading to the door. "It's not where you came from. It's where you're going. That is important."

They drove to Shelby, which was fifteen minutes away. Large homes with balconies and turrets dotted the streets.

"Look, the Bennett-Hill Elementary," Ambrose said as they pulled onto Bennett-Hill drive. "Was that the Bennett-Hill Bank? I wonder if they have a Bennett-Hill Baptist Church."

Paul thought about Abbot Jacob Mackenzie's family. Their name appeared in several places in Montana, at the church in Elan. Jacob's father had donated sizeable sums of money. The Bennett-Hills had done the same. They were in no need of Paul's inheritance from his mother. A trickle of worry nagged him. Would they think he was seeking them for their wealth?

"I don't know what religion the Bennett-Hills are. They have a family graveyard somewhere on their property. At least that is what Charlie told me," Paul said.

They turned onto a driveway that twisted and turned under the shade of oaks. The house stood majestic and large, with a balcony on every level. Immense columns graced the edges like bookends. A long deck stretched toward the double front doors. Three dogs, a chocolate lab, a spaniel, and a beagle, came running up to them as they exited the car. The dogs barked and circled. A lazy hound, resting on the top step, lifted his head and let out a howl, causing the other dogs to join the chorus. Ambrose tossed his head back and howled with the dogs.

A brief thought of having Ambrose wait in the car ran through Paul's mind. What impression would he leave at this meeting?

Paul remembered encountering the large man when he first came to the monastery. Ambrose had tossed him into the air. The fear and thrill of that meeting had bonded Paul to him. Ambrose's simple acceptance of everything he met caused Paul to dismiss his misgivings and move to the front doors.

Paul walked up the three steps, wiped his hands on his jeans, and rang the doorbell. Paul waited. Ambrose scratched the head of the lab.

The door opened. There stood a woman. Her face was smooth and her eyes large and brown. Her neck was a layer of wrinkles and Paul judged her to be ancient at least eighty. The black long-sleeved dress hung loosely on her frame. She wore a hat with two pheasant feathers sticking out of the side.

"I'm Paul Warner. I need to talk to someone concerning Sarah Warner."

"Come in. We're keeping the flies out." The woman clunked her way on thick heels.

Ambrose and Paul stepped inside, closing the door behind them. A large marble table adorned with fresh flowers filled the space with a light fragrance.

"Come, come, I will show you the family tree. It's worth a climb," the woman said. She turned to Ambrose and patted him on the chest. "A giant. An Ozark man, I guess, not one of us. Bennett-Hill men, handsome rogues, but weak as weasels."

"Nope, not one of your kin," Ambrose said with a bow. "I'm Ambrose Reed, at your service, miss."

"Bernice Warner, sir, a pleasure to make your acquaintance. Now come, come, let's chat about men and the past." Bernice latched onto Ambrose's arm like ivy to an oak.

She led them to a room, humming to herself. Paul followed,

watching Ambrose circle his finger to his temple, showing that he thought the woman to be crazy.

The room was rich with dark panels, and sunlight flowed warmly through the windows. Chairs circled an enormous fireplace. A musket hung over the mantle. A large black cat sat next to the cold hearth as if waiting for the warmth of a fire.

Bernice settled herself in a cushioned chair, placing her feet on the tapestry footstool.

"I figured this day would come. So, I guess you want answers," Bernice said. "I raised her."

Paul sat on the delicate French sofa opposite of Bernice. Ambrose squeezed in next to him. Paul held his breath. The love seat groaned but did not collapse.

"I was hoping you could tell me something about her."

"That isn't sinister," Ambrose muttered as Paul frowned at him.

"Sarah, sweet and pretty. Stubborn and strong, cunning and curious. You know Sarah died," Bernice said as she picked up a tiny bell that sat on a silver tray and rang it.

A woman appeared.

"Bring refreshments for my company," Bernice said.

"Yes, I know my mother died. She died when I was four years old," Paul said as he watched the woman calculate. Tension tightened her face.

"How?"

"Cancer."

A smile filled her face. Paul had never seen someone smile about cancer.

"Wonderful. David, you should not have come. Danger is here." Bernice glanced at the door and wrung her hands.

Remnants of fairy tales bounced into Paul's head, Sleeping

Beauty, being spirited away to keep her from the evil in the kingdom.

"I'm not David," Paul said. Why did she call him David?

"Yes, you are," Bernice said with a grin of an innocent child defending her make- believe friends.

No, he was Paul. He knew who he was. David was the dead baby on the certificate that Charlie found.

The refreshments arrived, wheeled on a cart. Ambrose filled a little plate with triangle sandwiches and balanced it on his knee. His pinky finger jutted out like an antenna as he slurped from the blue gilded teacup. Paul longed to turn the cup over and look at the mark. Was it a tiny blue half-moon? He was sure it was a Royal Worcester, which dated back to 1790. This proved his family had a long history. Charlie loved old stuff, and they had gone to sales and fairs in search of ancient items. Sometimes, it was a silver spoon, sometimes a teacup, or a quill.

"Always accept one's hospitality," Ambrose said in a hushed tone at Paul's disapproving look.

"If you know Sarah is dead, what do you want, honey?"

"I want to meet my father," Paul said.

The teacup in Bernice's hand fell to the floor.

The black cat flinched, his ears folded back on his head, and his tail twitched. He didn't move as if he was used to the drama of crashing dishes.

A woman appeared and cleaned the mess. The blue half-moon winked at Paul.

"It never should have happened. I should have been more diligent," Bernice said in a childlike whine. "Sarah didn't know her half brother was Sean. That's the danger of keeping the twins apart."

Half brother, his lineage, was worse than he thought.

"Love happens, mistakes get made," Ambrose said.

"True. Nellie will not like this. Oh dear, another Bennett-Hill treasure gone."

Two people are speaking in the foyer. He turned. The doorway was empty. A fan slipped out of Bernice's sleeve and snapped open. The air moved and Paul smelled roses, soft and faint. The voices drifted past the opened door. A man and a woman.

"I'm sorry, I didn't mean to upset you," Paul said as Ambrose helped himself to cookies.

"Devious old crone, smashing her adversaries, one teacup at a time," Ambrose whispered.

"You're not helping," Paul said under his breath. "I'm sorry about the teacup. I can pay for it."

"It's not your fault. It's a teacup. They have more."

"But it's a Worcester. A collector's piece," Paul said and then muttered, "worth over two thousand dollars." What wouldn't Charlie sell to have this piece in her collection? He wished now that they hadn't fought. She would appreciate this strange woman.

Ambrose set his cup down with careful precision and pushed it far out of reach.

"What are you doing here?" Paul asked. Wondering why Bernice Warner was here at the Bennett-Hill estates living with Nellie, his father's great aunt who had buried his mother and David with pen and paper.

"Honor, protect, defend," Bernice shouted, raising her fist above her head. The woman cleaning stifled a giggle before leaving.

"Bloodlines, boy. The Warners and Bennett-Hills came to an agreement. Twins were shared. The descending lines wouldn't die out. Isn't that just so clever?"

"More like creepy," Paul muttered.

Ambrose gave a shrug. "One man's coffee is another man's tea."

Her voice was deep and gravelly as she sat in her chair. "I have to be here to assure our lines continue. The family name must go on. The Bennett-Hills are not trustworthy. The female line is the key, one for you, and one for me."

Bernice fanned herself as she leaned back in her chair.

"You're right, it's the double yolk, not the rooster," Ambrose said.

Bernice laughed a loud belly laugh.

"The Bennett-Hill men are roosters, no doubt about that. It was a dark and stormy night. Sarah had two, Tessie one," Bernice said, her eyes shifted to the doorway. "She didn't leave. She's dead."

Paul looked at the golden eyes of the black cat, now slinking its way toward Bernice. Tessie, Sean's wife, thought Paul, what does she have to do with this?

"Who is dead?" a raspy southern voice asked. "Who are you confessing to, you addled woman? Have you no sense? Your tongue is dripping like a dog on a hot day."

She entered the room, her cane and heels hitting the floor in a three-step rhythm, dressed in white, pale and ghostly. Her eyes, a milky green, settled on Paul.

"Why did Sarah leave, Nellie? Why?" Bernice asked, her voice high-pitched and childlike.

"Sarah. Sarah is dead, you old bat."

In a soft and dangerous voice, Bernice said, "David is alive. David is here. Run, David, run."

Nellie's eyes fixated on Paul. This woman filled in the death certificates that had confused him and Charlie. Her relentless stare caused him to feel guilty about the grievous sin of his birth. She teetered close and Paul could smell lavender.

"Do you think we're fools? You can't claim to be a son of a dead woman."

The black cat stepped up onto the footstool, perched, and waited.

"I have birth certificates and death certificates," Paul said as sweat trickled down his back.

Bernice grinned the grin of a crazy woman as she murmured, "He knows the truth, Nellie."

"Keep quiet, old woman. Speak up, David. What do you want?" Nellie banged her cane on the floor as she unlocked her eyes from him and moved to sit in a straight-backed chair.

Paul felt his face go hot. "I want to meet my father."

"No," Nellie said, her eyes narrowing.

"I came to meet Sean. You put his name on the death certificate."

"I want you to leave."

"No."

"Sean is not your father. We don't know who fathered Sarah's bastard," Nellie said, leaning forward.

"Now that's not nice and a lie," Ambrose muttered.

"Who are you?" Nellie snapped as she turned her gaze to Ambrose.

"Ambrose Reed, bodyguard." Ambrose offered nothing else, not a handshake or a bow. He leaned back and crossed his arms over his enormous chest. The black cat's golden eyes blinked, reminding all he wasn't a statue.

"Take him home, Mr. Reed," Nellie said. "There's nothing here for him."

Paul glanced at Ambrose. He had come for answers. Irritation rose in him like an unreachable itch.

"Why did you have my mother declared dead?" Paul asked.

"She wouldn't obey." Nellie's green eyes flashed with anger.

She admits the truth. That was too easy.

Obey. Even in the monastery where obedience was part of the Rule, Abbot Jacob never forced him to obey. Is that what you wanted me to learn, Momma? What obedience is? Is that why you placed me in a monastery?

Nellie clicked her tongue, "Take him away, Mr. Reed."

"The boy deserves the truth, even if sordid and messy," Ambrose said.

"The truth is he was born here, and his mother left us," Nellie said. "The Truth is his mother became pregnant without my consent. She is an adulterer. The truth is, you are a powerless nobody. I killed you off once. I can do it again."

Paul gripped the sofa arm and let out a guarded breath. Charlie was right. These people made up their own rules.

"You're dead. Go back to your grave, David. This is not your home."

The name felt like a curse as it came from her lips. He narrowed his eyes.

No. He was Paul. Paul Warner, son of Sarah. Raised by the monks of St. Alberic's. He knew who he was.

Paul looked at the sour face of his great aunt Nellie. He saw no guilt or shame.

The black cat jumped onto the sofa next to him, breaking the tension.

"Nellie dear, settle. You'll give yourself a heart attack," Bernice said as she turned to Paul. "Are you aware that Warner girls have twins? First a girl and then a boy."

It occurred to Paul that Nellie had followed through with the Warner Bennett-Hill pact.

"Enough. This isn't Sarah's son. I don't care who he is, but Sarah and her child died," Nellie said.

"Nellie, this is David. Just look at him. He has his daddy's lips. Do you need your glasses?" Bernice asked in calm innocence.

Nellie's face froze as the truth glared at Paul. The psalm of boasting evildoers came to mind as sorrow filled Paul.

"Shut up, Bernice, I don't need my darn glasses," Nellie said as sweat glistened on her forehead.

Pride swelled up in Paul for the Warner woman who dare to face the lioness in her own den.

"My father doesn't realize I am alive, does he?"

"Your father has a son and no need of you," Nellie said in a frosty tone.

"Your opinion is noted, but you didn't tell him I was alive. You told him your story of lies." Paul ran his hand over the sofa's softness.

Nellie pulled herself up to sit straight in the chair. "He's a Bennett-Hill."

"What you have done is evil, forcing my mother to leave. All the lies you have told because of family lines and twins."

Nellie smiled with tight lips. "Who are you going to tell? On a dark and stormy night on October 24th, 1975, Sarah ran away, taking her baby. You have the death certificates, they died. Whom do you think they will believe? A dead boy or the people who were there? I reckon they will believe me. Be gone. You've become tiresome." She raised her hand as if shooing a fly from her sweet tea.

The black cat nibbled at the minced meat on the cart, brazen and hungry.

The time had come. Paul stood.

"Ambrose, let's go home," Paul said as he headed out of the room.

CHAPTER 43
SEAN BENNETT-HILL

Psalm 51: 5
You love evil more than good. Lies more than truth.

Ambrose followed Paul into the foyer.

"Call me dense as a bale of hay, but why are you leaving?" Ambrose asked.

"I'm not leaving," Paul said as he headed down a long hallway.

Two doors were to the right and one to the left.

"I feel like we are on *Let's Make a Deal*," Ambrose said.

Maybe that was true. One door led to his father. Is it a deal of a lifetime? Which door to choose? Paul realized he had little time. The clock at the end of the hallway dinged. The black cat opened the second door. Paul moved in that direction.

Here's hoping black cats are good luck this time.

"Wait here," Paul said, standing in front of a half-closed door. Paul left Ambrose in the hall as he stepped inside and closed the door behind him.

The man behind the desk looked familiar, an older version of himself.

"Excuse me," Paul said.

Sean Bennett-Hill looked up from the three stacks of paperwork. Paul assumed the three piles represented an order, read, reading, and unread. Sean's brow creased at the sudden interruption of his morning.

"Do I know you?" he asked. Sean stood and moved to the right of the desk. Paul heard the drawer open.

Crap, is he reaching for a gun? Stop it. Don't let Nellie spook you.

"No, you don't. I'm Paul Warner, my mother was Sarah Warner," Paul said. He swallowed hard. His throat was dry.

Sean shook his head. "You're misinformed. Sarah died in October 1975 with her son, David."

"No, she died in April 1980, and I'm her son, only she didn't name me David."

"You're mistaken. I was there."

"So was I. Did you see her dead body? I did," Paul said. He hadn't wanted to look at his mother. The reality of her death was hard to comprehend.

"No. I didn't, but there was a funeral. I carried the coffins. I would notice an empty coffin."

Paul remembered Charlie's delivery of her mother's ashes. The funeral home couldn't tell the difference. For all his self-confidence, Sean was wrong.

Sean's eyes narrowed. Paul wondered what he was contemplating. Was he revisiting that night twenty-two years ago?

"I have the death certificates," Sean said, his voice strong with emotion. The man liked to argue a point that was moot. It appeared they had something in common. How many times had Paul argued for the sake of arguing?

"I have a death certificate too, for Sarah Warner. It's not a fake."

"Are you accusing us of falsifying documents?" The man stood.

"No, you all have a tendency to fabricate the truth. You should talk to your informant. And my mother's great aunt Bernice, she has a different story to tell."

The man stiffened. Paul wanted to believe his father knew only the lies of his birth. But the nagging truth that his father was married and not to Sarah gave Paul doubt. He was unfaithful to his wife and got another woman pregnant. From the sounds of it, Sean had remained married to Tessie. That was a good move. Paul found that frightening and admirable that twenty-one years of silence surrounded the events of his birth. He had heard it said that some truths belonged in the grave. Only this truth did not. This family, his family, was unbalanced, out of kilter. They lied to themselves, to his father, and now to him.

"What do you want?" Sean straightened as he stood.

"I came to meet my father. You are my father."

"I'm not your father. Even if you're Sarah's son, that doesn't make you my son. We don't know who the father of Sarah's baby was."

We? Paul glanced around the room. Had he missed someone?

"You're the father of Sarah's baby. She told me so."

He didn't want to say you are a married man who got his half sister pregnant. He wished he had the finesse of words that Father Joannicus possessed. Paul stepped toward the family portrait, gazing at the young woman standing next to Sean.

Bernice's words shook Paul's brain. Warner women have twins, first a girl, then a boy.

"Who is that?"

"That's my daughter, DaVita, her mother, Tessie, DaVita's twin brother, Nicholas, and Shawn."

Paul stared at the picture. The hairs on his arms stood at attention. That was his sister. The man refused to acknowledge Paul as his son.

"This woman looks like my mother." Paul reached into his pocket, pulled out his wallet. He took out a worn photo of Sarah and him before cancer had eaten away her future. He watched the glimmer of recognition as he handed the photo to Sean.

In the hallway came the sound of a cane hitting the floor as Ambrose's voice rose, "Now, lady. That is not nice."

Ambrose could hold his own.

"What did Nellie do?" Paul said in a whisper. "I don't remember the night of my birth, but Bernice does. She might be confused, but she knows the family mantra, first a girl, then a boy. My mother was a Warner. That is Sarah's daughter, my twin sister."

Paul envisioned the scene twenty-one years ago. Great Aunt Nellie being insistent that Sarah give up one twin as the unspoken agreement between the families had dictated. Sarah refusing to separate the twins because she learned not to know your twin could lead to the complication she was now experiencing. Paul realized his mother thought his sister had died. Nellie must have walked the baby to Tessie, telling her this is your daughter, making a complete set of twins for the Bennett-Hills. The reality played out like a bad horror movie.

The door to the office banged open. Nellie stepped in, waving her cane over her head as if hoping to whack Ambrose, who loomed behind her.

Nellie had been right. He was nobody in this family, a name with no substance. But she was wrong. The truth would not go to the grave buried in her coffin. A sense of righteousness filled him. They didn't deserve his presence in their little drama-filled lives.

"What arrogance. I'm calling the sheriff," Nellie shouted as she rushed forward to the phone on the desk.

"Good idea, you do that. When they arrive, you can explain what or who is buried in Sarah and David's graves," Paul said.

Ambrose's eyebrows shot upward.

Sean continued to look from the photo to the wall. His jaw tightened.

"Auntie?" Sean asked, his voice betraying his hurt. He held the black-and-white picture in his trembling hand. His face softened. "Did Sarah live?"

Paul held his breath. But the next question didn't come. *Is this my son?*

"Whose daughter is DaVita?" Sean continued.

Nellie paused, phone receiver in hand. She answered, her voice a pitch higher, "Yours. Are you daft? She's your daughter. You were there. I handed her to you."

"No, Tessie had the babes in her arms."

"First a girl, and then a boy."

"Tessie is not a Warner," Sean's voice sounded as menacing as Nellie's was shrill. Silence hung like the crystal chandelier, threatening to shatter. "So many things occurred that night. The storm, both women in labor, baby Shawn had the croup, you, and Aunt Bernice sending the servants home early." Sean paused and gazed intently at Paul. "Who is this young man?"

"A liar, trying to cause chaos. There is nothing for him here."

Nothing for me here, yes. Finally, Nellie has spoken the truth.

"Put down the phone, Auntie, we need to talk," Sean said as he turned to Paul, handing him the photo.

"Keep it. I have others. You might need it to remember."

Paul waited for the words, *my son*, to come out of Sean's mouth. The man realized the truth. He wouldn't admit to this family deception, but Paul knew this was his father. Sometimes you waited and sometimes you acted. He had waited long enough.

"Shame on you," Paul said as he turned to Nellie.

"How dare you," hissed Nellie.

"How dare you kidnap my sister and lie to my mom? I'm glad she left. She was right to do so."

"Go away, take your lies with you," she said as she swung her cane.

Even if Sean had accepted him, welcomed him, there was treachery entangled with each truth. Nellie had lied and switched the babies for her own gain. These people were twisted.

Turning around, Paul held out his hand to Sean. The man shook his hand. No thrill of recognition passed between them. Paul's past rushed to his mind. The first time he saw Father Joannicus, standing in front of him, clutching papers and a battered old briefcase. He had formed an immediate connection to that man dressed in a black habit. Paul smiled as he remembered the thrill he felt when Ambrose walked into the room and tossed him in the air. The expectations he had when he took Jacob's hand.

"Ambrose, it is time to go."

"Proud of you, boy," Ambrose said as he followed Paul out the door.

The future, not the past, thought Paul. He couldn't wait to get home.

CHAPTER 44
PAUL AND CHARLIE

Psalm 126:3
Truly, sons are a gift from the Lord.

P aul stood in the graveyard next to his mother's grave. He placed a bouquet of red roses and white calla lilies in the urn.

"Sorry for not listening. You were wise to leave me here. I didn't get it until now."

Most people found it hard to understand a mother leaving her son with monks who had little knowledge or wish to raise children.

The gate screeched open, and Paul turned to see Abbot Jacob. His tall, lean frame moved up the walk to the secular side of the cemetery. He touched the top of his wife's headstone as he passed to stand next to Paul.

"Welcome home," Jacob said. "How's your mom?"

Home. St. Alberic's monastery. Home. Paul smiled.

"She's fine. Smarter than her son," Paul said, understanding that Sarah Warner left North Carolina for the right reasons.

"Thanks for taking care of Brother Ambrose."

"I couldn't say no. We were so close to Florida." Ambrose had a glorious time and Paul enjoyed watching him.

Jacob nodded. "You could gently remind him that mouse ears do not replace a cowl."

Paul laughed. He would suggest that Ambrose wear the ears when they watched movies together.

The old gate scraped, and Paul turned to see Charlie and Father Joannicus.

"Warner," Charlie shouted as she left Father Joannicus to run toward Paul.

She hugged him and then stepped back and punched him in the arm, hard. She had forgiven him. Her fragrance embraced him and he inhaled deeply.

"Welcome home," Father Joannicus said as he joined the group.

"Thanks. I learned this is the family I want," Paul said.

"That's scary," Charlie said, linking her arm into his.

"I have a sister. A twin sister."

"I knew it," Charlie said. "So, what is she like?"

"I didn't meet her. I'm not sure that will happen."

"Do you want that experience?" Joannicus asked.

"Yes, but not now. I can't justify rising from the grave and causing her life to change. I can't guarantee it would be a positive transformation for her."

The motto of St. Alberic's Monastery, coined by the saint himself: "Do because it is right, not because you can," glared in

Paul's mind. He had seen that line a thousand times every time he entered the monastery.

"I couldn't bring myself to say, 'Hi, I'm your twin brother; that guy who you thought was your twin is only your half brother. And our great aunts are evil. They kidnapped you and our mother is dead.'"

"Wise," Charlie said, leading the way out of the cemetery.

"I'm sorry it did not work out," Jacob said as they walked.

"I'm not. I didn't want it to work out," Joannicus said. "Call me selfish, but I didn't want to have to share."

"Don't be sorry. I'm glad it didn't work out. This is my home," Paul said. "You're my fathers." Both men smiled at each other.

Once, he had wanted Father Joannicus to be his real father, and today he knew that he was. He was grateful that Joannicus put aside his fears and embraced raising a child.

"They tried to tell me I was David," Paul said. "I'm Paul Warner. Those people in North Carolina make me uncomfortable. Maybe someday I'll met my sister, but not now. I don't think we are ready for that."

"You are wise. I was forty before I realized I didn't need or want family drama," Jacob said, sadness flitting across his face.

"Okay, I got news," Charlie said, squeezing Paul's arm.

A glance back at the monks told Paul this was not news to them.

"Yes, I'm going to Idaho," Charlie said.

"What's in Idaho?" Paul asked as they approached the church.

"St. Gertrude's Monastery."

Paul stopped and stared at her. Gothic still peeked out of her own styled clothing. She couldn't be serious. Yet looking at her face, she was. She wanted his blessing. Paul's heart sunk, and he drew in a deep breath.

"Well, don't just stand there like a baby hippopotamus with your mouth hanging open. Say something."

"When did you get the call?"

Charlie's face scrunched. "The call? You're joking, right? God didn't call me. If he did, I wasn't home to answer it. I'm going to find out if I love it."

"When did you decide this?" Paul asked, suddenly saddened. He stuck his hand in his jeans pocket and felt the little box he had slipped in there this morning.

"It's been on my mind for a few months. I would've told you sooner, but you ran off to Timbuktu. I'm glad you came back. I was hoping you would drive me to Idaho," Charlie said.

"Sure," Paul said.

"Excellent," Charlie shouted, and then she turned and hugged Joannicus and Jacob. "It's happening. Promise me you will come and visit."

"As soon as we can," Jacob said.

"When the Prioress says we can," Joannicus said.

She turned back to Paul. "What's wrong?"

Paul considered for a moment telling her the truth, that he came back to ask her to marry him.

"Nothing, I'm just surprised, but I'm aware of your fondness for wearing black, so it makes sense. If this is what you want, then I'm happy for you."

"Nothing will change. You will come to visit on the full moon. It's not that far away."

"Every month? Won't that interfere with your vocation?" Joannicus asked.

"No. You're all family."

"No. I'm your best friend. We are not family," Paul said. The Bennett-Hill drama had left him feeling vulnerable to love and siblings.

"Okay, don't get weird. I'm leaving you my church, to take care of until I decide. Don't dig up any graves," Charlie said, brightening. "I'll get my stuff and we can go."

Now? Paul nodded and let himself fall into her enthusiasm. Charlie jogged ahead. Paul sighed and handed Jacob the little blue box from inside of his pocket.

"Hold on to it for me?"

"Are you sure you don't want to take it with you?"

Paul hesitated and then glanced in the direction Charlie had gone and sighed. "That wouldn't be fair. She wants to try this."

"Good for you," Jacob said, placing a hand on Paul's shoulder.

"I don't know if it is good for me, but I can wait."

Jacob took the box and Paul turned to run after Charlie.

Joannicus grabbed the box before Jacob could slip it into his pocket. Opening it, he saw two white gold rings, feather inlaid.

"What did I miss?" Joannicus asked.

"Nothing. He will wait," Jacob said, still smiling.

Joannicus stared at the rings and then at Jacob. "Those are your wedding bands. You gave them to Paul. Was he going to...?"

Jacob nodded.

"But she's going to the monastery."

"I heard. I am proud of him. We raised him well."

The church bells rang, calling them to prayers.

"Now I don't know what to pray for," Joannicus said, shaking his head. "Grandchildren or her vocation?"

"Just don't pray for money," Abbot Jacob said. "I knew of a monastery that prayed for money and got the benediction of a child."

Father Joannicus laughed. "But this time, my friend, our hearts are ready."

Acknowledgments

Bringing these books to you has been a journey filled with excitement and joy. I will once again thank those who have made this journey possible, including my brilliant editor Maggie Sokolik, The Puget Sound Writers Guild whose members have been instrumental in getting my work to the well-plotted stage.

To my readers ,and there are so many, from my neighbors and those in my non-DNA-related family. Special thanks to Dave and Jane Stillman for their unfailing loyalty as readers and cheerleaders. I am looking forward to a growing readership and the opportunity to discuss my work with them.

If you are interested in a meeting, please contact me at:

Patricia@PatriciaMcClureNovels.com

THE SERIES: THE BENEDICTION OF PAUL

Thank you for reading Book 3 of *The Benediction of Paul*. Here is the entire series:

Book 1: *Winds of Life*

Book 2: *Less Thunder, More Lightning*

Book 3: *All for One Child*

Book 4: *Counting Coup: The Making of an Abbot* (prequel to the series)

www.ingramcontent.com/pod-product-compliance
Lightning Source LLC
Chambersburg PA
CBHW020500260626
47156CB00006B/1799